"Clay Reynolds is an arresting new voice in American fiction, a writer of scope, vision, and vigorous storytelling ability. *Rage* is a satisfying suspense novel of the time-bomb variety; it starts ticking on page one and goes off about three-quarters of the way through the book with a long, sustained roar. *Rage* contains the best sustained gunfight since Glendon Swarthout's *The Shootist*—readers will finish it gasping, wrung out . . . and eager for more." **—Stephen King**

"Ruthless, superheated . . . I couldn't put it down." —Dan Cushman
author of *Stay Away, Joe*

"A grisly, well-told tale."
—*Winston-Salem Journal*

"Memorable characters . . . compelling pace and tension." —Bryan, Texas, *Eagle*

"A murdered woman . . . a town that makes Peyton Place look like Green Acres . . . a master storyteller." —*Beaumont Enterprise*

RAGE

Clay Reynolds

A SIGNET BOOK

SIGNET
Published by the Penguin Group
Penguin Books USA Inc., 375 Hudson Street,
New York, New York 10014, U.S.A.
Penguin Books Ltd, 27 Wrights Lane,
London W8 5TZ, England
Penguin Books Australia Ltd, Ringwood
Victoria, Australia
Penguin Books Canada Ltd, 10 Alcorn Avenue,
Toronto, Ontario, Canada M4V 3B2
Penguin Books (N.Z.) Ltd, 182–190 Wairau Road,
Auckland 10, New Zealand

Penguin Books Ltd, Registered Offices:
Harmondsworth, Middlesex, England

Published by Signet, an imprint of Dutton Signet, a division of
Penguin Books USA Inc. Originally published as *Agatite*.

First Signet Printing, January, 1994
10 9 8 7 6 5 4 3 2 1

Cover photo by John Walker

Ⓢ REGISTERED TRADEMARK—MARCA REGISTRADA

Printed in the United States of America

PUBLISHER'S NOTE
This is a work of fiction. Names, characters, places, and incidents either are
the product of the author's imagination or are used fictitiously, and any resemblance to actual persons, living or dead, events, or locales is entirely coinci-
dental.

For my father
and all the good men

ag • ate (ag′it), *n.* a variegated chalcedony with curved, colored bands or other markings. Cf. *ruby.*

Prologue: The Town

In the Old West, when a man's destiny was open to whatever chances he could or would take, Agatite, Texas, sprang up on the north central plains as a major railhead and agricultural and ranching center. Over the years it remained prosperous while smaller communities around it died or were blown away and never rebuilt. When cattle, cotton, and oil were still being discovered everywhere else, the fertile Greenbelt soil of the Red River Valley yielded wheat and soybeans to add to the wealth of the barons already rich in horned, black, and white gold. Even though the Depression and the Dustbowl ruin of the plains took its toll in Sandhill County, almost everyone believed that those who picked up and moved to California were only the weak ones, those who lacked the whatever the hell it took to fight the weather, the banks, or anything else that stood in the way of prosperity.

Along with prosperity, of course, came what the respectable folks in town called the "undesirable element," for farming and ranching and oil wells brought with them the vulgar cowboys and drifters, roughnecks and wheaties, field niggers and mestizos, all of whom from time to time haunted the midnight alleys and streets and just as often populated the town's jails.

Once boasting almost ten thousand souls, Agatite now barely sustained half that number. Aside from the banker, the odd small businessman or insurance agent, the local law officers, and the handful of successful ranchers who had moved into town to live in brick homes, the populace was mostly made up of old people waiting to die and

young people waiting to get the hell out. The railhead
had moved away from Agatite, northeast to Tulsa, and
also shut down were the two small clothing factories that
once operated in the city because of the railroad's acces-
sibility. Agricultural goods, now using long-haul truck-
ing that came right out to the farm or ranch to pick up
crops or livestock for market, were only rarely stored in
the dozen or so elevators or the enormous stockyard near
the tracks in town, and the cotton gin that marked the
town's skyline along with the Agatite Hotel and the city
water tower had also been left to rust and neglect with
the reduced demand for cotton in a world clothed by syn-
thetic fabrics. The gypsum mine and mill, once boasted
to be the world's largest, was running at only three-
quarters production level, since the slump in the nation's
demand for wallboard had put a cramp in business. To
the old-timers who thought about it, and only a few did,
the town seemed worn out, used up.

The land around Agatite was also used up. All that
wasn't completely useless for crops or grazing had been
bought up by a small number of enterprising farmers and
ranchers, and all the oil that was pumped from it went
off to Houston companies that sent in an occasional ge-
ologist to live for a year or two but put very little else
into the community.

With Fort Worth far to the southeast, Abilene to the
south, and Amarillo stretching just as far to the northwest, the small town nostalgically remembered when it
had been called the "Jewel of the Plains," fighting an
all-out range war with Pease City, five miles away, for
the right to be the seat of Sandhill County. Once it had
been a stopover for aspiring governors and senators; even
foreign dignitaries had paused there, and once, Teddy
Roosevelt himself had whistle-stopped through and made
a resounding speech from the presidential train in front
of the depot. Now the town was merely a scar widening
the stretch of blacktop bypass known as U.S. 287, noted
chiefly as being the center of the last dry county before
northbound travelers reached the Oklahoma border.

Tourists coming from any direction groaned when they

sighted the city limits, noting with disgust that it was typical of any of the small towns that dotted north central Texas: dirty, small, dying. Greasy oil and dirt mixed with red clay and gypsum in the streets to form a kind of dustiness that even a rare spring day's stillness could not lighten or disperse. Travelers would move quickly through the main street of the hamlet, hardly slowing down for the blinking yellow light that marked the exact center of town, and they usually slowed again, considering briefly the dirt-encrusted Dairy Mart on the outskirts, across from the equally wind-battered and weathered motel The Four Seasons, across U.S. 287, and they would wonder if anything between Agatite and Amarillo or Fort Worth, Abilene, or Lawton could possibly be less appealing and whether they should just wait until they arrived at one of those more inviting metropolises.

Long before the railhead had removed to Tulsa and trains meant more than something to interrupt the flow of traffic on Main Street, time and progress had stopped in Agatite, and in some ways, the clock seemed to run backward. Except for a new Texaco or Gulf sign, a banker's new Oldsmobile or a rancher's new pickup, the TV antennae, and other small changes, there was little indication that the town was aware that men had walked on the moon, that hearts were transplanted, or that war had become unpopular. Old men fought older wars in the Goodyear tire store's air-conditioned waiting room, the domino parlor, or, on cool days, on benches placed strategically around the downtown area. And when they ran out of war stories, they replayed high school football games, compared the current team to the one that had actually won a state championship in 1966, and speculated on the worth of the nine- and ten-year-old boys scrimmaging on the playgrounds around the elementary school.

The WPA provided the town with a park, a football stadium, a post office, a city hall, and a county courthouse, where a broken statue of a Confederate infantryman stood guard, staring toward the empty streets of Agatite day and night. The Women's Club had erected a

sign near the highway years before, but the merciless
climate that brought winters with below-zero readings
and summers with one-hundred-ten temperatures, both
whipped by a vigorous wind from the Caprock, had swept
by it so often that even the most alert tourist had trouble
discovering that AGATITE IS A BIRD SANCTUARY.

Centuries before, when the Comanches roamed southward in search of respite from the cruel southwestern
windblown winters, or northward in search of antelope
or buffalo, they would pass quickly by the area that
formed the present township of Agatite, hurrying to cross
over Blind Man's Creek, disdaining to camp there because of the terrible winds, the sudden tearing thunder-
storms that could blow up out of nowhere and bring with
them vicious cyclones that ravaged the buffalo grass and
tore the occasional tree up from its roots, and the red
ants, rattlesnakes, cougars, and brown bears that hid in
the swamps around the creeks and rivers. Now such wild
animals, all but the snakes and red ants at least, had gone
with the Indians, and in their place mesquite had come,
brought north from the coast in the spoor of massive
cattle herds, spreading and encroaching upon every other
living thing in the whole area, covering the land, drinking its water, and giving the impression that hamlets such
as Agatite had been hewn out of the short, thorny forest
rather than that they had sprung up from the long-
forgotten waving grasses of the southwestern plains, as
they had actually done.

Once the people of Agatite had prided themselves on
their sociability. Every night people would walk down
the sidewalks of the neighborhoods the half mile or so to
downtown, where they would walk to and fro past the
still open shops, marveling over the latest in fashions in
clothing, autos, jewelry, while the kids wandered the
aisles of the Ben Franklin store, their eyes wide with
lusty wonder, and, more often than not, a nickel or dime
clutched in their hands, burning to be spent on some
trinket but held onto as long as possible almost as if the
waiting would make the value of their coin magically
grow. The population of this town had been confident,

even cocky, about its future, and on weekends when the outlying areas would yield up their folk to join the towns-people, the downtown was embued with a holiday spirit of optimistic vitality.

Now, however, things looked less bright. Although people still filled downtown during the day, they went about their business grudgingly, and at night they stayed home, squaring off in front of their color TVs and tch-tching the world's problems away. Stores downtown were closed by five-thirty, some earlier, and many had closed forever. Ben Franklin had put in a line of fabric to com-plement its previously tiny notions department, since kids saved their money nowadays for spending in the discount stores of Wichita Falls, and seemed to have little interest in the modest toy selection of the small five-and-dime.

By ten o'clock on any night, even Saturday, only a few teenagers scouted for each other in the streets, eventually parking on the lot in front of the Dairy Mart, talking about sex, beer, and the mysteries of the world they would find, they were certain, as soon as they put the skyline of Agatite behind them.

The adults of the town had grown familiar with some-thing they couldn't define or even articulate in any con-crete way. They felt that something, some power, some evil perhaps, but something greater than their compre-hension or ability to resist or control functioned beyond their TV screens, and they watched and waited anxiously every night for it to be revealed. Every Sunday they punched and prodded their kids into one of the seven Protestant churches in town and listened to their preach-ers talk about God and the eventual destruction of the world, but they knew that God didn't really worry the citi-zens of Agatite any more than politicians did. They were all too far off to pose much of a threat. What the popu-lace of this town worried about was that something out there threatened them in a way they could not imagine, something that would make their preachers' favorite texts from *Revelation* seem more like promises than threats. They fundamentally believed that it, or them, or what-ever was responsible for the erosion of the town, that was killing it as surely as the railroad had gone away and left them with no future to count on, would come someday and visit them in a horrible way.

They kept a watchful eye out for something that would serve as a concrete enemy—juvenile delinquency in their children, bootleg beer and whiskey from Oklahoma, atheism, drugs, sin. Every time they ate, bought clothing, made a judgment about a football game or a brand of soap, they felt the power of that unknown something creeping around the edges of the town. And every week began with the unspoken hope that before Saturday the revelation would be made, that they would understand and be able to face whatever it was. Behind the small talk of the town the fear lurked, and everyone seemed to sense it, but no one mentioned it, almost as if to speak such a fear might make its source a reality.

One thing they did talk about was how they seemed to lose people. The cemetery that lay gaping at the edge of town, conspicuous by its freedom from the mesquite thickets and its green grass, had more graves than there were residents in the small city. Children simply grew up and left. They talked about leaving from the time they were old enough to be aware that there was anywhere else to be. They either married and left, went off to college, or joined the army and never came back. Sometimes, they just went off. From the time they crossed the city limit line, they spoke of coming home in terms that were both reluctant and weary. Mama or Daddy had to be sick or dying for them to make that long trek from elsewhere, and when they did come home, they were not the same. They looked at their hometown with foreign eyes, eyes that understood what was going on *out there*, eyes that had seen and recognized the something that terrorized the town, perhaps eyes that had become a part of it. As soon as they had done their duties at the hospital or cemetery, they left, racing away from Agatite as if the town were some sort of trap, ready to spring and keep them there. They rarely came back again. They saw the fear in the people there. They had escaped it, and they didn't want to feel it again.

Of course, some did come home. But oddly, and ironically, the townspeople tended to shake their heads over
those who couldn't stay away. There must be something
wrong with them, they would say over a secret cache of
whiskey in the domino parlor or barbershop, probably
couldn't stand to be away from their mamas. Usually they
were the ones who came back to take over the family
ranch, the family business, or to live in the family way.
Only money or disgrace could really convince most to
return to live in Agatite forever.

In spite of the fact that businesses were failing in Agatite, the bank held plenty of money. The ranchers and
farmers, although fewer in number than in previous years,
prospered from their large holdings, and the workers in
the reduced labor force at the gyp mill and the cotton gin
had learned long ago to bank as much of their salaries as
they could to hedge against the time when they, like the
railroad workers, would face the expensive choice of
moving elsewhere to work or retiring early on an inadequate pension. The businesses that survived also prospered after a fashion, tied as they were to the agrarian
community, and they too, in order to encourage everyone
to "shop at home," deposited their profits in the First
Security Bank of Agatite, permitting the assets of that
red brick institution to remain impressive even as the
town died around it.

Life in Agatite, Texas, then, continued to proceed
without progressing. Like countless small towns across
the nation, it had enjoyed a rich and optimistic history.
Its children had fought in wars, and its ghosts were as
harmless and forgotten as the *History of Sandhill County,*
which lay musty and unused in the Sandhill County Library. The only excitement that came its way was the
odd Mexican girl who found herself with child by one of
the white boys on the football team, an occasional fist-
fight between local kids and the roaming wheaties, or a
marital spat that got out of hand. Agatite was a quiet
town, and the fear that lay beneath its surface and awakened its citizens late at night was never mentioned.

PART 1

You're wrong.—He was the mildest mannered man
    That ever scuttled ship or cut a throat;
With such true breeding of a gentleman,
    You never could divine his real thought,
No courtier could, and scarcely woman can
    Gird more deceit within a petticoat;
Pity he loved adventurous life's variety
He was so great a loss to good society.

            —*Don Juan*
              George Gordon, Lord Byron

1

Who would've known? Breedlove sipped the beer, which
was too warm, and leaned against the car, which was too
cool on his bare skin. She was still crying and had been
for more than an hour. The blackness of the sky all but
hid the oil derrick just a few yards off. He wished the
hell he'd never come out here with her. Captain of the
football team. Big deal! He *had* to prove himself, prove
something to someone. He felt like a louse, and his mouth
was sour and tasted like piss. Beer that was too damned
hot didn't help at all.

There was blood on his Levis, probably all over the
back seat, too. How in the hell was he going to explain
that to the old man? Easy? Shit. Easy. She was the one.
How in the hell was he supposed to have known? He
wished she would shut the hell up. It wasn't even fun!
He didn't even enjoy it, not the way everybody said they
enjoyed it. He couldn't even feel it with his jeans bunched
up around his knees, his boots jammed against the backseat's armrest, her pushing him away and pulling him to
her all at the same time. Shit.

His lips felt like hamburger from all the kissing. His
tongue was sore too. He could see the lights of Agatite
reflected off the northern sky, and he remembered that
they were all waiting for him back at the old Dairy Mart
parking lot. Waiting for him to come helling up, jump
out and begin to lie to them, the same way they had lied
to him, nearly every goddamn one of them. They had all
been out with her. But they had *lied*. Boy, they lied. He
knew, and he had the blood all over him to prove it. He
would have some laugh on them, boy! But he didn't feel

like laughing, not now, not with her blubbering all over hell back there.

The funny thing was that she really liked him. Him. The son of old man Breedlove, town drunk, town joke. What was funnier was that he didn't much like her. She was too prissy, too bitchy, too bossy. He only took her out because all the guys said she was easy.

She had been such a tease at school, even in the car at the drive-in. Grabbing his crotch, sticking her hand down his shirt when they started making out. Hell, she hadn't even done anything when he stuck his hand in her blouse, just let him feel away, pushing herself into him, saying, "No, no," from time to time, but not trying to stop him. Then when he worked his hand into her shorts, right past her underwear, she had only said, "Not here." Shit.

"Are you okay?" he asked in the vague direction of the dark window of the car. No reply. He could hear her crying. Yeah, she was a cock teaser all right. And now she was a crybaby.

"I trust you," she had said when he pulled up under the derrick and parked, turning out the lights and adjusting the radio on the old Chevy to KOMA, Oklahoma City. And then they had really gotten it on.

She had trusted him all right. She had trusted him to do exactly what he did, of that he was sure. And he wouldn't hurt her; he told her that over and over. Shit. But he didn't hurt her, not really. He just took her cherry, and now she was hurt plenty.

Hell, it was my cherry too, he wanted to yell at her blubbering shadow, hunched over, holding her blouse in front of her naked breasts and crying into it, and I ain't crying. Captains of football teams don't cry! Men don't cry! And I'm a man! Now.

But he didn't say anything. He reached into the front seat and grabbed his shirt, still wet from perspiration, and pulled it on. It was clammy on his back, and he inspected it to see if any blood had gotten on it as well. He couldn't see anything in the dark, though. He reached in again, this time opening the glove compartment and found a pack of Marlboros. Pressing in the car's lighter, he glanced at her again. She had stopped crying, and she was just sitting there, quietly staring and clutching her blouse. He could see her bare knees, and his eyes automatically traced the line of her thighs up to the darkness of her crotch until he stopped himself in disgust. That's enough of that, boy, he thought. You'd think you'd had enough of that for one night.

He stood up out of the car's window and strolled around front to get the rest of the beer. He finished it slowly, enjoying the smoke and the beer and the violation of Coach's rules more than ever before. Man, I've broken training all the way tonight, he thought, shaking his head and grinning humorlessly.

He heard her moving around, getting out of the back-seat and into the front. The radio played an Everly Brothers tune, and he waited until it was over before going around to the driver's side.

He got in and slammed the door. She was sitting with her hands in her lap, her hair falling down around her bowed head. He realized dumbly that she was still weeping, not blubbering like before, but weeping, like somebody had died.

"Hey," he said as softly as he could, "are you okay?" He put out his hand to touch her.

She jerked away from him, practically thrusting her head and shoulders out of the window to keep him from touching her. Her eyes were large with fear, but she suddenly regained control, started crying loudly again, and slumped back into the seat. "I wanna go home," she said through sobs.

He realized that he wanted to take her home more than anything else in the world.

He started the car and backed out onto Airport Road, then sprayed gravel from his tires getting away from the side road that led into the derrick area. He wanted to be witty, and he almost asked her if this meant that they were going steady. But he doubted she would take it as a joke.

Damn her anyway, he thought. He'd tried. What'd she expect? How was he supposed to know? It was all her fault, anyway. Prick tease. Bitch. As he drove back toward the lights of town, he found himself feeling very sad. He wished the hell she would stop crying.

II. Lawman
August, The Present

Sheriff Able Newsome of Sandhill County lazily rolled his Hava-Tampa Jewel from one side of his mouth to the other. He had mastered the art of shifting cigars from side to side without using his fingers some time ago. It was a studied technique that had a properly awesome and disarming effect on whomever happened to witness it. He particularly like using it on Newell Longman, the fat-assed mayor of Agatite, Texas, and Able's chief nemesis.

Able Newsome was a large man, muscular and not fat. He stood six-two, taller in his boots, and his broad, solid chest tapered nicely into a narrow waist that rested on powerful legs. His hands were large, but they could be gentle in the handling of small things. Clean-shaven, clear-eyed, Able Newsome was the sort of man law enforcement agencies like to use for their image. But Able didn't give a damn for image. He only cared about being healthy. His one vice was his cigars, and he ran five miles every morning along a country road, usually rising before dawn and going out to his storm cellar, where he kept a bench press and weights, in order to work out before his morning run.

He hoisted one copper-colored cowboy boot over the other, which was propped carefully on his desk, and enjoyed the comforting squeak from his two-hundred-pound mass straining the ancient swivel chair. It was to be another lazy summer day in August—dog days, somebody had called them—and he looked forward to the prospect of not having to venture forth from the office all afternoon.

A circulating fan hummed dreamily in the morning dust of the Sheriff's Office, and he felt himself becoming drowsy from the full breakfast he had eaten at the Town and Country Dinette, but a dull sense that there was too much to do around the office to permit him a nap kept him from moving over to the made-up bed in the holding cell that occupied the office's corner. He wasn't that interested in doing any of the work—papers piled ready for filing, and the usual reports that had to be typed and classified—but he stoically figured that staying awake and not doing it was better than sleeping and not doing it, and he fought off any feelings of guilt that began to rise.

Outside he could hear the sounds of a summer morning in Agatite—cars squealing to a stop on the sweating blacktop in front of the post office or City Hall, and down the hall a clatter of typewriters.

He plucked the cigar out of his mouth, rested the butt on a half-full ashtray, then pulled his revolver from its holster, grunting as he shifted position to reach it and causing the swivel chair to squeak. He had been out target shooting after his run that morning, something he rarely did, and the gun needed cleaning. With a mental grimace at having to sit up again, he lowered his boots to the floor and opened the desk drawer containing the cleaning kit.

The county courthouse had been designed in the mid-1920s, but the Great Depression had set in and it hadn't been built until the WPA came into town and constructed it. Able glanced up to the high twelve-foot ceilings and contemplated the asbestos tiles way up above the circulating fans. It was a comfortable office, smelling of old paper and tobacco, with just the right amount of clutter to make it look busy but not sloppy. Able Newsome liked his office, and he liked being sheriff. It was a comfortable position to have. It fit like a good boot. He held up his pistol, contemplating its blackness in the dim, dusty light of the Sheriff's Office.

The weapon that occupied his attention was a custom-made .44 with a bone handle inlaid with real silver. He had inherited it along with the badge he wore from Sheriff Ezra Stone Holmes, when the latter had retired back in 1952. Holmes told Able that he had killed some men with the gun, mostly bootleggers who chose to fight rather than to run when he caught them moving illegal whiskey through the county back during Prohibition. But one of the men slain by the .44, Able knew, had been a bank robber of national reputation whom the sheriff had gunned down as he was waiting on a sandwich he'd ordered from the counter girl in Central Drugs. Holmes had won himself a front-page picture in newspapers coast to coast for having removed a tri-state bank robber and killer from society, and the pistol, which Sheriff Holmes said had once belonged to one of the original Agatite founders, proved its worth as a weapon of stature and reliability. "It's a damn good gun," Holmes had told Able several times, "heavier than the regular pistols most sheriffs carry, but I like to know I can stop what I hit."

But Able had never fired the pistol "in the line of duty," as the phrase went, unless you counted—and he didn't—the shooting of old lady Carmichael's dog when Mrs. Carmichael was dead inside her house and the mongrel wouldn't let anybody past the front door. Able still remembered the incident with embarrassment. All the time he was taking aim at the mutt, he'd thought that it was silly to use the pistol when he had a perfectly good shotgun in the trunk of the cruiser. But he had gone ahead and put a slug through the dog's brain, spilling blood all over the old lady's porch and wincing to think of the comparison between Sheriff Holmes' bravery and his own weak attempt at subduing an angry dog.

Able broke down the pistol and began cleaning it, enjoying the smell of gun oil that came with the task. The bone grip was smooth and worn, and its custom design made the weapon hang easily in his hand. Secretly and silently Able hoped that he would never have to use the gun "in the line of duty" or any other line. He didn't want to kill a man with it, or, for that matter, another dog. It wasn't that he was afraid of killing some criminal; it was just that he had seen enough killing in Korea to last him a lifetime. What he mostly wanted to do with the gun was to pass it along to the next sheriff when the time came for retirement.

He replaced the cleaned gun in its holster and put away

the cleaning materials. Then he swung his body away from the desk, stood up, and yawned. By God, he thought, if I don't get started on the paperwork, I'll be asleep by noon. He strolled over to a smaller desk by the window and shuffled through the forms and reports he needed to deal with. There were the usual F.B.I., D.P.S., and local law enforcement bulletins and directives, and the prospect of sorting through them, separating the missing persons from the wanted criminals, then sub-classifying them into smaller categories bored him.

His eyes raised from the clutter of papers to City Hall, kitty-corner to the courthouse. A frown of frustration crossed Able's brow as he saw "Jingles" Murphy pull up in the city police squad car and shift his fat gut out onto the sidewalk. They have it all, Able thought sourly, feeling the breakfast that had previously been so com-forting grow heavy on his stomach. New goddamn cars, special riot guns, a radio dispatcher, renovated offices. Shit, they even have perma-pressed uniforms, not these butternut khakis we have to wash and iron.

He took a sheaf of reports, went back to his desk and got down to separating them into stacks.

A sudden series of shouts brought him back to the win-dow. He spotted City Patrolman Blair Phillips in a heated argument with a stranger dressed in Bermuda shorts and a golf shirt. The stranger's truck, a Chevrolet Suburban, was parked behind the squad car, and inside, Mrs. Stranger and two little Strangers peered in fear as Mr. Stranger ges-tured and yelled at Officer Phillips.

Phillips was standing quietly and allowing Mr. Stranger to vent his rage into the rapidly warming air. From the Sheriff's Office it was hard to tell what the nature of the argument was, but Able figured it was another speed trap problem. The tourists like Mr. Stranger were usually out-raged to be pulled over by a small-town cop. Usually Phillips and his counterpart, Clovis Hiker, would tap them if they were doing fifty-seven or better.

Shit, Able thought, the Highway Patrol gives them nine over. But not Jingles' boys. To pay for that shiny new squad car to complete their full trio of new vehicles, they had to increase their quotas, and Mr. Stranger wasn't too happy about being a part of Agatite's new revenue plan.

Soon Mr. Stranger ran out of steam, and, pulling a red bandanna out of his shorts, he wiped his balding head and was gently led by the arm into City Hall. He'll get twenty-five for speeding, Able calculated silently, and probably twenty-five more for abusing an officer of the law.

He grinned sourly. "Officer of the law," he said out loud—Phillips. Two years ago he was nothing but a street hood who probably had more citations than he'd written stashed in the glove compartment of his souped-up car. Somehow he seemed more threatening in a uniform and a squad car, Able thought, than he had been in greasy jeans and a hot rod.

Able's dislike of the two city patrolmen was the only point he and Mayor Newell Longman had ever agreed on. Both Phillips and Hiker were local toughs. Hiker hadn't even finished high school, and his reputation seemed to fit his face, scarred from a knife fight in one of the river beer joints over in Oklahoma that left him with only one good eye, the other being clouded and out of position. Both boys had made a practice of drinking too much, picking on the younger kids, and helling around town in their hot cars. Nobody liked them very much. Hiker had even been arrested once on a statutory rape charge when he was nineteen, but the girl's family had dropped charges after Phillips had "reasoned" with them.

When the police force had organized, Jingles was going to be the only cop for a while, but one blustery afternoon in October he had changed his mind and hired what he called the meanest sons of bitches he could find.

What had happened was that he got a call from over in what had once been called Nigger Town, or, officially, the Colored Section, but now was discreetly referred to as "across the tracks," that some white girls had had car trouble and some of the black boys were giving them a hard time. Able had taken the call while he was in the mayor's office, trying to convince Newell Longman that the Sheriff's Department needed a new cruiser more than Jingles needed a full-time dispatcher and communications system, and he had reacted too casually for the mayor's taste.

"I doubt there are any girls in trouble over there," Able had tried to explain to the fat, fuming mayor. "Sounds to me like a high school prank. What'd white girls be doing over there all by themselves in the first place?"

Newell wasn't in any mood to listen to reason. Seizing the opportunity to point out Able's inefficiency and to feed the fires of his own ill-hidden bigotry, he called Jingles and commanded that he go rescue these white damsels whose virtue was in danger of forced racial intermingling.

Jingles hadn't found any white girls in trouble, just as Able had predicted he wouldn't, but he'd taken the opportunity to roust a group of black youths at a neighborhood drugstore. Five of them had taken his gun away from him and were marching him down Main Street in his underwear and boots, making him sing the Agatite Eagles' fight song at the top of his falsetto lungs by the time Able was called in to rescue the chief of police.

By the time Able got to the scene, the boys had disappeared, and Jingles was sitting on the curb crying in indignation and shame, his pistol, which hadn't even been loaded, lying at his feet alongside of his bundled uniform.

Able drove over the tracks, but, as he expected, no one knew anything about anything. Even Old Samuel, the time-worn custodian of the First Security Bank, pleaded ignorance of any such thing, but Able detected a grin beneath the grizzled old Negro's frown, even as he denied that any of the Agatite boys would have such an idea about the much-respected chief of police.

By the time Able got back, Jingles had dressed and regained some of his composure, but he wasn't about to go back over the tracks, at least not alone, not even for something as sensational as a murder call, if there ever was one. He hid behind his excuse that all blacks looked alike to him, and he charged Able with the responsibility of finding those who had disgraced him in front of the whole town. But Able never did anything more about it, and Jingles decided it was best to forget the whole affair.

As a result of the day's events, however, Jingles got his communications system and a dispatcher to boot—his daughter-in-law, Chrystal—and now he could radio "officer in trouble" even if no one would come. He also hired two patrolmen, and he hit upon Phillips and Hiker because of their reputations. They would keep the kids in line, Jingles claimed, and they wouldn't take any shit from smart-aleck tourists, and they would kick black ass every time they got the chance. Their first official act, in fact, was to arrest about twenty black youths for running a crap game in the same drugstore where Jingles found trouble. The case was dismissed for lack of evidence. Not only were no dice turned up, but the arrested boys had less than fifteen dollars among them.

"What the hell kind of crap game can you have with no dice and fifteen dollars?" Judge Stokes had demanded of Jingles when he and his men had presented their offenders before the Sandhill County bench. "You leave these people alone!" Stokes had yelled at the three police officers. "They're good folks, and they don't need any of your ignorant, bigoted, hardheaded bullshit."

So except for a black trucker or tourist, no blacks were ever again brought before Judge Stokes' bench by the Agatite Police Department.

In fact, except for tourists and truckers, speed violators all, few arrests were ever made in Agatite. From time to time Able or Jingles would bring in some kid, but usually a quick call to the parents put an end to the matter and saved the city or county the cost of a meal or booking. Randy Tridell had taken Cy Breedlove's place as the town drunk since the latter died of exposure one cold December night, and Randy did enough maintenance work around the courthouse or City Hall in lieu of a fine, to make arresting him more of a prize than a chore. There hadn't been much serious crime in Agatite for a long, long time, more than a decade, really, or at

least none had been reported, and the "attempted" file
rarely resulted in an arrest being made. Usually a talking-
to was sufficient for most of the locals. There had been
a rash of prowlers the previous summer, and occasionally
a drunk driver would be picked up, or maybe a vagrant,
but there just wasn't enough crime in Agatite for two
separate law enforcement agencies. And that galled Able
Newsome.

He had managed to argue Newell Longman out of some
help for his own office. Sheriff Holmes' deputy-of-sorts,
Dooley, had died years before, and since he had worked
for practically nothing—room, board, and pocket
change—there were no funds to replace him. But now
Able had two deputies, both good men, who worked for
a third less than the city policemen made. They had to
buy their own uniforms and guns, and between them they
shared a single broken-down cruiser, a Chrysler, bought
secondhand from the Wichita Falls Police Department.
But Able was proud of their quiet ability to go about their
jobs with good manners, and he often bragged of their
stoical grace about accepting the shittiest work in the
county for less pay than they could have made in the gyp
mill, and their reputations for being honest, dependable
people.

One of the young men, John David Hogan, was a local
boy who had been halfway through law school down in
Austin when his young wife had developed complications
giving birth to their first child. He had dropped out and
moved home, seeking work to pay doctor bills and save
to complete his degree while living at home with his elderly mother. He was a particularly good man as college
kids go, but the child was sickly. Maribeth, his wife, had
gone to work at the First Security as a secretary, and John
David was frequently late going on duty and relieving
Vernon Ferguson, the daytime deputy.

Vernon had been rejected by the D.P.S. Academy for
bad knees and a possible heart murmur. He frequently
complained that those ailments hadn't kept him out of
the army or out of Vietnam, where he had served "with
valor," his papers said. But that was about all Vernon

ever complained about, or, for that matter, talked about at all. Vernon kept to himself and politely did his job with efficiency and decorum. Those things set him apart from anyone else Able knew, law officer or otherwise, but Vernon was also distinguished by another feature: he was black.

Old Samuel brought Vernon to Able as an applicant as soon as word was out that the sheriff's department was taking on deputies. That recommendation was enough for Able, as he had nothing but respect and admiration for Old Samuel, and he would have hired Vernon without his war record or impressive personal air that seemed to fill the room with authority.

Newell and Jingles had both shit bricks when they heard about Vernon. Newell called Able in and asked him in his irritating fatherly manner if he knew what the hell he was doing. Able simply said that this was an election year, and he didn't think it looked that good for the blacks in the community to be marching the chief of police down Main Street again, so he figured Vernon might come in handy. If Newell, or Jingles for that matter, didn't like it, Able added as an afterthought, they could go fuck themselves.

Newell had apparently taken that as enough of an explanation. He had even provided a new Buick cruiser for Able so the two deputies could share the used one from Wichita Falls, and the office was promised a secretary after the first of the year, although it was now August and none had been hired.

Able moved back to the papers on his desk, then wandered again to the window, lighting a fresh cigar, regretting briefly the one he had forgotten in the ashtray. He saw Mr. Stranger come raging out of City Hall.

The little man was literally shaking with rage and indignation. He was shaking a fist at the building and the window behind which he believed the fat chief of police and justice of the peace, Reilly Jameson, were counting and dividing the fifty-plus dollars they had just taken off him. Mrs. Stranger was yelling at Mr. Stranger to get back in the car before they decided to get him again, but he wouldn't be stopped, and he shouted as he edged toward the Suburban.

"Bunch of goddamn *thieves*!" Able heard in what he recognized as a northern accent. "I'm gonna stand by the goddamn county line an' warn people about you!" He reached the door of the Suburban just as Patrolman Phillips emerged on the City Hall steps. Mr. Stranger jumped inside and drove off quickly, but not, Able noted, quickly enough to invite another ticket from the grinning policeman. Inside the truck, as it disappeared around the corner of Main Street, Able could see Mrs. Stranger waving her arms and yelling at her husband.

Able sighed and went back to his paperwork. On top of the stack of bulletins was an update on the holdup gang that had terrorized small finance offices in the north part of the state. Only recently had it dawned on the Texas Rangers and the D.P.S. that the two robberies were committed by the same group of men. Each time they seemed to increase their armament, but other than their violent attacks on the small loan offices there didn't seem to be much pattern to their work, none except that they got away clean both times.

Able shrugged and tossed the bulletin into the "file suspense" basket for Vernon to take care of that afternoon. He didn't worry about holdups of small finance offices. The last establishment of such a nature in Agatite had closed down a year ago.

A fly buzzed into the office from the open hallway, and Able rose and went to close the door. He yawned again and suddenly realized that it was becoming hot in the building and went over to the wall switch to turn up the fans. His pocket watch told him it was more than an hour to lunchtime, so he still had time for a nap. He wondered idly what Sue Ellen would fix today, and he hoped it wasn't anything too heavy. It was too hot for heavy food. He didn't want to get fat like Jingles, who had a substantial pot hanging over his utility belt.

Eventually weakening in his resolve, Able wandered into the holding cell and lay back on the made-up bed, at first leaving his booted feet on the floor. Finally he pulled them up, adjusted the pillow, and began to doze. His pistol belt was uncomfortable, but he didn't think of removing it. He was almost completely asleep when the phone rang and he was summoned to come quickly to Hoolian.

2

As usual, Breedlove was short of money. His old man considered such nonsense as amusement parks to be about the biggest waste of money in the world. The grizzled old drunk had grudgingly given him five dollars, but a box lunch provided by the Agatite Eagles' Booster Auxiliary had taken two bucks, and he had immediately and foolishly spent one more for some cotton candy, a hot dog, and two cokes.

He sat idly on a concrete wall between the concession booths and amused himself by dropping large globs of spittle into the gravel walk, creating a miniature lake in the reddish, rocky surface and trying not to think about his troubles.

Craterville Amusement Park near Lake Lugart, Oklahoma, wasn't Six Flags Over Texas or anything, but it did have a bunch of exciting rides and a carnival midway that most kids in the region loved. Still, it was a summer place, and Breedlove felt the sharp bite of fall in the air, and the smell of the season's change was stronger than liquor. Something seemed odd to him about being there off-season, but he wondered if it wasn't just that he was broke and depressed that took the sparkle away from the park.

His depression was the result of a major fight he had had with her the night before at the dance after the big Olney game. He kept saying he thought carnival rides were for punks, and she, naturally, had called him cheap and said that he didn't care whether she wanted something or not.

He didn't want to tell her that he didn't have the money

to pay for a bunch of silly rides, and he wished she would just say she didn't want to go, and maybe they could go out to James Earl's and ride horses or something. But she kept talking about how she was so excited about getting to go to Craterville—the day trip was the Eagle Boosters' reward to the team, cheerleaders, and pep squad for winning District Championship—since she hadn't been there since she was a little kid. Then she had been too young to go on any of the really neat rides, so she couldn't wait for Breedlove to take her on them this time.

As Roy Orbison wailed over the loudspeakers at the Teen Canteen, they tried to keep the rhythm of the slow dance while they argued, but Breedlove felt something slipping in their relationship. She was getting pissed off as hell, and he was tired. The game had been a killer for him. His knee hurt where some big shit from Olney had clipped him, and the ref hadn't seen it or just hadn't called it. He had a headache from sampling some Coke with vodka in it that Phil Grimes had brought to the dance. Furthermore, he had worked for old man Coleman over at the Agatite Feed & Grain Store until ten o'clock every night for two weeks trying to make enough money to buy her a "sweet sixteen" present for her surprise birthday party the following weekend. He had spent all the money he made on a pendant with an opal stone in it. It was rested on his bureau at home, already wrapped and marked with a special note to her. And now she was behaving like a shit because he didn't have the money to take her on the goddamn Tilt-a-Whirl.

After the dance they had "broken up." Breedlove knew that neither one of them wanted it to happen, but happen it did. She had run off with two of her girlfriends, crying her eyes out, and they had all given him go-to-hell looks that girls can be so good at. He had gone to search for Grimes to see what he could do about getting drunk, but Grimes had already gone home.

They had both thought, he felt sure, that they could talk things over on the bus trip over to Craterville, but the goddamn boosters had separated the boys and girls because so many of the kids had brought along pillows in the predawn hours of departure, hoping to catch some sleep on the two-hour trip, and the chaperones were afraid that the idea of pillows and boys and girls suggested something nasty, so they hadn't seen each other all that day.

The park was nearly deserted when they got there except for the Agatite high school team and pep squad and cheerleaders. The men who ran the rides and games were glad to see the free-handed teenagers swarming over the grounds, and the kiddie rides quickly shut down in favor of the more thrilling attractions like the Tilt-a-Whirl, Octopus, or the ride of rides, the Hammer, which would spin adventuresome customers upside down as it spun in a complete circle of neon lights and spitting electrical noises.

There were other, tamer rides as well, but the Tunnel of Horrors was the major favorite for the young lovers in the crowd. They went through the swinging doors in the trams again and again, and the operator would deliberately stop it for a few minutes for the youthful smoochers in the darkness where skeletons and horrible masks would jump out at them, making them scream and grab each other even more tightly than they were inspired to just by the darkness and eerie music.

Breedlove got up from the concrete wall and wandered aimlessly around the amusement park, wishing he could find a place for a cigarette in secret, feeling the two dollars, now diminished by a wasted quarter spent in a ring-toss game, burning in his pocket. He occasionally caught a glimpse of her going around with Corky Poole, a pimply defensive end who had been after her ever since he moved to Agatite from Florida. They had been through the Tunnel of Horrors three times already, with her waving meaningfully at Breedlove each time the tram had bumped the swinging doors open.

Breedlove wanted to go over and punch Corky in his fat, greasy mouth and grab her and tell her the reason he didn't have any goddamn money. But his pride wouldn't let him. So he sulked around the midway and watched the other kids having a good time, frequently finding his steps leading him back to the Tunnel of Horrors.

Around noon the wind picked up some, and the fluffy clouds took on a hard gray metallic look that signaled a cold front moving in. He strolled back to the bus for his letter jacket which she had returned to him the night before by wadding it up and throwing it at him before she went off with her girlfriends. That was one good thing, he thought, as he wandered by the Tunnel of Horrors again and listened to the delighted screams of terrorized pleasure from inside. Bitch.

He walked up and down in front of the ride, trying to work up the courage to swallow his pride and make up with her, when suddenly he noticed the building next to the Tunnel of Horrors. It looked more like a little house than a midway attraction, and he ignored it as had most all the kids, electing instead to follow the neon lights and bright tent-tops of the other rides and games. The house had windows almost all around it, and a wooden porch that covered the front and side. He stepped up onto the porch and peered into the window and saw his reflection looking back at him. What the hell? he thought. He went around the corner, and then he saw the bill.

It was a twenty, scotch-taped to the window on the inside. Right above it was a sign—House of Mirrors—it was a maze! A trail which, if followed correctly would lead the customer through to the bill. It must be some maze, Breedlove thought.

In his jacket pocket he fingered the single one and change that he had left. Cokes, he dimly realized, were thirty-five cents apiece, for small ones, and they weren't planning to eat their box lunches until four o'clock, when they would go over to the picnic grounds near the lake. He'd have to choke his down dry or do without much of anything else until then. That twenty could make him rich!

Screams from the Tunnel of Horrors reached his ears as he stood in the rapidly cooling breeze that hinted of sleet later in the day. He could hear her above all the rest, and he could also, he imagined, hear Corky's idiot giggle along with hers. With the twenty he could take her on the goddamn Tilt-a-Whirl all she wanted. Even the Hammer, which Corky was scared of, he had heard.

Admission was posted as seventy-five cents for the House of Mirrors. That was three times what the other attractions cost. He suddenly saw James Earl Meacham coming over to him with Maggie on his arm, snuggling into his side against the cooling wind. James Earl hated carnival rides and carnivals in general. He and Maggie had sneaked back onto the buses after the kids had left and spent their time making out, from the looks of her messed-up hair and rumpled blouse. They talked about the House of Mirrors for a minute. Maggie said she had been over here last summer on a church outing and had tried it.

It was really tough to get to the twenty, she said. Nobody in the group had made it, but the manager did it for them just to show it wasn't a trick. She giggled and asked Breedlove if he was going to try it. He said no, and went over to get a Coke, and they went toward the Tunnel of Horrors, which by now didn't even stop unless people wanted to get on or off. The operator just took up more money while they passed by and rode the young lovers again and again.

Breedlove sat on a wooden bench and contemplated the House of Mirrors as he sipped his Coke, noting disgustedly that it was more ice than drink. Bright carnival music came from the Merry-Go-Round, but few if any kids were riding it. He glanced around and noticed Michael Perkins, last year's All State center, throwing up hot dogs and Cokes after his fifth ride on the Hammer with Millie Hogart, who was now standing by his side and trying between giggles to be helpful and sympathetic. They were all having such a damned good time, Breedlove thought sadly, and it was because they had money.

He had one dollar and forty cents left. Enough for a large Coke with his lunch and . . . and, he realized, a trip through the House of Mirrors.

No one was paying any attention to him, but if he

made it, and something inside him told him he could, he would have twenty bucks. Twenty bucks to blow!

Suddenly Virgil Hightower and his girlfriend Penny Ubanks sauntered over to the boardwalk around the House of Mirrors. They didn't see Breedlove. Breedlove didn't like Virgil worth a shit. He cheated in school, for one thing, and he had been caught masturbating in the locker room showers. The guys had all started calling him "Squirtgun" after that, but then he'd started going with Penny, a big-titted girl who was less good-looking than she was available. His tales of their sexual escapades had taken attention away from his perversion and his nickname, and more than one clean-living team member had hustled himself into the fieldhouse john to jerk off after one of Virgil's stories. Breedlove didn't believe much of what Virgil said, and he thought Penny was mostly a whore who only put out so she could hang around with the football boys and feel popular.

Virgil and Penny scooted around the corner, and Breedlove realized to his horror that they were going to try the House of Mirrors. He'd been thinking about it for too long, he realized, and they were ahead of him.

Without another moment's thought, he pulled the one dollar from his jacket pocket and rushed around to the ticket booth. A bored, fat woman with a dark line of hair on her upper lip took his dollar and smacked chewing gum at his hand stretched out for the quarter change. After a few seconds she jerked a pudgy thumb to a faded sign over the ticket booth that specified that adults were charged a dollar and kids under twelve only seventy-five cents. That left Breedlove only forty cents, he knew, but there was the twenty. He rushed through the turnstile into the maze.

Inside, the mirrors were more confusing than they had looked from the boardwalk. Breedlove found himself in dead end after dead end, and he could hear Virgil and Penny giggling and laughing around corners all the time, even though he never ran into them directly. At first he raced blindly through the glass maze, bumping into himself over and over again, once so hard he feared he'd broken the glass. Finally he found himself standing at an outside window, and he paused to catch his breath and gazed onto the midway.

He saw Corky and her going over to the Tilt-a-Whirl, giggling and holding hands. If he had found one outside wall, he reasoned, he could find the one with the twenty. With a renewed confidence, he turned to search through the glass hallways again.

His wrist smarted from where he had bumped into himself, and he began to lose track of time and direction. The air was stuffy inside the House of Mirrors, and he took off his jacket, almost laying it down before he thought better of the idea. This was too goddamn small a house for him to have been wandering around all this time, he thought. He'd been going over the same path again and again.

He stood still and tried to recall his route for the past few minutes. He thought he had it, and started out again only to become as confused and lost as he had been in only a few steps. All the mirrors looked alike. They were dirty and fly-specked in places, and they seemed to mock him with his own frustrated reflection, now growing increasingly sweaty and haggard as he tried to figure out where he had been and which way to turn next.

All at once an idea struck him, and he took his index finger and wet it in his mouth. Carefully, just above the eye level on the mirror to the right of the passage between where he stood and the next hallway, he marked a wet cross in the dust. It stayed marked. He moved into the next room of glass and did the same thing. Eventually he had marked five rooms, and when he encountered the same mark again, he turned left instead of right.

An overwhelming sense of progress swelled over him as he came upon unmarked mirrors and moved through the maze. Finally he began to understand a crazy logic that traced the pattern of the hallways. He went left, left, right, then right twice more, and then left again. Behind him he heard Virgil and Penny still giggling and fumbling around. They were apparently trying to find their way out. Good, he thought.

Suddenly Breedlove emerged into a room where the outside wall held the twenty. He stopped dead and looked at it. He was breathing hard. It was three steps across the room, then the twenty would peel off and all he had to do was find his way out. He wondered if he was obliged to tell the fat woman in the ticket booth that he had taken it, but he decided he wouldn't. They might not let him keep it.

He was already forming his approach to her. Maybe they could buy some hamburgers or chicken from the concession booths and throw away the cold box lunches. God, he hoped they'd have time to ride several rides.

He took a deep breath and stepped across to the window. Too bad, he thought, that nobody was outside watching him. He ran his hands around the bill, feeling the coolness of the glass beneath his fingertips and enjoying the anticipation of actually possessing the bill. He wanted to take special care not to tear the twenty, and he slowly moved his nails into place near the scotch tape. Then, incredibly, his fingernails slid right past the tape's edge. He clawed at it, but they passed again without resistance. All that was there was the smooth coolness of the glass. The bill wasn't there at all.

But he could see it. Still it wasn't there, not on the inside of the glass as it appeared to be. It was between a double pane of glass that covered the entire outer wall of the House of Mirrors. He couldn't get to it from the inside anymore than he could from the outside. It was a goddamn trick!

Frantically he ran his eyes up and around the pane of glass, but it was tightly sealed and puttied into place. There was no way he could get to the bill without breaking the window, and he briefly considered it. For a moment he made a fist and thought of simply pushing it through the pane, smashing the glass into splinters. But he could feel how strong it was, and he knew he could wind up cutting himself to shreds if he tried it. Besides, he thought, even if he did it, they would probably make him pay for it.

He leaned against the glass with his forehead, feeling

the cool which by now was coming in from the outside and giving the maze a chilly atmosphere. His breath fogged the mirror, and he reached up and made a tiny cross in the frosted circle. "Story of my life," he said softly.

On the midway the wind was whipping up dust devils and making the brightly colored tents flap. Some of the rides were shutting down, and the games operators were pulling down plywood shutters around their booths. He saw her and Corky talking to James Earl and Maggie in front of the Merry-Go-Round. Its music didn't penetrate the maze of the House of Mirrors, but he noticed that they were all huddling together against the chill of the wind. She was tightly snuggled into Corky's side, cold in spite of the fact that she wore his letter jacket.

Breedlove closed his eyes and thought of the forty cents in his pocket. All of a sudden the tears began to come.

II. Lawman
August

The swirl of white dust had not quite settled around the sheriff's big black Buick cruiser when Able Newsome climbed out and stood up straight. He didn't much like the Buick, since it forced him to have to readjust his pistol belt and straw hat every time he got in or out of it, and he was particularly aggravated by the dusty, all-weather street that was already settling on his copper-colored boots.

August heat hit him squarely in the face as he walked through the dust up to the door of the Hoolian Barber-shop, and the fabric of his shirt quickly gave up the cool from the cruiser's air conditioner and began to moisten with sweat. The dust made little puffs as he moved off the road that passed for a street across a bed of red ants toward the concrete porch of the shop, and he automatically cast a wary eye into the weeds alongside the ditch for snakes.

Outside the shop, in spite of the heat, a small knot of

men stood. Able recognized most of them by face if not by name right away. There was Mel Stephens, the barber, and Ray Clifford, still wearing his barber's apron with small clipped hairs stuck to it. Apparently he had actually been in the shop for a haircut for a change instead of the infamous three G's—Gossip, Guzzle, and Goofoff—for which the small establishment was widely known.

Ever since Able's childhood Mel had been the barber in Hoolian, and his shop had become one of the two remaining businesses in the small country community that once had flourished in an age before automobiles made travel into such municipalities as Agatite practical. All that remained of Hoolian now was the old barbershop and a combination garage and feed store on what used to be a street corner a block away. In fact, the other two men, whose names escaped Able for the moment, were probably from there, he judged, noting that one wore greasy overalls and the other carried a large socket wrench in one hand.

The Hoolian Barbershop was an institution in Sandhill County, even though Hoolian had ceased to exist sometime before World War II. The three or four stone or adobe buildings that remained were boarded up and in a state of advanced decay, and the one or two houses that hadn't been moved into Agatite in one or two pieces were falling down and choked by weeds and ant beds. As a functioning business, the barbershop was more of a gathering place than a hair-cutting establishment. Mel kept cold drinks on hand and a full rack of pornographic magazines. Anyone who stopped by could count on a game of dominos, checkers, or the latest gossip from around the county. His business was more talk than cut—everyone knew it—and it was regarded with suspicious eyes by the ladies of the county just as it was jealously guarded in its integrity by the men who frequented it as a place to escape the college kids, communists, and other riffraff the government suffered to exist in the world. It was also a place where a man could get an illegal drink in a dry county, although that was the best-known secret around.

Even Able knew it and looked the other way. After all, it wasn't hurting anybody, and people had been drinking at Mel's a lot longer than he'd been sheriff.

In order to keep solvent, Mel had to start cutting the hair of the migrant farm workers, mostly Mexican-Americans, mestizos, who moved through the county from time to time. The two shops in Agatite wouldn't let them in the door as the workers reportedly had lice and greased their hair so much. Even the black shop wouldn't take the Mexican-Americans, but Melvin kept a special set of scissors and combs under a purple fluorescent light that was guaranteed to purify, and on Friday mornings and some Wednesdays he would take them if they could get off work and if there were no white customers ahead of them—or behind them, for that matter.

No one particularly liked the idea of the dark-skinned men coming into the Hoolian Barbershop, but Mel made the situation easier on his regulars by instituting a set of rules for the mestizos. They had to wait out on the porch, regardless of the weather. They paid double what the white customers paid, and if they needed to go to the rest room, they had to use the outside johnny behind the shop.

The johnny was anything but inviting. Stuck forty feet behind the back wall of the barbershop in a patch of Johnson grass, tumbleweeds, and red ant beds, it challenged even the most desperate individual's resolve not to unzip and piss in public. Wasps and hornets buzzed around the tin roof, and the path was so narrow and cramped by high grass and weeds that even the dullest imagination had no problem envisioning eight-foot rattlers lying in wait on either side.

Mel did nothing to clean or maintain the facility in any way, and the stench from the trench underneath was discernible from fifteen feet, even though no one could remember anyone using it in years. Mel had installed a commode in a storage closet in the back of the shop some ten years before. But it was strictly reserved for his white patrons, particularly those he knew. He had hand-lettered an "Out of Order" sign, which permanently dangled from the closet door's knob, and while Ray and others who dropped by for conversation ignored it, the sign directed other, less desirable clientele to the filthy johnny out back. It was a standing joke among Mel's regulars. Most of the Hispanic patrons avoided it by waiting until they got home or, if their needs were particularly strong, by heading for the outcroppings of mesquite in the pasture beyond the small outhouse.

On this particular August morning, however, a young Mexican lad had come into the shop and was immediately sent out to the porch to wait until Mel completed the finishing touches on Ray's diminishing locks. After a bit, the boy stuck his head indoors and asked permission to use the toilet, but Mel had shaken his head and hooked his thumb out the back window of the shop toward the johnny. "Not working, a-meego," he had said, while Ray giggled like an idiot. "Have to use the crapper."

A few minutes passed while Mel and Ray exchanged jokes about mescans, and suddenly the boy burst back into the shop's door, screaming breathlessly in Spanish and half pulling and half pushing Ray and Mel out the door in the direction of the johnny.

Two minutes later Mel called Able Newsome.

Hoolian is only about a fifteen-minute drive from Agatite, and Able made it in normal time. He didn't know what was going on out there, but he figured it wasn't too serious, in spite of the loud, confused phone call from Mel. The old barber wouldn't say why he wanted the sheriff to come, only that he'd better come quick, and in the background Able could hear someone shouting in Spanish and Ray yelling for him to "speak English, goddamnit."

So when Able Newsome arrived and approached the men in front of the shop, he wasn't in too good a mood. He envisioned his lunch being spoiled by this stupid country drive in the heat to fix some squabble between Mel and the mestizos, and he looked with less than his usual tolerant feeling toward the small brown boy squatting on the concrete porch of the shop. "So what's up this time," he asked in general. "What is it, Mel?"

The whole group exploded in explanation at once, and

Able almost had to scream to get them to talk one at a time. Finally he got the information he sought.

"Who found it?" he asked the boy.

"I did," the youngster answered, dusting off his trousers which were conspicuously cleaner than Ray's or any of the others standing around him. "I went in, and there she was. I slammed the door. . . ." He trailed off.

"You know her?" He directed the question at Mel, noting that the boy looked scared and sick, but Able felt instinctively that the youth was worried because he had unwittingly stepped into a white man's mess and figured, all things being equal, he would be blamed. The men were all quiet, watching both Mel and the boy as they shuffled around.

"Well?" Able repeated the question and glanced at them each in turn.

"How the hell should I know?" Mel shouted at Able, then realized how loud his voice was and lowered it. "I didn't stand there and study her none, for Chrissake!"

Ray shook his head slowly. "It's pretty bad, Able, pretty goddamn bad."

Able shifted his weight and took a deep breath of the superheated air around the shop. He felt sweat running from under his arms down his sides. "Did you call an ambulance?" he asked.

"Ambulance?" Mel shouted, and started to guffaw, then caught himself. "You go take a look, Able!" he demanded, moving his hand up to wipe his mouth. "She ain't needed an ambulance in quite a while. You go take a look."

Able stood looking around the faces of the group of men, pivoting his body and holding his hand on the butt of the holstered .44. He realized that they were all waiting for him to go and look. And why didn't he? That was his job, wasn't it? He also realized that from the garbled accounts of what was waiting for him to look at, he didn't want to. He knew he would rather do almost anything than go back there and look into the outhouse. But he also knew that he had to go and look. And he had to do it right then.

Sweat ran down the side of his face and he could feel the wetness of his shirt under his arms. He stood one minute more, listening to the traffic over on U.S. 287, to a dog barking like hell someplace, sounds of cicada, grasshoppers, his own breathing, his own heart beating.

He had seen plenty of death in Korea. Lately, he had been finding more and more old people who had died or killed themselves in houses remotely placed around the country. He remembered the old lady who had been dead and whose dog he had shot. She had been there for three days when he burst into the front door. She had been on the floor, near the telephone, reaching for it when her heart burst. And he had seen car wreck victims, victims of violence of practically every kind, inflicted with all sorts of weapons. But something in him didn't want to see what was in Mel's outhouse.

His eyes moved around the group once more, and he swallowed hard. His mouth was dry, and he wished he could ask Mel for a sip of some of the whiskey he knew the old barber kept in the back room, but he also knew Mel would deny having any, and the whole group would be shocked at Able's breach of county etiquette. The dog in the distance stopped barking, and Able wondered why. Then, without a conscious command from his brain, he found himself walking around the side of the shop toward the overgrown path that led to the johnny in the back.

The four men and the boy hung back a little. Able paused where the path to the outhouse entered the weeds and turned on them. "You men wait here," he said, pointing briefly at Mel, noting that Ray had a pint bottle sticking conspicuously from under his barber's apron.

"Don't worry, Able," Ray snickered. "We ain't gonna look again."

"Then shut up," Able ordered, madder at himself for sounding angry than he was at these buffoons who were lollygagging around, waiting to see what his reaction would be. "You two, go on home, unless you got business here or know something about this," he said to the two mechanics who were standing behind Mel and Ray. They slunk off around the side of the shop.

Able turned to face the path again. The door hung at an odd angle, probably a result of the boy's slamming it shut. It was slightly open, revealing nothing of the interior. The grasshopper sounds increased as he became aware of the white-hot heat from the noonday sun, the breathlessness in the atmosphere. Somewhere the dog, or a different dog, had begun barking again, a rasping, frantic bark that indicated that it had discovered an interloper in its territory, maybe a prairie dog, snake, or other dog. Maybe a man. Able rested his hand on his pistol butt again, then quickly withdrew it, not wanting to gain more snickering comments from the country hicks behind him.

Fear overcame him and he fought it back with difficulty, noting that his stomach was heaving already in anticipation of what he was about to see. He felt a knot forming in his throat, and his tongue felt like an old, dry rope, fruitlessly attempting to wet his lips. Finally he stepped onto the path, instinctively looking for snakes and listening for the warning rattle that would blessedly postpone the task at hand, but none came.

The grasshopper sounds ceased abruptly as his legs brushed the tumbleweeds and cactus and Johnson grass strands, and he set his jaw, walking as deliberately as he could toward the outhouse door.

The smell hit him from about fifteen feet, and he involuntarily reeled back from it, recognizing it immediately from the battlegrounds he had walked on. It was the smell of carrion, of death, of rotting human tissue, or corpse, bloated, bursting, exploding at a touch.

Awful as it was, it gave him an eerie feeling of familiar comfort, and the fear receded. He felt he could deal with what was beyond the door of the johnny now. It was going to be bad, he knew, but at least it was familiar. There wouldn't be anything there he hadn't seen before. More quickly now, he moved to the outhouse door and grabbed it to open it.

The weeds and overgrowth resisted his moving the door to a fully open position. He looked down to see what he could do to make it clear the strands of vegetation that had wound around the rotten bottom of the jamb. He pushed harder, and the door came completely off its hinges in his hands, and his attention shifted to prevent falling over with it into the tumbleweeds. He dropped it into the weeds in a cloud of dust and splinters, and then automatically, before he thought about what he was doing, he looked up, into the outhouse's interior.

"Jesus Christ on a crutch!" he said, drawing air in through clenched teeth. "Bleeding Jesus Christ on a goddamn crutch."

3

I. Breedlove
1969

The Greyhound became a missile of silver against the hot
Texas sun. Breedlove sat behind the gray-tinted windows
watching the fields zip past him. He had the old feeling
again: of his father sitting behind his three-day beard,
smelling of cheap whiskey, trying his damnedest to look
disapproving as he said, "All young men . . . how do
you think you came into the world? . . ." and trailing off
and lighting another Camel and shaking his head.

Breedlove remembered all the kids in school laughing,
kidding around about it. Her and him. Well, hell, who
wouldn't believe it? They had been going steady for two
years, hadn't they? What the hell else did going steady
mean other than screwing, getting ready to get married?

By no one really thought *she* would marry the son of
Cy Breedlove, the town drunk, not unless . . . not unless
. . . not unless she got knocked up—there, it was said,
at least to himself. He had knocked her up. Then she *had*
to marry him. That's how it looked anyway. But that
wasn't how it was.

He looked out the bus window at the wheat fields.
There had been a lot of rain this spring, he knew. Too
much for the wheat. They hadn't been able to get it out
of the fields in time, and now they'd have to plough it
under. God, he knew about that—the thought made him
sweat. He had spent too many hours on top of a tractor
ploughing wheat stubble under. But this year there would
be more than stubble, and that would be hard on the
farmers and, indirectly, on everyone else. But Breedlove
didn't really care. In fact, he took a perverse pleasure in
the misfortune of those who fought the heat, mesquite,

and rain of north central Texas. Somehow it seemed just that the farmers in Sandhill County would lose their asses this year. He had sure as hell lost more than they ever would.

As he settled back into the plush seat of the Greyhound and closed his eyes, he contemplated his future. He had a fifty-dollar bill, a bottle of whiskey, and a job waiting for him down near Anson. He was pat.

In his mind the picture of her father coming over to Breedlove's house that evening crept in. He wore thick glasses, her father, and he had entered the filthy smells of the Breedlove home, noticed with a sniff the empty bottles his old man had left out in plain view, the unwashed dishes, clothes scattered all over the worn-out furniture, and then he suggested they go out onto the porch.

"It's okay, son," her father said. "Everyone makes mistakes. You kids made yours, and now you've got to live up to your responsibilities." Breedlove remembered shuffling his feet in the growing dusk and wishing the man would simply go away. "I've spoken to Hillis Potter, and he said you could go to work in the lumberyard. It's not a lot of money, at first, but you're a bright boy, not like . . ." He trailed off with a shrug and a glance toward the ramshackle house where Cy Breedlove snored in the back bedroom and waited until full dark when he would start drinking again, "And I'm sure you'll be a good provider for, uh, my daughter, uh, your wife, and, uh . . . family," he finally finished and lit a pipe that seemed to fog his glasses.

Sure, Breedlove thought, listening to the night sounds around them and watching his pipe smoke in the streetlight's silvery haze, everyone makes mistakes. But that was one mistake he didn't make. He got the hell out. That very night. He didn't want to work in any goddamn lumberyard, and he didn't want to marry her. So he just packed a duffel bag his old man had brought home from the service and split.

Now, after six months of wandering around in Fort Worth, Dallas, and finally Wichita Falls, he had found a guy who was hiring for an oil drilling team down around Anson. The guy advanced him fifty, gave him a pint of good whiskey, and bought him a bus ticket.

The worst part of it, he believed, was pretending that it was all his idea, to get married. He didn't even get asked about anything. He went over to see her just like he always did after two-a-days, and she and her mother, who never spoke to him either before or after she knew her daughter was pregnant, would be sitting there, making plans, picking out patterns of silver and china, colors for bridesmaids' dresses, all that shit. He wasn't even asked what church he wanted to do it in, not that he gave a damn. She was a Methodist, he knew, but he never went to church except on Easter and Christmas.

He wondered what she had named it. "It" was always *it*. Never him or her, only it, a shapeless thing in his mind that would never have a name or personality but that always would be a part of him. But it was an it, a *thing* that screwed up his life and kept him from ever going home again, not that he wanted to. After all, his luck was changing. He had a fifty, a bottle, and a job.

Trying to forget, he squeezed his eyes shut. The girl in the seat behind him reached over and touched his shoulder, and he almost jumped straight up. She wanted a light, and she gestured with her cigarette rather than ask for it. He concentrated hard as he fished out a lighter from his pocket, trying to keep his eyes away from her breasts as they strained against a college sweatshirt, trying to think of something to say, to ask her, anything to prolong the moment she drew sexily in on the cigarette. The moment passed, however, and she leaned back and began leafing through a magazine.

Just for a moment the image of her, standing in the Methodist church, surrounded by her father, her friends—*their* friends, he corrected—and her mother who had finally broken down and asked him, "Uh, is your, uh . . . father . . . planning to come to the, uh . . . wedding?" appeared in the eyes of the girl who had asked for the light. But he turned quickly and faced forward.

Had she cried when he didn't show up? She probably

did. She always did cry easily. Her father was probably
pissed as hell, and her mother—well, she was probably
relieved. Better to be the grandmother of a bastard than
the in-law of the town drunk.

He opened the paperback he had found in the bus station's men's room and tried to read it, but the words
didn't seem to go together on the page, and he finally
realized that it was written in French. That figured, he
thought, dropping it onto the empty seat beside him, and
he briefly considered asking the girl behind him about it.
Maybe she spoke French. But he shook his head. He
didn't need any more trouble.

II. Lawman
August

Sheriff Able Newsome reached out his hand to steady
himself on the outhouse's door jamb, but as soon as his
fingers and palms made contact with the ancient wood,
he jerked them back as if he had been burned by a horrible heat. From inside the ramshackle building came an
imaginary furnace blast, floating on the odor he had
smelled before, now sickly sweet and stronger, wafting
past him in waves he was certain he could see. As his
eyes adjusted to the dusky interior of the building, he
moved his hand to his throat and then to his mouth, as if
to hold back the contents of his stomach, which were
churning and threatening to erupt.

A habit people who discover a corpse inevitably have
is to stare at the face, hoping, perhaps fearing, that some
life improbably might remain. Able's eyes, however, refused to find the face, and they fell to the toilet seat,
from which they began to rise toward the horrible aspect
he knew he would sooner or later have to see.

The woman hung suspended by a frayed piece of electrical cord that had been tied to a rotting beam over the
one-holer. Her feet dangled inches from the toilet's opening, and one shoe was missing. The remaining pump was
half off, hanging impossibly on her toes. Her stockings

were streaked with some dark substance, and one was torn in gashes, although her leg didn't seem to be scratched. Able's mind unreasonably documented that she had been well-dressed, noting the peach-colored suit with the slit skirt, now torn and stained, and the frilly white blouse she wore under it. The front of the blouse was ripped open, but her slip and bra were intact, and her arms, which hung loosely by her sides, were unbound. Her hands were, in fact, open, not clasping anything, and Able noticed, again bothered by the conspicuous details of the whole scene, that she wore heavy peach-colored polish and that three of her long, well-manicured nails were broken off at clean ends. But try as he might, he could not continue to force himself to dwell on the facts of her lower body, and his eyes continued their ascent.

Above the frilly collar of the blouse her neck was stretched an incredible length, the weight of the body having pulled her torso away from the skull without breaking the spinal connection. The electrical cord was buried so deeply in a dark brown scar under her chin that it almost disappeared into the folds of rotten skin, and her hair hung straight down, dark and matted, and framed her open mouth.

Her eyes were completely gone, the open sockets dried and dark as if they were holes without bottoms, and her nostrils were flayed open with creases running horizontally across both cheeks below her open, sightless stare. "Birds?" Able wondered aloud, his voice little more than a choking whisper.

Her jaw hung open in a silent scream, with the lips shriveled back from the teeth, some of which seemed broken, but no scream was possible. For inside the open mouth was an enormous wasp's nest, filled with eggs and covered by the Indian-red insects busily tending their home.

Able watched the wasps, horribly fascinated, then his eyes fell down her body again, trying to collect details, facts, clues if there were any. He looked about the floor of the outhouse for a purse or a wallet, something to identify her; then, unable to stop himself, he raised his head again to stare at the eyeless face, the mouth filled with paper chewed and digested by hundreds of tiny insect mouths, and he felt the bile of the morning's breakfast fill his throat and mouth.

Able half-turned and half-stumbled down the path away from the johnny. He was dimly aware of the constant barking of the dog he had heard before, and the whole area swam before his eyes.

Ray and Mel and the Mexican boy stood watching him, oddly pale and cool in the intense heat. Able reached their feet and dropped down to one knee, prepared to vomit, but he brought all his will to bear and forced the vileness in his throat back down. He fished a handkerchief out of his pocket and wiped the sweat off his face and neck.

"Did anybody touch anything?" he asked when he could trust his voice to sound reasonably normal. He stood up.

"You gotta be kiddin'," Ray piped up. "I gotta tell you, Able, I worked burial detail on Guadalcanal, an' I never—"

"Shut up," Able cut him off, and Ray cast his eyes down, remembering that Able was a bona fide war hero, not some back lines shit detailer, and had probably seen worse, much worse, than Ray had.

"Who the hell is she?" Mel asked Able, as if the sheriff would know.

Able didn't say anything for a moment, then he turned slightly so he could see the outhouse. From where he stood nothing of the inside could be detected. It was simply a black hole, made darker by the reflection of the sun off the building's tin roof. "Who knows? Who can tell?" he said quietly.

Mel spat out some tobacco juice from a plug he had been working. "I wonder how long she's, uh . . . ." He looked at the outhouse and didn't finish the thought.

Able picked up the thread. "How long's it been since anybody's been in there?" he asked Mel.

"Hard to say," Mel said, scratching his groin and then wiping his chin, which was dripping juice-laden spittle.

"Last time I remember anybody *askin'* to use it was last winter. 'Course, people come by when I ain't here an' use it, I reckon. *I* sure as hell never go out there."

Able glanced quickly at the Mexican boy, who was looking at Mel with open contempt, and he suddenly was embarrassed. "Y'all go wait in the shop. I don't want nobody goin' near that outhouse till we check it out."

"Don't have to worry 'bout that," Ray said, turning to walk around to the front of the building and pulling the Mexican boy along behind him.

Mel stood his ground for a moment, still scratching his groin and shaking his head. "Wish them people would find someplace else to make their mess," he said, starting to turn and follow Ray and the boy.

"What'd you mean?" Able asked sharply.

"Niggers," Mel said definitively. "Goddamn nigger bitch picks my place to hang herself. Now what're people gonna think?" He spat derisively into the gravelly soil.

"What makes you think she's a nig—that she's black?" Able asked, suddenly interested. Mel looked at him incredulously.

"You seen her, didn't you?" he asked.

"That's normal," Able said, sighing. For a moment he thought Mel knew more than he was telling, but apparently not.

"People, *white* people, turn black when they, uh, decompose in the heat. It's normal. She *might* be black, but I don't think so."

"Well, I'll be damned," Mel said, spitting again on the ground. "Shouldn't you cut her down or somethin'?" he asked.

"I don't want nobody touchin' nothin'," Able repeated. "She's been hangin' there for God knows how long, and another hour or two won't make her or anybody else any difference." The thought of having to touch the horror out in the johnny made his stomach churn dangerously.

After one more look into the dark interior of the johnny, Able went around the other side of the building to the cruiser. He had left the windows up, and as he opened the door and sat down, the superheated air inside almost choked him. The foul smell of old cigar smoke was intolerable, so he learned out the door. He turned on the radio and keyed the mike, wincing at the hot plastic when it burned his fingers. He was completely covered with sweat.

Well, he thought, at least he hadn't puked his guts out in front of these guys. He wondered if they had when they saw her.

"Chrystal?" he said into the mike.

"Now, Able, you know that Chief Murphy wants you to use official procedure on the radio," her whining voice lectured back at him.

For a moment Able tried to remember his official call number assigned by Jingles Murphy to the sheriff's department, but his head was swimming with the heat and the suddenly recalled vision of the outhouse and its contents. "Goddamn it, Chrystal, let me talk to Murphy right now!"

"Okay, okay," she said, and he pictured her jumping when he snapped at her. She was Murphy's daughter-in-law and dumber than a hammered thumb. She was pretty, though, in a trashy sort of way, and Able correctly figured that one or both of Jingles' patrolmen were banging her in the holding cell every chance they got in spite of her happy marriage to Jingles' wimpy son. That boy was no more of a prize than his father was, and she was no better a dispatcher than Jingles was a police chief.

After a long time she came back on. "S-219? S-219? This is HQ calling S-219."

"God*damnit,* Chrystal, if you don't put lard-ass Murphy on right now, I'm gonna come in there and braid your tits," Able yelled into the mike, immediately regretting his loss of temper. Sweat was running into his eyes and mouth, and he felt almost frantic in the heat.

"My God, Able," she said, shocked by his unusual vulgarity, "what's wrong?"

He said nothing for a moment, his anger preventing any reasonable comment or explanation. He never called Murphy on the radio, for just this reason—having to deal with this silly, horny little bitch and all the goddamn *Dragnet* jargon Murphy had invented.

"Chief Murphy is in disposal at the moment," she finally said curtly when he didn't answer her. "But you shouldn't talk to me like—"

"Listen, Chrystal," Able broke in, "you tell that fat-assed Murphy to get in his fancy new police car and hightail it out to Hoolian right now. I'll be waitin' for him in front of the barbershop. Tell him *now!*"

"Okay," she said, and he had another thought.

"And call Doc Pritchard and get him out here too." Able mopped his brow with his thoroughly soaked handkerchief.

"Today's his day off," Chrystal said, and Able knew she was still stinging from his rough language with her.

"I don't care what today is."

"Jeff Randall's taking his cases," Chrystal offered. Randall was a young doctor who had just come to Agatite to help Pritchard with his work load. Pritchard was older than God, and retirement was long overdue.

"I don't want Randall, I want Pritchard, and you just by-God find him and get his ass out to Hoolian along with Murphy." Able was getting weary of arguing with this stupid girl. "And send along one of Murphy's thugs, too," he added, clicking off the radio before she could argue with him or ask him who in the world he might be referring to.

For a moment Able sat steaming in the merciless sun, then he turned the radio on again. He knew Vernon would be there, and sure enough, in response to his simple mouthing of the man's name into the mike, the deputy answered. Able gave him instructions. "Chrystal is looking for Doc Pritchard," he said. "See if you can help her out, and get him and you out to the Hoolian Barbershop right away."

"Right," Vernon said, and Able knew he was gone. Goddamn good man, he thought. No nonsense, follows orders, and can be depended on. *He* ought to be chief of police.

Able looked up into the blazing sun. Insects sang incessantly from all around him, and he could hear the hum of Mel's window air conditioner trying to cool inside the building in spite of the incredible heat swirling around outdoors. It wasn't even past noon yet, and it was well over a hundred. He reached again for the radio mike. "Chrystal?" he said.

"Yes, Able," she responded without nonsense. "I'm workin' on Doc Pritchard, but I think he's fishin' out to the lake."

"That's good," Able said, "Vernon'll be along in a minute to help you find him. Listen, call Sue Ellen for me and tell her I won't be home for lunch."

"Now, Able," she started, her voice sounding petulant, "that's *personal* business, and you know that Chief Murphy—"

"Chrystal," Able cut in before hearing the official line from Jingles Murphy, "please call my wife and tell her I won't be home for lunch, that I'll call her from the office later."

"Well, okay," she said, then she started a lot of over-and-out talk, which Able didn't want to hear, so he cut the radio off.

He got out of the cruiser and slammed the door, then pulled a Hava-Tampa Jewel from his shirt pocket. As he unwrapped it, he recalled again the sight of the woman's mouth, her eyeless sockets, her torn stockings. Every detail was etched on his memory, and he wondered if he'd ever get rid of it. This is one hell of a mess, he thought, and there's some sleepless nights going to come from it.

Slowly he went inside the shop to begin questioning the men.

III. Farmgirl
August, One Week Later

Cassie softly closed the barn door behind her and slipped out of her sandals to allow her feet the sheer pleasure of walking across the soft hay on the floor between the stalls. She loved the barn, and lately she had gotten into the habit of sneaking away from the house while the baby took her morning nap. Some days she would wait almost too late and then have to go flying back to the house and the heat of the kitchen to finish preparing dinner for Claude and his boys, who always arrived in time to watch *As the World Turns* on the miniature TV while they shoveled in the fried steak, corn, mashed potatoes and gravy she prepared for them almost every day. She hated that particular dinner, but she found that roast beef, chicken, or almost anything else took longer to cook and made the kitchen even hotter in summertime. And they never seemed to complain. If I put cardboard and cat shit down in front of them they'd just wash it down with iced tea and never look up, she sometimes thought.

The barn was always cool in summer, and it was warm in winter when the house shifted its season along with the weather and changed from bake-oven to icebox. But it was harder to get out here in winter. Claude didn't work that much then, and he would spend the whole afternoon puttering around the house and grounds rather than in the fields cursing the Mexicans or trying to get the best of the ever-present mesquite and Johnson grass.

She sat down on a haymow she had made several days before by tearing apart a couple of bales and spreading the sweet alfalfa grass in a corner. From inside her blouse she fished out a blue note sheet, now creased from being folded and unfolded so many times. She read her aunt's letter for the tenth or fifteenth time that morning. It was almost too good to be true, and she pretended to swoon with delight, falling deliciously back into the hay and allowing the sweet farm smells of manure and animals, trapped in the barn's cool darkness, to waft over her. Far above in the rafters she spied a bird's nest. She suspected it was an owl's nest, since she had heard one of the nocturnal creatures for several nights in a row, but she didn't want to know about it. Owls killed chicks, and Claude killed owls. Claude killed everything he touched.

Cassie wiggled her toes in the hay and pulled her skirt up to her waist. She lifted her legs, one at a time, in high arcs over her body, allowing them to swing free and naked from the printed skirt as she admired the bright red toenail polish she had applied the night before. She wished her thighs and hips still matched the girlish beauty of her feet, but they didn't. She was fat, she thought, old and fat, and not yet thirty.

Somewhere beyond the barn's walls she could hear a tractor chugging loyally away. That would be Claude. He liked to work the field closest to the house whenever he could. That way he could know if any of the boys quit early or took too much time getting away from the house in the morning. Each of them was somewhere between the house and the river, each on a tractor, trying to break concrete-hard ground, making it ready for planting again. Claude worked his land hard. Claude worked the boys hard. Claude worked everything he owned hard.

Cassie often found it hard to believe that she was here, on a farm in the middle of Sandhill County. She was what she had never even considered being, a farm wife. When it had finally dawned on her sometime before she and Claude had married that this was the life he had planned, she still hadn't realized what it would mean, how hard it would be. Rising before dawn and starting to cook breakfast for a bunch of hammer-handed men who were unappreciative and untalkative, who slurped down coffee and fried eggs and bacon all in one gulp, who wiped their plates with their toast or biscuits, then who wordlessly filed out of the kitchen, leaving dirty dishes and empty coffee cups in their wake for her to clean up—all that had been bad enough. But then to see them come back at noon, dirty, streaming sweat so badly they had to take off their shirts and gobble up their dinners in their underwear, often without doing much more than running cold well water over their faces and hands, their eyes glued to the portable TV set in the kitchen, talking only to ask for more food or to comment on what job needed doing next, what crop looked good for next season, or what machine was near to breaking down—that had been worse. Then, in the evening, just as the sunset robbed them of available light, the tractors and pickups would come roaring into the dooryard, and they would stumble down from their machines and half-stagger and half-fall into the kitchen doorway. They splashed water all over their heads and arms and sat down at the table half-asleep and tried to eat whatever new five-course meal she had been working on all afternoon, and often as not they fell asleep at the table before the pie was cut. It was enough to make her cry, and she often did cry as she wearily wiped the sweat from her brow over the steaming sink full of dirty dishes.

"Men have it tough, Cassie," her mother-in-law had told her as they were working in the kitchen the first week after she and Claude had moved in. Mrs. Crane was old and tired and near death, although no one but Mrs. Crane knew it. "You got to see to it they're well fed. Food is the fuel of the body. You remember that."

Cassie had remembered it. And after Mrs. Crane was gone, after Cassie had become Mrs. Crane, she learned what it meant. It meant working from sunup to sundown and after, taking care of the chickens and the barn stock, nursing the baby all night long and changing diapers and washing clothes and cleaning the house and, of course, washing dishes, mountains of dishes. "Men have it tough," she was fond of telling the baby while she worked away in the kitchen and her daughter crawled around in the muddy boot prints on the yet-to-be-mopped floor. "But women . . . Shit!"

Claude had changed the moment she married him. All through high school they had been the number-one couple to watch for marriage. He had been a star on the football team, and she had been the school mascot, dressed up in a big Eagle outfit with plastic feathers and funny rubber feet, leading the cheers with the cheerleaders, feeling proud that Claude was helping lead the team to victory and that she was cheering Claude.

Then there had been graduation for Claude, and she had two more years to go. She didn't date a single other boy the whole time he was off at Cisco Junior College getting his associate's degree. He came home every weekend anyway, and they would go out after the games and get a Coke and talk about being married and "owning their own place" and being free and happy.

But then they got married, and right away they moved in with his folks because his father had had a stroke and fallen off his tractor and been dragged halfway across a field and two pastures before it stopped in a clump of mesquite. Now the old man sat in his room and peered with his one good eye into his own TV morning and night. She would think his mind was as gone as the use of his right side except that when she went in to change his sheets or bring him some food he would reach out and grab her by the ass. When she would squeal and slap his hand, half his mouth would grin, and he would say something she never could understand, making the half of his mouth drool even more than it ordinarily did.

That was about the only victory she had won over Claude. She put her foot down about even going into the old man's room after one of his pinches raised a large purple welt on her hip, and Claude was forced to hire a practical nurse to take care of him full time. Her name was Earnestine Sitwell, and she had two passions in life: TV game shows and ice cream, usually taken together. But at least old Mr. Crane was one burden Cassie didn't have anymore, even though he was one more mouth to feed, since Mrs. Sitwell didn't cook at all.

Then Mrs. Crane began to die. Cancer. And every night after Cassie had washed the dishes and mopped the kitchen floor, she and Claude would drive into Agatite and sit in the darkened hospital room and watch her rot away. It was then that Claude began to really change. As his mother faded away from him, he slowly became his father by degrees, he naturally expected that Cassie would become Mrs. Crane in spirit as well as name.

That might not have been bad for someone else, for Mrs. Crane was a fine woman, a good woman. Cassie had always loved her. But *she* was Mrs. Crane, and Cassie was Cassie. And she didn't plan to wind up in a hospital bed with her kids sitting around watching her die. At least not until she had lived a little.

Her eyes lit on a nest of wasps way up to the beams of

the barn, and she watched with fascination as the Indian-red insects flew back and forth building their home. All those males working for one female, she thought idly. Now that's the way to live. Or at least a partnership, the way the birds do it. Not this. Not just me busting my ass to feed a bunch of thankless farm boys and Mexicans. That's not fair.

Claude had two brothers, both of whom had their own places nearby. On rainy days or during the winter when the field work was stopped or slowed, when Cassie felt she should have a break too, they would all come over to the house and sit around the wood stove in the living room and drink beer and eat. They'd talk about last year's crop, next year's crop, what they should have done, what they would do. They'd sit there from dawn to dusk, moving only to go to the bathroom or get something from the table to eat, a table Cassie was expected to keep filled with bread, meat, pies, cakes. She had asked Claude why they didn't go to one of their homes sometimes, and he'd looked at her like she was crazy.

"This *is* their home!" he told her, as if she'd asked why they didn't walk on somebody else's feet.

"Well, where the hell is mine?" she'd screamed back at him, and he'd slapped her. Slapped her!

It was the first time he'd ever hit her, and she could sense by the look in his eyes when he did it that it wouldn't be the last. She made up her mind to leave him right then, and she was surprised how easy the decision was. It had been in the back of her mind all along, and now she was prepared to do it. Then, with a horrible premonition, she waited. The next week she went into town to see Doc Pritchard. She was pregnant.

When the baby came it was dead winter, and Cassie was permitted two weeks in bed before she had to get back to her routine. Her sisters-in-law had come by to help out then, but they hadn't been back except for a Sunday dinner, which Cassie herself had to cook and clean up after while they sat around the table and smoked cigarettes and gossiped. She knew they didn't like her much. She and Claude had the Home Place, and he hadn't

had to pay a dime for it. The brothers, Francis, Jr., and
Thomas, had both been obliged to pay handsomely for
their farms. The old man had loaned them the money,
but he'd insisted they pay back every cent. And now
Claude had the old man's farm *and* their money. Of
course, Claude had the old man, too. But they didn't
seem to think much about that.

Her own mother and father came out to the farm hardly
at all. It wasn't that they didn't approve of Claude. Her
father publicly acknowledged that she had made a "fine
match, a damned sight better than her sister did," which
wasn't saying much, since her elder sister hadn't made
any match at all but found herself pregnant by a high
school sweetheart who left her standing flatfooted and
big as a barn in the Methodist church while he took off
for parts unknown. But all that had happened years ago
when Cassie was still a child, and she wasn't even sure
where her sister was now, she had "the baby," as her
mother called her teenaged grandchild.

No, it wasn't her marriage that kept them away. It was
the farm, the sight of their daughter, for whom they had
had such high hopes, working herself into an early middle age when she could have gone to college; living in a
house without air conditioning or decent heat, working
like a galley slave for a farmer with whom neither of
them could hold a decent conversation. Dinners at her
home had become few and far between as well, since
Claude would simply stuff his face, then bury himself in
a magazine or TV program until about nine o'clock, then
remind Cassie that it was going to be "an early 'un"
tomorrow and hustle her out the door. Her parents hadn't
done much more than drop out to see them once or twice
a month since the baby came, and they almost never
stayed to supper.

The baby, named Claudine, had just added to Cassie's
work load. She was only another one of Claude's possessions, like Cassie herself had become, and she had to
tend to it the best she could, careful not to damage it or
let it fall into decay or neglect. Eighteen-month-old
Claudine was just so much livestock around the place,

like the chickens, the cows, he pigs, and the herds of dogs and cats. Something to be fed, watered, and cleaned up after. Something with which Cassie was too tired to play or cuddle. In fact, Cassie never thought of the baby as *Claudine* at all. She was just something else to do every day.

Claude was remarkably generous about some things. Every Saturday he would give Cassie a wad of bills to take to Agatite to spend on whatever she wanted for herself or the baby. At first she bought dresses and shoes. A virtual wardrobe had filled the ancient chiffonier in their bedroom. But soon she stopped. She had no place to wear them. Claude had no time or tolerance for social outings other than maybe a drive-in movie in Agatite, or, on special occasions like birthdays and anniversaries, a trip into town for the rib-eye platter at the Town and Country Dinette. Something about their old dented and dirty GMC pickup parked beside a crackly speaker at the Eagle Drive-in took the fun out of a new dress, so she gave most of the dress-up clothes to the charity rummage sales at the church.

She soon learned that the chief difference in Saturdays and Sundays and other days of the week was that the boys only worked half-days on Saturdays and usually took Sundays off, unless it had rained the week before. She was expected to cook something special for dinner and supper on both days, regardless, which meant it was actually more work, and the damned cows still had to be milked, the eggs had to be gathered, the chickens and pigs had to be fed on those days just like any other day of the week. Such a schedule usually ruled out church, unless there was a special reason like a revival or a neighbor's baptism going on, and it meant that the Friday night football games that had been so much a part of their courting lives were just like anything else she wanted to do—impossible. They lasted too late, were too far away, or Claude was just too tired to go. To tell the truth, so was she.

Generous as he could be about giving her money, Claude could be hardheaded about other things. He let her have an electric mixer for the kitchen only after her mother had given her one. They had a washing machine, but she had to hang out the clothes on an outside line or in the kitchen when the dust was blowing or rain threatened, which meant she had to iron most of everything before it was fit to wear. And Claude liked to have his work shirts starched so stiff they would cut you if you ran a finger along a seam. He also liked khaki, and it stained badly from the least little thing. Claude wouldn't wear a stained shirt to kill a hog in, so she usually wound up buying him new ones and slipping them in with the old. If he ever noticed her efforts, he never mentioned it.

The house itself had been built by Claude's grandfather sometime before World War I, in which Claude's two uncles had been killed. It had no air conditioning of any kind other than a couple of noisy circulating fans, and the only heat came from a couple of wood stoves, one in the living room and one in the kitchen. Some rooms had no electrical outlets at all except for a naked bulb hanging from the ceiling, and the hot water heater was so small that Cassie had to heat water on the stove to bathe the baby unless she got her in before the boys had cleaned up for the night. She felt like she was living in the dark ages, and she complained to Claude about it often.

He refused to modernize the house, at least as long as the old man was living. That's what he'd told her, anyway. She thought he didn't want to do it because he was afraid his brothers wouldn't approve. Of the three of them, he was the only one making any money with a farm, and he felt their resentment as much as Cassie did when the subject of success came up. So they banked their money at the First Security Bank of Agatite and lived the way his parents had lived, and their parents before them.

Even much of the farm equipment was antiquated. Old Man Crane had finally bought a new tractor ten years before, but it was now breaking down a good deal. The other two tractors were of such rare vintage that Cassie often heard the men in town tease Claude about it. His favorite was an ancient International Harvester with fifteen gears, only three of which worked, and it made a noise like a bucket full of chickens when it labored in the field. The newer John Deeres were handed over to the boys, but they were constantly burning out clutches, throwing bearings, or just breaking down in a variety of mysterious ways, and Claude would roundly curse them as he tried to patch them up. Nothing short of one simply disintegrating would make him buy a new one, however.

They owned three pickups, none of which ran all of any week without breaking down, and Claude was forever borrowing parts from one and slapping them on another, to try to keep at least two of them working.

After eight years Cassie had had enough. She was going to leave Claude, and that was that. Her problem before had been that she had no place to go. Her sister hadn't even written home for more than five years—her last letter, in fact, had been from a motel in California, and Cassie wasn't even sure what city she had been moving to. She didn't dare ask her mother or father, so she didn't even consider trying to find her. But then Aunt Annie had come to her rescue and invited her to come to San Marcos. It was a Godsend.

Cassie didn't worry too much about Claude coming after her, and even if he did, she had no intention of returning to the farm. For more than eight years the farm and the TV had been her primary contacts with the world, and she wasn't going to break out of that prison just to be returned to it.

She got up from the haymow and looked out through a crack in the barn wall. It wasn't even eleven yet, and she figured she could stay for a while longer. The barn had become a refuge for her, and she would miss it in San Marcos, but maybe she wouldn't need a refuge, she told herself. She ran her hands up and down her body, feeling her belly, noting how her breasts had sagged since the baby was born. Having the baby and eating all the food she cooked had been her ruin, she knew, and while the first was purely and simply a mistake, the second was just plain silly. Well, at Aunt Annie's she could diet, lose about twenty pounds, and soon she would be pretty again.

Aunt Annie said the college in San Marcos was a good one, a place where she could study to be a nurse, a teacher, or anything else she decided she wanted to be. She also told Cassie she would watch Claudine while Cassie went to classes or worked. It would be heaven! Taking Claudine hadn't been her exact plan, but she supposed she'd better. After all, the baby was her own daughter, even if she hadn't wanted her in the first place. She wondered if her parents would approve. Probably not, she thought, shaking her head and smiling grimly to herself. Divorce was right next to harlotry on their list of evils. It was going to kill her mother.

When Cassie married Claude she had been a virgin. So had he—she knew that. Sex had been a thoroughly boring experience for both of them, and it had become more and more infrequent in their married life. She tended to think a good deal of the problem was that his parents, or at least the old man, were in the house, and he had simply climbed on top of her and grunted and groaned for a while, then rolled over and gone to sleep. She couldn't remember the last time he'd kissed her.

A month before they married, she had gone to Doc Pritchard for some birth control pills for her cramps, and her mother had insisted on a long talk about her sister, but Cassie had learned that lesson long ago. The lectures about ''fooling around'' had begun with her first period and didn't stop until a year after she was married. She kept taking the pills for a long time, but Claude's interest in sex was so sparse she didn't worry about getting pregnant. Then Claudine was born, and Cassie started taking them again, religiously. There would be no baby to mess her up this time, even though she had not had relations with Claude except once since Claudine's birth.

Sauntering lazily back to the haymow, swishing her hips to make the skirt fly randomly about her legs, she began to think of Adam Moorely. She wondered what would have happened if she had given him a real chance. Claude had never much liked Adam, and she wondered if he knew about her secret "romance" with the class freak.

Adam had always been chubby and had played no sports. He was never elected to anything, and he won no contests. Nobody paid much attention to him, least of all Cassie or Claude or any of the "in crowd" as they liked to call themselves. He wasn't ugly or anything, except for the horn-rimmed glasses he wore that made him look like a great owl. But he was always stuck up, conceited, and he stayed by himself most of the time.

One afternoon she had been home from school with a cold. Almost everyone had gone over to Iowa Park for a basketball game, so she was shocked when her mother told her the telephone call was for her. She was even more shocked when the caller identified himself as Adam Moorely.

They had talked for *hours* and *hours*. She recalled she was fascinated by him. He seemed to know so much about everything. After he hung up, she realized that he never told her why he called, but it didn't seem to matter. They had enjoyed such a wonderful time that she didn't even feel guilty about it or anything. But she didn't tell Claude. She didn't know why; she just didn't.

Adam called back the following Tuesday, late at night, after ten, and they had stayed up talking until her father came into her room and yelled at her. Adam's voice was smooth and confident on the phone, and he seemed to be tender and interested in what she thought about things. They talked about philosophical stuff, deep stuff, music and art, and all sorts of things she never discussed with Claude, or, for that matter, with any of the "in crowd," who always seemed to agree on everything. She was in awe of Adam's perception of things, and she found herself looking forward to his phone calls.

She didn't tell Claude about Adam's calling her, and when she ran into her nighttime telephone "date," as she came to think of him, in the halls at school, he would just speak quietly and move quickly away from her like she was a snake or something. Sometimes, though, she thought she saw him hanging around the vestibule near her locker, peering down the hall through his horned-rimmed glasses to see if she was coming. She would move toward him, and suddenly he would speak from a distance and scoot out the door in the opposite direction. In person he was so different from the man of the world who called her three or four nights a week and talked until sometimes two or three in the morning that she had trouble connecting the two personalities.

If he didn't call, or if her father restricted her calls to punish her for some adolescent misdemeanor, she found herself miserable and longing to talk to him. If, at the same time, her father grounded her, she felt guilty that she didn't miss Claude as much as she did her conversations with Adam, and sometimes she would secretly dial his number and talk, hidden under the covers in her bed, just to fulfill whatever need inside her he answered.

Their telephone romance went on for more than a year. He was in Claude's class and was due to graduate with him and go off to college, only he wasn't going to Cisco or A&M or even Texas Tech. He was going to Tulane in New Orleans. He wasn't that good a student. His grades were low B's and high C's, with even a D or two to balance his two or three A's in English and journalism and history, but when she mentioned this to him, he laughed.

"Grades in high school mean nothing!"

"But how can you get a scholarship without them?" she asked, amazed at his nonchalance.

"The only thing grades get you in hick towns like Agatite is these local yokel scholarships that mean nothing!" Suddenly he became serious, and she tingled. "It's the money that counts, it's the meaning behind the scholarship. I got this one for entering an essay contest. One scholarship will get me another. Just hide and watch!"

She asked him to read the essay to her, and he happily obliged. And then once or twice a week he would call her just to read things he had written and was preparing for contests or scholarship competitions. Sometimes he simply called to read things he had himself read and thought were poetic or interesting or romantic or beautiful. His voice would make her excited, sexually excited, and she would recline in her bed and listen to him read with a vision of a romantic hero on the other end of the phone rather than the pudgy, spectacled, unpopular boy who actually spoke to her.

After nearly a year of nocturnal long-distance meetings, she took advantage of him in a way by asking him why he'd called her on that first night.

"I thought the answer to that would be obvious," he said placidly.

"Be serious, Adam," she said. "I just have wondered, that's all." She suddenly felt sorry she was pushing it.

"Well, Cassie, to tell you the truth, I called to ask you for a date," he said.

She was shocked at first. The thought of going out with him had never occurred to her. She was Claude's girl. Everyone knew that. At first she didn't know what to say, then she recovered.

"Why didn't you?" she asked, trying to keep her voice from quavering.

He didn't speak for a moment, and for the first time in all their conversations she sensed his confidence slipping. "Well, I'd uh . . . I didn't think you would go out with me."

"Why not?"

"Well, hell, Cassie—" He had never sworn while talking to her. She smiled and felt her stomach tighten in anxious excitement. "You're Claude's girl. Everybody knows that. You and he . . . well, uh . . . you're you and he."

"What do you mean?" A danger light went off in her head, but she ignored it and went on. "Why haven't you asked anyway? You kept calling back."

"Look, Cassie," he explained, "You know I like to talk to you, I like to have somebody to talk to, to read my stuff to. You're about the best friend I've got. I just didn't want to screw it up."

"How?" The danger light was flashing wildly inside her head by now, but her ego kept her going. She felt herself getting wet between her legs. This was incredibly exciting.

"I didn't ask you because, uh . . . I haven't asked you because . . ." and for the second time he was at a loss for words. Then what he was trying to say, that he hadn't asked her because he was afraid, dawned on her. Afraid of Claude? How silly. Claude wouldn't hurt anybody, not for her. Would he? She didn't think so, but the idea was even more exciting and her breathing became faster and faster. She decided to continue to ignore the danger light and take one more step.

"Because why?" She wanted him to say it, to confirm Claude's value to her as a protector, a knight who would do battle for her.

"All right!" he said suddenly. This wasn't what she'd expected. "Let's go out. Let's meet. Not in Agatite, but somewhere else. Kirkland. We'll go to a show, have a hamburger or something. What do you say?"

The reality of what he was asking suddenly sank in on her along with the significance of the cruel joke she was playing on him. She knew she would never go out with him. It was out of the question. She was Claude's girl. He would be furious. He would . . . he would . . . he . . . What would he do? Well, it didn't matter. Claude was her boyfriend. They were "engaged to be engaged" as soon as he got back from Cisco. She was one of the most popular girls in school. She couldn't go out with this nobody, this unpopular lump of conceit. How could she explain it to any of her girlfriends? They would laugh her right out of the "in crowd." Kirkland was another town. No one would recognize them there, but Claude would know. He'd have to know. It'd be like cheating on him to meet Adam anywhere, especially Kirkland. Kirkland was where Larry Haynes and Linda Fitzpatrick met to check into the Ramada Inn. No way, José.

"I can't, Adam," she said, feeling the excitement drain from her, leaving her stomach feeling flat and empty.

"No. I didn't think you could," Adam said, and the sadness in his voice almost made her cry.

"Claude, well . . . Claude and I have plans," she said lamely.

"Oh, well I know it, my dear!" His voice began to rise. "He's a shoo-in for the gyp mill scholarship, just like those other assholes who will scoop up the big bucks here in Hicksville." He paused to take a deep breath and then went on, speaking rapidly. "Their daddies and mommies have been putting up and putting out for them for the past eighteen years, and probably none of them will make it past his sophomore year. And all you little cheerleaders will follow them around like a pack of lap-dogs, begging for them to throw you a bone because you've got big blue eyes and bigger tits. Jesus Christ! Are you blind? They don't care about you, any of you, and only a handful of you are worth caring about! I picked *you*! You're the prettiest, the smartest, the best! But I'm Mr. Nobody who never gets elected to a goddamn thing. Whose picture in the yearbook will be followed by a blank space because he wasn't among the ass lickers who followed the football boys around and held their jock-straps!" His outburst stopped, and she believed he must have been crying. She was stunned. No one had ever dared such heresy before. It was almost blasphemous to say what he had said in Agatite.

"Adam, please, I never—" She stopped when he cut her off.

"You silly, hicktown bitch!" he exploded. "Don't you know I'm in love with you?"

The telephone slammed down in her ear. He never called her again, and he avoided her at all the graduation functions he attended, which weren't many. During the summer he took a construction job, and he left for Tulane in the fall.

She wanted to call him before he left, to wish him luck if nothing else, but she didn't have the courage. She had felt strange about the last conversation for a long time, realizing, perhaps, that he might be right, but knowing that, right or wrong, she didn't have the convictions he had and couldn't follow him down his path. After all, he was leaving. She was staying, for two more years anyway, and she had to have her friends, her popularity. Then maybe she could afford to believe he was right. But she never had the chance. Claude, who got the scholarship just as Adam had predicted, had stopped his education when he finished his two-year degree from Cisco. Most of the other "assholes," as Adam had called them, didn't even make it that far.

She eventually forgot about him, however, and then just last week she had run into him in the First Security Bank. His mother had died and he had returned to handle her affairs. Cassie had gone in for just a minute to pick up a draft for some shoats Claude was buying, and she was, as usual, between dinner and supper.

Adam emerged from the bank's offices, wearing a tweed jacket and smoking a pipe. He had a small mustache and was sporting fashionable glasses. He wasn't fat anymore but appeared tall, lean, and tan, and—she gasped when she realized it—*handsome*. She almost didn't even recognize him at first. He moved with confidence and vigor and smiled briefly as he passed her, leaving a smell of tobacco and musk in his wake. He didn't recognize her.

She noticed in the mirrored wall behind the teller's cage that it would have been a wonder if he had known her. She hadn't had the time to fix herself up at all, and she had the baby perched on one overweight hip. Her skin was splotchy from too many rich foods, and her eyes were baggy and dull. She saw a broad-faced farm girl stare back at her from the mirror, dressed in a bright, tacky, printed blouse and a pair of dirty jeans with baking flour streaked on them. Her hair was pulled back into a dirty set of barrettes, and she could see the need for new tinting and cutting.

When she came out of the bank, she saw him talking to Wayne Henderson over by the hardware store. She walked deliberately down the sidewalk to where they were standing, even though it was out of her way, and she passed slowly by the two men. Adam flashed another smile that said, "I wish I could remember you, but I can't. Hello anyway," and turned back to his argument with Wayne. She crossed the street and saw him get into a small red sports car and pull out and drive off. Cassie wondered if he was happy now, and she also wondered how different her life might have been if she had met him in Kirkland that night.

The chugging of Claude's tractor reminded her that it was time to go in and start boiling the potatoes for dinner. Her plan was a simple one. She would fix dinner, wash the dishes, mop the floor, then, after leaving a note for Claude—she owed him that much, she guessed—she would take whichever pickup was running today and go into Agatite and get on a bus for San Marcos.

She would take two thousand dollars out of their joint account in the bank, and to that she would add the nearly four thousand dollars she had saved from the Saturday money Claude had given her over the years. That should be enough, at least enough to get her and Claudine to San Marcos, hire a lawyer, and rid herself of Claude and his goddamn farm forever.

She rose, brushed the hay off her skirt, and slipped back into her sandals. Her bags were already packed and waited for her in the root cellar. She had taken care of that yesterday when Aunt Annie's letter came. It was too good to be true. She was actually going.

Pushing the barn door open, she felt the August heat sweep over her, and she made her way slowly toward the house. She could hear the baby crying, and she silently cursed Mrs. Sitwell for not watching her as she'd said she would. "I wonder who'll milk the cows tomorrow?" Cassie asked the clucking hens around the back porch. She mounted the wooden steps leading to the kitchen.

4

I. Breedlove
1971

The movie was over at ten-thirty. The lights came up.
Everyone began to rise and stretch, preparing to leave.
Breedlove got up from the seat where he had been
sprawled for seven solid hours. His back was stiff from
the old, broken seat. His legs hurt, his feet tingled as
circulation returned to them, and his eyes burned under
the bright floodlight that illuminated the torn and faded carpet. Stretching, he watched several couples pass on their way
out, laughing, talking in low whispers and giggles.

He tried to remember something about the movie that
had been funny, but he couldn't. After all, he'd only seen
it three times, three and half if he counted the part where
he came in and went to sleep. What the hell? It was
cheaper than a motel. He shouldered a duffel bag and
filed in behind the last people to leave.

Through the darkened lobby the exit was shown by
green and blue lights from the cigarette and soft-drink
machines. A girl, dark-haired and dark-eyed, cleaned the
popcorn machine with a white cloth. He tried to look up
her skirt as she strained up to wipe the inside of the glass.
Her legs were skinny. She was too young. The manager,
keys in hand, glared sourly at him and coughed disapprovingly. Say something to me, Breedlove silently dared
him, returning his glare with a gaze of determined trouble; say something to me, asshole.

The door clicked locked behind him, and he suddenly
realized that he was on the sidewalk with no place particularly to go. The street was wet. It had been raining. The neon
marquee glittered in the puddles of the concrete sidewalk,
and he regretted losing the shine on his new boots. But it

couldn't be helped. Finally the marquee fizzled and went out, plunging the front of the theater into darkness. Breedlove lit a cigarette, cupping the flame of the match in his hand, even though there was no wind.

Down the empty street he saw through the gray smoke he blew from his nostrils the flickering neons of the bus station. Too bad there wasn't more to do in these small towns while waiting for a bus, he thought. But what the hell? What should he expect? He drew in deeply on the smoke and hefted the duffel higher on his shoulder.

A carload of teenagers passed him, and he briefly caught the tinny sound of their car radio or tape deck playing something loud and rhythmic. They splashed past him, laughing and shouting to each other from inside the sedan. Hippies, he thought derisively. Goddamn longhairs.

Flicking the cigarette butt into the gutter and hearing it hiss, he moved slowly toward the bus terminal through the darkened street, splashing through an anonymous puddle. As he walked it started to rain again.

II. Lawman
August

The two Agatite Police squad cars screeched to a parallel stop on the old, dead-end street in front of the Hoolian Barbershop. Sheriff Able Newsome from his vantage point on the steps of the barbershop's concrete porch marveled at the flashing lights and bright paint jobs on the new machines. An old resentment flashed in his mind as he watched Police Chief Jingles Murphy move his fat body out of his car, wince against the heat, and tug his straw cowboy hat down over his eyes.

"What the hell's so important, Able," he yelled as he slammed the car door, "that you got to cuss Chrystal out about it? An' why in hell don't you keep your radio on monitor so I can call you back?"

Able noted with perverse pleasure that the police chief and his deputy both had left their windows up, just as he had before. Only now the thermometer next to the barbershop's door registered 110, not the comparatively cool 100 it had when Able arrived. Ten degrees could make one hell of a difference in August in Texas. Officer Phillips came up behind his chief, his hand on his gun butt, looking, no doubt, for lurking gunmen behind every clump of Johnson grass.

"Well?" Jingles waddled up to where Able sat on the concrete steps. The chief was breathing heavily just from the short walk from the car, and Able changed his mind about briefing Jingles to prepare him for what hung in the outhouse. He had already warned Mel and Ray to stay inside the shop when the chief of police arrived, knowing they had nothing but contempt for the fat man, and he had sent the Mexican boy on home—if a deserted box car on a siding near Kirkland could be called a home—after getting his statement and personal information, such as it was.

"It's out back," the Sandhill County sheriff said as he stood up, moving his Hava-Tampa Jewel from one side of his mouth to the other, noting with satisfaction Jingles' eyes as they followed the maneuver. Able's khaki shirt was completely soaked in sweat, and he had spent the better part of the past half hour trying to expunge the black, mummified face of the woman in the outhouse from his mind's eye without any success. "Go on. Take a look."

"Go have a look, Phillips," Jingles ordered, jerking a thumb around the side of the barbershop, noting and nodding to Mel's and Ray's faces peering from the window.

"I think you better go look for yourself, Murphy," Able said evenly, stretching his impressive form up to maximum height. "This is big. Really big."

Jingles shuffled his feet and looked indecisive for a moment, then suddenly turned and stalked around the side of the building with Phillips in his wake, his hand still ready on his gun. "It's in the outhouse," Able said, following Phillips at a distance. "Don't touch anything."

"Don't tell me how to do my goddamn job, Able!"

Jingles yelled from over his shoulder, and Able silently
followed them as far as the back corner of the barbershop. He leaned against the building as he watched them
move directly up the path to the old johnny.

By the time they arrived at the open door of the outhouse, Jingles was moving quickly. Suddenly his eyes
focused and he realized what was inside and abruptly
stopped, something Phillips, who had been hustling to
keep up with his chief, didn't expect. The patrolman
bumped hard into Jingles, and for a moment the two tot-
tered on the brink of the outhouse's threshold, and Able
feared that they were going to fall headlong into the dark
interior. For a horrible second the sheriff imagined Jingles grabbing out to break his fall and finding the legs of
the rotting corpse, pulling the whole putrid mess down
on top of both of them, and before he could stop himself,
he yelled, "Look out! Goddamnit!"

But Jingles thrust out both hands and found the jam of
the open door, and with a reserve of energy he stopped
their forward progress. Then they froze, Jingles' head
moving from the feet to the head of the hanging corpse,
and Phillips, his face staring over the left shoulder of the
police chief, following the path of the latter's eyes. Able
could perceive their slow recognition of exactly what they
were seeing, and he fought back an involuntary gag.

The duo stood in silence, staring at the horror in the
old johnny, mesmerized as if by a Medusa, and Able
dropped his cigar and ground it out with his boot. Incom-
prehensibly he reminded himself that he was hungry. He
had missed lunch. He listened for the dog he had heard
earlier, but the only sound besides the insects was the
distant traffic on U.S. 287 and the silence surrounding
the two policemen.

Suddenly the silence and their frozen figures broke at
once with the sound of retching, and Phillips, who was
a full head taller than Chief Murphy, hunched his shoulders and began to give up his stomach's contents. Hearing the patrolman's coughing and retching, Jingles turned
about-face and received the vomit down his shirt front.
Gagging, he pushed Phillips directly backward, and the

younger man fell headlong into the weeds and cactus alongside the path that led back to the barbershop. Then the chief tried to step over the flailing legs that blocked the path, became tangled, and almost fell on top of the still regurgitating patrolman. Stumbling through the confusing and kicking limbs, he finally broke free, fell down almost onto his face in the dirt of the path. Then he climbed back up and ran down the trail, wiping his shirt front with violent gestures and jamming a fist into his mouth to try to keep down his own substantial lunch just taken an hour before at the Town and Country Dinette.

Phillips, recovering from his nausea, suddenly came to his feet, and with one horrible glance from his eyes, now revealed since he had managed to lose his dark glasses—Able couldn't remember ever having seen Phillips without the military-style sunglasses—broke into a dead run right behind the stumbling Jingles. He bumped into him again and actually tried to climb over him as the chief of police fell into the briers and Johnson grass at the mouth of the pathway. Jingles tripped him up, however, and in an attempt to regain his own balance and footing, appeared to be trying to climb the struggling patrolman like a ladder. But his stomach, no longer restrained by concentration and his pudgy fist, emptied its contents, and he fell back to his knees, retching and puking onto the gravel and dirt and red ants around the opening that led to the outhouse. It was almost a full two minutes before they recovered themselves enough to find their way back to where Able stood, still leaning against a corner of the building. But at last they arrived, covered with dirt, tumbleweed, cactus needles, vomit, and sweat, where the sheriff stood, no longer able to repress a smile.

"You *shit*!" Jingles screamed at Able. "You goddamned *shit*! Why didn't you tell me what we were walking into?" He glared at the sheriff, trying to straighten his utility belt and pistol and wipe the remaining flecks of half-digested food from his uniform blouse.

Phillips simply sat down on the gravelly ground, uncomfortably near a red ant bed, and with a wary eye on the insects, cradled his head in his hands.

"Why didn't you *tell* me, you son of a bitch?" Jingles was livid. His cheeks puffed out, and his hair was standing up in places. His hat lay near the outhouse door, and Able wondered how long it would be before he sent Phillips to get it.

"Tell you what?" Able asked innocently, hearing for the first time the hysterical laughter coming from Mel and Ray inside the barbershop. "You're the by-God *investigatin'* force in this county. At least that's what you and your brother-in-law keep tellin' me." Able liked to remind Jingles that his position had been created by Newell Longman, mayor of Agatite and brother of Jingles' wife, as often as he could.

"This is *county*, goddamnit," Jingles cried, starting to regain his composure slowly, "your jurisdiction, not mine." He looked at the back window of the barbershop, where Mel and Ray were making no attempt whatever to control their mirth or disrespect for the Agatite chief of police. "Get up, Phillips, goddamnit," he barked at the patrolman. "You're actin' like some kinda goddamn pussy."

He pulled a bandanna from his pants pocket and began wiping his mouth and face. "Go get my hat, Phillips," he ordered, then turned back to Able. "That is, unless you don't think you can handle it." He tried to grin, but it wound up being a sneer.

"That's by-God horrible," Phillips interjected as he pulled himself to his feet and began trying to clean himself off. "Who is she? How long—"

"Don't know nothin' yet," Able said. "I sent for Doc Pritchard, and he might be able to tell us something."

"You call the D.P.S. too?" Jingles asked. He didn't like the idea of people making decisions without consulting him first, even if this, technically, was Able's jurisdiction.

"Harvey Connally will be over in about thirty minutes," Able replied. Connally was the local Highway Patrolman, stationed in Agatite, responsible for the area between that city and Kirkland, thirty miles away. "But he said we should go ahead and try to handle it without him. He's got more to do than he can take care of already."

Jingles snorted and lit a cigarette, glancing with distaste at the outhouse. "Jesus, Able," he said, blowing smoke out through his nostrils, "that's somethin'."

Able nodded and shifted the Hava-Tampa Jewel to the other side of his mouth. "There's some bad dreams there, all right."

They didn't say much for a while. Phillips fetched Jingles' hat, which had unfortunately taken the brunt of his regurgitation, and was assigned the task of cleaning it off. That done after a fashion, he began pacing back and forth behind the barbershop, peering intently into the tumbleweeds and briers and Johnson grass on both sides of the path. The white-hot heat of the afternoon bore down on them, and they stood and smoked in silence, listening to the insect ambiance around them and the traffic over on the highway, until Phillips finally broke their individual musings. "Who do you figure for this, Able?" he asked.

Jingles looked up suddenly from the toes of his ruined boots and peered at Phillips. "What?" he asked.

"This ain't no ordinary murder," Phillips went on, ignoring Jingles and talking directly to the sheriff.

"What makes you think it's murder?" Able asked, genuinely interested in Phillips' comment. Phillips had always been so low in his estimation that he never considered that he might have an original thought. In fact, he hadn't said anything at all to him the whole time he had been an Agatite patrolman. But he had assumed immediately that the woman had been killed, not killed herself, in spite of the appearance of the body. Able was anxious to hear why Phillips jumped to that conclusion, but before he could get an answer, Jingles cut in.

"You dumb shit," the fat chief of police said, spitting on the ground. "This is a suicide. People don't go around hanging murder victims in old shithouses." Phillips started to protest, but Jingles waved his hand and silenced him. "Go in there and ask that asshole Mel if he's got a hot towel or something to clean off my shirt." Phillips shrugged and moved around the front of the building.

"These young punks," Jingles complained as Phillips disappeared. "They're brought up on TV and shit, and they think every piddlin' little ol' traffic ticket they write should come out like some TV cop show.''

Able said nothing in reply. ''Hell, he's already tore up that new car,'' Jingles went on, ''an' Hiker ain't any better.''

When Able failed to reply again, they fell silent. Phillips returned with a *dry* towel, and a dirty one at that. Jingles roundly cursed him and stalked around to the front of the building. Able trailed along, glad for an excuse to get out of the sun. He wasn't about to leave the glare of the afternoon heat until Jingles did, even though he was beginning to feel woozy from all the excitement and missing lunch.

''Wait around there and make sure nobody touches anything,'' Jingles ordered Phillips when he reached the shade of the concrete porch. Able assumed he wasn't talking to him as well. He damned well better not be talking to me, the sheriff thought.

In the comparative cool of the barbershop's porch, Jingles called through the door to Mel, ''Bring us a couple of beers out here,'' and he raised his eyebrows to Able to get the okay. Some protocol was still being observed, Able thought with mild amusement.

''Just Coke,'' Able yelled in through the glass, and Mel nodded.

Jingles knelt down by a water faucet and wet the towel, wiping it first across his balding head and then down his stained shirt front. Mel brought out a pair of iced Cokes and handed them over. ''You know I ain't got no beer, Murphy,'' he said.

''Shit you don't,'' Jingles sneered back at him, taking the Coke anyway. ''An' Able an' half the county knows it. Goddamn sign out front ought to read, 'Haircut, Coors, or Cutty Sark.' ''

Mel smiled at Able, and Ray put his head out the door. He was still wearing the absurd barber's apron. ''What's the matter, Chief? You need a little bracer? Maybe you ain't got the *stomach* for this kind of work?''

''Fuck you!'' Jingles yelled, and Able turned away. ''You tellin' me you saw it an' didn't puke your guts out?''

"Hell, no," Ray said, smiling and winking at Mel, "but I ain't *paid* for bravery and valor above an' beyond the callin'. Able here, he didn't puke."

"Maybe he didn't have breakfast," Jingles snorted. He drank a mouthful of Coke and spit it out onto the dirt in front of the porch. "Now you two old farts get back inside an' stop interferin' in police business."

"Yessir," Ray said, offering a sloppy salute, and he and Mel went inside, grinning and giggling openly.

Jingles sat heavily on the edge of the porch and lit another cigarette. "Now, Able, about that jurisdiction thing, there could be an awful lot of paperwork here . . ."

Able braced his shoulder against a post. He knew what was coming. Once recovered from the shock of seeing the corpse, Jingles began totaling up the possible notoriety he could obtain from this little investigation. Technically, he had been right in the first place. This *was* county, and therefore a sheriff's department matter. But Mayor Newell Longman had made it painfully clear two months ago that *capital* cases should be handled by the police department, even if they occurred outside the city limits. That had been fine with Able, since the closest thing to a capital crime committed in Sandhill County was an occasional shooting or car theft or something, and the paperwork *was* enormous.

This was different, however. It intrigued him. The whole time he had been waiting for Jingles to come helling up and take charge, which he was clearly preparing to do, he had begun asking himself questions about the dead woman. Who the hell *was* she? What sort of sickness provoked somebody to do that to herself? Why an outhouse? She was well dressed, possibly wealthy. Why? Who? How? How long had she been hanging out there? A week? Two? Longer? How long did it take for a body to turn black and for wasps to build a nest in a corpse's mouth? That was a big nest. You didn't see one of those built in a day or two. Then there was the vision of her gaping mouth, filled with swarming insects, the empty sockets staring into the darkness of the place that kept coming back into his mind, and he wanted to gag again.

He was glad he hadn't thrown up in front of these country clowns. It was a source of pride, but he knew the experience wasn't over yet. He'd just as soon give this over to Jingles and his band of fumbling cronies, but the feeling passed suddenly when he remembered Phillips had suggested it wasn't suicide. Why had Phillips immediately assumed it was murder? Able knew he had to find out, and he also knew he couldn't turn this over to the police department and let them bungle it.

"What you mean, Murphy"—Able finished off his Coke, then went on—"is that there's gonna be an awful lot of *newspaper* work on this one."

Jingles' eyes narrowed suddenly, then softened. "Ah, shit, Able, I don't want no glory. I just want to get this thing cleared up. I thought—"

"I think we better work together on this one," Able said suddenly, spotting Vernon's cruiser turning off the highway onto the former Main Street of Hoolian. "You can talk to the press if you want. It's yours all the way. But don't try to cut me out. I'm in."

Jingles set his jaw for an argument, but at that moment Vernon drove up and the chief of police shifted his interest.

"Doc Pritchard's comin'," Vernon called as he paused to roll down the glass in his cruiser. "He's out to the country club lake, fishin', an' he won't be here for an hour or so, if that's okay?" Vernon began walking up to the barbershop porch. "What've you got?"

"It's around back, in the shithouse," Jingles piped up, rising quickly and shooting a look at Able that told him not to interfere. As Vernon moved around toward the back, he whispered, "You had your fun with me, so don't screw this up." Able shrugged. He wasn't worried about Vernon.

They followed the black deputy sheriff around to the back of the shop and waited at the mouth of the pathway while he strolled up to the outhouse door. Phillips joined them. The heat was worse, Able noted, and the sounds of the insects seemed almost deafening. Phillips and Jingles were both grinning at Vernon's back as he moved deftly and quickly up the path.

When his deputy arrived at the outhouse's door, Able

thought he noticed an almost perceptible stiffening of Vernon's shoulders, and he watched as the black man's head moved from her feet up to her face, but Vernon didn't reel back, swear, or run away. In fact, he offered no outward signs that he had seen anything extraordinary at all. He slowly reached into his pocket and pulled out a pack of cigarettes. Lighting one, he took another long look, and then he came calmly back to the trio of men who waited at the path's entrance.

"You told him she was there!" Jingles accused Able disappointedly. "Shit. You warned *him*!"

"He didn't tell me anything," Vernon said, walking up close to Jingles. Ever since his embarrassment at the hands of the teenage boys in Agatite, Jingles had been noticeably uncomfortable around black men. If they were old, small, weak, or scared, he was a tyrant. But if they were large, self-confident, and manly, he was intimidated. Vernon always intimidated the chief of police. "What'd you expect me to do? Yell, 'Feets, get movin', an' haul ass?' " Jingles looked helplessly away. "Shit, I seen worse in Vietnam. Lots worse." Vernon drew on the cigarette, then caught Jingles' eye. "You think I'd barf or somethin'?"

"Hell, no, Deputy. Why would *anyone* do that?" It was Ray's voice coming from the now raised rear window of the barbershop, where he and Mel were again overcome with laughter.

"You shut the *fuck* up!" Jingles cried at them, his face turning red in the heat.

"Mel," Able spoke up. "You an' Ray stay inside an' get drunk or whatever the hell it is you do in the afternoons when we ain't around. But shut up that laughin' an' foolin' around. We got a dead woman out there an' a lot of questions to ask, an' 'less you got somethin' to say that's helpful, shut up an' stay out of the way, or I'll ask Vernon here to take you into town an' introduce you to the lockup. Okay?" Looking like a truant officer talking to schoolboys, Able wagged his finger at the offending two men, who sheepishly pulled the window down and retreated into the shop's interior.

"What'd you think?" Able asked Vernon, ignoring Jingles, who was still fuming in the heat.

"I think it's too goddamn hot to stand around here and discuss it," the black deputy said, and Phillips laughed.

"Now there's wisdom a mother could be proud of in her son," Jingles said, and Able noticed his deputy's face tense as he tossed his cigarette butt down on the ground and stomped it out. "I swear, Able," Jingles went on, "with help like these two, it's a wonder the whole damned town hasn't fell apart."

"I'd say she's been out there a couple of weeks at least," Vernon went on as if Jingles hadn't spoken at all, "She's definitely mummified. I saw that happen to some VC in Nam."

"Do you think it's a suicide?" Phillips asked Vernon directly.

"Why? Don't you?" Able cut in before Vernon could answer.

"Well"—Phillips glanced to see if Jingles could hear him—"for one thing, how'd she get up there? I mean to hang herself? I didn't see no stool or ladder or chair or nothin'."

Able was impressed. He hadn't noticed the absence of some kind of prop either. One thing was damned sure, he thought, she didn't hoist herself up there and tie herself off on the cross beam.

"Another thing." Phillips was warming to Able's reception of his theories. "Her clothes were torn and stained—blood, maybe?—an' the scratches on her legs, like she had a fight or somethin', or was drug through these tumbleweeds here. I was lookin' for a snatch of cloth or somethin'." He rocked back on his boot heels, pleased to have finally presented his ideas to somebody who would take him seriously.

Vernon was nodding in agreement. "I doubt she hung herself there, Able," he said. "Phillips is right. How'd she manage to tie that cord off and then hang herself without somethin' to stand on? Somebody helped her, that's sure."

Able took a long look at the former street hood who

wore the policeman's uniform. He hadn't ever respected
him at all, not even as a hood. He'd always been a bully,
and the uniform and gun and car seemed just to give him
license to do it with more formality. He'd never struck
Able as even being very bright either, but this was good
stuff. Able hadn't thought of any of this. Maybe he'd
been wrong about this young punk. Maybe the young
punk was growing up. "You two take a look around these
weeds," he said to Vernon and Phillips. "Watch out for
snakes, and don't touch anything you find. Connally is
on his way, and he might have some other ideas." They
started off, and Able grabbed the patrolman's arm. "That
was real good, Blair," he said. "I didn't think you got
that good a look in there."

The patrolman grinned sheepishly. "I don't reckon I'll
forget that for a long time, Able," he said, then became
serious. "I seen some pretty bad shit around here—traffic
wrecks, and old man Pearson's body after his cats had
been feedin' on it for a week. But that wasps' nest . . ."
He trailed off, shaking his head and moving away, beginning to sweep around the outhouse.

Vernon was already taking the other half of the sweep,
looking for clues. Jingles leaned against the corner of the
building smoking, and Able wiped sweat from his eyes.
It was turning into a long afternoon.

III. Merchant
August, One Week Later

Wayne Henderson slowly moved his broom back and
forth in front of his hardware store and enjoyed the cool
air of the shady side of Agatite's Main Street. Cars and
pickups moved slowly up and down the paved street.
Pulling in and out of parking places, they jerked in stops
and starts as pedestrians jaywalked in front of them. It
was an hour of the morning Wayne normally enjoyed because it reminded him of a time when he was a boy coming "to town" with his grandmother on her weekly
shopping trip.

Wayne's grandmother had lived way out in the country, five miles from the paved farm-to-market road that ran southwest of Agatite. Once a week she would pile Wayne and his sister, Pearlie, into a battered 1936 Ford and drive them to town. She would stop first downtown and walk slowly up and down Main Street, speaking to people she met, and buying cloth, thread, or maybe a new pair of cotton stockings. Sometimes she would stop at the hardware store for something more substantial, and she almost always found a "pretty" for Wayne and his sister at the Ben Franklin store.

In his memory it always seemed to be summer when they came to town.

By the time she had finished her shopping, the heat of the summer sun had become intolerable, even to small children, and they would climb into the old Ford and putter down to Rayson's Grocery so she could pick up her weekly supply of "vittles," as she called them, and usually a popsicle for Wayne and Pearlie, before heading back to the farm and a supper of fried chicken or baked ham.

When he graduated from high school, Wayne had enrolled in Baker School of Business over in Wichita Falls, and with his graduation certificate from there, he went to work as the assistant manager of the Main Street Hardware Store, owned and operated by Mr. Greely. Wayne often wondered if he had any real first name—even his tombstone read simply "M. Greely," and Wayne never heard anyone call him anything else.

When Mr. Greely died, Wayne used his savings to buy the store from Mr. Greely's daughter, who had come home from Chicago to sell everything as soon as possible and take her mother away with her. He got it for about half what it was worth and had been running it ever since. There was a while when he thought he would be drafted, but he was exempted when he claimed he had nightmares and walked in his sleep. He had to talk it over with three Army doctors, none of whom believed him, Wayne knew, but he stuck to his story and finally was declared unfit for military service, except in cases of National Emergency, which Wayne didn't expect.

Now he was the sole proprietor of Henderson's Main Street Furniture & Hardware, and he hired no assistant manager. He kept his inventory records carefully up-to-date so in case anything happened to him no one could buy it for the cut rate he had paid, even though he wasn't married and there could be no one but the First Security Bank to sell it for him—Pearlie had been killed in a car accident his senior year in high school.

He had worked hard in the business, and it had paid him well. He spent little money on his life-style, preferring to live in a garage apartment in an old section of Agatite, and to walk to work rather than to drive. He did own a car, but it was a "stripped down" model, a 1963 Chevrolet Biscayne, which boasted no luxury other than a heater, and even though it was more than twenty years old, it had fewer than twenty-five thousand miles on it. He wore the same clothes to work each day, white shirt and black trousers, black tie, and Sears Best Workshoes, and he ate a tuna fish sandwich at the Town and Country Dinette or at Central Drugs each day for lunch. He skipped breakfast, and usually a heated can of Campbell's soup for dinner was more than he could eat. He didn't like television, and he checked out books from the Sandhill County library to fill his evenings, for he never went out, socially or otherwise. He hadn't seen a movie in more than fifteen years.

In a time when middle-aged bachelors were considered "queer," Wayne Henderson was content to allow the small town to form whatever opinions it would about him. He never thought about sex at all. A slight figure of a man, he had not been popular in high school, and his only attempt at a date had been a disastrous affair at the Senior Picnic, when Sally McMichaels had wound up going home with another boy when Wayne refused to kiss her on the hayride that followed. He joined no clubs, no lodges, had no friends, man or woman—except his cat, Otto, a stray who had decided the stairs leading up to Wayne's apartment were going to be home, and who had refused to be discouraged by Wayne's attempts to drive him off.

Wayne had no passions in his life, no desires. Even the money he religiously deposited and counted in the pages of his ledgers and checkbooks had no meaning, as money. It was merely a convenient set of figures by which he could measure his life's work, a chart of profits and losses that meant nothing in terms of buying power or access to luxury and comfort. Dollars were merely numbers, exact, predictable, impersonal, and he was totally unaware of the gossip he caused at the women's clubs and card parties and around the domino parlor and country club bar because he was an "old bachelor" who preferred the company of an alley cat to that of the town's eligible females.

His single joy, in fact, was his recollections, and every summer the sweeping reminded him of Mama Henderson and his childhood, which he had decided was the best time he would ever have. It relaxed him. He let Warren, a boy he hired to take care of the heavy work, handle the snow and ice in the winter, but in the summertime he found the shady side of Main Street soothing and nostalgic. "It is pleasurable," he often said.

This particular August morning, however, Wayne Henderson was not thinking about Mama Henderson or popsicles or his youth. He was disturbed about two separate and unrelated problems. First of all, he was developing an ulcer. Secondly, he had to go to a funeral. Either of these was sufficient to depress him, but both together formed a lump in his stomach that aggravated it even more than usual, and the rhythmic swinging of the broom seemed to accentuate his pain.

The ulcer had been brought about by overwork, Doc Pritchard had told him. "You need a vacation, Wayne," the old medical man had said as he handed Wayne his shirt after his examination. "You're a textbook case of workaholicism. You've got high blood pressure, a bad back, your 'indigestion' is a duodenal ulcer that needs immediate attention, maybe surgery. All the Pepto-

Bismol in the world won't cure it, and it could kill you. Hell, man, you're not that old.''

Wayne shook his head. It was true. He hadn't had a vacation since he'd taken over the store except for one quick trip down to Laredo to buy some Mexican lighting fixtures. That had been a total bust, too, since the market for Spanish design in Agatite proved to be more limited than he had imagined, and the fixtures were wired so poorly that he had wound up spending more than he paid for them to restring the wires and make them safe. To boot, when he got back, the kid, Warren, had screwed up the books and lost a whole shipment of fishing tackle by refusing to accept it because he didn't know Wayne had planned to enlarge his line of sporting goods. It had been a complete disaster and had done his stomach pains no good either.

To leave again, even for a day or two, meant leaving that idiot kid in charge again. Kid. Hell, Wayne thought, he was almost twenty, but he still had pimples and didn't know enough to clean the shit off his shoes. Wayne couldn't leave without closing the store, and that meant losing maybe a couple of thousand. He had the only hardware store in thirty miles in any direction, and he made good money. He couldn't let people get in the habit of shopping at the cut-rate place over in Vernon.

He was counting the potential loss when he realized that Doc Pritchard was still talking.

"Now all this prescription will do is relieve some of the stomachache," Doc said. "What you're going to need is surgery if you don't take some time off and relax. Go fishing, man. That's what I do. Hell, you don't even play golf." He saw Wayne's eyes go blank again. Probably figuring the cost of a country club membership, Doc Pritchard thought. "Wayne," he said, "listen to me." Wayne raised his eyes, and Doc sighed and went on as sincerely as he knew how. "You don't want to mess around with this thing. You could lose half your stomach, or worse." Wayne was gone again, looking right at him, but gone. "Hell." Doc Pritchard became disgusted and turned away from his patient. "You'll lose a month flat on your back at the hospital. Then what'll happen to your store?''

That, at least, had gotten through to Wayne. A *month*! What would happen then? Warren would run the whole thing into the ground, and if he closed, his customers would find the cut-rate places in Vernon or Wichita Falls worth the drive, even if they didn't give local credit, interest free. He'd lose a fortune either way. But a vacation! Golf! Shit. Where would he go anyway?

Wayne promised himself that instead of a vacation he would just slow down, let Warren do more of the heavy work. He had put in a line of furniture right after he bought the business, and moving those sofas and tables around was backbreaking. Maybe, he half-promised himself, he'd start taking a regular afternoon off a week, and Warren could call him at home if he had any questions, if something came up he couldn't handle.

But on this Wednesday, the first planned afternoon off, he wouldn't be at home mowing his landlady's lawn with one of the new self-propelled rear-baggers he had just gotten in, or napping on the Luxury Lounger he was trying out with an idea of stocking. He would be down at the First Baptist Church attending Bill Castlereigh's funeral.

Wayne's dread of funerals went back to his childhood along with his pleasant recollections of Mama Henderson. Before he and Pearlie had gone to live with his grandmother, before his mother ran off with a man from Altus, Oklahoma, and his father had gone after her, getting himself shot to death in some bar in Oklahoma City, his parents had ben strict Church of Christers. They had dragged him and Pearlie to every service, Sunday and Wednesday night, held in the yellow brick church on Grove Street. He had sat squirming in prickly wool suits as the preacher screeched and screamed about the horrors of hell and the wages of sin, punctuated by toneless, unaccompanied singing and the occasional ''Amen'' shouted from some half-asleep soul in the congregation.

But the church funerals had been the worst part of it. For some reason his mother had been fascinated by them, and she would dress up both kids and march them down front in the pews to sit and listen while the preacher droned on about the virtues of whatever corpse lay encoffined in front of the pulpit. Wayne had curiously watched the weeping families mourn for whoever had died, wondering all the time what all the crying was about, since from what he could understand, the "departed" had gone on to a better and happier existence, although Wayne in his youthful innocence never could exactly understand where the place was.

After a measure, the droning was deemed sufficient, and the congregation would sing another off-key hymn, and then they would all pile out into steaming hot cars and caravan out to the Sandhill County Memorial Cemetery. There the "departed" would be prayed and sung over again before being lowered into the red clay soil, and Wayne would have to spend an hour getting the mud or dust off his Sunday shoes.

It seemed like all funerals, like all the trips to Agatite with Mama Henderson, had been in the summertime. And the pleasant memories of trips into town were often balanced by the sticky, hot memories of burying the dead. That is, all the memories but one.

When Wayne was seven, a man, a drifter, was found starving and nearly frozen on Agatite's Main Street. He languished in the county hospital for nearly a week before a combination of pneumonia and exposure and starvation brought him to what Wayne's mother called "the death throes." In the course of his demise he was visited by every minister in Agatite, even the Catholic vicar, but it was the Reverend Hays who had made the greatest impression on the dying man. In the final moments of lucidity the drifter agreed to "give his soul to Jesus" and be baptized in the church.

Over the objections of Doc Pritchard and several nurses, the Reverend Hays and a couple of deacons bundled up the old man—his name was Roosevelt Grady—and trundled him out into what people were calling the worst norther in memory. The temperature hung at the zero mark, and the wind howled down the streets of

Agatite as the preacher drove Grady over to the church, where a party of the faithful had been roused from their warm living rooms to witness this last-minute conversion and soul saving of one of God's chief sinners.

Wayne, Pearlie, and his mother had also come, his father refusing to go out in such a storm for such nonsense, and they were in the first chorus of a hymn when word was whispered around that Roosevelt Grady had arrived.

Inside the church the temperature was below freezing, it being mid-week and the heating system not having yet caught up to the expanses of the sanctuary. Wayne and his family had come wrapped in coats and scarves, and they huddled on the front pew beside other frozen brothers and sisters of the congregation. The hymn was faltering through the vaporized breaths of the icy building's occupants, and Wayne watched fascinated as the light played in the smoke that came from people's mouths.

Just as I am, without one plea,
But that Christ's Blood was shed for me,

The curtains of the baptistry opened, and Wayne saw the Reverend Hays wade down waist-deep into the icy water behind the partial glass panel that fronted the tank. Hays was wearing rubber waders and a scarf around his neck, but his hands were turning blue from the freezing water. He had to return to the concrete steps to help Clarence Underwood bring Roosevelt Grady down into the baptistry. He was still wearing his hospital gown and was only about half-conscious, and several of the women in the congregation averted their eyes as Hayes and Clarence held him awkwardly up, trying to keep him from slipping and exposing more of his bare backside to the hymn singers than was already visible through the slits in his hospital garb.

And that Thou biddest me come to Thee

The icy-cold water had an awakening effect on Roosevelt Grady. His eyes opened wide, and he began strug-

gling to get free from Clarence's hold on his hands and
now from the grip the Reverend Hays had on his head
and shoulders. But his illness had weakened him, and
with a minimum of effort they maneuvered him to the
center of the tank.

Oh Lamb of God, I come, I come.

"Brother Roosevelt Grady, by your Profession of Faith,
and Acceptance of Jesus Christ as Your Personal Savior, I
baptize you, my brother . . ." Reverend Hays began. But
Grady had had enough religion for one occasion, and
he began to struggle violently in the tank, sloshing water
out onto the carpet behind the pulpit, and all over the
shirt of the Reverend Hays. "In the Name of the Father,
the Son, and the Holy Ghost." Hays placed one hand in
the small of Grady's back and the other on his forehead.
Grady's arms flailed wildly, splashing water all over Hays
and Clarence, who had begun to lose their grip in the
numbness of the icy bath, but somehow the minister
managed to hold on and dunked Grady into the tank.
Whatever strength the old man's body still possessed
came suddenly to bear.

Feet and arms whipped out, thrashing the water and
knocking Clarence back onto the baptistry's stairs and
pushing the Reverend Hays away, causing him to lose his
footing and sink to his neck in the freezing water. Grady's arms beat the air above the water, and he tried to
stand, splashed down again, and finally gained his feet
and stood up.

Wayne would never forget the horrible expression on
Grady's unshaven face as he lunged up for air, gasping
and working his toothless jaws in bewilderment. He
hoisted himself up as high as he could, steadying himself
on the glass front of the baptistry, and peered out through
the spotlights into the darkened church at the small group
gathered to witness the formal saving of his soul.

"God fuckin' *damn*!" he spluttered through a wracked
and choked throat, spraying water and spittle as far as

the feet of Wayne and the others in the front pew. "What are you people tryin' to *do* to me?"

Silence fell on the church as if a thunderbolt had sealed their doom. Several people looked to the ceiling as if they expected God to open the building like a tin can and vent His wrath on them directly. The Reverend Hays, now on his feet and trying to compose himself, but shivering so hard he could barely speak, waded over to Grady and placed a dripping hand on the old man's shoulder, now naked since he had kicked off the hospital gown in his struggles.

"Brother Grady—" Hays began, but Grady would have no part of it. He spun around on the Reverend Hays and punched him squarely in the middle of his face. Clarence, who had also waded down toward the candidate for baptism, caught Hays full in his arms, and they both went completely under the waist-deep water, flailing and sputtering, trying to escape Grady, who now was swinging wildly in their direction.

All of a sudden the strength left Grady's body, and he turned and hung both arms over the partial glass partition, looking out into the congregation, gasping for air, completely naked.

"You're all a bunch of fuckin' lunatics!" he said. Then his legs gave out and he collapsed, sliding back into the water of the baptistry. He was dead when they fished him out.

Wayne and Pearlie were sent to an arctic Sunday School classroom with the other children while the adults tried to decide what to do about all this. Clearly, Grady had died as a result of the icy water and the exertion he had put forth resisting baptism. Some of the older women began debating whether he was baptized at all, since he had not let the Reverend Hays complete the rite. The Reverend Hays, shivering and chattering in a blanket to the similarly clad and now sneezing Clarence Underwood, nursed his broken nose and stated flatly that of course he was baptized, and it was a blessing that they had gotten to him in time.

No one mentioned what Grady had said, his language,

or his blasphemy uttered at the point of death, but Allen
Underwood, Clarence's brother and one of the most respected members of the church, worried out loud about
whether *they* had killed him. Most shouted that down,
but their voices weren't that convincing, so they swore a
vow before God not to repeat what had happened there
that night. And they were told to warn their children.
Doc Pritchard would be informed that Grady had expired
just after the ceremony. God's Will be done.

Finally the Reverend Hays recovered himself suffi-
ciently to decide on a plan of action. He called Doc Pritchard and Everett Hardin, Agatite's only mortician, and
the body was soon pronounced dead and picked up and
made ready for burial. The church paid for the service,
and those present scurried around, awakening more
members and finding flowers. The church was warming
up by four in the morning when about half the congregation filed in for the funeral of Roosevelt Grady, age
unknown, who had been taken into the arms of the Lord
at the point of accepting Jesus as his Personal Savior.

At the graveside Everett Hardin's gravedigger, grumbling and complaining about the unnecessary overtime
and climate, had managed to scrape a hole from the frozen ground in Pauper's Corner, and Roosevelt Grady was
laid to rest with the Reverend Hays and Clarence Underwood and almost a hundred congregation members
wheezing and sneezing a handful of hymns over his coffin
as the winter sun rose.

The memory of that ludicrous funeral, of Grady's flailing arms, and the splashing water, had haunted Wayne
all his life. He had refused to commit himself to Jesus
Christ or to anything that would lead to a baptism, and
after his mother had run off and he had moved in with
Mama Henderson, he had refused steadfastly to join her
at church services. Further, at her funeral, and at his
sister's, he had absented himself, claiming stomach pains
for the former, and pleading the flu for the latter. He
couldn't abide the idea of being inside a church at all.

Sometimes, at night, he would awaken from a dream
of Roosevelt Grady's funeral. In the dream Grady's coffin

would suddenly stand up on end, Grady, his face dripping water from the baptistry, would be revealed from behind the swinging lid, and his horrible eyes would open. His hand would slowly raise and point directly toward Wayne, and he would open his mouth to say something. But he never did. Instead his hollow, toothless jaws would stay open and water from the baptistry would dribble out. Wayne would be terrified. He would awaken in a cold sweat, remembering the icy stare of Roosevelt Grady from the nightmare even later the next day. He hated the dream, and he always had it right after a funeral. He had had it Monday night when he served as a pallbearer for that damned girl they found out in Hoolian, and he would have it tonight. Twice in one week. He shuddered at the thought.

Suddenly Wayne realized that he had been sweeping he sidewalk longer than usual. The sun was heating up, and the pleasant and unpleasant memories of childhood had disappeared along with the shade on the storefront's side of Main Street. Normally the sweeping gave him such pleasure, he thought, but not today. It was the damned funeral. Just because he had foolishly agreed to join the goddamn Chamber of Commerce's Goodwill Committee. He'd had no idea that funerals would be a part of it. Pallbearers to half the goddamn county, it seemed. Ironically, it had been Bill Castlereigh who had talked him into joining. Now it was his body Wayne would carry that day.

Wayne walked slowly into the store, pausing only to straighten out a display of camping equipment in the window. Then he stalked back into the gloom of the back.

Warren shot him a careful look when he approached that said, "Look, see? I'm working," as Wayne placed the broom back on the display rack with its companions. He used a different one each day. No sense wasting a good item. He'd just knock off a few cents if anyone noticed that one of them was soiled. Not much traffic in them anyway. Rayson's Grocery, now run by Rayson, Jr., undercut Wayne's price on household products like brooms.

Warren went back to taking inventory on guns and ammunition in the store. It was a twice-a-month job, although the government didn't require it nearly so often. Mr. Greely had been the one to stock guns, and Wayne would have stopped, but he recognized that this was the only place in town, one of three in the whole county, where people could buy such equipment. He got a lot of trade in camping and hunting accessories from the gun customers, and he had nearly five thousand dollars in inventory tied up in it. Still, Wayne didn't like guns. He'd never fired any kind of gun in his life or been around people when they did. Papa Henderson had been killed in a hunting accident before Wayne was born, and Mama Henderson wouldn't allow any kind of gun on the place, even a toy gun. Wayne didn't even like to handle the guns he carried, and he made Warren count every bullet, every rifle, shotgun, and pistol in the store every two weeks. He feared being robbed and learning that some kid had shot up somebody with a firearm stolen from his store. But so far nothing like that had ever happened.

"When you get done there," he said to the boy, "dust off the furniture room, then go to lunch."

Warren nodded, not wanting to lose count and wishing the skinflint would allow him to use one of the calculators he stocked to make this tedious job easier. Warren didn't really mind working for Wayne, but he resented his boss's stingy nature. He recognized that he could make more at the gyp mill or even farming, probably, than Wayne paid him, but he also knew that if he held on long enough Wayne would die or something, and Warren would be the only man in Agatite who knew hardware and furniture. Such knowledge, however, didn't come because Wayne taught him anything. To his boss, Warren knew, he was hired help. That was it.

Even if Wayne didn't die, however, Warren had a plan to go over to the First Security Bank and borrow enough money to buy one of the cut-rate franchises that had sprung up in the small towns nearby. He figured he could put ol' Wayne out of business in six months, maybe less.

But in the meantime he bided his time, working his ass off for Wayne and learning all he could about the business.

"Did Adam Moorely call while I was out front?" Wayne asked as he checked the supply of fishing lures on a shelf behind him.

"Nope," Warren said absently.

"If he comes in while I'm not here, remember to get cash from him. His mother's account is in the register there, and you check it to make sure of the amount. Don't take a check. He tried to give me a check twice already, drawn on some goddamn California bank. Don't take a check, understand?"

"Sure, sure," Warren said, finally realizing he had lost count and would have to start over. "Why tell me? You'll be here, won't you?" He suddenly remarked, and brightened and said, "Oh, hey, that's right, today's your first day off." Wayne turned away toward the weather stripping and made a mental note to restock. "You got a date or somethin'?"

Wayne turned around and looked hard at Warren, trying to decide if the kid was being smart. Then he remembered he was wearing a good suit instead of his usual outfit. "No," he said quietly, "I gotta go to a funeral. Pallbearer for Bill Castlereigh."

"You just went to a funeral, didn't you? On Monday?" Warren was starting to count again. "That girl they found out to Hoolian. Hanging in the crapper. Shi—I mean shoot! That was gross."

"People die. People have funerals," Wayne said with finality. He didn't want to discuss it or even think about it, and before Warren could say anything else, he said hurriedly, "If you don't quit doodling around, you won't get your lunch. Get a move on." Then he moved to the garden tools to see if he had enough spades and rakes in stock for the winter season.

IV. Breedlove
1973

Breedlove heaved into the rusty commode and sank to his knees. Cold sweat accented the fever on his forehead. The brown vomit spilled off the porcelain, yellowed by the urine of a generation of inaccurate drunks, and onto the stained and cracked tile floor. Raising his head, he fixed his eyes on a dirty Rollowipe and felt nausea come over him again. His empty stomach heaved a warning not to try to force anything into it for a good long while.

He wanted to go home. He wanted to sleep in a clean bed with people in the next room who gave a good goddamn. The three condom machines mocked his misery with pictures of semi-naked women and claims of wild adventure. He felt like he wanted to die. He was certain he wanted to die—here, in a dirty bar in a town the name of which he forgot the minute he hitchhiked across the city limits line.

He forced himself up onto wobbly legs and flushed the commode, but it wouldn't do anything but burp and gurgle and threaten to run over onto his boots and make a mess. He stepped back. He splashed water in his face from the sink's tap and dried himself on his shirttail. Drawing water into his hands, he forced himself to rinse the taste of vomit from his mouth, and then he remembered why he had told her—what was her name?—that he wanted to go to the john.

Digging deeply into his Levis pockets, he located a quarter, his last money besides the ten-spot sewn into the lining of the top of his boot, and he paid a machine labeled "Pecker Stretcher." A white miniature litter with a red cross on it fell out of the till when he turned the crank, and he felt sick all over again. It had been a stupid, dumb kid mistake—like coming into this bar and trying to pick up something had been—he was too young and he knew that she knew he knew it. He was a goddamn fool. Goddamn these machines! he thought, put-

ting more water into his mouth and spitting it out all over
the floor. Don't swallow! He looked into the mirror.

Staring back at him was a thinly bearded, red-eyed,
uncombed mess, but around the corners of his mouth,
beneath the pitiful and scornful expression, was the
shadow of Breedlove. Captain of the football team. Stud
Breedlove! Son of a bum! Son of a bitch! Now he was a
bum all by himself.

He wiped his eyes clear and left the men's room,
emerging into the glaring red jukebox lights of the bar.
He almost ran back inside as another wave of nausea hit
him. He felt strangely sober and looked around for Mar-
cia—or Mildred—or whateverthehell her name was. He
spotted her at the bar, sitting beside a fat-faced truck
driver who had looped an arm around her waist and was
whispering and laughing into her ear. She was laughing
too, pouring another beer into her glass, and apparently
unaware that she had promised to leave with Breedlove.
Hell, he had been a truck driver too, and a cowboy, and
a dishwasher, and a farmer, and a roughneck . . . and
. . . and . . . and he had just finished his last job cleaning out cattle trucks—maybe this guy's truck.

Glancing at him from the corner of her eye, she picked
up her glass and sipped it, showing no hurry and no
inclination to leave. Fuck her, Breedlove thought, bad
whiskey, bad women, bad-assed truck drivers. He could
end up dead. No piece of ass was worth that risk, especially not some honkytonk honey with that many miles
on her.

The cold, wet air of the Texas autumn chilled him as
he left the bar. He leaned against the bar's door and lit a
cigarette, but the taste of ashes in his mouth made him
throw it away. He wondered what the name of this goddamn town was. Turning up the collar of his Levi's jacket
against the cold, he tried to remember the name of the
fleabag where he'd left his stuff. Along U.S. 287 a semi
screamed by in the whipping wind.

5

I. Breedlove
1976

Sunlight crept silently into the cheap pattern of wallpaper, that had been invisible in the darkness. Breedlove sat in a ragged, overstuffed chair and looked at the whore turning in the bed where she slept. She had been pretty damned good for a Mex, he thought with pleasure. She had known how to make him feel good. Like a man.

He was amazed at how sober he felt, and he reached for another cigarette, almost trying to force the headache he was sure he deserved after all he'd drunk the night before. As he concentrated, he found he couldn't remember much about the night before, and he especially couldn't remember how much he had had to drink. He'd always heard that you could build a tolerance for the stuff, and maybe he was. He knew he had *opened* two bottles, but he couldn't remember if he had finished both or, for that matter, even one.

The whore turned again in her sleep, revealing a thigh briefly, naked under the dingy sheets of the cheap hotel's bed. Her hair looked stringy and dirty, but he really didn't care. He hadn't had a good lay in a long time, and she had been damned fine, even if she wasn't white.

He'd gotten a dose off the last white girl he had slept with, a hippie-chick up in Colorado. She had a van and said she liked to do cowboys for fun. They'd had fun, he guessed, but he'd been drunk then too. And he really didn't remember much, since he'd passed out sometime during the night and she'd thrown him out somewhere near the New Mexico line. But he remembered the burning sensation when he peed, and he remembered the dripping embarrassment of having to get it treated. It had taken two months and many dollars to pay for that night's fun. But it had taught him a lesson. He stuck to professionals, whores who knew how to keep themselves clean and show a man a good time without giving him something to remember them by.

He briefly considered grabbing his pants and getting the hell out of the room before she woke up and expected him to hand her the fifty—or was it a hundred?—he had promised her last night. It didn't really matter, he knew, since he only had about thirty bucks, and he still had to pay for the room. He didn't intend to give her more than twenty, and he expected a fight. But that sort of turned him on, and he knew that she might be his last lay for quite a while. He had a job in the oil fields again, and when he went out on a job, sometimes it was weeks before he could get into town and scout the local talent.

He studied the sleeping woman. She had nice skin, even if her hair did look dirty. Her skin was soft and clear. He rose and moved over next to the bed, allowing his penis to stand completely erect over her dozing face. It made him feel suddenly powerful to stand over her with an erection, knowing she would awaken in a moment and reach up and grab it and take it in her mouth. He almost couldn't stand the thought, it was so completely delightful.

After a moment she opened her eyes and looked up past his erect member toward his face. Instead of reaching for him, she smiled and showed her bright, uneven teeth and raised the sheet, revealing small, almost shriveled breasts with sunken nipples surrounded by long single hairs, and his eyes fell away down to a long cesarean scar running from her skinny midsection down to her sparse pubic hair. He winced when he saw the scar, the stretch marks covering her abdomen, and the dirt under her fingernails as she began massaging her pathetic breasts and trying to entice him.

Hell, he thought, his erection beginning to shrink away, he'd probably get a dose from her too. But he closed his eyes and slid into the bed next to her. As he entered her, he pushed the smell of body odor and stale cigarettes away and found himself believing she was someone else. For the next few minutes he was home.

II. Lawman
August, The Present

At three o'clock old Doc Pritchard stood on the front porch of the Hoolian Barbershop wiping his hands on a wet towel. Jingles sat nearby sipping a beer he had finally talked Mel out of, and Able leaned against the support post of the barbershop's porch, silently shifting a Hava-Tampa Jewel from one side of his mouth to the other, contemplating his copper-colored boots, and allowing his mind to wander.

"Well, Able," Doc Pritchard said after drying his hands on another towel, "I can't tell you much right now. She's definitely dead, and she's been that way for a good long time."

"You go to medical school to learn that?" Jingles asked. He was out of sorts. First of all, he had learned that Able had let the Mexican boy go after a few questions. He had been under the impression that Mel or Ray had found the body, and when he learned that it was an itinerant farm worker, he was hell-bent to make an arrest. Then, when Harvey Connally had arrived, he had hardly spoken to the chief of police, preferring to deal only with Able, a man he knew and respected. In fact, when he left, he put Able *in charge* of the investigation, even though his word carried no weight with Jingles. Still, the policeman was rankled.

Then Doc Pritchard had shown up and things went worse for Jingles. Pritchard had ignored him, causing Jingles to erupt finally in a childish explosion of temper, insisting that jurisdiction or no goddamn jurisdiction, this was his by-God case and his by-God investigation, and Able was by-God along for the by-God ride.

It had been an unfortunate outburst, at least in terms of timing, since Doc Pritchard's immediate reaction had been calmly to assign Jingles to the removal of the body and to order him to do it as quickly and quietly as possible. That had soured Chief Murphy's mood completely and turned it from impish to ugly.

As the two subordinates, Vernon and Phillips, bagged the body, which had nearly fallen apart when they cut it down, Jingles stood a safe distance away, yelling at their every move and gagging when he got a whiff of the noxious odor. When the three of them finally got the body loaded into the back of Pritchard's station wagon—which served Sandhill County as a coroner's car the same way Doc Pritchard served it as coroner, occasionally and infrequently—Jingles had almost lost his voice due to the loud questions he had demanded of the men concerning their parentage and competency.

Pritchard had examined the body in the outhouse before they cut her down, and now he had washed his hands and wanted to talk to Able, a cool and reasonable man if he ever knew one, in spite of his thoroughly soaked shirt and sweat-stained straw hat.

"I swear, Murphy," he said as he tossed the towel toward Mel, who dropped it as if it contained the plague, "you're a worse pain in the ass than piles." Doc Pritchard was nearing seventy, and from behind his glasses his eyes appeared pale and watery. He had been the only physician in Agatite for years, and now his role as coroner was an honorary position he held to keep his hand in until young Jeff Randall could gain experience and, most importantly, the trust of the area's population.

"Able," he continued, turning his back on the fuming chief of police, "it's hard to tell anything out here. I don't know what killed her, but strangulation seems like a good bet from the look of things. I'm gonna take her into the hospital and do a proper autopsy, and I should know more in a couple of hours, although it could be a couple of days before everything is in. I may have to send some stuff to the D.P.S. lab down in Austin unless I run into something solid first. I'd say offhand that she's been dead at least three weeks, maybe longer. Your deputy's theory about murder may be right. I don't see how she could hang herself up there, but if she was poisoned or something, we may never know. There's not a drop of blood left in her, or any liquid for that matter. She's almost totally mummified." He paused for a moment. "Of course, that's both good and bad."

"How so?" Able asked, moving his cigar from one side of his mouth to the other and making a mental note to congratulate Phillips on his theory's second from the doctor. It was Phillips, not Vernon, who thought of it, and even Doc Pritchard had found it hard to believe that a former street hood could think that quickly.

"Well, it's good to the extent that the exterior of her body, skin, so forth, the solid parts, bone, cartilage, along with the major organs, will be intact—dried like fruit. If she'd been outside where all kinds of varmits could've gotten to her, there wouldn't be anything left to work with, and she'd likely have burst and been picked clean by birds and ants and such. Her bones would've been scattered, too. Same would've probably happened if she'd been buried, 'less, of course, she'd been buried deep."

"Jesus God!" Jingles gagged into his beer.

"But without blood," Doc Pritchard went on, ignoring the chief of police, "that's the bad part. It'll be hard to tell if she was drugged or, as I said, poisoned, or drunk, or anything. I still should have some stomach contents, though, and there are other things as well, tissue samples and—"

"Jesus H. Christ!" Jingles set his beer down and hung his head between his knees, mopping his balding pate with an already soaked bandanna.

"—there's brain tissue to look at, as well as her heart. All those things can reveal a lot even without blood and body fluids," Pritchard concluded.

Jingles got up quickly and went inside.

"What can you tell me about her? I mean, we got no idea who she is," Able said, smiling as he watched through the shop's window Jingles finding his way to the barbershop's toilet.

"Well," Doc Pritchard said, wiping his chin and pulling out a tooth-scarred pipe and a small can of Sir Walter

Raleigh tobacco, "she's a white woman, I'd say young, maybe twenty or so, though she could be some older. She's about five-two, but that's hard to tell. I'm judging from her leg length, since her neck's stretched so, and from what I can tell, she'd been beaten pretty bad, but whether it was bad enough to cause her death, I can't say, not now. Like I said, I imagine she was strangled by that cord."

"But you think Phillips might be right about murder?" Able asked, glad to have given the patrolman credit for his idea.

Doc Pritchard lit his pipe with a wooden match. "That ain't my department."

"The way her clothes were torn, and the fact that there wasn't anything to stand on, the scratches and so forth. The stains . . ." Able trailed off, realizing that Doc Pritchard had noticed those things too.

"Well," Doc said, puffing contentedly and thoughtfully, "normally, in a hanging like this"—he nodded toward Jingles, who had emerged pale and looking decidedly unhappy—"the victim will tear at his clothes, especially around the neck and chest areas. It's involuntary, like voiding the bowels. I don't know, though, since she didn't get through her underwear or anything, and as for the lack of something to stand on, she might have managed to wedge her feet along the side boards or something. Although that doesn't seem likely. Remember, her feet would've cleared the seat of the john by a good twelve inches, give or take, before her neck stretched."

Able pulled out a soggy notebook from his breast pocket, and the stub of a pencil, and started taking notes.

"She'd broken some fingernails, too, no, three." Pritchard chuckled at his unintentional pun, "but the others looked well manicured, and polished. I looked around a bit, but I didn't find the broken ends, and they'd be considerably long. Some varmint might've carried them off, which ain't likely, if she broke them in the struggle with her clothes or fooling around with the cord. Her front two teeth seem to be busted, and, like you say, there's the scratches on her legs. She sure as hell didn't do that herself, and she didn't beat herself up. Those stains might be blood. By the way, did you find her other shoe?''

Able shook his head and flicked his cigar butt into the weeds. There were so many questions, and he had no answers.

Doc Pritchard stopped talking and stepped down off the porch in the direction of his car. "I'm getting too old for this shit, Able," he said, "and it's too damned hot." Able nodded. Pritchard turned after glancing up at the sky that was almost bleached white by the sun, "Connally said to call you with the autopsy report." He opened his car door.

"Oh, he did, did he?" Jingles was wiping his mouth with his much-soiled bandanna. "Well, Mr. High-God-Almighty-Coroner-from-Sandhill-County-because-we-ain't-got-no-better, this is *my* goddamn case, and I'm taking over jurisdiction, and you can by-God call me with your goddamn autopsy report!" He was out of control, furious, and frothing a bit at the mouth.

Doc Pritchard pulled on his pipe and blew the smoke out into a halo that formed around his gray head, "I don't think your stomach can take it, Murphy," he said, calmly contemplating the soiled shirt and trousers of the Agatite chief of police. "I'll call you, Able, and you can water it down for Dick Tracy here." With that he got into his car, slammed the door, rolled up the windows, and roared off toward Agatite.

III. Rancher
August, One Week Later

In the shadows of the darkened living room James Earl Meacham III sat sipping a strong bourbon and water. He had his feet up on a coffee table that had been hand-hewn with an ax—"carved" was not the right word—from an oak tree by James Earl Meacham, Jr., the week World War I had started. The living room itself was part of a house that, in fact, had been hand-hewn by James Earl

Meacham I, or by his men, and it sat on a ranch that had *itself* been hand-hewn out of buffalo grass and prairie scrub by the self-same James Earl Meacham *Numero Uno*.

Although in possession of a few window-unit air conditioners, the house was naturally cool even in the midday heat of an August sun, and James Earl, who usually was out among his cattle or worrying over some other aspect of ranch work, found the sensation of sitting in the big old house sinfully comforting. He wondered why he had spent so many days out in the heat, sweating blood over some damned cow when he could have been sitting right here, his socks up on his great-granddaddy's hand-hewn coffee table, sipping extra-smooth bourbon, and enjoying the cool of his great-granddaddy's hand-hewn house.

The house sat on a knoll that was little more than a gentle rise of ground from the expanse of prairie around it. It, too, had been hand-built, *on demand,* the family story went, of his great-granddaddy's bride, Esther Meacham. She had wed the big, sunburned cowboy-turned-rancher in St. Louis after a whirlwind courtship, and they had taken riverboat, train, and finally stagecoach to get to Agatite so they could ride a buggy out to the ranch in the spring of 1890. The legend said that she and her new husband arrived at ranch headquarters about noon, and she took one look at the flat, barren, sun-cooked, and sleet-cooled prairie broken only by an occasional mesquite tree—they had only been occasional then—and a flat-board-augmented soddy planted squarely in the center of two windmills, and she had refused to get down from the buggy.

"Let's get one thing straight, Mr. Meacham," she was supposed to have said sweetly as the fumble-mouthed ranch hands stood around playing with their hats in their gnarled hands, marveling at the new mistress of the ranch. "I'm not living in some sort of Comanche hogan."

James Earl Meacham I was supposed to have been dumbfounded, and he suddenly started pointing out the virtues of living in a house that was naturally cool in summer and warm in winter. He also corrected her—Comanches didn't live in hogans—but she opened her umbrella and turned away from him.

"When you've built a proper house," she said, "then you can expect a proper wife to live in it. In the meantime I shall take up residence at a hotel in Agatite, if such an improbably named *ville* has such an establishment fit for a lady."

The ranch hands began to snicker among themselves, but she cut them short with a cold look. Then, sweetly turning to her husband, she added, "And I think I should fancy a white house"—she pointed vaguely in the direction of the windmills with her umbrella—"on a hill."

A *hill*! As far as the eye could see, the rolling prairie was broken only by an infrequent mesa. There wasn't a hill in miles! But a hill she would have, with a big white house on it. And the snickering ranch hands soon turned to cursing this frilly woman from "Saint Looie," as they actually hand-built a hill with shovels, wheelbarrows, and enormous sod squares cut right out of the prairie and backbreakingly toted up to the site. In all, it took two months for the hill, and by that time a San Antonio architect had come up and made drawings that would become a marvelous combination of Spanish and Texas ranch-style housing.

Built with natural ventilation and double insulated with specially treated cotton, it was cool in the hottest afternoons, and in the wintertime the three enormous fireplaces with special heat vents brought warmth to the whole house. The system still worked, almost eight decades later, as James Earl Meacham III sat in his living room and contemplated the many years he had spent there, enjoying both the beauty and the comfort of his ancestrial home.

Like his great granddaddy, his granddaddy, and his daddy, James Earl Meacham III was a prime beef rancher. He no longer drove steers to market the way his ancestors had, nor had he fought Indians, although he had been in the U.S. Cavalry, modern style. But he had never seen combat, either, finding that his expertise in spotting good beef and knowing about crops and feeds had landed him a fine job as a food purchaser for the Army's Quartermaster Corps, and a transfer out of the Vietnam-bound Seventh Cavalry.

He rose to make himself another drink, strolling, or really sauntering, over to the fancy hand-hewn bar his daddy had built from twisted scrub cedar. In fact, he thought as he topped off the highball glass with unwatered whiskey, the whole damned house was a by-God collection of hand-hewn, hand-built, hand-sewn, and hand-made objects created by his parents, grandparents, great grandparents, or the people who worked for them. Furniture, samplers, antimacassars, counterpanes, bookshelves, paintings, picture frames, even the goddamn toilet seats in their extra-large indoor bathroom—the first in Sandhill County—were all hand-something-or-othered, just like the house and the hill it sat on.

But, James Earl Meacham III thought as he surveyed the room around him, I haven't made one fucking thing. He didn't work with his hands. He was a gentleman rancher, a businessman. He didn't have time for any by-God hobby shopping. He *did* have a hand-made bank account in six goddamn figures—and he flashed a handsome smile that became him.

He took a soft sip of his drink. It was too strong and made him wince. That's okay, he thought, I'm not going to work today. He sauntered again around the living room, looking at old photographs, steer horns, and other silly bric-a-brac his forebearers had seen fit to place on the walls of the room. He was long and lean with black hair and blue eyes. He was clean-shaven and had long, slender fingers that hooked easily into the belt loops of his expensive, western-cut pants. He stood easily in sharp-pointed boots, of which he had six pairs—and not one of them made from cowhide—up to better than six feet three inches. In short, he was carelessly handsome, brutally strong, slick-tongued, and sharp-minded. He loved the rodeo and rodeo events; he preferred the bucking broncs. He had won a silver belt a few years ago from

the Texas Amateur Rodeo Association, which said he was
the best bronc rider in the whole by-God state.

He had taken the ranch left to him by his father, Edward Seaton Meacham, which *he* had acquired in the year
of his majority when James Earl Meacham, Jr., and his
wife, Rose, both died within a year of each other of in-
fluenza and heart attack, respectively. The reason for the
gap of one generation in the progression of James Earls
had been that the intended namesake had been born both
dead and with a cowl on a howlingly cold January night,
and superstition forbade giving any other child the name
planned for the dead one. So he had been buried nameless, and it was up to the second born, Edward Seaton,
to continue the tradition.

When Edward had taken over at twenty-one, the ranch
was still suffering from the Great Depression ravages of
drought and low money for investments, and it had taken
him most of his life to put it back together and make it
work. When he himself had died after being snake-bit
while hunting down a heifer in a remote pasture and lying
there for three days before anyone found him, James Earl
had been twenty-five, and one of his first official acts as
the new master of the ranch had been to move his mother
into a hospital for the hopelessly insane—he hated the
word asylum—in Houston. Her mind had snapped for no
apparent reason in 1955, shortly after James Earl III was
born, leaving him brotherless and effectively motherless
most of his life. But she had given him her dark beauty,
and, he often thought, her sense of the ironic.

He had grown up normally, otherwise, if being a su-
perstar is normal. He played football and made varsity
as a sophomore. He had been president of every club he
joined, and he had dated the prettiest cheerleader, Maggie Stokes. He was All-State for three years in a row,
and he had gone to Texas A&M as his daddy and granddaddy had before him, joined the Corps, as they had,
and majored in animal husbandry and ranch manage-
ment, as they had. The major difference was that he received special permission in the Army to stay in school
for two more years, and he took a master's degree in

business. He recognized that he had to know more than the north end of a southdown mule to make it ranching in a modern world.

His military career ended early when he received a hardship discharge after his daddy died, and he came home to take over the ranch. He married Maggie, and, after committing his mother, they had moved into the Big House as all the Meachams had called it, although James Earl III liked to think of it as "Miz Esther's House," because that's really what it was. He had thrown himself into ranch work. That was when the trouble started.

The whiskey was nearly gone in his glass, and he contemplated making himself another drink, telling himself he really didn't need it, and then giving up and deliberately losing the argument. He sauntered over to the hand-hewn bar and neatly banged his leg on the hand-hewn coffee table, then poured the glass full again. It wasn't his intention to get drunk or even high. He merely wanted to drink, and since Agatite and all of Sandhill County was dry, home was about the only place he could do that without driving over to Oklahoma or Wichita Falls.

The drink poured, James Earl Meacham III maneuvered his way up the stairs of the house, careful not to slosh the whiskey onto the Persian rug runner or to repeat the injury to his knee, which was now throbbing dully from its meeting with the coffee table. At the top of the stairs he turned to walk down the hall, softly padding in his stocking feet, and peeked into the half-open door that was Maggie's bedroom. They had slept apart for the past five years. He saw her lying naked on top of the hand-made counterpane, and he admired her beauty. She had the blondest hair in the world, he thought. Golden. Her eyes were brown and rich, like chocolate. She was by-God beautiful. There was no denying it, and a part of him wanted to go right into the room, take her, naked, into his arms, and make love to her. A big part of him wanted to do that. That's the bourbon talking, he said to himself, egging me on because it knows that a part of me is still in love with her.

But another part of him, a smaller but more powerful

part, knew she was a tramp, a goddamn whore and a tramp. That was the truth, and he knew it couldn't be denied any more than her beauty could. He realized that the other part of him would always be kept down by the truth of that fact.

Maggie and he had started going together in junior high, and they continued the romance throughout Agatite High School. They were an ideal couple—Most Likely to Succeed, Most Handsome Boy, Most Beautiful Girl, Mr. and Miss Senior Prom, Homecoming Queen and Escort two years in a row, an unprecedented accomplishment for the Eagles' Homecoming tradition. She had gone to Baylor, while he had gone to A&M, and they had made violent, passionate love in motel rooms in Waco, College Station, and all points in between or wherever else they happened to be, a habit they had started years before in the scattered hay barns of the Meacham ranch. They had literally fucked their way across Texas, each time renewing the passion they had discovered in each other when they were barely fourteen.

They had dated other people, of course, "during the week." After all, she was the most popular girl in her sorority, and he had a reputation to keep up, too, but he never believed that she slept with any of the Baptist nerds who took her out for a Coke on a week night anymore than he thought she knew about his trips to La Grange or other whorehouses with the guys in the Corps—maneuvers, he had called them. But he was a man, and he didn't much care whether she knew or not.

When he went into the army, she had cried bitterly and taxed her father's—Judge Stokes'—bank account, flying around the country to meet him wherever he was and could get leave. And when his father had died and he came home, they had married in one of the biggest by-God shows Agatite had ever seen. Half the town came.

Maggie turned in her sleep, and he crept away from her door. After twelve and still asleep, he thought, but she probably needs her sleep. She's probably all tuckered out from fucking the brains out of whomever she was out with last night. Probably was pulling a train for the whole goddamn football team, he thought, grinding his teeth a bit. She was a whore. A by-God tramp. That he knew. "At least she wasn't with Bill Castlereigh," he said aloud, and chuckled.

He drained the bourbon as he padded down the stairs. He wouldn't drink another one, he promised himself, but he now knew what he would do. He needed to be clearheaded, and he sat down on the sofa and pulled on his boots. This was an excellent idea, he thought, to take the day off and just relax around the house.

He waited awhile and finally gave up the fight and made himself another drink. He caught sight of a photograph of his senior year team. He silently named each player in line, wondering where they all were now. "We could've made state that year," he said to the picture, "but we didn't have the guts." He sipped the drink. "And we didn't have a quarterback, either," he finished, and placed the glass carefully on top of the bar. "Women," he said to the empty glass. "Women fuck up everything."

Finally he heard what he was waiting to hear. The shower upstairs was running. Maggie was up.

He moved slowly over to the mantlepiece and took down his great granddaddy's .10-gauge shotgun with the dual hammers and—he chuckled when the thought crossed his mind—hand-hewn stock.

He broke the breech, checked it, and walked carefully if somewhat unsteadily up the stairs to Maggie's bedroom. Her bathroom was smaller than the oversized one of which the Meachams had been so proud, since it was added after the house was built. He walked in, pushing the door full open with the end of the twin barrels. Steam came from the shower's hot water as Maggie washed the smell of whomever she had been fucking the night before down the drain.

"Maggie darling," he called loudly enough to be heard over the running water.

"What the hell are you doing home?" she asked as she pulled the curtain back, revealing the soft lusciousness of her body. Suddenly her dark, chocolate eyes wid-

ened as she saw him standing there with the shotgun
pointed directly at her flat abdomen. "James Earl?" she
said.

As the twin hammers fell on their percussion points,
she screamed and fell back against the blue tiles of the
shower stall.

IV. Breedlove
1978

Gingerly touching the eye that was black and swollen,
Breedlove shifted his position on the hard bench so it
wouldn't bite his ass so much. One of these days, he
thought, you're gonna get in real trouble in one of those
bars.

"You'd better learn to drink, boy," the cowboy had
yelled at him as he pitched him out into the mud of the
parking lot. That was the problem, Breedlove thought,
he'd already learned to drink, but too well.

The goddamn bus was going to be late again, so he
would be late getting into Abilene. He'd missed one job
because of a whore, and now another one was about to
go because of another goddamn bitch.

He'd gone into the bar with about half a buzz, excited
because he'd found a job so easily, just hanging around
the truck stop. This guy named Miller had walked up to
him and offered him a roughnecking job. It was great.
Then he'd gotten a bit too drunk, spending all his reserve
cash, except for enough to buy a bus ticket, on booze
and on that whore in the bar.

What a setup for a fool like him, he thought, again
touching the bruised eye and hoping it would go down
before he got to the job. The bar, bedrooms in back—all
he had to do was give her twenty and go back for a
quickie. But not that quickie, goddamn it. At first it had
seemed all right. She had taken down his pants, then got
a basin full of warm water and started washing him all
over down there. He got hard as hell, then he came,

shooting all over the place. She had called him nasty, dirty, and then she wanted to keep the money.

"But you ain't done nothin'," he yelled at her. "I ain't done nothin'!"

"What you call this, honey?" she had yelled back as she wiped semen from her upper chest.

They had continued to yell at each other for a while, then the cowboy came in, and he took a fist full of nickels and started hitting Breedlove all over. He came at me like a goddamn windmill, Breedlove recalled, hitting me in the eye and throwing me out in the mud. Shit.

He'd lain there all night and missed the first bus out. Now he looked forlornly down the highway for another. It was too damned hot to work anyway, but hell, a body has to eat, he told himself.

The job was near Agatite, too damned close to home for comfort, but hell, it'd been a long time since he left. He was a different person now, he believed. He'd grown a beard, which he hated, and he'd just take a room in Kirkland and ride out to the job with some of the guys or hitch every morning. He was an accomplished hitchhiker. He'd stay close to his room and stay sober. Sandhill County was dry anyhow, and he could save up enough to get down to San Antonio for the winter, maybe Corpus.

In Kirkland there'd be no chance of running into the old man, or her. The wall of the makeshift bus station in the jack-leg town he found himself in had flowers on the wall. Not wallpaper, but painted flowers, each hand-done. It reminded him of the wallpaper in her house, out on the sleeping porch. What with the creaky old air conditioner going full blast and her parents and sister way off in the main part of the house, they could get away with anything on the big old sleeper sofa while they were supposed to be doing homework or watching TV. And they had, too.

He smiled when he thought of the feeling he had, walking up to the Dairy Mart parking lot where all the guys were, them horny-the-hell bug-eyed, lying about what they had almost done out on Airport Road, and him, swaggering like a real boss stud, telling them how he'd just had his horns clipped *again,* and how they would like it if they tried it.

He remembered those warm nights, drinking all the rodeo-cool green beer, talking about going to college. Hell, he'd have been All-State for sure that fall, and they couldn't help but go all the way with him carrying the ball. A scholarship would've been a sure thing. They would jack him around about being pussy-whipped, but they'd really be jealous because he was going with one of the prettiest girls in school, and her old man had money to boot. Him, the son of a drunk, whose mother was dead, whose future was simply a matter of a job unless he could make it with such a rich girl or win a good scholarship.

He realized that he wanted those times again, the talk about the best of the crop on varsity, and all and all. And her, watching him across the classroom, turning red at the least thing he said to her, wanting him to put his arm around her and touch her hand every chance he got. She knew he belonged to her, and he knew she belonged to him. They knew that nothing could be more wrong and still be as right as things were between them. Then things went to hell, all of a sudden.

She turned up crying and blubbering. She had always been a crybaby, from the very first time. Her old man—his old man, staying sober and respectable, even going down to the church, for a whole week just out of pride and anger. No. He couldn't go back. Not after leaving the way he did. All that was history now.

The heat of the afternoon made the flowered wall waver and shimmer. Miller had said he'd leave for Agatite from Abilene today, at three-thirty, sharp. "Ain't waitin' on no drifters, though," he had warned. It was after one and the bus still wasn't here. His eyes hurt like hell, and he wanted a drink. That cowboy had caught him just right, just like in the movies. It felt like he'd used a baseball bat.

6

There had to be something wrong somewhere. Breedlove had been playing the same poker with the same bunch of assholes for months, and he had never, never drawn four of a kind. There was nothing else showing in the seven-stud game. Nothing.

He looked around the table. Two fives here, a jacks-possible there, but nothing like a full boat or even trips. He had two sevens showing and two down, and two cards to go. Hellfire! Maybe his luck was changing.

He bet cautiously, trying to keep a serious but casual look on his face, although he knew his hands were shaking. One fold, then another—no, you don't, you mothers—the jack and fives stay. The Okie with zilch raises ten bucks. What could be sweeter? The jacks-possible stays, and the five raises ten more. That pot must be damned near three hundred bucks by now. Four sevens! *Shit!* Two more cards—two more chances to build the pot.

His next card was a king, and he felt good about that. No help for anybody else, but his hand still looked only fair and hid dynamite! This time the jacks-possible calls his bet, and the fives raises twenty. What the hell could he have down? It didn't matter—sevens beats fives—build the pot. The sweat under his arms trickled down his side in spite of the fact that it was nearly freezing outside the drilling shack. One more card and he could quit winners, and quit rich! The fives dealt it to him down. He didn't even need to look at it, but to keep up his bluff, he raised its corner carefully and pretended to peek slowly.

He had planned to groan loudly and really suck them

in good, but when he saw the card he groaned for real. What the hell? Another seven? A club! What the hell was going on here? He casually checked his hole cards, two sevens down, a spade and a heart. He checked the last card again, the seven of clubs. Two sevens up and three down! Jesus!

He almost laughed out loud, but he caught himself and studied the faces across the table. The jacks-possible was a dude who had been playing and losing all along, for months. No way he could be a cheat. The fives had dealt him the bogus seven—in fact all five of them—but he knew the guy. Breedlove had needed a friend on this job, and the fives had been it. He was honest, Breedlove thought, and he only won from time to time, never getting a big pot. The Okie was too stupid to double-deal or cheat; besides he would stay as long as he had anything to bet with—at least he always did—that's why they asked him to play.

Even if the move was to suck him in with too good a hand to fold, who could beat him with any potential combination showing? What was the point? Who? Why? Breedlove wanted to jerk them each up by their collars and ask each one to his face. But he just sat.

The sweat under his shirt turned cold, and he began to see himself accused of cheating and unable to deny it—convincingly, anyway. He could call a misdeal, right now, but that would mean he'd lose that pot. No, he would have to just fold the hand. But he had almost a hundred of his own money out there by now, and he needed that pot. It was getting to be time to move on. He had been here too long.

He slid five dollars out on the table and waited breathlessly. The jacks-possible folded. Good, that cut down the odds. If everyone would fold, he could claim they'd been bluffed and never show his hole cards! Damn! He suddenly thought. The fives raised twenty—it must be him!—the Okie calls but doesn't raise. See the twenty and get the hell out, Breedlove said to himself with an urgent internal voice. He waited for a moment, fingering the few bills remaining in front of him. Hell no! he suddenly heard his internal voice shout. Up fifty and fuck you!

As the others called his raise, he fished into his Levi's jacket pocket for a cigarette. They finished their muttering and grumbling as they dug into wallets and pockets for extra and hidden cash to finish their betting round, then sat back to wait. He flipped over two of the three hidden sevens, waited as they gasped, and smiled. He never took his eyes off the fifth seven—the extra club—and he waited for the storm to break.

The Okie cursed and fell backward off his bottle case. The jacks-possible blew out loudly through his teeth and began raking in the cards, and the fives only muttered and shook his head in a grudging compliment to the way Breedlove had played the hand.

Breedlove grinned and said nothing. He scraped the bills and coins on the table toward him, carefully scooping up the bogus seven of clubs in the process. As quickly and with as much stealth as he could, he stuck it under his watch's wristband.

Pulling his jacket cuffs down, he announced that his time was up. Standing and buttoning the jacket up tight, he moved slowly toward the door, awaiting the outraged reaction he was sure was about to come. Fives complained about his quitting winners but said nothing else. The others acknowledged that Breedlove had lost enough times to quit while he was ahead for once, and he closed the door of the drilling shack behind him with a sigh of relief.

Outside the wind cut across the gray sky in one final effort to make winter a permanent state of affairs on the Texas prairie. He flicked his cigarette away and lit another, cupping the flame of the lighter in his hands as he contemplated what had just taken place. There was no percentage in hanging around here. They were bound to discover the light deck soon, and then they'd want a replay of that hand. Or worse, he thought, they might just decide to tack a piece of his ass to the drilling shack wall. They were a rough crew.

He quickly counted the more than seven hundred fifty

bucks that he had scooped up from the pot. He added that to the six hundred or so he had left in a cigar box in his room in town. For the first time in his life he had money to travel on. He was tempted to try to find Calhoun, the foreman, and collect this week's pay. Goddamn Calhoun, Breedlove thought, for holding back a whole week's pay from the first just to keep them from doing what Breedlove was about to do—run out on him.

Well, it was just too damned bad. The poker winnings more than made up for it, and he didn't dare waste any time listening to Calhoun try to talk him into staying on. It was a good time to travel. The season would be changing soon, and it would get goddamn hot out here. Give me the cold, Breedlove thought, pulling his hat down low on his eyes, I'd one hell of a lot rather shiver than sweat. He was tired of roughnecking anyway, and rodeo season was coming on. Hell, he'd always wanted to try that.

He stuffed the bills into his wallet and turned his coat collar up against the wind and began moving toward the highway. As he got closer he saw a car moving slowly against the wind—probably a preacher, Breedlove thought, judging from the slow pace and condition of the old Ford. He waved and began moving toward the highway at a more rapid pace. When he lifted his arm, the wind caught the card and it scraped against his wrist.

Maybe they would figure out that the deck had been screwed up all along. Maybe they wouldn't even notice it tonight, he thought as he tried to run against the wind. The extra seven hadn't been detected in more than an hour of playing, so why should a light deck suddenly seem odd? It didn't really matter. He was through with the oil fields no matter what. But they'd still kick his ass if they thought he cheated. That had been the biggest pot he'd seen on that table.

He reached the shoulder of the highway about fifty yards in front of the car and found himself breathing heavily and barely able to lift his arm. The dude ranches up in Colorado would be opening in a few weeks. Maybe with the cash he could get a cowboy outfit and a job up there. Those rich women from the East were always looking for a cowboy to play a little "buckin' bronc" on their pampered backs. And some of them were even willing to pay for the opportunity.

The car weaved a bit, then pulled over and stopped to wait for him. He almost fell over, trying to run against the wind. He would be damned glad to get out of Texas and that goddamn wind for a while. Colorado sounded good. Real good. He wanted to get away from the damned oil-field workers who thought that because they had grease all over their clothes and under their fingernails they had to fight anybody who didn't. He'd lost three teeth on this job just from hanging around with that bunch of assholes back there, trying to pick up some of the girls in the local towns. Shit, Colorado sounded like heaven.

The old Ford had a preacher in it all right, and Breedlove slid into the passenger side with a smile at the old minster behind the wheel. They drove along for a while in the silence of the car, which was fighting to stay on the road against the caprock wind that came in a steady stream of angry wailing, assaulting whatever dared to rise above the sandy ground along the highway. Finally the old man glanced into Breedlove's lap and smiled.

"Lucky in love?" he asked, nodding.

Breedlove looked down at the card protruding from his watchband and sweat broke out again on his forehead. Somehow in his confusion, he had picked up the wrong card. Lying in his open palm was the seven of hearts.

He now wondered if he would have time to get into town and clean out his gear and get back on the road before those idiots accused him of cheating them. He knew it would be no good trying to explain what had happened to him when they caught him. They'd kill him. Or they'd make one hell of a try at it.

"How far you goin'?" the old man asked him.

Breedlove thought briefly about the six hundred in his room, about his clothes—everything, in fact, he owned. Then he replied by repeating the question, "How far *you* goin'?"

"Why, Amarillo, if this norther don't blow me off the road."

"Mind if I just ride along with you?" Breedlove's shoulders sagged with the weight of resignation and loss. Fucked up again, he thought bitterly. Hell, I can't even cheat to keep from cheating.

"Welcome the company," the old man declared.

They rode along in silence for a while, the wind whistling in through the car's imperfect window seals and battling with the inadequate heater.

"It ain't none of my business," the preacher said, "but I've never found there was much percentage in card playin'." He glanced down again at the seven of hearts in Breedlove's hand.

Breedlove crushed the card and wadded it into a ball. "Me neither," he said. "Me neither."

II. Lawman
August, The Present

On the return drive from Hoolian to Agatite, Sheriff Able Newsome began to have serious doubts about his job and whether or not he was really interested in keeping it any longer. He and Sue Ellen had a bit of savings put away, and he thought about simply calling it quits and finding something else to do. He had never had such thoughts before, and he realized that the cause of it all was Chief of Police Jingles Murphy.

When Able graduated from Agatite High School in 1946, he found himself in a unique position for a young man. His only brother had been killed in Europe, and his father, a widower for years, had a heart attack shortly after the Army telegram brought the news home. At barely eighteen, then, Able found himself in possession of the family business, a dairy, which had fallen into neglect since his father died. Able eventually sold the dairy, which provided him with enough money to tide him over until he decided what to do with his life.

He went through the money rapidly, spending it in all-night poker games and in gin mills in Wichita Falls and Lawton, Oklahoma, and before long he was shocked to see how little was left. He took a job at the gyp mill near town, but he found out quickly that he hated the work, the boredom, and being a nobody. He met Sue Ellen Fulbright at a dance following a high school football game between Agatite and Pease City. She was chaperoning the Pease City kids at the dance held in that town after the game, and he was driving the football bus and had to hang around. To his surprise, he fell in love.

They were married in 1949, but he still found his life vaguely dissatisfying and frustrating. He sat around their apartment and watched himself get fat on Sue Ellen's cooking. When the Korean War broke out, he drove down to Fort Worth and enlisted in the Marine Corps, leaving early in the morning and not even telling Sue Ellen he was going to do it. Getting killed in Korea, he figured, was better than being ground down in a gyp mine. And after some hysterical crying, even Sue Ellen turned out to be a champ about his leaving for war. She also made sure she was pregnant before he left, so he would have some reason to come home, she told him.

Korea had proved to be his making. He found himself charging up a hill with about fifty other guys. Finally, with his hands blistered from the superheated barrel of the Thompson submachine gun he was carrying, he discovered that he was the only human being standing up as far as he could see. Most of the fifty guys who had started up the hill with him were dead, and the North Koreans had either been killed or had broken and fled before this giant Texan with a smoking machine gun. He didn't know much what to do, but before he could decide, another bunch of guys came helling up behind him and brought a chicken colonel in tow. Another group arrived with cameras, and they all started slapping him on the back, yelling that he was the greatest hero since Audie Murphy, and talking about medals. The colonel threw his arm around him and had the camera guy take pictures; then they went down the hill through the human carnage that littered it, and some congressman showed up from nowhere and a hundred more cameras flashed around them.

They were shaking hands and smiling, holding up the still smoking Thompson.

He received the Silver Star and a Purple Heart, although the only wound he could find was an infected blister that had developed two days before. The congressman was pushing him for a Medal of Honor, but Able came to before they could go that far, and he wrote to the congressman and told him that he hadn't done anything but be confused and scared shitless and that he didn't want any more medals or hero stuff and that he flat wouldn't accept them. But then the hometown paper had picked up the pictures and stories, and when the Purple Heart came through, so did his discharge papers. He went home to a hero's welcome. He was now a somebody, a man with a reputation for a courage and a bravery he knew he had never felt.

That same year old Sheriff Holmes had announced his retirement, and Able was pushed and prodded into running. He agreed, mostly because he couldn't stand the idea of going back to the gyp mill, and now Sue Ellen and Angela, his baby daughter, were expecting another arrival who would be Theresa, born the following Christmas.

He was unopposed in the election, and Able found himself sheriff of Sandhill County. Holmes hung around the office for about six months to teach Able what he needed to know about sheriffing, telling him stories about chasing bootleggers and runaway husbands and kids, serving eviction notices and protecting public property from the goddamn high school delinquents in town, until Able couldn't stand it anymore, couldn't stand the sight of the old man shuffling around the courthouse office, his pipe continually steaming behind him, looking lost and sad as he contemplated another, much younger man sitting at his desk, wearing his badge.

One morning Able had simply had enough. He told Holmes that he had a lot of work to do and asked him to come back later, like maybe next week.

An internal wince always went with the memory of that morning. Holmes stood stunned in the middle of the

office, facing Able with a horrible look of understanding.
He slowly removed his gunbelt, which he had continued
to wear even after Able's election, and placed it rever-
ently on the desk between him and Able, then turned and
walked toward the door. Able remembered that he limped
on a bad knee and used a cane, and when he reached the
door, the ancient sheriff turned and revealed tears in his
eyes. "Good luck, Able," he said in a quavering voice.
"Keep the pistol. I hope to God you never have to use
it." Then he left. The next day he packed up and went
on a fishing trip to Colorado and the Northern Rockies.

Able had intended to apologize and ask him around
again when he got back, but he never came back. He was
dead of a heart attack in a month.

Able had run unopposed in every election since, up
until five years before, when Newell Longman's brother-
in-law, Keith Murphy, ran for sheriff on the same ticket
where Newell was running for mayor of Agatite. Able
had actually felt the need to campaign that year, but he
just couldn't bring himself to make speeches about how
good a sheriff he was, so he didn't. He allowed some
friends to put up poster-sized letters around the county
saying that he wanted to remain in office and continue to
do the same job he had always done—which, the letter
said, was a good one—and he was finally convinced by
his children that bumper stickers would be worthwhile
and okayed the printing and distribution of about five
hundred of the stickers that read, "Able for Sheriff."
Even though Murphy hammered posters and signs on
every pole and fence post, held rallies, and gave away
barbecue and fried chicken, and even went on the county's only radio station every hour on the hour for a solid
month before the election, Able won hands down, de-
feating Newell's brother-in-law six to one.

Murphy had his revenge, however, forcing Newell to
keep peace in the family if not in the county by appoint-
ing him chief of police for the City of Agatite and then
ramrodding through the city council an appropriation for
equipment that would have funded the Sheriff's Department for five years.

Keith Murphy had immediately been dubbed "Jingles" by the town's smirking populace, owing to a resemblance between the portly chief of police and Andy Devine, as well as to Murphy's insistence on wearing a tremendous amount of equipment on his person that jingled when he walked.

The speed zone in Agatite was two miles long and slowed highway traffic out on U.S. 287 to a plodding 30 mph, but the two miles before and after that zone were prime areas for blind corners and billboards, and Newell had decided that an investment in sophisticated radar would substantially increase city revenues, something he needed to do since he had to deal with the burdensome expense of the new police equipment.

When Able refused to sit out in the heat and cold and catch speeders, Newell had handed the job exclusively to Jingles, who made it a passion in his life. He brought in between ten and twenty motorists a day during the vacation season, and at least three to five during the off months. Able hated the whole idea of a speed trap, and while he recognized that going faster than fifty-five mph was a violation, he also knew that he rarely drove his cruiser less than seventy when he was out on the highway and county roads, and he knew that Jingles and his two patrolmen were fond of higher speeds too.

Vernon's voice crackled over the radio, and Able answered. The deputy wanted to let the sheriff know that he was going to go off duty and that John David would be coming on late since his baby was sick again and his wife wasn't home from work yet. Normally that wouldn't have bothered Able, especially since he knew that Phillips and his partner in crime, Clovis Hiker, would be on patrol, thus at least keeping up the appearance of law and order in Agatite, but today it did bother him.

The dead woman in the outhouse in Hoolian posed a serious problem in Able's mind. All the unanswered questions of the afternoon ate at his sense of everything-in-its-place order. He was anxious to get back to the office and await Doc Pritchard's call. He desperately wanted the old man to tell him that it was suicide, that she was eaten up with cancer, or that her husband had beaten her up so badly that she had just killed herself. Something. Anything. But deep inside him he knew she had been killed, murdered. Phillips had been absolutely right. This was pure-dee murder. Murder. Cold blooded and brutal. In his county.

Oh, there had been killings enough in Sandhill County. Marital spats that escalated into arguments that escalated into shootings or knifings, the odd farmer shooting a poacher or thief on his land, or, Able thought with a shudder, the poachers shooting back. He recalled Old Man Cooper's blasted body, the result of a running gun battle fought with kids stealing watermelons twenty years ago. And there had been suicides before. Shotguns in the mouth, overdoses of pills, and one other hanging—a salesman from Amarillo who, distraught over his failing career and his wife's infidelity, had checked into the Four Seasons Motel and hanged himself from the shower head. But that had been relatively clean, easy. Not like this.

This was First Degree, Pre-Meditated, Murder. Somebody had killed that girl, then he had hung her in the outhouse. Or, at least, he had knocked her out and hung her there. The thought of her waking up at the point where the electrical cord tightened around her throat and starting to struggle was almost more than Able could bear. He wondered who in this county could do such a thing. Who in the *world*, he almost asked aloud, could do such a thing?

Able had never had to deal with a murderer, a pathological killer, who might slay his victim and hang her in an outhouse in the summer heat. There was something frighteningly sick about it all, and Able suddenly felt old and tired. "Hell," he said to the steering wheel, "I'm damned near sixty, too old for chasing killers all over the country." He was tempted to dump the whole thing in Jingles' lap, let him handle it top to bottom, just walk away and forget it. He had every reason to, he knew. But he couldn't.

The vision of the woman kept haunting him. The wasps, the empty eyes, the smell and the heat. Her bro-

ken fingernails and torn clothing, all of it, kept coming
before his eyes, and he knew he had to find out who did
this, this gruesome—that was the word for it—gruesome
deed.

God, it was hot, he thought, as sweat, generated just
from the walk from the car, ran down his forehead and
into his eyes. Well after five o'clock and still over a hundred. He shook his head as he opened the door to the
courthouse and went in to wait for Doc Pritchard to call.

III. Preacher
August, One Week Later

The Reverend Dr. Randolph P. Streetman inhaled deeply
on his Pall Mall cigarette, allowing the smoke to sear his
lungs before he released it into the atmosphere of his
study. He scratched his unshaven chin and ran his fingers
through the two or three strands of hair that inadequately
covered his bald head. Before him on his desk was a
sheaf of papers pertaining to William Castlereigh, and
Dr. Streetman was thoroughly frustrated.

In a few hours he was to preach a eulogy over the body
of William—Bill, everyone called him—Castlereigh, and
he knew less about the man after poring over the information in the church member's file than he had known
before he started. He was in a real quandary, and he
didn't know what he was going to do at two-thirty when
the services for the departed man were to begin.

Dr. Streetman was very upset over not having faced
the problem squarely from the beginning. But it was a
natural mistake. He had thought he knew Bill Castlereigh, or at least he thought he knew enough about him
to say the appropriate words, draw the appropriate ex-
amples, and make the appropriate rituals appear correct
enough to bury the man. But when he had sat down and
begun to make notes for the eulogy the night before, he
had realized that he didn't know much of anything.

William Castlereigh? he thought for the fortieth time
in the past hour, and he crushed out his cigarette in his

ashtray that was now growing full. Who are you? Who were you?

He remembered vaguely that Castlereigh had joined the First Baptist Church of Agatite nine years before along with his wife, Wilma, and his two daughters, Catherine and Belinda. His letter of membership, which Castlereigh himself had presented to Dr. Streetman, had come from the First Baptist Church of Youngstown, Ohio, but a routine phone call made earlier this morning to inform that congregation of the departure of one of their former members had revealed that there was no record of a Bill or William Castlereigh or any of the family ever being there. It was possible, of course, that some mistake had been made. But by whom? How?

Dr. Streetman lit another cigarette, and he noticed how his office was filled with smoke. He made a mental note to open a window, in spite of the August heat, to air it out, and to be absolutely certain to empty the ashtray into one of the large manila envelopes in his desk and to throw it away in the outdoor incinerator before he went home. Smoking was his one sin, a self-indulgence he picked up while a student at Hardin Simmons College in Abilene, and one he guarded with care and enjoyed only in the privacy of his church office or while on vacation where no one knew he was a minister of the Lord.

He had been the pastor of the First Baptist Church of Agatite for almost twenty years, and he had a reputation for decorum and propriety in the community. To allow even a rumor to go abroad that he *smoked* would be intolerably damaging, and he always took special care to conceal his habit, even from his wife and children. He kept breath fresheners in his pocket at all times, air freshener in his desk, a special spray to freshen his clothes, and he washed his hands and face in the church's men's room before entering his house.

Agatite, for him, had been a "temporary" post, a punishment position, really, which he stoically accepted because of a one-time indiscretion. He had been an Army chaplain, and he had had the misfortune to be arrested along with about twenty other GIs near Fort Hood, Texas, at a riot in a bar where prostitutes were working. Actually, he *had* been at the bar seeking a prostitute, but he could not explain then why he had been so motivated any more than he could now. He didn't get a chance to find out, either. He had barely walked into the bar when a fight erupted, and the MPs had come along with the civilian police and arrested everyone in sight. Having thoughtfully removed his chaplain's insignia before he went in, he was shunted along with the offending GIs to the stockade and booked and jailed until morning. The charges had amounted to nothing, especially when the GIs all said that he hadn't done anything except walk into the place at the wrong time, but word had leaked out to the Southern Baptist Convention, and when he was discharged six months later, he found himself unable to locate any church that would have him—any, that is, except the First Baptist Church in Agatite, since the former pastor had retired due to sudden illness, and no other minister was remotely interested.

Here in this outpost, away from the libraries in the seminary and universities he had loved so much, he was shelved and forgotten. His "temporary" status was permanent, and vaguely he felt he deserved it.

His wife, Gladys, and their two children, Tom and Suzie, had moved along with him, of course, the latter two now away at Baylor, and he had settled long ago into a resigned understanding that his one slipup, innocent though he may have been, had ruined him. He would never have a shot at one of the really large churches in Dallas or Houston, and he was never to do much more than minister to the small-town needs of his congregation.

So he indulged himself with cigarettes, preached three sermons a week, performed marriages, funerals, baptisms, visited the shut-ins, the hospitalized, the bereaved, administered the church's business to the best of his disinterested ability, which he felt was considerable, and prayed for the strength to overcome self-pity, an emotion that drove him more and more often these days to the seclusion of his office and the secreted packs of

Pall Malls tucked carefully away in hollowed-out books on his library shelves.

Today, however, the problem of Bill Castlereigh's funeral plagued him, and he was smoking far, far too much. He had visited Wilma, both at the funeral home and in her home, but she had provided him with no information whatever. So overcome with grief was she that all she could do was blubber and squall when he offered to pray with her, and he had to obtain all the funeral arrangements from Everett Hardin's file on Castlereigh, made out by the deceased nine years before when he first came to Agatite.

Again Dr. Streetman turned over the pages in front of him and began to jot down all he knew about the dead man. Castlereigh was forty-eight years old, but no place of birth was indicated on the funeral home's form. It was blank. He had weighed 184 pounds, stood six-two, had brown hair, brown eyes, and was in good health. Under occupation the words "Business Consultant" were listed, but what sort of business? Dr. Streetman didn't really know, and no one he had asked in the past two days knew either. The family's names followed under the "personal information" section, but that didn't help much, and there really wasn't much else besides his address in Agatite, his phone number, and the fact that he had both a savings and a checking account at the First Security Bank.

Normally, in situations like this, Dr. Streetman could extol the virtues of the departed as a Christian, as a family man, as a good husband and father. But he couldn't this time. He knew he would choke on the words. Bill Castlereigh had been inside the First Baptist Church only twice or three times in the past nine years, he had refused to contribute to the building fund, and he had spent almost every Sunday playing golf at the Sandhill County Country Club, drinking heavily, it was reported, after a round, and betting on the Sunday afternoon football games.

As for his Christian virtues as husband and father, Dr. Streetman knew that such tripe wouldn't work either. Although he didn't, as a matter of principle, traffic in gossip, in his capacity as minister of the largest denomination in Agatite he had been obliged to council a number of women of his congregation who had been ''loved and left'' by the handsome Bill Castlereigh. Almost from the first year of Castlereigh's residence in Agatite, women had come to Dr. Streetman for council about what to do about their infidelity to their own husbands with the now deceased business consultant. Some were even carrying a child fathered by Castlereigh and wanted to know the moral consequences of abortion or putting up a child for adoption.

It wasn't as if there had been a steady stream of such forlorn souls; in that case Dr. Streetman would have had to take the decidedly unpleasant action of calling Castlereigh in and speaking to him of his extramarital affairs. Certainly not all women had named Castlereigh as the source of their distress, but enough had, either through hints or direct mention, for Dr. Streetman to detect a recognizable pattern. By the time they came to Streetman, however, they were no longer involved with the man. The love affair, if one could call it that, was over, although Dr. Streetman often wondered if it amounted to much more than a one-night stand in many cases.

Few of the women involved were beautiful or striking in any way. They were often dowdy and average-looking, and they ranged in ages from young girls to old maids nearing fifty. And they all blamed themselves, not Castlereigh, confessing, to the preacher's shock and dismay, that they ''should have known'' about Castlereigh from his reputation as a lady's man and should have had better sense.

What Dr. Streetman could never have known and was too timid to find out by inquiring of his fellow clergymen in Agatite was that he was not the only pastor who had been beseiged by women in emotional or physical trouble as a result of a liaison with Castlereigh. Indeed, there had been a steady stream of female complaint, more of which had ended in the divorce courts than Dr. Streetman thought, concerning the curly-haired business consultant who had blown into town nine years before and had systematically begun to try to sleep with every woman he met. Nor was Dr. Streetman the only person ignorant of Castlereigh's background. No one in the community really knew who he was or where he came from or what he did for a living. They only knew that he had a reputation as a "cocksman," as they termed it at the Goodyear Tire Store's back room, seemed to be very successful in whatever business he practiced, and was well liked by almost everyone.

William Castlereigh had come to Agatite with his family and a blank-sided moving van nine years before on a cold February day. They had bought a large house on Grove Street, not far from the Church of Christ, and, as the rumor mongers of the city were to proclaim very quickly, paid *cash* for it. They drove large, expensive cars, dressed well, and bought whatever they needed for the house—appliances, furnishings, dishes, and so forth—with cold cash, the remainder of which they deposited in the First Security Bank in exchange for an electric blanket and a set of stainless steel flatware.

Bill Castlereigh joined the country club right away, where he soon became a familiar figure on the sunbaked golf course, around the clubhouse, and at the bar, the only place in Sandhill County where a legal drink was sold. He was a member of the Chamber of Commerce and the Lion's Club, and he spent his time away from these activities around town by slapping backs and shaking hands with everyone he met, when he wasn't in his small, side-street office that stated on its glass door simply and enigmatically, "William Castlereigh: Professional Consultant."

Who or what he consulted was a mystery, but whatever it was, it seemed to serve the dual purpose of making him available for golf seven days a week and providing him and his family with a comfortable living. It wasn't long before the town gossips knew that certain women were visiting his office for consultations that were neither professional nor necessarily moral, but nothing could be proved, only that some of these same women took long vacations, sooner or later sought divorces, or found themselves depressed and unhappy for inexplicable reasons.

These rumors were more whispered than spoken, however. And Castlereigh managed to avoid irate husbands, if there were any; charges of illicit conduct, or any other public smear of his name. It wasn't so much that the people of Agatite didn't know what he was doing as much as it was that they didn't want to admit it. Besides, as Jingles Murphy was fond of saying whenever the subject came up, "It takes two to screw," and it was no skin off his ass if some of the "fee-males" of Agatite wanted to get poled by a professional consultant, just so long as nobody got hurt, or it wasn't *his* wife who was involved. But in the end somebody did get hurt because of Castlereigh's philanderous activities, and that somebody was Bill Castlereigh.

Wilma Castlereigh, while her husband "consulted" with the women of the town, developed a large but far more secret reputation of her own. Her husband spent little time at home, and her two teenage daughters were usually out on dates or at football or basketball games until very late. They were the first two girls at Agatite High to date without parental curfew, a fact that scandalized their friends' parents as much as it caused family arguments about "what the Castlereigh girls do" all over town. But, as a result of giving her daughters the freedom they wanted, Wilma found herself alone much of the time.

She found her pleasure in the college boys who returned to Agatite for weekends or holidays, and it was known among the youthful visitors from the region's colleges and universities that "serious amusement" could be found by knocking on Wilma's back door any time Bill Castlereigh's big Lincoln was not in the driveway.

There was a strong feeling in the community that the Castlereigh marriage wasn't real. They almost never appeared anywhere outside the house as a couple. They even shopped separately. She stayed home and screwed college boys, and he went to his office and screwed housewives. The girls were probably just as promiscuous, although both had steady boyfriends and attended church regularly, but neither seemed to rely on their parents for much of anything. The lack of information that perplexed Dr. Streetman also perplexed school officials, who found that aside from barely legible copies of transcripts, the girls had no official records at all. Most of the information required of transferring students, such as health records, birth certificates, and baptismal forms, appeared as poorly made copies of affadavits sworn out and signed by unreadable signatures but soundly confirmed by Castlereigh and his wife.

It was almost as if the whole Castlereigh family had been created nine years before and suddenly dropped on Agatite from a clear sky, full-blown and developed as a nuclear family. Questions about their past always received immediate, cheerful, and believable responses, but when notes were compared later, the questioners learned that the answers they had were contradictory in many details.

There was no way of verifying the information without confronting Bill or Wilma and calling them liars, and the girls didn't seem to invite questions about their lives before they moved to Agatite, referring to where they came from as "back home," and former occupations and places as something or somewhere we "did" or "were" once.

A small town respects individual privacy, on the face of things, anyway, and even though rumors floated around from time to time, suggesting that Castlereigh was really an extortionist who got away with a bundle of cash from a big East Coast business, a hit-man-turned-state's evidence-informant in exchange for a new identity, or a Russian spy who had defected and was now being kept in secret by the State Department, no one ever approached them directly about any discrepancies in their stories or questions about their backgrounds. The main reason was that they were both so very well liked.

Even Bill's death didn't change things, and like Dr. Streetman, many in the town were desperately trying to recall something significant to say about the man, even though the circumstances of his death seemed to confirm the rumors that had floated around for years.

Another thing Dr. Streetman did not know about Bill Castlereigh was the total particulars concerning his death, and if he had known, he would have needed something stronger than Pall Malls to shore himself up for a eulogy. Wherever Bill Castlereigh had come from, or whoever sent the cashier's check for $5,000 each month to the First Security Bank for deposit to his account, or whatever he did behind the glass door of his office, one fact of Bill Castlereigh's life was undeniably proved in his death—he was a sex maniac.

His and Wilma's sexual relationship was both frequent and full, but it wasn't enough for Bill. When she realized how voracious her husband's appetite for sexual adventure was, Wilma struck back, first by taking various men in town into her bedroom, but then finding the youthful bodies of college boys more to her taste. She had flaunted her flings in front of Bill, but he had laughed at her, knowing that his desire for sex was unrelenting, and trying to understand her attempts to make him jealous. She had continued her college boy affairs more out of habit than desire for them, but she took no real pleasure in her couplings. She merely used them to pay Bill back for all he did at his office on the side street downtown, in tawdry motels in nearby communities, or even in the backseat of his big Lincoln.

None of the women Bill bedded meant anything to him at all. Once he made a conquest, he usually cast his partner aside, returning to her only occasionally and after a long wait. There were sometimes ugly scenes of recrimination, especially when the woman turned up pregnant, owing—in his mind—to her own carelessness. He wasn't insensitive, however, and by picking up his office phone and making a few mysterious calls long distance, he could arrange a discreet abortion or, in the case of some of the single women, a home for unwed mothers. He paid for everything, but he never discussed divorcing Wilma or marriage with his often tearful lovers. He patiently and incredibly tried to explain to them that, in the final analysis, he loved his wife.

When he drank, Bill's sexual desire often overcame him, and he had been known to go beyond the bounds of discretion. But he usually didn't drink that much in public, except on Sunday afternoons at the country club. It was on such an afternoon that his weakness for women finally brought him and his sexual adventures to an end.

It was a particularly hot August afternoon, and as was his usual habit, Castlereigh had finished a round of golf with Dr. Jeff Randall and two other regulars of Sunday morning golf. They sat on stools at the country club's bar, the "Nineteenth Hole," sipping their third round of cocktails and speculating about the body of the girl found hanging in the outhouse behind the Hoolian Barbershop the previous Wednesday. Behind the bar, through a plate-glass window, the club's lifeguard, Vicki Jefferies, was preparing the pool for its one o'clock opening time.

All summer on Sunday afternoons Bill had been on the same stool, sipping cocktails and watching the bikini-clad and deeply tanned girl sweep the bottom of the pool, adjust the ropes, and test the water's chlorine level. Her long red hair spilled down her tawny back, and her breasts strained against the bathing suit's halter. His eyes greedily moved up and down her body that was glowing from perspiration due to her work efforts, and he focused and concentrated on the rise of the pubic area, imagining what it would be like to slip those briefs off and view her nakedness, to touch her soft, beautiful body, and finally to devour her, literally, running his mouth and tongue all over her before fucking her unconscious.

Sitting there, thinking about her, made him shiver, and the erection that automatically came with such thoughts was poorly concealed by his double-knit golf pants. More than once that summer after watching her for hours as she sat sexily and pertly atop the lifeguard's tower over the pool, the plastic whistle nestled in the perfect cleavage of her breasts, he had driven in a frenzy to his office, summoned whatever woman he had been cultivating through his friendly and affable manners, and plunged

142 *Clay Reynolds*

violently into her almost before she could get undressed in the stuffy confines of his office.

This particular afternoon, however, Bill Castlereigh faced a problem. There was no woman to call, no one to serve as a physical substitute for Vicki Jefferies. He ordered another double scotch and water and enjoyed the chafing of his hard penis against the material of his trousers.

Vicki Jefferies was indeed a beautiful woman. Home for the summer, she was preparing for her senior year at the University of Texas in Austin, which, she hoped, would include some honors on the varsity swim team. She was in excellent condition, and she had been honored the previous spring by being named Blue Bonnet Belle, a distinction reserved for the most shapely beauties on the giant campus in Austin. She had a regular boyfriend from Houston who was working offshore this summer, and they had agreed that the "safest" place for a woman of her beauty was a secluded country club lifeguard's job near her hometown. There she could practice her swimming, live with her folks for the last time before marriage the following summer, and avoid the temptation to date eligible men who might compete for the future engineer's place in her life. The last person on her mind that morning was William Castlereigh.

Bill drained his double scotch and ordered another, and Jeff Randall took time out from his vivid description of Doc Pritchard's autopsy of the corpse found in the old crapper to comment that Bill seemed to be drinking for two that day. But Bill didn't respond to the remark. His eyes were now fixed on the shapely behind of Vicki Jefferies, and his thoughts were just as fixed on what it would be like without the lime-green bikini bottom covering it. He continued to sip his drink for a few minutes, finishing the reorder and demanding another loudly. When it came, he gulped it suddenly, then rose from his stool and awkwardly moved toward the sliding glass door that led from the bar out to the pool.

Jeff Randall noticed that Bill was walking funny, stiffly. But Jeff assumed Bill needed to go to the men's room, and he called out, "Hey, Castlereigh, you're goin' the wrong way. Pool's already full!"

Bill turned and looked at his golfing partners at the bar, and they all noticed the craziness in his eyes, the bulge in his pants, and the almost mad tone in his voice when he said softly, "That's what you think."

They turned back to their drinks and did not see him move through the door, removing his shirt and unbuttoning his pants. He crossed to the end of the pool by the diving board where Vicki was having trouble with the pool vacuum hose. She had not seen him. They didn't notice him talking to her, or hear what she said as he moved to grab her and she escaped his reach and plunged into the pool. But they did turn around when they heard the splash he made as he followed her into the water.

His pants unzipped and open at the waist made swimming awkward, but his size was sufficient to put him in arm's reach of the girl. She was flailing about and trying to kick away from this madman who had come out of the bar, unzipped his pants, revealed the largest erect penis she had ever imagined possible, and announced, "I want you. Now! In the equipment room. Quick!"

She knew who he was, of course, and she was dimly aware of his reputation. One of her old classmates—among others, she was sure—had related tearfully the details of an afternoon session in his office the previous summer. But Vicki wanted no part of it, and her panic at being so suddenly and openly approached had confused her. "Get away from me!" was all she could manage to say before leaping into the pool's deep end.

Now wrestling and trying to tread water at the same time, the man and woman were awkwardly struggling in the pool. The trio at the bar had stopped their chatter and joined one or two others in peering out through the glass, not wanting to believe what they were certain they saw, yet feeling the vague need to do something about it.

Suddenly Vicki eluded Bill's grasp, losing her suit's bra in the process, and she tried to lift herself up on the side of the pool, revealing her naked breasts to the men in the Nineteenth Hole. "Help me!" she tried to scream, but her lungs, having gotten used to fighting for breath, refused to support her voice, and before she could concentrate enough to repeat her plea, Bill grabbed her by the waist and pulled her back in.

Jeff and several others scrambled for the sliding door, finally spilling out onto the pool's side just in time to see Vicki kick Bill violently in the stomach and wrench her torso out of his hands. He grabbed again, finding purchase on her bikini bottom, and she began twisting and turning in the water, finally kicking free of the suit and propelling herself to the pool's opposite side, where she lunged up out of the water onto the tiled edge.

Bill began splashing after her, the bikini pants still in his hand, but by now his trousers were completely down around his ankles, and his shoes had filled with water. He was desperately trying to swim toward her figure, which stood in naked shock on the pool's edge. The whistle dangled from her neck and her eyes were wide with fear. Suddenly he stiffened, grabbed his chest, and sank to the bottom.

For a horrible moment there was silence around the pool. After the violent splashing and cries of the struggle, the water was remarkably quiet, and the figure of Bill Castlereigh, now bobbing on the bottom, the bikini bottom still clutched in his hand, seemed mesmerizing and almost peaceful. Vicki, completely naked and shaking with rage and terror, lifted her eyes from the pool to see the gaggle of men on the opposite side. Some were standing, staring dumbly at Bill's form; others had raised their gaze, however, and were now just as silently glaring at her. She didn't know what to do.

"Damn it!" Jeff Randall finally found his tongue and began kicking his shoes off. "Somebody do something before he drowns." His voice seemed to bring Vicki to action, and without hesitation, she dove into the pool and brought Bill to the surface, where the men helped her haul his dripping body onto the tiles along the edge. Then, as Randall raced to the dressing room for his doctor's bag, she performed mouth-to-mouth resuscitation on Bill's lifeless body, her large breasts brushing against his naked chest as she met his lips and tried to force air into his water-filled lungs.

Vicki's efforts, however, like Randall's when he returned with an injection of adrenalin for Bill's heart, were useless. William Castlereigh had died of drowning caused by heart attack, in an attempted rape of a twenty-year-old lifeguard of the Sandhill County Country Club.

Of course, the official version did not go like that. Officially, he died while swimming to cool off after a golf game. The combination of exercise in 100-degree heat along with the icy-cold water of the club's pool had simply caused his heart to burst, and he drowned before Vicki or anyone else could get to him. Everyone there was willing to go along with this version of events rather than risk a closing of the club by the county's do-gooders, who regarded it as a den of iniquity anyhow. The time of death was even fixed at one-fifteen to indicate that the pool had been legitimately open.

Of course, Vicki had to resign her position. The club couldn't keep a lifeguard who let a patron drown, and when Able Newsome drove out to investigate the death, he found her unwilling to talk about the whole thing, preferring to go home right away, where she packed her bags and drove all night to meet her boyfriend in Houston. Able wasn't that big a fool, and he was certain that her attitude hid something sinister. He also noticed that she was in street clothes, not a swim suit, when he arrived, and that she didn't even want the lime-green bikini when one of the club managers brought it, dripping and wadded up, out to where the sheriff was interviewing her. But he had nothing to go on, and he only wondered if he would ever know the whole story.

Dr. Streetman didn't have a suspicion that the facts surrounding Bill Castlereigh's death were bogus. But what he did know was that at two-thirty that afternoon the church would be filled with mourners. He knew that Bill Castlereigh, in spite of the rumors and mysteries, had been one of the most popular men in the city, well liked by both men and women, and that it was about as close to a "state funeral" as this small town would ever see. He had already been warned that the floral orders were going to set a record, and he knew his eulogy had to be first-class.

But what to say?

The Reverend Dr. Randolph P. Streetman lit another Pall Mall and continued to rub the stubble on his chin. The information he had was worse than useless. It was ludicrous. Finally, with a sense of resignation, he reached for his Bible and turned to the book of *Solomon*, hoping to find there both wisdom and a text for his upcoming sermon.

IV. Breedlove
1983

"The main thing to remember," Joe Don McBride said as he rolled down the window of the Coupe de Ville, "is that nobody gets hurt, especially shot. I mean, they give you twenty to life for that. But armed robbery, shit. That's a cakewalk. Maybe out in five on good behavior, maybe two if you get a good lawyer."

The Caddy shot across the vast no-man's land between El Paso and San Antonio, a place so desolate that when the Spanish Conquistadores crossed it in search of El Dorado, they drove stakes in the ground to mark their way back. On this summer night, however, there were no Spanish stakes to guide anyone back home, only the green mileage markers of IH-10 as it snaked lazily across the naked plains. Breedlove sat sleepily on the passenger side of the big automobile, stealing sips from a bottle of Blackjack Old #7, which was comfortably secure in a cooler between him and the driver, Joe Don, who joined his companion in chasing the whiskey with a steadily diminishing supply of Coors beer. The two men held no illusions about cities of gold or about much of anything else. They had both lived too much to dream of easy money.

Joe Don drove the Caddy with one finger. The cruise control was on, and he crossed his legs under the uptilted

wheel, leaning forward to change the tape from John
Denver to Herb Alpert. "Never could stand that queer,"
he growled as he slipped the Denver tape out into the slip
stream and swiveled around to take another sip from the
bottle.

"Is he queer?" Breedlove asked casually, opening another Coors and flipping the pop top out his own window.

"Everybody from Colorado is queer," Joe Don said
with certainty.

Breedlove didn't like the comment. He had always
liked Colorado, and the two or three times he had drifted
up there, he had liked the people he met. Even if he'd
gotten a case of clap from a hippie chick up there years
ago, he still thought well of the place. She was from
someplace else, too, he remembered.

He was getting nervous about Joe Don's foul mood.
The more he drank, the uglier he got, and the uglier he
got, the faster he pushed the Caddy. He had the cruise
control set on ninety now, and he was toying with the
button again, obviously contemplating higher speeds. But
other than the anger, there was no sign the sour mash
was having any effect on him at all. He just drove too
damned fast.

They had met the day before, really the night before
the day before, and Breedlove was amazed that they had
fallen in together. He hadn't been much for traveling
companions over the years. Sometimes he would get
along with a girl for a while, but he never had traveled
with a man. Men tended to get him into too much trouble, and they usually got around to asking too many
questions about where he had been or what he was running from. Women just kept their mouths shut when they
were told to. But you didn't tell a man, especially one
like Joe Don, who had a hair-trigger temper, to shut the
fuck up.

Breedlove had been hitching back to Texas from California. Going out there had been one freaky mistake in
itself. He had just gone, using all his cash to buy a bus
ticket out and to eat well for once in his life. He got to

L.A. and felt so damned lonely all of a sudden he couldn't stand it. He went out to Malibu, using his last twenty for cab fare and a hot dog, and finally found the beach.

Eating the cold hot dog and walking up and down on the sand, looking at girls and old men and the Pacific, he recognized that it was prettier than the Gulf of Mexico, that the girls were better-looking than those the trashy beaches of Texas attracted, and that, on the whole, California was a goddamn nice place to be. But the girls, prettier or no, were shitty. He had no luck picking up anybody, and the final couple of hours before sunset, when he rolled up his pants and waded out into the surf to try to make some conversation with a couple of likely-looking females who turned out to be about fourteen, somebody stole his duffle bag with his extra clothes and stuff. At least they left his boots, he had glumly thought as he tried to wipe the sand off his feet.

He had hitched all the way to the highway, then to Flagstaff with a trucker, and down to Phoenix with a guy in a van. The last ride had handed him a twenty when he let him out in front of the Nite Life Lounge on Phoenix's city limits. "Hey, man!" Breedlove had said, shaking his head and trying to avoid the twenty-dollar bill being thrust toward him. "No. That's okay."

"It's cool," the driver said, continuing to hand him the bill until Breedlove finally accepted it. "I've been down before. I'd take you home an' give you a meal and a place to crash, but my ol' lady don't understand."

Breedlove waved his thanks as the van pulled off to drive back into Phoenix. Then he went into the dark, smoky bar, hoisted himself up onto a barstool, and ordered a beer. At the bar a dark figure slumped over and drooled on a napkin.

"Hey, Texas!" the woman at the bar suddenly yelled at the figure. "Either order up or get the hell out. You're taking up space." The dark figure looked up and sneered at her, and she scowled back.

Breedlove suddenly felt generous. He'd been in that position before—broke in a bar with no place else to be

and no place to go—and he heard himself ask the shad-
owed man, "You really from Texas?"

"Yeah." The dark man turned slowly toward Breedlove's voice, and even in the dim light of the Schlitz beer
sign and clock, Breedlove could see he was about done
in, wasted. "Wanna make somethin' of it, fuckface?" A
long scar cut down from the man's eye toward his jaw,
making a deep ridge that flamed in the beer sign's light.

"I don't wan' no trouble in here," the woman said, suddenly moving down the bar away from them. "Willy?" Willy
was about the biggest man Breedlove had ever seen. Half-
Indian, half-Mexican, Breedlove guessed as he noted the long
greasy hair braided down Willy's back. He wore his shirt
split open down the front, revealing a hairless, powerful chest
covered with a tattoo of a fish holding a lightning bolt in one
fin. He rose from the stool where he had been sitting and
flexed his arm muscles as he brought two enormous fists
together in front of him.

"Bring me another beer," Breedlove said quickly to
the woman, "and whatever he's having for him." He
gestured to the scarred man.

"Blackjack," the dark man said, not taking his eyes
off Breedlove.

Breedlove felt himself become increasingly uncomfortable under the man's stare, but finally the woman
brought the drinks down, and he turned away from the
man and contemplated the whiskey glass. Willy returned
to his stool.

"Look, honey," the woman said to Breedlove as she
lifted his glass and mopped the formica top underneath,
"don' let ol' Texas sponge off you too long. I don' care
myself how long he sits here, but Mavis—that's the
owner—she'll give me hell if she comes in here an' he
ain' got a drink in front of him. She'll sic Willy on him
sure 'nough."

Breedlove nodded, glad to concentrate on something
besides the dark man she called Texas.

"Go find a pimple to pop, you old whore," Texas said
in a growling voice. She started to argue but moved away

instead. Breedlove sipped his beer, watching the dark man watch him from the corner of his eye. He'd been in situations like this too many times, he told himself. This was goddamn dangerous. When the hell was he going to learn to mind his own business and keep his mouth shut? The wrong question or comment could set this guy off but good, and Willy didn't look like the type to care who started a ruckus. He was just going to finish it.

"So what's it to you?" the dark man said, downing his drink with a quick gulp but keeping one eye on Breedlove all the time.

For a moment Breedlove didn't know what to say, then he realized he hadn't answered the question he had been asked, if such a question demanded an answer. "Oh, nothing," he said. "It's just that I'm from there, too. Texas, I mean."

"So're lots of people," the dark man responded, gesturing to the woman for a refill and raising his eyebrows toward Breedlove for the okay. Breedlove nodded. "About half the dumb fucks I've ever met are from Texas one way or another," he concluded as the woman approached with the bottle.

Breedlove sighed to himself. There was no pleasing a man like this. He'd let him have one more drink, then get out. At this rate the twenty wouldn't last long enough for a package of Fritos, let alone a meal of any kind.

"You're from Agatite," the dark man said suddenly, "ain't you?"

Breedlove was so startled he almost fell off his barstool. He'd always run into people who knew of Agatite, small and insignificant as it was, but this was the first time since he'd left years before that anybody'd ever guessed he was from there. He was sweating and nervous.

"You're—don't tell me." The man rubbed his scarred cheek. "Brownlow—uh, no . . . Breedlove?" He smiled in a sinister way. "Right?"

Breedlove nodded in amazement, trying to find a name to put with the face he saw before him and fighting the temptation to run out the door of the bar.

"Well, I'll be goddamned," the man said, and he jumped down from the bar in Breedlove's path and thrust a hand out toward him. "You don't remember me, do you?"

Breedlove gasped out a denial of the charge, even though it was true, and he shook hands with the mystery man. Before he could say anything more, the woman was back at their end of the bar to make sure this wasn't more trouble.

"Fanny," the dark man said as he pumped Breedlove's hand, "I want you to meet an ol' acquaintance of mine." She stared at him, more amazed by his change in attitude toward her than by the information he was offering. "Best goddamn quarterback the Eagles ever had. Probably the best all-round pussy-getter, too? Right?"

"Uh . . . yeah," Breedlove said, quietly trying to sort this out in his mind. He was too confused to be embarrassed. Was he being made fun of?

"Joe Don," the man said. "Joe Don McBride. Uh, no, Franklin, you knew me as Joe Don Franklin. Kirkland Cowboys. Class of '66. I played defense against you two seasons. You almost broke my goddamn collarbone my junior year runnin' over me for an eighty-yard t.d. Goddamn!—Who'd a-thought? Where the hell you been? What're you doin' in this hole in the ground?"

Suddenly, like a door opening in his memory, Breedlove recalled the short man standing in front of him. Joe Don Franklin, number 11 for the Kirkland Cowboys. He was All-State defense three years running, in spite of his size. He hustled, and he hustled hard. He stopped more runs than players twice his size. He was like a bulldog—grabbed hold and didn't let go until the ball carrier fell with him. "Tough as nails," Breedlove heard Coach warn him before the yearly game with Kirkland that opened every season each fall. He remembered running over him, and he felt guilty, since Joe Don had been caught looking the other way in a fake. Breedlove could have gone around him, or even simply knocked him aside, but he went over him to prove to the tough little man from Kirk-

land that "Big Bad Breed," the Eagles' star quarterback
and captain of the team, had what it took.

"Uh . . . California. L.A. I'm on my way back to
Texas," Breedlove stammered out.

"No, you dumb shit." Joe Don remounted his barstool
and picked up his glass. "I mean *all* this time. Shit, it's
been damned near fifteen years, damn near, more even.
Where you been? Last time I saw you—"

"Uh, here an' there," Breedlove cut in. He didn't want
to explain his history to this scarred man with slurred
speech.

"Lessee," Joe Don continued as if Breedlove hadn't
spoken. "You were a year behind me, right?" He wrinkled his brow and rubbed his scar. "An' you made varsity your freshman year. Last year we could do that in
our division? Right? So we played against each other
three—no, two years. You didn't play my senior year. It
must be my junior year you ran over me like a goddamn
train."

"Uh . . . yeah, I guess so." Breedlove was amazed at
the glow in the man's eyes. His scar seemed translucent
in the red lights.

"I remember now. You knocked up some girl and took
off. What was her name?" Breedlove let the question
pass without comment. "Man, that took some guts. Left
her full up as Boulder Dam and took off, football hero
and all." He grinned broadly. "Shitfire!" He lifted his
glass in a mock toast and ran his tongue around its empty
bottom.

Breedlove began to squirm. This was exactly the conversation he wanted to avoid. He'd been able to put her
out of his mind for years now. There were no more
dreams, no more worries. It was all coming back, here,
in a dirty bar in Phoenix, and he didn't like it. He didn't
like it at all. He also felt his stomach rumbling. The beer
seemed to harden inside him. He hadn't had a meal in
two days, just junk.

"You go to 'Nam?" Joe Don asked him, shooting him
a look across his empty glass and setting it easily down
on the counter.

"Uh . . . no," Breedlove responded. It was always a hard question to answer.

"How the hell you get out of it?" Joe Don's mouth hung open. "You didn't go to college."

"Well . . ." Breedlove drained his beer glass. This was the hard part. It sounded too good to be true. "After I left, uh . . . I just kept movin' around. I kept going from job to job, and I guess they never figured out where to send my draft notice to. I never even registered. Nobody told me to when I turned eighteen, and nobody ever asked me about it after that. I was in Mexico for a while, but nobody ever said anything to me about it."

"Fuck me to tears," Joe Don said suddenly and laughed a high, piercing laugh, a laugh tinged with madness, Breedlove thought. Apparently Willy thought so, too, for he looked hard in their direction. "Why didn't I think of that?" Joe Don wiped tears from his eyes, and the scar glowed again. "Why didn't we all?"

They ordered another round and talked for a while, but while Joe Don downed his drink right away, Breedlove sipped his and mentally tallied the bill. After about a half hour of small talk, they turned to Joe Don's past, and Breedlove felt relieved. He loathed talking about his aimless life of the past decade and a half. In a way, it was embarrassing. In a way, it was painful. But, he believed, it seemed mostly boring. It bored his ass off to think about it, and he could see no reason why anybody would be interested in it more than he was. Joe Don, on the other hand, found his own background fascinating, and he kept Breedlove entertained with colorful escapades and adventures, about half of which, Breedlove guessed, were manufactured, and about half of which, he also figured, were exaggerated out of proportion to the abilities of the short man he saw sitting before him. It seemed that Joe Don Franklin, or McBride, had spent the years of his youth doing even less than Breedlove had.

They hadn't really known each other in high school, except in the way rival teams know each other's star players. Breedlove vaguely recalled meeting Joe Don in mid-

field and tossing a coin for the kickoff, but that hadn't
been the man sitting on the stool in a dirty bar in Phoenix. It had been a kid, shorter and more muscular than
he, who had grinned and offered his hand in sportsman-
ship years ago. The scarred, bitter, and vulgar man who
talked through the whiskey on this summer night was no
relation to that boy, Breedlove realized. But then, he had
no relation to the boy who had taken the hand and grinned
back either.

The scar that ran down Joe Don's face, he told Breedlove, was the result of one hell of a firefight.

"I got this," Joe Don said, gesturing to his cheek,
"for bein' a 'hero.' " He grinned sardonically and ran
his finger the length of the scar. " 'Nam. I carried three
ol' boys one at a time across a rice paddy while gook
mortars was blastin' hell out of us."

Breedlove looked away. He was embarrassed for the
little man who continued to tell his war story, elaborating
the details and emphasizing his own heroism, not only
in that battle but in others, digressing from time to time
to color his account with tales of Saigon prostitutes and
to compare them to the girls he had had in Japan, Hawaii,
and back home. Joe Don's voice continued, undaunted
by his companion's inattention.

". . . when I was in Huntsville." Joe Don finished a
sentence and Breedlove realized that the old football
player had moved back to Texas and was now recounting
a life that had led to armed robbery and prison. Breedlove tried to focus his attention on what Joe Don was
saying, but the stories tended to run together, and they
all had the same theme: how much Joe Don had done,
how many women he had slept with, how many men he
had hurt in fights, and how many times he had been
"royally screwed," even though he didn't deserve it.

He laughed his high, crazy laugh. "Shit, man, I'm on
parole." He dropped his voice low on the last word. "I
ain't supposed to leave Austin let alone Texas!"

They were on their fifth round by this time, and Breedlove had started to develop a strong sense of kinship with
this scarred old adversary from years before, even though

he still had trouble seeing him in his helmet and pads. He was growing so tired of being alone, of thinking he was the only one who had trouble in his life, that it was refreshing in a way to find that someone else had been through some of the same kind of troubles. His own life hadn't been much better than Joe Don's, he recognized, and while he had avoided prison and Vietnam, he had left towns in a hurry before, more often than not with either a bruise or black eye to show for his trouble. Also, he realized, he admired Joe Don's ability to turn his life into something more than a boring story of dingy motel rooms, hookers, and ball-busting work. The bullshit might be running deep in here, Breedlove thought, but at least it's good bullshit.

"Why'd you change your name?" Breedlove asked, recalling the original confusion.

"It was changed for me," Joe Don said. "I was adopted, or I was supposed to be. I'm really from Louisiana, an orphanage down around New Orleans, place called Gretna. I never knew my folks, never knew nothin' about them. But this family from Kirkland name of St. John took me in. I'd lived for two years with a family name of Franklin for a while, an' they told me my name was Franklin. I just thought it was, so the St. Johns called me Franklin, too, for a last name, you see? So they was goin' to adopt me, but the name was all confused, an' by the time they straightened it out, I'd graduated, an' it didn't really matter. See?" He looked sadly around, then continued, "I was goin' to go to college, but I couldn't get a scholarship because I was too light. Shitheads only wanted defensive players that weighed more 'n one-eighty, so I joined the Army. They didn't care how much I weighed. Made my foster dad, ol' St. John, mad as hell. But he couldn't find me, on account of I had found out through an Army lawyer that my real name was McBride, an' I changed it back."

Breedlove knew his money was running out, and he figured he had about enough with the change in his jeans for a hamburger if he could find a cheap place. He stood up as if to leave, but Joe Don continued talking.

"You know what was funny? We—the St. Johns, that is—lived right smack dab on the county line. We paid taxes in both counties for the farm, what taxes my old man could pay, that is. Could've gone to Agatite High! Wouldn't that have been somethin'?" He laughed. "Wouldn't that have been somethin'? We'd have played with each other instead of against each other. Some of my brothers and sisters did go to Agatite instead of Kirkland. You know any of 'em?" He reached out and grabbed Breedlove's arm. "Hey, where you goin'?"

"I don't know," Breedlove said truthfully. "I ain't got but about three bucks left, an' I'm hungry as hell."

"You just wait right here, ol' buddy from Agatite, Texas," Joe Don said, suddenly bounding off the bar-stool, all his previous haggard look now gone in the glow of the whiskey. "Gimme those three smackers an' wait about an hour."

Breedlove hesitated, but then he figured, what the hell? He'd gambled on poorer odds before, and he shoved the three wrinkled bills over to him. He figured he might have enough silver for one more beer, and he prayed his rumbling stomach would tolerate an hour's wait before it received something more than suds.

More than two hours passed, and Fanny and Willy were giving him long, hard looks before Joe Don burst back into the bar. "C'mon," he said, pulling Breedlove away from the single glass of flat, warm beer he had been care-fully nursing. "I ain't got all night." Breedlove got up and followed him out to the graveled parking lot, where Joe Don gestured toward a new black Trans Am T-Top parked just outside the door. "Get in," he said. "Ain't this somethin'?" He was grinning expansively. "Just like Burt fuckin' Reynolds."

The car was stolen. That much Breedlove was sure of, but before he could think of any way to get out of riding in a car he had knowingly helped steal by giving the thief stake money, Joe Don walked over to the bar's door and flung it wide open.

"Hey!" he yelled into the dark interior. "You cock-sucking greaser!" He stood up as tall as his short frame would allow him. "How'd you like to kiss my rosy-red ass?" He slammed the door hard enough to crack the painted over glass in the center that advised minors to stay out of the establishment, and Breedlove sucked his breath in hard and jumped into the Trans Am without opening the door. He scraped his knee badly, and he visualized the pounding Joe Don and he would probably be receiving from Willy's giant fists.

Joe Don stepped neatly to one side of the door, and in a few seconds it burst open and Willy fairly jumped out onto the threshold, legs spread apart, fists clenched. His mouth hung open, and drool dripped from his teeth. Joe Don took a half-jump and placed the toe of his heavy work boot squarely in Willy's crotch. The kick was delivered as if the short man were punting a football, and his left leg jumped off the ground with the force of the delivery.

Willy drew into himself with pain, and Breedlove heard a rush of air as the giant inhaled and prepared to scream. But Joe Don didn't give him a chance. As Willy's head lowered into his chest, Joe Don kicked him again, this time catching him across the bridge of the nose with the boot's steel toe. Breedlove heard the wet splotch as Willy's nose broke, and as Willy's head snapped up, pulling the bulk of his body with it, Breedlove saw blood already spilling out of the nostrils and mouth. He was hurt bad, Breedlove thought, hurt real bad.

Continuing his backward momentum into the bar, Willy crashed onto the inside floor, and Joe Don slammed the door, catching the big man's shins and causing them to draw up. Then Joe Don scampered around the Trans Am, expertly vaulted into the driver's seat, and started the engine, jerking the shifter into reverse. "Fuckin' Mescan," he said as he sprayed gravel all over the front of the Nite Life Lounge. "Should've killed the son of a bitch." He jammed the stick shift into first gear and laid down a strip of rubber as the powerful automobile peeled out onto the blacktop highway. Then he laughed the high, mad laugh Breedlove had already come to hate.

"Shit!" Breedlove let out a long, slow breath, realizing that he hadn't dared breathe since he saw Willy standing in the bar's doorway.

"Hell," Joe Don said, shifting gears and winding the car out to sixty before easing the shifter into fourth, "that ain't nothin'. Once I saw a guy my size take on a man twice as big as ol' Willy. It ain't the size, it's the surprise!" he concluded in a mock black dialect.

Breedlove realized he was sweating in spite of the cool evening breeze that came through the open car. "It just comes down to who's the toughest son of a bitch," Joe Don said, grinning, his scar glowing green in the dashboard lights, and Breedlove forced a grin of his own as well. His stomach turned over, and he thought he must be hungrier than he'd ever been before.

They ditched the Trans Am in Deming, New Mexico, and picked up a Buick Regal, which took them only as far as El Paso, where they found the Cadillac. Joe Don's technique for stealing cars was almost foolproof, but it took guts. Lots of guts.

Back in the desert near Phoenix, Joe Don had explained how it worked. He reached into the console of the Trans Am and pulled out a pack of unopened Marlboros. "Nice taste," he said, "my brand," and he punched the car's lighter. They stopped for burgers and beer and a bottle, and Breedlove bought a cooler and ice out of a wad of bills Joe Don produced from his greasy jeans. "This stealin' ain't stealin', really," he announced, belching through cigarette smoke. "It's more like borrowin'. No shit!" He settled back and pushed the speedometer needle up to ninety. The interstate melted beneath them. "It takes time, 'cause you have to know your mark. You see, in every city of any size there's a place where the big studs take their girlfriends—you know, one of those motels where they charge by the hour and clean sheets are extra. You just ask around at some bars, and sooner or later some bartender will let you in on the place, and you go there and wait for the car you want to show up."

"Then you steal it?" Breedlove asked.

"No, dumb shit, you wait." Joe Don broke the seal

on the whiskey and drank deeply. "These dudes don't want anybody to know they're there, so I just wait around until I see a car I want, wait until they're inside—long enough to get started a little—then I bust in and take the keys. Away we go!"

"Just like that?" Breedlove couldn't believe that somebody with the balls to drive a Trans Am and screw his girlfriend on the sly would give in to a short, greasy cowboy without a fight.

"Man, they beg me to take it." Joe Don laughed his high shrill laugh again. "By the time they get their pants back on, call a taxi for Honeybuns, make up a story for wifey, call the cops, and try to figure out what they're going to say they were doin' there in the first place, I'm gone. They don't really want the cops to find me anyway, 'cause I'm liable to tell the little woman how it really was in the ol' Fuckaway Lodge and Mount-her Court. He don't even want them to find the car much, 'cause the insurance pays off an' he gets a new one anyhow, an' everybody's happy. Meantime, we got wheels!"

Breedlove whistled through his teeth. "You don't have to, uh . . . hit him or nothin'?" he asked.

"Shit, no!" Joe Don said, flicking his butt into the airstream above their heads. "My number one rule is nobody gets hurt!" He pulled another cigarette from the pack and shoved it out toward Breedlove, who took it and punched in the lighter. "I just banged on the door real hard like I'm the cops or somethin', and it opened right up. Those dollar-a-bang joints got nothin' in the way of locks anyhow—too many junkies use them to check out in, an' the crazies who hook the wrong way with some whore—anyway, I just bust right in an' there they are, humpin' till hell won't have it. She was a looker, too. Big tits. She starts to scream, and *he* shoves a pillow over her head. Damned near smothers her!" Joe Don laughed again. "He asks me what I want just like I popped into his goddamn office to set up a game of golf. I was just gonna take his keys, but since he was so obligin', I told him to hand over his money, too." He took another pull from the bottle.

Breedlove stared at the vanishing white stripes of the highway and wondered aloud, "And that's it?"

"Well, you gotta get the whole picture," Joe Don said in mock seriousness. "He stands up, still has a hard on, too, right? An' he asks me real polite if he can keep his other keys while he's pullin' his wallet and stuff out of his pants. I tell him, 'Sure, what the hell?' All the time his piece of ass is lying there lookin' for all the world like I'm John Dillinger or somebody, an' I ain't even got no gun or nothin'. Not even a knife. So I take the money an' the keys, an' I push him into a chair an' go over an' run my hand all over her. An' she *moans*. I mean, no scream, just a nice moan, like she really dug it. You know? Man, it was all I could do to keep from runnin' a finger up her, or droppin' trow an' jumpin' on top." He pulled again from the bottle and flicked his cigarette over his head. "You know, I'll bet ol' Mr. Nice-an-Polite would've just stood there an' watched. Probably he'd have jerked off in the bargain." Breedlove felt himself growing tight in his crotch and pulled at his jeans. This was probably bullshit, he thought, but it was a good story. Joe Don could tell a good story!

"So I ask him," Joe Don went on. " 'What if I want her, too?' " He laughed again. "And the bastard just shrugs! Man, you should have seen the look she give him." He pulled another cigarette from the pack and punched the lighter. Breedlove noted that they were making almost a hundred. "I'd like to've had her, too. She had real nice tits, an' she was soft. But that's sloppy seconds, friend, an' it would have violated my basic number-one rule: *nobody gets hurt!*"

Breedlove was confused. Back in the bar he had dismissed half of what Joe Don told him as pure bullshit, and this sounded no less fantastic than the war stories or long tales of sexual prowess being demonstrated all over the Southwest. But here was the Trans Am, he had a roll of bills left in his pocket, and from the way he drove, relaxed, without a care in the world for a cop stopping them for speeding, to say nothing of the amount of liquor he had consumed, he obviously wasn't worried a bit about attracting attention. Either he was telling the truth, Breedlove concluded, or he was crazy.

But in Deming the scam worked right in front of Breedlove's eyes, and again in El Paso. Joe Don offered to let Breedlove try it, but he wasn't that interested. He figured his luck would lead him into a room with a karate expert or something. In fact, Joe Don had a bit of trouble in Deming when the Regal's owner objected to Joe Don's fondling the girl. Breedlove watched the whole scene in a state of disbelief from the open door. The guy was big and fat with a large hairy belly and a proportionately large penis. When the short man reached to touch the girl, the fat man suddenly moved toward him. Joe Don slammed him back against the wall with violent force. The look of terror on the guy's face impressed Breedlove, but before he could wink, Joe Don was outside with the keys to the Buick and a fist full of bills to boot.

"It's all in the technique," Joe Don explained to Breedlove as he fiddled with the Buick's tape deck. "It's like a fuckin' poker game, but you gotta make your move and make it hard. He's naked, so he can't run no bluff at all. You gotta make him think you're hurtin' him even when you're not. An' you gotta convince him you can hurt him a lot worse if he stays in the game. Nine times outta ten they fold. But if they don't, you gotta be able to back your play or you're fucked over."

Joe Don, Breedlove realized, talked tough, and Breedlove knew that in a fight Joe Don would use whatever tactics he thought he needed to win. Joe Don had no illusions about his abilities, and he didn't bluff. He was small, and he compensated for his size by being tough, the same way he had made All State as a defensive player in high school. If it came to it, he would blow somebody's head off before he gave up. He had handled Willy by surprising him. Dirty fighting, maybe, but who ever won a clean fight? Breedlove certainly hadn't, and he had a broken nose and several scars to prove it. Whatever exaggeration Joe Don used to gild his own lily didn't fool Joe Don. He knew damned well what he could and couldn't do, and he just wouldn't play if he couldn't win.

Breedlove vowed never to cross him, because if he did, he might have to kill him to keep him from killing Breedlove. If that happened, Breedlove realized, he'd be in sorrier shape than ever before.

In El Paso they acquired the Caddy. As night swept westward around them, Breedlove began to doze. Joe Don had talked a steady stream since they left El Paso. They had taken turns driving and sleeping, but he was having trouble falling off, not so much because of Joe Don's rambling voice, but because of what lay ahead. Joe Don kept talking about his big deal in San Antonio, the people they would meet there. He was vague about specifics, but Breedlove sensed that what he had in mind was seriously illegal. He figured he could ditch Joe Don when they got there. This was a dangerous son of a bitch, Breedlove said to himself more than once as they continued to move into Texas; that much was clear, and since he himself hadn't ever been arrested for any crime more serious than vagrancy or hitchhiking, had never even spent a night in jail, he wasn't anxious to get involved.

But his conscious mind kept nagging at him as Joe Don droned on about techniques of robbery and assorted felonies, about how famous criminals from the James gang to the Symbionese Liberation Army had fucked up. Breedlove was already an accessory to theft, driving in a stolen car spree that traversed two states. How much deeper was there to go?

For once, he thought grimly, you may have gotten yourself into something you can't just walk away from.

7

I. Breedlove
1984

"If 'nobody gets hurt,' " Mike Dix asked as he crushed out his cigarette in the Holiday Inn ashtray, "then what the fuck do we need guns for?"

Joe Don looked up over his glass of Blackjack and smiled at Breedlove. It was a good question, Breedlove thought, one he himself had wanted to ask Joe Don a hundred times in the past six months, but one he feared to ask because he knew it would sound cowardly. But Mike didn't fear much of anything. He was a greasy, stupid-looking ex-hippie with broken teeth and a scraggly beard, but he had twice Joe Don's weight and usually scared the shit out of Breedlove.

"Sometimes, Dix," Joe Don said slowly, his scar flashing as it frequently did when he got mad or excited, "you're a first-class ignoramus, you know that?"

"Look." Mike rose up to his full six-three and flexed his muscles under a faded Rolling Stones T-shirt. "For the past six months you've been yammering about how nobody's gonna get hurt, an' now you're talkin' about a fuckin' arsenal." He grinned and looked at Breedlove for corroboration. "It ain't consistant, man."

"Well," Joe Don said, taking another sip from his bourbon and fishing a joint out of a shirt pocket, "I don't know about you, but I don't exactly relish the idea of walkin' in there with nothin' but my dick in my hand an' sayin', 'Please, can we have about eighty grand or I'll pee all over you.' "

"But 'nobody gets hurt,' " Mike said, mimicking Joe Don's higher-pitched voice.

"That's right." Joe Don nodded and lit the joint, inhaling deeply and passing it toward Breedlove, who waved it off toward Mike.

"So what happens," Mike said, "if one of these yokels pulls a shotgun out and starts blowing up the joint?" This last had come out as a high squeak as he tried to hold in the smoke.

"In that case," Joe Don answered as he received the joint from Mike's hand, "you gotta shoot back, and it cannot be helped. But it ain't gonna happen."

"How the hell do you know?" Mike blew smoke across the room toward the bullfighter on the painting over the double bed where Breedlove sat.

"Cause I *know* these places, man, an' all they got is some old fart of a guard who probably don't even carry a gun. They'll all lay down if you yell at 'em. *And* we're talkin' *loan companies,* not *banks* or armored cars—at least not yet—an' carryin' guns just ain't the style of loan company clerks."

Mike took the joint back from Joe Don and lay back on his own bed. Joe Don also moved onto the bed where Breedlove sat cross-legged. He closed his eyes and lay back. They were all tired. The night before three Mexican hookers had kept them up. Mike had brought them in, and God only knew where he found them. They were wild as hell, and they had swapped around and smoked grass with them until daybreak, when Joe Don suddenly turned mean and kicked them out on their asses. He had flung fifty dollars, the last of their cash, out the door after them and laughed like hell when they banged on the door and cursed him in Spanish.

They had gone to sleep then, and sometime in midafternoon they woke up and began drinking and smoking again. Breedlove was hungry. It seemed it was always hunger that he associated with Mike and Joe Don, especially Joe Don. He'd been hungry when they met, and he couldn't recall having a full stomach since. About all he could think of that Joe Don kept around in ready supply was booze, and God, they had enough booze. He wondered where they would get the money to eat on. He found that he worried about where the money would come from about as often as he worried about food.

Joe Don had insisted that they stay clean in Texas. Still, they had boosted two cars since leaving the Caddy they took in El Paso in a drainage ditch near Uvalde. Even though they wiped the whole car down in case the cops tried to take fingerprints, Breedlove felt very tense knowing that the LTD parked outside the motel room was also stolen and that he was only a hairsbreadth away from prison.

And Mike did nothing to add to Breedlove's feeling of security. The dirty, obnoxious man had met them at a motel in San Antonio the night they pulled in, and since then he'd breezed in and out of their lives with easy freedom. He tended to show up every time their money was low with grass and, not infrequently, girls, and after he had stayed around a couple of days, he would leave without a word, often in the middle of the night. When Breedlove had questioned Joe Don about Mike's peculiar behavior, Joe Don had only grinned and said, "He's crazy as a three-dicked dog at a fair."

Mike bothered Breedlove. He was as big as Joe Don was small. He was well-built and told Breedlove that if he didn't work out more he would wind up flabby. He was ugly, extremely ugly, Breedlove thought, and he usually was dirty. All his clothes seemed to be combinations of faded and patched Levi's and T-shirts naming one rock group or another. He told Breedlove he had played with several rock bands from coast to coast, but none of them had made it big while he was with them. The one or two that had potential, he carped, had sold out to that "c&w shit," abandoning their true rock-and-roll traditions. He said he was a bass man, and he didn't like all that twangy guitar and Willy Nelson bullshit.

He had been in Vietnam, but a line unit, Long Range Reconnaissance, he claimed, which was where he met Joe Don. "I thought he was a fuckin' faggot," Mike had laughed when the two recounted their adventures to Breedlove. "But we got good and drunk and then good and stoned and we went out and found a couple of gook

whores and had a fucking contest.'' They both laughed
at that. ''He could get me coke or grass or whatever else
I wanted, and then we got in trouble a couple of times.''
They had run into each other in a Houston bar after Mike
had been released on parole, and they had more or less
kept in touch since through phone calls and prostitutes
they both knew in various towns.

Mike loved grass, and he loved sex, and he took both
in large portions. The whores he brought around usually
served for all three of them, and Breedlove had no complaint, really, even though he rarely got to go with any
of them before Mike had ''sampled'' the merchandise,
as he demanded to do. The drugs, however, made Breedlove nervous. He didn't have a moral thing about grass
or even the hard drugs. He'd been around plenty of it
over the years, but something in him wouldn't let him
take even a hit from a joint or even pretend to. He didn't
really know why; he didn't try to analyze it; he just found
some secret pride in his abstinence and held on to it as
best he could.

After a while the grass and continued drinking took its
effect on Joe Don, and he dozed off. Mike rose and
looked over at Breedlove, who had buried his nose in a
Playboy and was trying not to think about food. ''You
wanna go down on the river an' pick up some snatch?''

''With what?'' Breedlove asked, thinking that picking
up some hamburgers or fried chicken sounded like a better idea.

''Ain't you guys got any money at all?'' Mike's snag-
gled teeth gave him the impression of always snarling
when he spoke.

''He threw our last fifty out the door behind the whores
this morning,'' Breedlove said, looking back at the magazine. He saw no reason to hide the fact that the only
money they had had for the past six months had either
been stolen or given to them by the greasy man who now
wanted to know if they were really broke. ''I had about
twenty when I met him in Phoenix, and I ain't had shit
since.''

''Fine fuckin' mess,'' Mike said. ''He's talkin' about

buyin' some decent hardware, an' y'all don't have a pot to piss in.'' He picked up a jeans jacket and pulled it on over his T-shirt. ''C'mon, pussy.'' He snatched the magazine from Breedlove's hands. ''It's about time you guys earned your keep around here.''

Breedlove felt a lump rise in his stomach and swallowed hard, but he got up and pulled on his boots and followed Mike out the door and into his van. They pulled out onto IH-10 and soon were cruising around the fringes of downtown San Antonio. Soon Breedlove became confused about where they were. Mike made so many turns and circles he was totally turned around. All the time he kept complaining that Breedlove couldn't find a decent radio station. It was getting later and later, and Breedlove was feeling sick without any food in his stomach. He wished Mike would get hungry too, but he showed no signs of it.

''Shit,'' Mike said at last as they passed a convenience store, ''These places all got drop safes and the assholes who work in them don't know the combinations. It's too late to hit a liquor store. Shit.'' He turned another corner. ''You gotta gun, or does ol' Nobody-Gets-Hurt allow you to carry one?''

Breedlove smarted under the implication that he was Joe Don's pet spaniel or something, but he admitted, ''No, no gun. He said we ought to stay clean while we were in Texas.''

''Oh, yeah?'' Mike stopped at a red light. ''What about that Ford in the parking lot?'' Breedlove said nothing. ''Fuckin' amateurs,'' Mike concluded, spinning his tires when the light turned green.

They drove in silence north, away from downtown, and emerged on San Pedro. A large nightclub with expensive cars in the lot emerged on their left just beyond Loop 410, and Mike wheeled the van in behind a Jaguar. He jumped out of the van and sauntered into the club. Breedlove had just about made up his mind to get out and follow Mike inside when the big man emerged from the door. He stepped into the van and slammed the door.

''No money in there,'' he said. ''Too many fuckin'

credit cards. I'm not gonna get my ass shot off for thirty-five bills and a handful of change.''

They continued to cruise around the city's north side, pulling into two more places, but both times Mike said no. Finally they began cruising Loop 410, and soon a drive-in theater loomed in the distance. The marquee was advertising adult films, and from the height of the highway, Breedlove could see that both theaters were full of cars.

"This is it," Mike said, and he pulled the van off the freeway onto an exit ramp. They circled around and turned into the driveway of the outdoor theater. A car full of people was in front of them in line, but it soon pulled on into one of the parking lots for the screen, and Mike eased the van up close to the ticket window, reaching down under his seat and pulling up a small leather bag at the same time.

"How many?" the girl behind the window asked. She was young and alone, and she looked out the window of the booth and smiled a toothy grin at Mike's ugly face.

"All you got, sweetie." Mike sneered at her, and she reeled back. He reached into the leather bag and pulled out a small revolver, and Breedlove jumped in shock. "I want all the cash, both windows," Mike announced, "and I want it fast. Make a move, honey, and I'll blow your titties off."

For a moment she stood paralyzed, but Mike gestured with the pistol and she moved quickly to open the cash drawer. She neatly stacked the bills on top of each other, then she turned around and emptied the other till. She handed the stack of money to Mike, who took it with his free hand and tossed it to Breedlove in the other seat.

"You want the change, too?" she asked, her voice trembling a bit.

"Naw, honey." Mike leaned out the window of the van and leered in at her. "Just unbutton."

"Huh?" She stared at him in shock.

"The blouse, cutie pie." Mike gestured with the gun, "Take it off. I want to see them nice titties I almost shot off."

"No! Please, no!" she begged, her hand going up to her throat. Lights from a car suddenly came through the back window of the van.

"Let's go!" Breedlove hissed at Mike. "C'mon, man, let's go!"

Mike glanced into his rearview mirror and shrugged. "Okay, sweet pants, maybe next time." He leered at her. He threw the van into reverse and backed out at a high speed, narrowly missing the car pulling in behind them. Breedlove was thrown around in the seat as Mike swung the van into a 180-degree turn and hit the shoulder of the access road to 410.

Soon they were back on IH-10 heading back downtown. "Now for some fun," he shouted to Breedlove, who was trying to reassemble the money into stacks to calm his shaking hands.

He couldn't believe what had just happened. He had participated in an armed robbery! Nothing in his experience had prepared him for the ruthlessness of the man who drove the van he now rode in. He frantically searched his mind for an escape route. Maybe he could just run away, he thought, get lost in downtown San Antonio. But the idea didn't seem to take. The whole episode was so unreal. He couldn't believe it had actually happened. A few minutes ago they had been flat broke and out of gas; now they had what looked to be damned near five hundred dollars, and it had all gone as smooth as silk. He couldn't decide whether this was good or not, but he figured, with his luck, it would turn sour any minute.

"Think maybe we could get something to eat?" he shouted at Mike, who only looked at him and laughed.

They parked the van on a side street and waited around for a taxi to come by. When one did, they piled in and told the driver to find the nearest tavern that served food. The one the driver took them to was off South St. Mary's, deep in the San Antonio barrio.

Mike explained to Breedlove as they drove that the pistol wasn't real. "It's a starter pistol," he whispered to Breedlove as the driver turned a corner, "like they use to start track meets. I don't like carrying a real gun. I'm on parole, too. Only I ain't jumped the way ol' asshole did.''

They paid the cabbie from the wads of stolen bills stuffed into their Levis, and walked into the bar. Breedlove was nervous about being in a bar on San Antonio's south side, but he didn't know what to do. He had lived in the city some three or four years before, but he'd stayed on the north side of the downtown area. The south side was just too dangerous for whites, he had been told, and it was especially dangerous after dark. He glanced at the bar's clock. It was damned near ten o'clock.

Breedlove didn't notice the angry stares the two white men received going into the bar. His eyes immediately fixed on a large bowl of hard-boiled eggs next to a jug of hot links. "Hey, food," he said to Mike, but the big man ignored him. Breedlove had peeled off a couple of bills from the wads in his pockets so he could pay for whatever they got without having to show all the cash, and he plunked down the bills on the bar and began hungrily devouring the links and eggs while Mike ordered some beer.

"Joe Don's gonna be pissed as hell about the van," Breedlove offered through a full mouth.

"Fuck him," Mike said, sipping his beer and fingering an egg but not breaking the shell. "We can boost another one tomorrow."

"Boost?" Breedlove said, looking up into the mirror over the bar and noticing for the first time that everyone else in the place was Mexican-American. "I thought you said you borrowed it."

"Yeah, well, the chick I borrowed it from is gonna be back from Dallas tomorrow, an' she might not remember she loaned it to me," Mike said, and grinned widely at Breedlove, revealing his broken teeth and reminding Breedlove how truly ugly he was.

They stood at the bar a while longer, eating eggs and "scopin' *chicitas*," as Mike put it, but no unattached women came in. Finally he rose and walked over to the pool table and put a quarter down where four swarthy men were playing.

"Winners," he said, smiling, but the men hardly looked up.

When they finished their game, he walked back and grinned at them, strolled over to a rack of cues and selected one, measuring it with his eye. "C'mon, Breed," he said loudly, waving his partner over.

Breedlove had started to move when one of the players spoke up. "This is a private game." Mike turned a bit to face him. "Gringo."

"The hell you say." Mike smiled a big, snaggle-toothed grin and shifted his weight to seem as affable as possible. "Well, *amigo*, what does it take to get in?"

Another of the men, a younger one with a sweat shirt that the sleeves had been cut out of, stepped forward. "You have to know your father's name," he said, and he crushed out a cigarette butt with his toe.

Breedlove stood up. He had been in too many bar fights in his life not to know what was coming, and he dreaded it. A small spot just above his left eye began smarting from the memory of an old fight that had left him blind for two weeks.

Mike was still smiling, and he looked at the two other men who were now inching forward behind the first pair. They inverted their pool cues and were holding them like clubs. "Hey, Breed," Mike called, making Breedlove wish he could sink into the floor, "these fuckin' bean-eaters are callin' me names!" He strolled lazily over to where Breedlove stood, turning his back completely on the angry quartet behind him. "Now that's freaky," he said, still grinning and speaking loudly enough to be heard over the Mexican polka music on the jukebox. "This must be some kinda club for queer Mescans, or somethin'." One of the men began to step forward and raise his cue a bit. "I mean," Mike went on, speaking even more loudly, "we been here almost an hour an' we ain't seen one little ol' seen-yor-reeta come in an' wanna sell her spick cunt so she can get some good white meat. I mean—"

He was cut short. Sweat Shirt clubbed his cue high and swung from the side, like a batter, catching Mike squarely on the ear with a loud *thwack*.

Breedlove jumped when the pool cue connected. He knew Mike had the starter pistol stuck in his belt under his jacket, but he also knew these guys meant business. No bluff would work now. Mike was completely out of his mind, Breedlove thought in a panic, and now he was out of action and these four honchos are gonna clean my plow.

When he settled a second later, he was shocked to see that Mike was still standing there, still grinning at him.

The blow had broken the cue stick and sent its end flying over the bar. It narrowly missed a woman on one of the stools, and now her boyfriend was shoving her into a booth near the back of the room. A trickle of blood ran from under Mike's hair down his cheek, and he reached up and touched his ear, then began a slow turn toward the four men who still stood with their feet planted and their cues held like weapons in front of them.

Breedlove sighed to himself and stood up, doubling his fists and trying to look as tough as he could. He hated the idea of what he was going to have to do, and he had little doubt that in a very few minutes one or more of these big Mexican-Americans would be pounding the shit out of him.

But as soon as he gained his feet, Mike put up his hand, shook his head, and gestured for him to be seated. "I'm gonna clean this place out, Breed," he said in a cold, calm voice, "an' that asshole—" he pointed toward Sweat Shirt—"is gonna loan me his car. Right, Pancho?"

Sweat Shirt was visibly unnerved by Mike's cool speech and because he hadn't gone down from such a blow to the head. But he quickly regained his composure. He reached down into his Levi's pocket and came up with a knife, opened it, and crouched in the classic pose of a knife fighter. "C'mon! Come *on*, *cabrone*!" he said.

The next few minutes passed in slow motion for Breed-

love. Mike casually walked over to the crouching and
weaving Sweat Shirt, still grinning his broken-toothed
smile, and slowly raised his leg, bent it, and brought it
down hard on Sweat Shirt's knee before the smaller man
could react. Breedlove heard the kneecap pop loudly, and
he watched Sweat Shirt double up in pain, screaming out
as he began to fall. He wasn't all the way to the floor
when Mike's arm snaked out and grabbed the wrist of
the hand that held the knife. He brought it up, twisted it
slightly, making it pop loudly also when the bone inside
snapped.

One of the other men, the one who had spoken first,
backed up slightly and prepared to swing his cue, but
Mike did a bit of a jig, hopping up on one leg and bringing the other around in a full circle, connecting his boot
heel with the man's jaw. As he fell, the other two men
started looking for an exit from this terrible fighter they
had foolishly challenged, but Mike became a whirlwind
of arms and legs, kicking and striking them as they held
up their cue sticks in useless defense.

Suddenly it was all over. Mike stood in the middle of
the foursome, two of whom were unconscious, and
grinned at the other two, who watched him with frightened eyes as they cradled broken elbows, sprains, and
bruises. Sweat Shirt was one of these, and Mike reached
down and grabbed him by the neck of his shirt and pulled
him semi-erect, making him cry out in pain.

"What kind of car you drive, *amigo*?" Mike asked,
shaking him a bit like a broken doll. Sweat Shirt said
nothing, just clenched his teeth, and Mike grabbed his
hair and pulled his head back so far Breedlove was sure
his neck would break. "Answer me," Mike said calmly,
still smiling a friendly smile and speaking in a calm
voice. "Answer me or I'll snap your neck like you was
a Mescan chicken." He pulled back another inch. "*Pollo*.
Dig?"

"Camaro," Sweat Shirt gasped out in pain.

"What color? Where are the keys?" Mike asked, tug-
ging Sweat Shirt's head back even farther.

"Yellow.'78. Yellow. Keys in my pocket," Sweat Shirt

said quickly. "On the side, parked on the side." He was close to passing out, Breedlove knew. He'd felt such pain, and he felt sorry for the kid being punished by Mike's cruelty.

"Gimme!" Mike said, holding his other hand out. He was now holding Sweat Shirt completely by the hair, forcing pressure on the broken knee. With his good arm, Sweat Shirt dug into his pockets and came up with a key ring. "Now, you can pick this up on North San Pedro sometime next week, say Friday, okay?" Mike said as Sweat Shirt's face turned pale. "Okay?" Mike repeated, and Sweat Shirt tried to nod in his tightly stretched position.

"Hey, thanks a lot, man." Mike said, sounding suddenly serious and sincere, and he released the hair in his hand, dropping the youth onto the floor, where he lay unconscious.

The other people in the bar had backed up against the wall during the fight, and they now began looking curiously at the men on the floor, wondering if any of them were dead. Mike strolled over to where Breedlove, himself in a state of shock from what he had seen, still sat on the stool, and reached past him for a bar towel, which he placed on his bleeding ear.

"Hey, Pancho," he called to the bartender, "gimme some ice in a towel." The bartender complied. "Now, listen to me," Mike said to the bar's customers at large while he pressed the ice pack to the side of his head. "This man's my witness." He pointed to Breedlove. "He'll testify that ol' Pancho *numero uno* over there started all this, an' then he was so damned sorry he loaned me his car. I ain't stealin' nothin', an' all you beaners saw him hit me first."

The bartender nodded and moved back against the mirror. Mike hooked a thumb at him and announced, "Anybody who thinks anything different went down had better take a look at ol' Pancho number two's license." He touched Breedlove on the shoulder and they walked calmly out the bar's door.

They found the Camaro parked on the side of the tavern and got in.

"Runs like shit," Mike said as he backed out and drove onto South St. Mary's, "Goddamn Mescans don't know how to take care of a car." Breedlove nodded in agreement. He didn't know what to say or do, and dumb compliance seemed to be the only course of action that didn't strain his mind.

"Ol' Army trainin' pays off." Mike laughed as he wheeled the car through downtown San Antonio. Soon he found the entrance ramp to IH-10 and headed east toward the Holiday Inn.

"Listen," Mike said as they neared the motel, "you got the cash, so you go check us out. They got a good look at that van more'n once, an' it'll be connected to the movie holdup. We gotta move, even though I ain't officially registered. No point in pissin' off ol' Joe Don any more'n we have to." He pulled into the motel lot. "I guess I'll be stickin' with you guys full time now. Make sure you don't get into any trouble."

Breedlove got out of the car in front of the motel office and went inside to check out. He paid the bill in cash and noted that it was after midnight. Mike had gone to the room to get Joe Don up and pack their junk. Pack, Breedlove thought, that's a laugh. Between them they didn't own enough stuff to fill a cardboard box. In fact, he thought as he looked down to his boots, I'm wearing everything I own in the world.

He left the office and strolled out to the edge of the parking lot. On IH-10 traffic going to Houston or El Paso sped by. He felt it would be easy just to walk across the access road and up onto the highway, stick out a thumb, and hitch a ride out of this crazy business he found himself tied up with. All through the past six months with Joe Don talking about this loan office he knew about up in the north part of the state that they could take so easily, Breedlove had just let it all go. He'd never believed any of it. It was just more of Joe Don's bullshit, he'd thought. When Mike would drop in for a couple of days, the talk would always center on that, but Breedlove just figured it was Joe Don's way of getting Mike's attention. He never thought Joe Don was capable of pulling anything like that off.

Now he wasn't so sure. Not after tonight. After tonight Breedlove knew one thing for certain. He knew Mike Dix could pull it off, and he was fairly sure that with Mike along, Joe Don would go through with it.

The cars and trucks up on the interstate tempted Breedlove more than ever, and he started strolling slowly across the access road, stopping again on the grassy area on the other side. He couldn't decide what to do. He had almost three hundred dollars in his pockets, and he wouldn't have had any of it without Mike. But something about it was too scary, too damned scary.

His thoughts raced back through the past. He'd never had anything, and he'd spent most of his life like a criminal, although he'd never committed any crime, or at least any crime worth running from like he'd always run. It would be nice to have money, even if he had to steal it, enough money to have some things he'd always had to just dream of. He didn't know.

"Hey, Breed!" Joe Don's voice hollered at him from across the motel parking lot. They were getting into the Camaro and waving at him to come on. "You takin' a piss or jerkin' off?"

Jerking off, Breedlove thought as he turned and started jogging toward the car, just jerking off.

II. Lawman
August, The Present

"She was Eileen Kennedy." Doc Pritchard's voice rasped its weariness over the phone. "From Agatite, I think, originally."

"How the hell did you find that out?" Able Newsome couldn't contain his amazement. For a silly moment he imagined Doc Pritchard opening her up and discovering her name sewn into her skin like a mother would do for a child on her way to summer camp.

"A miracle of medical science." Doc Pritchard laughed into the phone, and Able imagined him puffing away on his pipe. "She had a class ring from Agatite High on, and her name was in it. Engraved on the inside. It could be somebody else's, but I doubt it. Too good a fit."

"I'll be damned." Able thought about her hands hanging beside her body. He remembered now that she'd worn a ring, as well as an ankle bracelet and some other doodads, but he hadn't thought much about them. Maybe he was getting too old for this job. "What else did you learn from your lab work?"

"Well," the old doctor went on, "I doubt it was a suicide, but that's your department, not mine. Death was caused by severe cranial trauma complicated by—you don't want all this in official medical bullshit, do you?"

"Save it," Able said. "Get to the point."

"Death was caused by a severe blow to the head, in fact several." He paused to check his notes. "Three or four at least, complicated by a strong blow to the jaw. Her jaw was totally busted. But her skull was cracked open like a cantaloupe, and her tongue was bit completely in two, hanging by a thread." Able remembered the wasps, nest. "Looks like she was hit pretty hard with something. Could've been a board or a rock or a hunk of metal of some kind. It's hard to tell. I got some flakes of debris—could be paint of some kind—out of the wounds, but her hair had all kinds of dirt and shit in it, so it's hard to tell if it came from the weapon or not. I can tell you it wasn't no typical 'blunt instrument' or nothing. It was too irregular." He paused again. "There was also a pretty good bruise on her chin, like I say. Her jaw was broke. Two front teeth busted, too. I'd suspect a fist did that, but again, it's hard to tell before the lab results come back. I'm gonna have to send this in to Austin. About all I can tell you for sure right now is that somebody knocked the shit out of her or she took one hell of a queer fall."

Able had brought out his battered notebook and was jotting down the information Doc Pritchard had given him, cradling the receiver in his shoulder. "Was she raped?" he asked.

"No sign of it. Her clothing was torn up some, so were her stockings, but her underwear was all there, just like it was supposed to be, and there were no indications of bleeding or beatings on her body. I didn't check further for rape, but I can if you want. It just would seem odd for a rapist to dress her back up or even clean her up, especially if he'd killed her already."

"No," Able said, "that wouldn't make sense. Anything else?"

"Well . . ." Doc Pritchard paused and took a breath. "She was likely killed one place and hung up in the outhouse after she was dead." Able thought of the Mexican boy. "But you could figure that out from the lack of blood around. She's been dead about three weeks.

"She had a watch on, and somehow it worked itself around under her coat—it was one of the kind you wear around your neck—a necklace watch, you know?" Able thought of the black, stretched-out neck and shuddered. "Anyhow," Pritchard went on, "it was smashed and stopped at six thirty-three p.m. on July twenty-third. It was one of those quartz jobs—day, date, you know?"

Doc Pritchard coughed. He sounded tired. Able said nothing and waited for him to go on, "She had eaten a pretty good meal that day from the looks of her stomach contents, but it'll take the lab to say what it was. There were no other broken bones, aside from her nose, which was busted pretty good, and one finger that had been fractured, but that had healed and had happened years ago. Three fingernails had been sheared off, almost like they'd been cut. Normally I wouldn't even note that, but the others are all done so fine, polished and manicured, you know, that I think it might be important. I took a look at one of them under the microscope, but I didn't learn nothing. Might not amount to nothing anyhow. But, Able, that's about all I have. There'll be more when the lab stuff comes back from Austin. Let's see, this is Wednesday—that'll be next Tuesday at the earliest. I'd bet on a murder. Still, that ain't my department."

So it wasn't a suicide, Able thought, feeling the bile rise in his stomach that now seemed alternately hungry and ill.

"I'll send over an official version of all this tomorrow, but it won't be complete." Doc Pritchard concluded, then interrupted his good-bye. "Oh, by the way, the boys from the newspaper and TV are probably on their way over. Apparently Mel got into some kind of tangle with Murphy, and he called up Wichita Falls, and they rode hell for leather over here. I had Jeff Randall talk to them, but he sent them over to Harvey's office, but he ain't there, naturally, so they'll likely be on your doorstep in a few minutes."

"Thanks for the warning, Doc," Able said, "and the fast work." Able's mind was working already. He hung up as Doc Pritchard welcomed the thanks; then he began searching his files.

It took him a few minutes to locate the flyer, but finally he found it: "MISSING: EILEEN ELLEN KENNEDY," and it was dated, sure enough, July 27. He ran quickly over the description: She was five feet two inches tall, blue eyes, brown hair, and weighed about one hundred ten pounds. She was born in Agatite, September 19, 1958, but moved to Oklaunion, Texas, after her parents were killed in a car wreck in 1979. There she worked as a secretary for a small finance company. Something stirred in Able's memory. She was last seen by her only living relative, a maiden aunt in Memphis, Texas, whom she had been visiting on the afternoon of July 23rd—it fit—before leaving to drive back to Oklaunion to join a group of people at a catfish supper. She never arrived. When she didn't make her usual phone call to her aunt— one Miss Violet Kennedy—by the next morning and didn't arrive at the catfish fry, the D.P.S. was contacted. The a.p.b. went out on the 27th—normal for missing persons of her age.

Able searched through his files for an update. He found one, dated a week later. Her car, a 1975 Chevrolet Vega, had been found burned out and abandoned beneath a bridge over a nameless dry creek east of Wichita Falls.

Her purse was in the car, but there was no sign of Eileen Ellen Kennedy or of foul play other than, of course, the burned vehicle. Melted credit cards seemed to discount any theory of holdup as well. Another update, only ten days old, indicated that nothing had turned up in the case, and it had been referred to the Texas Rangers for further investigation. She was still missing.

Able picked up the phone and called the sheriff in Oklaunion. When the youthful voice answered, he remembered what had stirred in his mind as he went over Eileen Kennedy's missing person report. Thirty minutes later, his memory's information confirmed, he called Jingles and ordered—he had to order—him to come over. Jingles had seen the TV truck pull up at the courthouse and had headed them off, furiously denying rumors of murder and rape in Hoolian and denying charges leveled by Mel that the police department was covering anything up. He broke off from his interview, however, when Able called, and in a few minutes stormed into the sheriff's office.

Able noticed that Jingles had changed into a fresh uniform and was now awkwardly smoking a cigar and trying to look official. "What the hell is so important?" he demanded as he blew into the office, unceremoniously slamming the door in the face of a questioning reporter and camera crew.

"I thought you might like to know who our lady is," Able said, unflapped by Jingles' agitation.

Stunned by the statement, the chief of police sat heavily in one of the wooden office chairs and waited, the cigar smoking full steam.

"Her name was Eileen Ellen Kennedy, graduate of Agatite High School, class of '76. She moved to Oklaunion after her parents were killed in a car crash, took some courses at the junior college in Vernon, went to work at the Holiday Finance Company. She's got no kinfolk except one old-maid aunt over in Memphis. Last winter she was involved in that robbery where the sheriff got killed. You remember. She was the one who tried to shoot the lights out of one of the gunmen and wound up scared to death and damn near shot everybody else. She went to visit her aunt for the day last month—on the twenty-third—left there around three o'clock in the afternoon, and was never seen again.'' Able paused and enjoyed the total shock registered on Jingles' fat face, then he added, ''At least not till today.''

''So why'd she kill herself?'' Jingles said, trying to cover his amazement that this man he'd just described as a ''hick sheriff''—off the record—to the reporters outside had managed to come up with so much information without even leaving his office. Suddenly he groped around and came up with a theory. ''Was she still fucked up over that robbery? In the head, I mean?''

''I don't think she did kill herself, not based on what Doc Pritchard had to say. He thinks it's murder, and so do I.'' Able spoke evenly, noting that Jingles was prepared to explode in a denial of Pritchard's ability to do anything other than smoke a pipe. Then he added, ''That is, unless she beat herself to death after hitting herself hard enough to break her jaw and bite her tongue off, then hauled herself, dead, across a weed patch to an outhouse, found an electrical cord, and hanged herself on it, then broke off a couple of fingernails and tore open her clothes just to fool us.''

Jingles mouth, which had been open in protest, snapped shut. Able went on reading his notes from the autopsy report, and the chief of police simply listened and smoked his cigar. Finally, when Able closed his notebook, Jingles stood up and dropped his cigar butt into a spitoon in the corner. ''Well,'' he said as he paced the room for a moment, ''who do you figure killed her? The Mescan?''

Able barked out a short laugh. ''No. I got no idea who killed her, or why. But I'd sure like to find out. It wasn't that kid. I'm sure of that.'' He leaned back and enjoyed the squeak of the chair.

''You want to talk to the press?'' Jingles looked a bit scared. Now he had to go out and admit that, after consulting with the ''hick sheriff,'' he had been incorrect in his denial of murder. He realized he was going to look stupid, admitting that he had no evidence to the contrary, and the facts had been dug up by the very man he had been criticizing only minutes before.

"Nope." Able didn't move. "I told you out in Hoolian. It's your show. You can have the glory. All I want is the killer."

"You're a class-A son of a bitch," Jingles said, without humor or emotion of any kind appearing on his fat face.

"Naw, Murphy," Able drawled, "I'm jus' the little ol' county sheriff. Like you keep tellin' me."

Jingles started over toward the door.

"If you want, I'll call the aunt over in Memphis and get her over here for a positive i.d.," Able said, and Jingles turned and looked helplessly at him. "Or you could send somebody over to Oklaunion. But we ought to get that by tomorrow." Jingles opened the door without replying and waded out into the swarm of reporters.

It was growing dark in the way only an August day can in north central Texas. The lengthening shadows of the trees and buildings offered shade that belied the heat that remained from the day's broiling temperatures. Able called Sue Ellen and told her he would be home for a late supper, wincing when she acknowledged his message without protest or question. She's a good woman, he thought, too damned good for me. She had put up with an awful lot all these years.

John David radioed in to let Able know he was at last on duty and that Chrystal Murphy had announced all the details of the day's events to any and all who had a C.B. to listen in on and who wanted to know. Able went over to his office window and looked out over the lawn. A few cars traversed "the drag," as the teenagers had long ago dubbed Main Street, and Able saw Wayne Henderson threading his way through the gaggle of reporters who clogged the steps of City Hall as he tried to make his way home. Dr. Jeff Randall's Pontiac pulled into a parking space on the courthouse square and idled for a minute, then pulled out to follow the small blue sports car that zoomed around the corner and headed east out of

town. Maggie Meacham, Able thought. Poor James Earl.
Church bells from the Baptist and Methodist towers
rivaled each other to announce seven o'clock in the evening air, and Able spotted the first lines of cars beginning to pass each other and honk on the street.

Life went on in Agatite, oblivious to the horror that
had been hanging in the Hoolian outhouse for almost a
month. He knew he wouldn't sleep easily for a while.
Maybe he should retire. But he wanted to find Eileen
Kennedy's killer. He wanted to punish him, not for killing Eileen Kennedy, a silly girl who probably picked up
the wrong hitchhiker or maybe had been involved in
something more serious. He wanted to punish the son of
a bitch for leaving that grotesque, gruesome *thing* out in
that awful, stinking outhouse for Able to see.

He watched the darkening town beneath him, and suddenly he felt the warning convulsion. He ran into the
holding cell and leaned over the open toilet. He heaved
and heaved, but there was nothing on his stomach to come
up but a half-mouthful of bile. Through blurred, teared
vision he saw the dead face of Eileen Kennedy, the dry,
crusted, empty sockets staring at . . . at . . . at what? At
her murderer? At the dismally plain wall of the inside of
a vintage outhouse? He saw the open, flared red nostrils,
breathing nothing, smelling nothing, unaware of the awful stench around her, the noxious fumes she herself had
caused. Would she have been embarrassed to have been
found like that? She probably would have. He heaved
again, and again his entire body shuddered with the violence of the convulsion. He saw her face again, her teeth
bared in a death grimace, her black lips boys had probably kissed or wanted to kiss pulled back in a sardonic
grin, wrapped around . . . around . . . around the wasps.
He heaved once more, a violent tearing reaction that
wracked his stomach muscles and sent pain upward to
his shoulders, neck, head. His throat seared with the hot
bile from his empty stomach.

A tongueless, toneless scream, stopped by a torn and
lacerated tongue, cut in two by teeth that now gripped
the nest of stinging insects, he thought. "Mother of

God," he muttered aloud as he sat down on the cell's cot and forced back another convulsion. His mind wandered over the hanging body of Eileen Kennedy once more. He studied it the way he had studied the nude bodies of girls dancing in nightclubs that catered to GIs in Korea and Japan. He saw it in translucent detail, memory providing part, imagination filling in the gaps. Why hadn't he noticed the ring? What was happening to him? He closed his eyes, squeezing them tight to expunge the vision, but it became stronger in the darkness of his lids, clear and vital, and he knew the nightmares would be far worse than he ever imagined.

He moved from the cell back to his desk. He wondered what the press would do with this. What would the headlines read?

Slowly he reached into his desk where an ancient pack of Camels waited for moments like this, times when he couldn't face another cigar. He lit one, drawing the smoke into his lungs. Eileen Ellen Kennedy. Who killed you? Why? He wondered if he would ever know, ever find the man, confront him, blame him for the vision he knew he would carry in his mind for a long time. As the cigarette burned down and threatened to ignite his fingers, he expertly flicked the butt into the spitoon in the corner. He was only a county sheriff in a remote corner of an enormous state. His jurisdiction was limited. His resources were nonexistent. Will I ever meet him? he wondered; will I have the chance to ask him why he did this to her? To me? He lit another Camel and smoked it down, trying to make his mind a complete blank. As this cigarette, too, burned down and joined its predecessor in the spitoon, Able sighed and filled the high ceilings of his office with blue tobacco smoke. "I doubt it," he said to the swirls of exhaled smoke.

III. Banker
August, A Week Later

Lunch was over and Alexander Bateman heavily seated himself in the chair behind his all-mahogany desk in the First Security Bank of Agatite, Texas. Outside, the heat baked the downtown afternoon, but inside the bank the cool, comfortable *refrigerated* air conditioner, a recent installment in the building, kept Alexander cool, almost cold, and he enjoyed that. For one of his personal indulgences was three-piece suits, and now he could wear them at his desk all day long and not "offend," as the commercial used to say.

He owned six three-piece suits, and he had just been measured for another by his personal tailor in Wichita Falls. He particularly liked the all-business look of such a suit, the many pockets for cigar cutters, matches, a watch—which hung, not incidentally, from a Phi Beta Kappa key—breath mints, the key to Irma McElroy's apartment, where he had been taking his Wednesday lunches for the past five years, and even the odd business card some pushy salesman or client might jab at him, which he didn't want to keep. But mostly he liked three-piece suits because he was fat, and he believed that they made him look thinner.

Irma is trying to take weight off me, he thought. Yes she is. Wednesday lunch this Wednesday had been light—cottage cheese and lean roast beef with iced tea. Then a brief rubdown, and then—But Alexander felt his loins stir, and he didn't want that, so he pushed thoughts of today's lunchtime away from his mind and bent his attention to the cigar he was gently rolling in his puckered, fat lips.

Havanas, he thought guiltily. Illegal as hell, but he had paid for them. Imported from Argentina, with Argentine lables and wrappers added to disguise them, they were for special clients, special dinners, and, of course, Wednesday after lunches. He lit the cigar with a wooden match—no lighter fluid to spoil the bouquet—turning the cigar slowly in the flame to make sure of uniform ignition, and then he drew in deeply.

Often he felt naughty about his Wednesday lunches with Irma and about his illegal cigars, but sometimes he justified his infidelities with the slim, trim Irma easily, as easily as he found he could enjoy a truly superior smoke. After all, he would tell himself whenever he felt a qualm of guilt, it wasn't his fault that his dear wife of twenty-five years, Maddy, had gone to seed. It wasn't that she was merely fat; a lot of women had fat, and Alexander was enough of a realist to know the truth about his own body. It wasn't that she had developed a rather dark and full mustache—fuller than he could grow on his round pink face—and it wasn't even that she had become dull, plastered to the goddamn TV all day when she wasn't out spending his money in one of the dozen or so "boo-teeks" she had discovered in neighboring towns. It wasn't any of these things. It was all of them. Maddy was all the things that Irma wasn't and, Alexander felt sure, never would be. And that wasn't his fault, he reasoned, any more than it was his fault that the government wouldn't allow him a decent Cuban cigar without breaking the law.

Irma was discreet, as discreet as the rich taste of the Havana Stout, and discretion was something Maddy could never be accused of. Maddy talked about his corns, his balding head, his indigestion, even his goddamn piles, and she didn't much care to whom she talked about them. She told people how much he weighed with the same easy freedom she discussed how much their new car cost, how much the goddamn vacation to Mexico City that she had carped about for so long had run him, probably told them how often they made love, for Christ's sake. No. She probably didn't do that much anymore, since he hadn't had the stomach to force himself into her bed for more than a decade, and the one time she had said something timidly about his absences, he had blithely told her that he thought he had become impotent. She had probably had to look that up somewhere before she blabbed it around too, he thought. Anyway, she hadn't bothered

him about it again. And it was just as well. It wouldn't
have done her any good.

Abstinence had been hard at first. And it was difficult,
he knew, for a fat man, even a rich one, to find love in
a small town with someone other than his wife. He had
contented himself with his "business" trips to Dallas or
even California, and the wild ecstasies of prostitutes who
hadn't cared how much he weighed, or, for that matter,
whether he was rich or not, only that he had the price of
a good time and wasn't some kind of freak.

Then, about five years ago, Irma had walked into his
bank, alone, widowed, in need of a job, but with no
marketable skills or assets. None, that is, besides an
extra-fetching pair of legs, some fine red hair—dyed, but
who cared?—and some pretty blue eyes. He had suggested lunch. She had suggested her place, a small apartment over a garage behind old lady Moorely's house.

Old lady Moorely was a semi-invalid who drew her
blinds only at dusk, and the setup was perfect. The bank
held the note on her house, which was kept up-to-date
by her globe-trotting son, who sent irregular checks to
the bank from all over the place. Alexander could have
called the mortgage in arrears a dozen times, but owing
to his arrangement with Irma, he never did. And then,
two weeks ago, the old lady died, and now Alexander
was in control. Moorely came into town and was happy
to let the banker buy the house for twenty-five cents on
the dollar. He had no idea he let it go so cheaply, and he
probably didn't care. His checks had been turning up bad
ever since he hit town and started trying to cover his
mother's outstanding debts. He was so anxious to con-
clude the deal, grab the money, and get back to his third
wife in New York or California or wherever the hell she
was divorcing him from. Alexander chuckled at the
thought of how neatly all this had come together. He
could now set Irma up in the house, and he could rent
the garage apartment for three times what it should bring
to offset the house payments. It was too beautiful to be
true.

With such pleasantly secure thoughts dancing inside

his head, Alexander leaned back and ran his hands over
the wood of his desk's top, which was, as he always liked
it to be, void of clutter or need-to-do work. His eyes
trailed through the cigar smoke until they fell on his ap-
pointments calendar, and his good mood ceased abruptly.
A frown curled down around the end of his Havana cigar,
and an ash fell unceremoniously onto the vest of his three-
piece suit. Today was Wednesday, and that *kid* was due
any minute to talk about that college loan. Well, shit,
Alexander Bateman thought, that spoiled the afternoon.
He had hoped to sneak away early and play a round of
golf or something as soon as Moorely came by to drop
off the papers he was supposed to have signed.

Alexander scowled out the Flex-Glo tinted windows of
his office that gave the searing August sky a softer, almost cool look. But he wasn't fooled by the tinted windows. Too damned hot anyway, he thought, and besides,
nobody'll be playing this afternoon until much later. Everybody and his dog will be at that funeral. But maybe
the kid would be quick and he could get out anyhow.

As he debated he relaxed a bit, enjoying the refrigerated air of the bank. No, he decided, his business with
the kid would *not* take long, but it was going to be
damned unpleasant. Damned unpleasant. At least it gave
him an excuse to miss Castlereigh's funeral. Funerals always spoiled his whole week. It was better to lose a few
hours dealing with business than ruin a whole week.

Almost as if his thoughts summoned the fact, his in-
tercom buzzed and Maribeth Hogan announced that the
kid was here to see him. She unfortunately called him
the "one-thirty appointment," not revealing his name,
and Alexander's mind flew briefly around trying to pin it
down. What the hell was it? he asked himself. He knew
the last name, of course, but he was going to have to be
unpleasant, and his business sense told him never to use
a last name when he was being unpleasant, not in a small-
town bank.

Before he could open his drawer and check the manila
folder inside, the door opened and the kid walked in. He
was nervous, and he had his hand stuck out in front of

him for a shake as soon as he crossed the threshold. A
grin was pasted on his face that said, "I sure do hate
eating this shit, but God, if it'll get me what I want, I'll
eat it and love it."

Alexander struggled to his feet and waved off the hand
by gesturing to the upholstered leather chair on the opposite side of the mahogany desk. The chair had been
chosen especially because it was the most attractive piece
Alexander could find in all of Dallas—that is, it was the
most attractive and the most *uncomfortable*. He had
hunted long and hard for it to put to use a pet theory he
had developed—person applying for a loan *should* be uncomfortable, by-God; he should feel like he was on the
fucking *rack*. For years Alexander had lazed in his opu-
lent office desk chair and eased his sore hemorrhoids into
cushy leather and foam, but his supplicants, as he liked
to think of them, writhed in agony on a chair that was a
real butt buster. He liked the vision of the poor, sand-
streaked, and sun-baked farmer, straw hat turning in his
gnarled hands, squirming around trying to find a comfortable position in that chair, knowing, as Alexander's
piggish eyes roamed over the form and took count of
everything he owned in the world, that in them lay the
fate of his dry-land dirt farm, his family, his life. It was
a wonderful device, Alexander thought; it gave him
power, it let these hick assholes know who was by-God
in charge, and it afforded him the ability to smile and
joke and be a good ol' boy with them while the chair
created all the discomfort that was necessary.

Farmers, small businessmen, homeowners, anyone
down on his luck had sat there along with proud papas,
dreamers, schemers, and cheats, all sweating and
squirming, trying to find a place for at least one cheek
to rest where the leather upholstery wouldn't bite their
asses, but there wasn't one. Alexander had found a chair
that looked as inviting as a chaise longue, but it felt like
an all-weather road. Now the kid sat there, and Alexander noticed that he wasn't squirming at all. He was just
leaning back and calmly, if somewhat nervously, waiting.

For the briefest moment the banker studied this supplicant. He was thin, too thin by pounds, Alexander thought. But he wasn't bad looking, and on second thought, he wasn't badly proportioned. At least he wasn't some kind of freak, some doper. Then he'd have all kinds of trouble with him. And he wasn't some minority. The bank wouldn't have some goddamn organization all over it the way it had when Alexander had turned down Elmer Johnson, that black son of a bitch. The NAACP had been on the horn with a lawyer before Johnson got back to Niggertown, Alexander angrily remembered. No, this was just a kid. Catholic, but no ethnic source showing, just a white, small-town asshole wanting a couple of thousand bucks for college.

The kid sat waiting as Alexander fished the manila folder from the desk and slowly opened it and started reviewing the application. He was wearing a squeaky-clean sports shirt and a pair of shiny pants. His shoes were brightly buffed, but they were worn shoes, and the polish couldn't hide the rundown heels and battered toes. Alexander noted with a pang of sympathy, which he quickly squelched, that it was the exact same outfit the kid had worn the week before when he applied for the loan. His hair was unfashionably long, but it was neatly trimmed on the ends, and it was clean. He had shaved close, cutting himself a bit, from the looks of the red marks on his neck and chin, and in his pocket was the tip of a ball-point pen, probably to sign the note with.

"Well, David," Alexander began, glancing up from the application.

"Danny, sir, uh . . . Daniel," the kid added eagerly. "David's my next youngest brother."

How many rats did old man O'Hara have? Alexander wanted to wonder out loud, and he fought back a smile, "Oh, I didn't know you had a younger brother."

"Yessir," Danny offered informatively. "There's eight of us, all told, uh . . . living at home, and Juan, too."

Alexander vaguely remembered the total from the application, and he remembered Juan, a baby Able Newsome had found in a garbage can outside the courthouse three years before. Some damned Mexican family had dumped him here in Agatite rather than take him north where more work waited. More likely a bastard the mother didn't want and was too ashamed to keep. The O'Haras had taken him in with their brood and even started adoption procedures, and all those kids and the old man lived in a dirt-floor shack surrounded by junked cars and two outside toilets. Alexander didn't think they even had electricity, since he'd seen the old lady parked in front of the laundromat so often. They were poor as cowshit and proud as turkeys.

But they had a reputation in the county as being "good people even if they *are* Catholic," a phrase Alexander had heard often enough to come to half believe. People ought to know their limitations, though, Alexander thought, ought to know when they didn't have the money to do what they wanted to or thought they should do.

"Well, uh, look David, uh, Daniel," Alexander said as he spread the folder open and fanned the application forms out in front of him on the desk, careful not to place any of the papers where the kid could see them, "I've talked this over with the board of directors"—Alexander leaned back and desperately enjoyed the final puffs of his Havana cigar—"and, as you know, money's real tight right now. We're facing a possible economic slowdown again this year or early next, maybe even a depression, who knows? And there's talk of a wage-price freeze coming up next year . . ."

Alexander droned on, talking economic gibberish, watching the disappointment build in the kid's eyes. He knew the "no" was coming; why didn't he get to the point? Well, Danny my boy, Alexander silently lectured the young supplicant as his mouth continued to spill out arguments, business. The reason why is business. "And the bottom line, David, is that we—that is the board— doesn't feel the college loan is really in line with the kind of banking we ought to be doing."

"Look, Mr. Bateman." The kid's eyes were flashing around the room, glancing at the plush office, the stuffed marlin, the stag's head, the college momentos. "I explained all this to you last week. I got this special church scholarship for St. Mary's down in San Antonio. It's no good anyplace else. . . ."

Just like the goddamn Catholics, Alexander thought, give a kid a scholarship to one of the most expensive schools in the goddamn state.

"But it only covers tuition. I still got to buy books and pay room and board, an' they won't let me work the first year. That's part of the deal. I'll pay you back, every cent. The government *guarantees* the loan, pays the interest. They won't let me borrow from the school or nothin'. Jes—Gee, it'd mean so much to my folks if I could go. None of us ever could before, ever had the chance. . . ."

Alexander leaned forward in his chair and stubbed out his cigar. This was the kill. All the bullshit about the board of directors had been high and deep. The goddamn board didn't know enough about banking to shit and go blind. He made all the decisions, always had. That's why this bank made money! "It's like I said, David, the board just doesn't think that college loans are good for business."

Suddenly the kid grew frantic, leaning forward and almost rising from the uncomfortable chair that hadn't had any apparent effect on him at all. "But you made one to Janey Pruitt and to Ray Richardson and even to Ella May Hargrove, an' I got better grades than all of them."

Alexander leaned back in his executive office chair and put both hands behind his fat, balding head and pursed his flabby lips. Then he dramatically brought his hands forward and folded them over his Phi Beta Kappa key and looked down at the file folder on his desk. He sighed deeply.

All of what the kid said was true, and it caused a sudden pang of sympathy. But it had no effect on the decision. That was irreversible. Never change your mind, Alexander always said to himself. Beneath the form in the folder lay the kid's transcript from Agatite High School. He had graduated fifth in a class of eighty-five. Not that bad. His family were decent people, even if they were poor as Job's goat and dumber than ploughed ground. He probably *would* pay back the loan, with interest, but he wasn't going to get the money. There simply wasn't enough profit in it. He could work his way through school the way most of the kids from Agatite had to do. Most of them went to one of the local colleges or junior colleges, working hard and paying their own way. Why should this little son of a sodbuster be different? Because he was Catholic? Arrogant little asshole.

"David," Alexander began, breaking the silence that had fallen following Danny's plea, "I don't doubt your good intentions. I don't doubt your abilities. And I don't doubt that you'd do well down there at St. Mark's. . . ."

"St. Mary's," Danny said flatly.

"St. Mary's," Alexander corrected himself. "But the bottom line is good business, boy. You simply don't have the collateral." God, how I love this, Alexander thought. It must be like playing a big fish like that big marlin on the wall. He personally didn't know. He hated fishing, and he had bought the trophy at the same furniture store where he had found the uncomfortable chair that didn't seem to be helping him out a bit with this kid.

"Daddy said . . ." Danny started in a whisper.

"Speak up, boy!" Alexander ordered.

"Daddy said he'd—he'd mortgage the farm," the kid blurted out.

Alexander had to struggle with himself to keep from laughing out loud. Mortgage the farm! It was ludicrous! The damned farm was already mortgaged to the hilt, probably for more than three times what it was worth, and the old man was in arrears two months at the moment for some new tractor parts he had bought to help him get ready for planting the previous April. Mortgage the farm! Alexander was amazed at the simple audacity of the idea. It sounded like something out of a melodrama. Mortgage the farm, indeed!

"I'm sorry, David," he finally managed to say without a trace of a smirk. "The board's decision is final." That was it, and Alexander breathed a sigh of relief. It was positively orgasmic, he thought. The big fish was landed.

All that remained was the blow to the head. "Maybe you could work for a year, save your money. Or maybe you could take some courses over to Vernon."

Danny shook his head and stood up. He was thin, but suddenly Alexander felt dwarfed by this kid in shiny pants and a pair of worn-out shoes. "It won't work," he said, "I wanted to go there to be a lawyer. The plan just won't work any other way. I can't earn enough even for tuition if I have to drive over and back all the time. The loan was the only way." He began to turn to go out. "That's it," he said softly.

Alexander felt something odd about the way things were developing. He was supposed to dismiss his supplicants, they weren't supposed to simply get up and walk away. That was the primary value of the damned chair. They were so relieved to be off the hot seat that they didn't mind when they didn't get the money. He hoisted his bulky body up onto his feet and shoved out his hand. "Look," he said as cheerily as he could, "no hard feelings. It's just business, boy, that's all."

Danny kept moving toward the office door, his back turned toward the banker's hand, his head down. "C'mon, David," Alexander said coaxingly.

The kid swung around sharply, his head snapping up, and his clear brown eyes locked on Alexander's pudgy face. "Danny, goddamn it! Daniel, you cheap, fat prick!" He spat out the words. His fists were clenched. He spun around quickly, ran his hands through his hair, visibly composing himself, then walked out the office door, shutting it quietly behind him.

Alexander was stunned. In his twenty years as a banker no one, *no one,* had ever used such language to him in his office, not even directed toward someone else in his presence. He was an elder in the Presbyterian church! Sweat broke out on his forehead, and he lurched around the desk toward the closed door. He was about to yell back at him, but all words faded in his mind and were replaced with a vision of himself flinging open the door and yelling, "Yah Yah!" at the back of the retreating boy.

Instead he stopped with one hand on the doorknob, pulled a handkerchief from his pocket, mopped his face, and shakily lowered himself into the attractive, uncomfortable chair. An unfamiliar emotion rose in him, and he gripped the arms of the chair as he felt nausea accompany it. What was it? Guilt? He couldn't believe it. He never felt guilty about this sort of transaction. It was just business. He had a responsibility to his depositors, and to his employees. He couldn't just go around handing out money to every kid who came in and claimed there was no other way. There were other ways: scholarships, ROTC stipends, government grants, work-study. Hell, there were ways this damn kid hadn't even heard of yet, hadn't even explored. Why should it be the bank's responsibility to fund his education? Alexander squeezed the bridge of his nose between two fingers. It wasn't the bank's fault that his old man was poor. So it wasn't the bank's fault that the kid couldn't go to some fancy-dan college.

Still, Alexander wondered what had caused the outburst. He hadn't been rude, and he hadn't been unsympathetic. He had said no, but surely the kid had known that he would. It should have been obvious.

The little shit was just *trying* to make me feel guilty, a voice in Alexander's head answered. Yeah! That's it. He was trying to get me to come around out of guilt. What the hell right does he have calling me *cheap*? College loans are just bad business. There's no real percentage there, anyhow. The damned kids move away from home and never come back to put money back into the community. The others the kid had mentioned, the Pruitt girl, the others—their parents were fine, upstanding people in the town. Hell, Bob Pruitt was an elder, too, and Alexander bought his refrigerated air conditioning for the bank from Terry Richardson, at a considerable discount. Mable Hargrove was Maddy's bridge partner. Shit, those loans were good for other business. What did old man O'Hara have to offer but dirt under his nails and the ruins of a '59 Edsel he somehow kept running? What concern should he show if the kid was ignorant of other financial alternatives? He wasn't the goddamn guidance counselor of Agatite High. Where was the goddamn priest who got him the scholarship and got his hopes up in the first place? Why didn't *he* tell him what he needed to know?

Business is business, Alexander thought, not wiping the nose of every shirttail kid that comes slinking in here. He was right. The kid cursed him out, and it would serve him right to have to get a job at hard labor at the gyp mill, work in his old man's fields. Teach him that he's not the only turd on the old toothpick, by-God!

Suddenly Alexander felt much better. He shifted his weight and realized that he was sitting on the hot seat, the uncomfortable chair, the shit seat. It didn't feel as bad as he remembered it feeling when it was new. Maybe it was getting worn out—or broken in. Maybe it was time for a little business trip down to Dallas to find a replacement.

He reached over the desk and took another Cuban cigar from the humidor. This is a two-smoke day, he thought as he neatly clipped the end with the cutter and replaced it in the vest pocket of his three-piece suit.

He rose and looked down at the chair again, lighting the cigar slowly and savoring the smoke. Yessir, he said to himself, about time for a replacement. I wonder what ol' Irma's up to this weekend?

IV. Breedlove
One Year Before

Breedlove felt decidedly scared. He also felt decidedly stupid. Even though the temperature in the small office of the Friendly Finance Company was cool, a trickle of sweat dripped down from his forehead onto his nose and hung there, not heavy enough to fall off but making its presence known, and forcing him to cross his eyes to look at it. He shook his head slightly, but it remained there, suspended. He didn't dare move his hand up to wipe it off. This was a crazy, nervous bunch, and a sudden move might bother them, spook them into some sort of stupid action, so he just watched the droplet and felt miserable.

On the floor four people—three women and an old man—lay stretched in prone positions, their heads down. One of the women was trembling. Breedlove let his eyes wander over to Mike Dix. Mike was perched on a stool he had dragged from behind the counter; he was watching the street, then moving his eyes down to one of the women whose legs were just far enough apart to reveal her hips and crotch under her hiked-up skirt. Breedlove suddenly felt embarrassed and disgusted, and he wanted to yell at her to put her legs together, for Chrissake! But he didn't. He said nothing and concentrated on the droplet of sweat that was becoming heavier and heavier on the end of his nose.

Behind the counter Joe Don McBride pushed the manager of the finance office around and ordered him about in loud whispers. Breedlove couldn't hear everything Joe Don was saying, but he could see the scared-rabbit look in the manager's eyes, which seemed to get larger and wider every time Joe Don poked him with the short-barreled pistol he held in the manager's ribs. Joe Don was a full head shorter than the manager, and he probably weighed thirty pounds less, but Joe Don had the gun, and he was letting the manager know who was boss by jamming him with it from time to time to punctuate his whispered orders and threats.

Breedlove looked down disbelievingly at the end of his own arm and studied the heavy pistol he gripped loosely in his hand. He had no sense of holding it, and it only casually covered the trembling figures on the floor. It was a nifty pistol, he thought, and he could faintly smell the gun oil from it as he waved it back and forth over the bodies he guarded. It had belonged to the security guard—the old man member of the prone quartet—and now it belonged to him. There would be some discussion about *that* later, he thought, but it was he, he reminded himself, who had come into this job armed with a cap pistol because that dumb shit Joe Don had spent too much of their money on cars and the getaway plan, and Breed-

love figured he had earned it by taking it off the guard in
the first place.

All of a sudden he noticed that the guard's pants were
becoming darker gray around his crotch and inner thigh.
Poor bastard's wet his pants, Breedlove thought casually,
and he looked over to see if Mike noticed. But Mike was
still focused on the legs and thighs of the secretary's
splayed figure. He's a fucking sex maniac, Breedlove almost said out loud, looking into the bloodshot eyes that
peered out from under a carpet of long, dirty, tangled
hair. Fucking sex maniac. Today, Breedlove decided, I
like him even less than usual, and I think I'm more scared
of him, too. He's liable to do anything. As they had
walked down the front of the office, Mike had taken a
moment to study his reflection in the store's window,
"Too much booze, too many drugs, not enough pussy,"
he'd diagnosed and laughed at the same time. He was
crazy. That much Breedlove was sure of.

"You're gonna open that fuckin' safe, an' you're gonna
open it right now!" Joe Don's voice suddenly rang clearly
and with a deadly distinction in the small office.

Breedlove noticed how Joe Don was jamming the pistol even harder into the manager's ribs. He's going to ruin
that suit, he thought. It was a nice cream-colored suit,
well-made, and the oil from that cheap pistol was going
to stain it for certain.

"For Chrissake, Tom, open the goddamn safe!" It was
one of the women on the floor, but which one Breedlove
couldn't tell.

"Watch 'em," Joe Don shouted at Breedlove, and then
lowered his voice in a sinister imitation of every cheap
Western Breedlove had ever seen, "If one of 'em twitches
an eyelash, waste 'em." Breedlove felt stupid again,
waving the pistol with sudden quickness over the figures
on the floor.

"Right!" he said, trying to sound tough.

Planning for this afternoon's robbery had been Joe
Don's passion for months. It had taken on the aura of a
game, something that reminded Breedlove of playing cops
and robbers with kids at school when he was a boy, and

even now, as he stood in the middle of the office covering the prone figures on the floor with a stolen pistol, he couldn't quite shake the feeling that they were all ten years old and their mothers would be calling them to supper.

But as he looked down at the pistol again, he knew it was no game. It looked like a .357 magnum, but he'd never seen one except on TV or in some cop's holster, and he knew he didn't know shit about handguns. He had wanted them to carry shotguns, but Joe Don had nixed that idea right off.

"One blast from a .12-gauge and you splatter some poor son of a bitch's guts all over the wall," he had announced like an expert. "Not that I mind killing one of these turkeys, but you know my first rule of business, 'Nobody gets hurt!' " He grinned reassuringly. "I don't want to shoot nobody if we don't have to, an' if we have to, I don't want to kill 'em."

Breedlove had gone along with this logic, even though he believed that a .45 or a .38 would likely be as deadly as a shotgun and was one hell of a lot harder to aim, but in the end they didn't get much in the way of armament at all. They got one snub-nosed .38 and a .22 cowboy pistol Mike carried. Breedlove wound up with a realistic-looking cap pistol because they ran out of money, and the only shotgun was a sawed-off 20-gauge Floyd carried in the car. But the other accessories Joe Don had insisted on were there. They all wore cheap suits, ties, gloves, hats, and even overcoats, even though it must have been over a hundred in the shade out in the street.

"The coats and cheap suits will throw off descriptions," Joe Don had explained when they all protested about having to put them on and wear them in such heat. "Everybody looks the same size and weight." All the clothes smelled of mothballs and other musty, dirty odors, since they had come from secondhand stores and junk shops, and Breedlove felt himself becoming slightly nauseated by the rising stink from his own heavy, hot outfit.

Joe Don had Tom on his knees at the back of the office,

stuffing bills from the safe into a duffel bag. Breedlove looked down at his four charges. The guard was now breathing funny, and the stain on his pants was enormous. Breedlove noticed lots of small, broken veins on the old man's cheek and briefly thought of his father, the old drunk. The guard's eyes were watery and he lay with his face on one side of the carpet gasping a bit. Christ, Breedlove thought, he must be over sixty. What the fuck's an old drunk like this doing guarding a finance office?

"You okay?" Breedlove asked the guard, touching his foot with the toe of his boot.

"You leave him alone!" One of the women, the one with the exposed crotch, looked up at him with an expression of absolute hatred on her face. "You just leave him alone, you son of a bitch!"

Breedlove started back, the heat from her hate almost overwhelming him.

"What in the name of bleeding Jesus is goin' on up there?" Joe Don yelled as he pushed Tom toward the front of the office into the well at one end of the counter. Tom looked scared, tired, and Breedlove thought he might pass out at any moment. He was panting. "Christ!" Joe Don yelled at Breedlove. "Keep that bitch quiet!"

The woman put her head back down, but Breedlove felt more stupid than ever, especially since he had felt sorry for her when Mike was looking at her. "You want me to gag her?" he said, trying to keep the sarcasm out of his voice.

"No, damn it." Joe Don turned away. "Just watch 'em, and if she mouths off again, blow her ass off." He grabbed Tom by the lapel of his jacket and kicked him behind the knee as he fell through the well, knocking him down across the two other women and partly onto the elderly guard who grunted loudly when Tom's body weight hit him. Tom's shoulder and chest covered the guard's fouled trousers; neither man moved at all. That suit's ruined now, Breedlove thought.

When Tom fell, one of the women screamed, and Joe Don reached out and grabbed her hips through her skirt.

She stiffened immediately. "That goes double for you, bitch," he hissed at her. "Got it?" He squeezed harder, grabbing a fistful of her hip in his hand. She nodded up and down and stifled sobs of pain as he let go. The guard mumbled softly.

"Watch it, fellah," Breedlove barked at the guard, touching the old man with his toe again, proud that he thought to speak before Joe Don had a chance to jump on him.

"Keep an eye on 'em," Joe Don said, moving over toward Mike. "You got that *stuff* ready?" he asked him, speaking loudly and emphasizing the word carefully.

"Right," Mike answered, taking a brown bag from under his overcoat. As they fussed with the bag, Breedlove kept his eye on the five bodies on the floor. The old guard was white and covered with sweat. Breedlove was sure he was having a stroke. What if he dies?

Before he could examine the old man more closely, Joe Don called him over to the door. "Okay, folks, y'all can get up now," he said in an almost congenial tone as if they had been hiding their eyes, waiting for a surprise of some sort. The bodies began to unpile and crawl to sitting positions, eventually pulling themselves up to their feet. The guard sat up also, but he didn't look good at all, and he kept grabbing his left arm. Breedlove moved over to Joe Don and Mike, and Mike took one quick look out at the street, then announced, "Do it."

Mike moved off the stool, and Joe Don countered behind him. The secretary who had exposed her legs jammed a fist into her mouth as Mike approached the clutch of employees, but he ignored her and swept off the papers and junk on top of the counter, hoisted himself up and over it, and moved over to the desks, taking out a large wire cutter and began cutting the phone cords leading to each desk. A sign had fallen in the pile of junk, and Breedlove read, "We Make Borrowing Money Fun!"

"Are there any more?" Mike asked in the general direction of Tom, who was now standing and holding a hand on his sore ribs.

"Don't ask *him*, for Chrissake!" Joe Don yelled, "Look!"

Mike looked into the office and even went into the back rooms. "That's it," he called out.

"Okay," Joe Don said, moving over to Tom and pulling him over to the door. Joe Don's scar was aflame with the excitement he was feeling. "See this?" He rammed his finger into a gob of gray sticking in the inside of the door's jam. A red wire ran from the center of the gob to the strip of burglar alarm tape on the window, and a white wire hung loose. "You know what this is, asshole?"

Tom looked at the gob dumbly. "Plastic explosive?" he asked like a kid in a science class.

"That's right, shit-for-brains." Joe Don grinned at him, widening his scar in a red jag across his face. "*Plastique*! It'll blow the shit outta you if you fuck with it." Tom stepped back involuntarily, bumping into Breedlove's gun and then, jumping forward, almost bowling Joe Don over. "You silly shit!" Joe Don yelled at the manager, grabbing his lapel again and throwing him up against the women. Tom tripped over the guard and almost knocked them all down like a bunch of dominos. "Now your phone is out, an' when we leave, we're gonna attach this little white wire to the outside lock. Anybody opens this door, you're all gonna fly to the moon! An' in case you get any ideas about bustin' this window with a chair or somethin', this alarm tape's connected too, an' the whole damned building's gonna go up!" Mike had moved back over the counter and lazily stood watching the dumbstruck hostages.

"The back door's connected, too," he said, "So just forget it." Tom looked uneasily out the window.

"Now, get this straight," Joe Don said in a low, threatening voice. "We don't want to kill nobody. We got the money, nobody got hurt, an' we're takin' off, so just hang around an' play post office or somethin' till the cops get here. I'm not kiddin'. This shit will blow you into little pieces."

The employees of the Friendly Finance Company

looked convinced. "Gimme your keys," Joe Don snapped at Tom.

Tom was cracking. He didn't move. "Gimme your fuckin' keys!" Joe Don yelled at him, waving his pistol around wildly. After a long minute one of the women turned and began going through Tom's pockets. She came up with a jangling ring of keys and threw them on the floor at Joe Don's feet. He reached down and picked them up, then gestured for the woman to come over to him. "Which one?" he asked.

She came slowly over and took the ring of keys, selecting one and then holding it out. Joe Don moved quickly and draped an arm around her, allowing his gun to fall down her chest with the barrel nuzzling the end of her right breast. Snaking out his tongue, he ran it into her ear, then he said in a loud whisper, "Sure you don't wanna come with us, Sugar? You got great tits, an' we'd be ever grateful."

With a frown of disgust she pulled away from him, and he raised his hand to strike her, but Breedlove suddenly found his nerve. "C'mon, let's go!" he said as urgently as he could.

Joe Don turned and looked at him hard to see if it was a command or a request, and deciding it must have been the latter, strode over to the door and began fooling with the gob.

Finally they stepped outside, feeling the heat of the street hit them squarely, like a wall. They pocketed their pistols, and Joe Don made a large business of attaching the wire with electrician's tape to the lock. He turned the key and threw it down on the sidewalk, tantalizingly close to the curb, and they all piled into the '72 Bonneville parked there. Floyd sat at the wheel, and with a glance into the mirror, he dropped the shifter into drive and they spun out of the parking space onto Main Street.

"Those dumb fucks'll sit there for days!" Joe Don laughed his high, mad laugh that Breedlove had come to dread, and suddenly the tension was broken. "Sixty-nine cents of Play-Doh, an' they'll sit there till hell freezes over." They were all laughing now. They had actually done it! Mike reached down onto the floorboard and came up with a six-pack, and Joe Don passed around cigarettes. They were hysterical with laughter as the car pulled out onto the highway and headed west.

The highway widened at the edge of town, and the Bonneville picked up speed. They rocked along at fifty-five, Floyd careful not to pick up a cop for driving too fast. He held the wheel easily, not even drinking one of the luke-warm beers Mike had offered him, for fear a passing patrol car might spot it.

Floyd Tatum was about as black a man as Breedlove had ever seen. Even the palms of his hands, usually pink on most of the Negroes Breedlove had known, were dark, and his eyes were deep brown, flecked with small veins that gave him the impression of looking out through tiny red spider webs from the blackness within him. He had met Joe Don in Vietnam, and while Joe Don allowed as how he'd never much cared for "members of the colored persuasion," Floyd was accepted readily into their gang. He was tall, graceful, and he never said much to anybody.

When he joined them for the first time, he sat down in a circle they had formed in the motel room in San Antonio and spoke softly. "All I ask you guys to do"—he looked around at the trio, gazing into each of their eyes— "is that you treat me like you treat each other and don't call me names. I'll do my share of the work, take my share of the risk, and I expect my share of the take." They sat silently, not answering him and feeling a little embarrassed by his formality, when he added, "If you do that, we'll get along. If you don't, I'll kill you." Breedlove knew he meant it. "One more thing," Floyd said, smiling a bit. "I don't go inside. All I do is drive. If I go inside, I'll get my black ass shot off in the redneck heavens you guys are planning to knock over."

That was acceptable to everyone, for Floyd's main talent lay under the hood of a car. He could do anything with a car, and cars were vital to the success of any robbery in the sparsely settled areas of north central Texas where they were planning to work. They all knew that.

Joe Don had wanted to buy new or at least good used cars, steal them if they couldn't buy them, but Floyd had laughed at that. He went around to junk yards and salvage shops and read the newspapers of three cities, putting together the cars they would use for their job. When the Bonneville had been towed into the garage at the house in Iowa Park they had rented as their hideout, Breedlove had almost laughed out loud. It was gutted inside, and the engine was a mass of junk—loose hoses, and wires that tangled and seemed to go nowhere. But in a week it was running, and the three of them scoured more junk yards for seats, body parts, even a passably complete top for the old convertible. Floyd had even painted it, explaining that it had to blend into traffic, and the rusty spots and dents would show up too easily.

"But this is the most important thing," he had lectured them as they sat around the garage and watched him work magic on the old wreck. "Nothin' must be stolen, and you never pay the first price." They had, therefore, haggled with junk and salvage dealers across Texas and southern Oklahoma for parts for the old Bonneville, and then for the big Mercury, and finally for the van, until they were all running.

The week before the robbery Floyd had invited them out into the garage where the two restored cars sat. "She'll do a hundred and fifty top end," he said, running a hand over the newly painted fender of the Bonneville, "and the shocks are heavy duty. So 're the springs." He moved over to the Mercury, but kept looking back at the Bonneville. "I also rebuilt the suspension, figuring if we have to get away in a hurry, we'll need a smooth ride for shooting back. The only problem is the gas mileage—it's shit the way I've got her souped up. But there's not much I can do about it and keep the power." They had nodded like schoolboys in a museum as he moved to open the door and sit inside the yellow Mercury. "She's fast, too, but I didn't do much to the suspension or body. She'll go farther than she'll go rough, but I think she'll do, since we ain't planning to take her off the highway. What we're going to need her for is speed more than anything.''

He got out and opened the garage door where the van sat parked in the driveway. It had black tinted windows each with miniblinds, and was painted bright red. Breedlove thought it looked like a rolling whorehouse, and he said so, but Floyd only laughed.

''She's stock,'' he said. ''She's not fast, but she's comfortable, and I think we could hide her in Dallas or Houston for a week just by driving her around.'' It was amazing that the three junks they had towed in from salvage yards had suddenly become such attractive vehicles. ''But here's the beauty of the whole thing,'' Floyd said as they admired the interior of the van. ''Legally, none of these cars exists.''

''What d'you mean.'' Mike spoke up. He didn't like Floyd much, and he didn't care much whether or not the mechanic knew it. ''They're not stolen.''

''Naw,'' Floyd said, flashing white teeth. ''They're not stolen. There's not a stolen part on any of them.'' He turned and opened his great arms. ''They don't exist because none of the vehicle identification numbers match. They all go to different cars. Even the plates are altered. Man, they couldn't trace one of these cars to anybody.''

When the cars were finally ready, Joe Don gave them all the final plan. Floyd, of course, would drive and would wait for them in front of the finance company office. Mike would watch the street from inside, and Breedlove would hold the hostages until Joe Don got the money. ''If nobody panics,'' Joe Don had coolly told them, ''we should make a clean getaway. And,'' he added, grinning, ''nobody gets hurt.''

Their money, coming as it did from petty larceny and minor holdups carried out by Mike and Joe Don, each in his own particular fashion, had begun to run low. The rent, cars and parts, and other incidental expenses, including the motel rooms in which they had to meet when they were hunting for parts and other necessities, the cheap suits and overcoats, gasoline and food had taken

all but about seventy bucks of their original reserve. That
was all, in fact, they had left for weapons.

Breedlove would have said something angry to them
about not thinking about it sooner, but he realized his
position was weak. He had not participated in any more
robberies since the one incident at the drive-in movie in
San Antonio; he'd gotten himself a job washing dishes in
a couple of restaurants to bring in a few bucks rather than
take another unnecessary risk with the madman he had
come to believe Mike Dix was. In fact, he'd wanted to
pull out more than once, but he knew he was in too far,
and he feared that they wouldn't let him go. Ironically,
he was relieved when he realized that they would have
no guns, as he was also afraid they might have to use
them in spite of Joe Don's constant assurance that no one
was to be hurt. But Mike found the .22 on sale in a
Wichita Falls K-Mart for twenty bucks, and the .38 had
turned up in the classifieds in the same city, a bargain at
thirty dollars, which they had talked down to twenty-five.
They got the cap pistol at a Ben Franklin store in Iowa
Park and they were set.

When they'd walked into the Friendly Finance Company in Jolly, Texas, they'd had only two dollars and
change among them. The beer and cigarettes had taken
the last of their funds, but now in the smoothly running
Bonneville, cruising west through Wichita Falls on U.S.
287, they had a white duffel bag full of bills and silver
dollars cleaned from the tills of the small lending company.

The inside of the Bonneville was stiflingly hot as the
three "inside men" changed from their overcoats and
suits into more comfortable and less conspicuous attire.
Breedlove squeezed into his Levi's and yoke shirt, Mike
into Levi's and a T-shirt that announced "ZZ Top," and
Joe Don into a rather plain set of khakis and a sports
shirt. Changing clothes in a moving car was a tricky
business, but they needed to take care of it quickly and
get ready to change cars.

Breedlove thought he had dropped the pistol he had
taken from the guard on the floorboard of the backseat,

and he began searching for it. It turned up between the
seat and the armrest, and he checked it quickly and stuck
it into his belt under his shirt. It looked stupid as hell,
he thought, but he wasn't about to give it up, not now.
He didn't reason that his cut of the take would buy him
a mountain of pistols, only that he had won this one by
taking it off the guard, even if the guard had been old
and sick. He couldn't get the picture of the old man out
of his mind, however, and the vision of him pissing all
over himself kept haunting him. But the pistol seemed to
comfort him.

By the time they had changed, they arrived at the small
roadside park where the Mercury had been left that
morning. They hadn't said much since finishing the beer,
and they continued their silence as they stuffed the suits
into one of the barbecue grills near the picnic tables and
poured gasoline all over them. Mike struck a match to
light the bundle of cheap clothes, and Joe Don opened
the trunk of the Mercury and stuffed the duffel inside.
Floyd started up the Mercury, and soon they were on
their way, still keeping an uncommon silence among
them, passing back through Wichita Falls in the opposite
direction from their original escape.

When they passed through Jolly, Joe Don lit a cigarette
and Breedlove held his breath. They came even with the
street where the Friendly Finance Company waited, and
they looked down toward the small office, almost exhal-
ing together when they saw no one nearby, no police cars
pulling up in front, nothing to indicate that a major armed
robbery had taken place a half-hour before. When Jolly
disappeared behind them and blank highway loomed
ahead, Joe Don finally laughed his high, crazy laugh and
broke the silence.

"Sixty-nine cents worth of Play-Doh!" he screamed
out. Breedlove thought Joe Don was going to choke on
the words, he was laughing so hard. They all joined in
the mirth, but it was unlike the laughter of relief they had
enjoyed when they'd pulled out of Jolly. The shock of
what they had done had worn off, and now the realization
that they were actually going to get away with it was

giving all of them a euphoric high. They suddenly began talking all at once, laughing and slapping each other on the shoulder, reliving moments of the event.

"By God, we *are* something!" Joe Don screamed through fits of laughter.

"Once"—Floyd had to shout to make himself heard over the din in the car—"a sheriff's car came by, and I thought we'd bought it."

"Did you see ol' Tom's face when I showed him the *plastique*?" Joe Don cried.

"Man, I'd like to bang that little secretary," Mike said, pulling at the crotch of his Levi's.

"That old man guard pissed all over himself," Breedlove said, and immediately a wash of guilt came over him. He felt he shouldn't have said that. It seemed private. He felt ashamed.

"Which one?" Joe Don asked.

"The guard," Breedlove said, then more softly, "The old man."

"Which *secretary*? Asshole." Joe Don corrected him. He had been asking Mike.

"The one with the big tits. The blonde. The one you snuggled up to," Mike laughed. "She was wantin' it too. You should have seen the way she opened up her beaver through the whole thing on the floor. Man, she was hot!" He turned up his beer and drained it. "Maybe next time we'll take hostages," he said, tossing his beer can out the window.

"Hey, man," Floyd yelled, no longer mirthful. "Stop that shit! You want us to get stopped for littering?" Mike started to laugh. "I'm not shittin' you, man." Floyd's eyes narrowed in the mirror as he cut Mike off. "Don't throw nothin' out while I'm in here."

"Naw, no hostages," Joe Don said quickly before Mike could get angry and respond. "They get in the way. They get hurt. Man! Nobody got hurt! Do you realize that? We got away clean, and *nobody got hurt!*"

"I think that old man had a stroke," Breedlove said softly, halfway hoping no one would hear.

"What old man?" Floyd asked, turning slightly, a cigarette dangling from his mouth.

"The guard," Breedlove said, suddenly feeling too tired even to check out Mike or Joe Don's reaction to what he was saying.

"Shit," Joe Don said suddenly. "That ain't our fault. What if he did? The main thing, man, is that nobody got shot! *We* didn't hurt nobody!" He looked around at the three men in the car, then he finally settled his gaze on Breedlove's face. "Right?"

Breedlove let less than a second pass before he responded with a nod. "Right. Nobody got hurt." Joe Don grinned and his scar flashed. Breedlove stared out the window of the car, watching the sunbaked mesquite flash by along the side of the highway. No, he thought, nobody got hurt, at least not yet.

PART 2

He entered in the house—his home no more,
   For without hearts there is no home—and felt
The solitude of passing his own door
   Without a welcome: *there* he long had dwelt,
   There his few peaceful days Time had swept o'er,
There his warm bosom and keen eye would melt
Over the innocence of that sweet child,
His only shrine of feelings undefiled.

               —*Don Juan*
                  George Gordon, Lord Byron

1

I. Breedlove
The Present, Eight Months Before

Winter shrieked down the main street of Oklaunion,
Texas, bringing with it billows of dust and tumbleweeds
from the cedar breaks and fields north of the small town.
Inside the Holiday Finance Company, Breedlove stood
holding a nickel-plated .45 automatic on five nervous and
frightened people, three employees and two customers of
the small loan office, while Joe Don McBride pushed Alvin Atwood, the company manager, up and down the
counter, prodding him with the barrel of a long-john .38
special. Mike Dix, like the time before, watched the
street through the door, only this time he didn't have a
stool to sit on, and he didn't have the time to pare his
nails and gaze up the skirt of some woman who didn't
have sense enough to keep her legs together.

This time Breedlove kept the hostages standing up.
There were too many windows in front for them to lie
down and maybe tip off a passerby to what was going on
inside. In fact, the whole face of the building was one
big plate-glass window, and even though the twenty-five-
mile-an hour icy-cold blasts that raced down the street
kept people indoors or hurrying past with collars turned
up and hat brims down, Breedlove didn't want to be
caught looking at the floor when the local law drove by.
And he was about half sure the sheriff or somebody would
ride by at any moment. He wanted the greenhorn deputy
who was supposed to be on patrol, according to Mike's
information, anyway, to see folks standing around, looking as natural as they could be made to look at the point
of a gun.

This time there was more tension than the last, and the

whole operation had a sour taste from the start. Just like last time, there had been the carefully drawn map and the detailed plans, and just like last time, there were the car switches arranged. Breedlove could see Floyd behind the wheel of the big Chrysler out at the curb; the exhaust trailed quickly into the blowing wind and disappeared into the dust rushing south. This was a by-God blue norther, Breedlove thought, and the weather was supposed to be "cool but fair." What else was going to go wrong?

Plenty had gone wrong already. Besides the weather, there had been the goddamn customers, he mused, shifting the .45 from low at his side to a slightly higher position in order to remind his charges that he was "armed and dangerous," as the phrase went. There were two of them. A sickly-looking old lady and a guy who looked like a football coach, wearing a by-God Ban-Lon shirt and a windbreaker with the local high school emblem on it like it was seventy degrees and sunny outside instead of ball-busting freezing wintertime in north central Texas.

"This dude, Alvin Atwood," Joe Don had said back in Dallas while he picked his teeth with a toothpick taken from the Wendy's Old-Fashioned Hamburger bag, "is a ripoff artist."

Mike had almost fallen off the bed laughing at that, Breedlove recalled, and he also remembered how stupid it was for them, a bunch of second-rate robbers, to condemn a man for making a few honest bucks loaning money, even if his interest rates were too high.

"He loans money to teachers and other state employees against their monthly paychecks," Joe Don continued, his scar widening as he warmed to the story. "Then he goes around to the schools and places 'long about the fifteenth when folks are strapped for a few bucks, and offers to let them borrow more against what they got comin' on the first. Then, on the first, they got to pay it all back. Every blessed penny, plus a healthy little interest charge, *plus* a goddamn handlin' fee."

"So?" Floyd belched his hamburger and went back to

the motel room's table where he had a C.B. radio disassembled. "Sounds s.o.p. to me."

"Maybe so," Joe Don went on, lighting a cigarette and blowing the smoke out through his nostrils, "but after a few months folks find that the little fucker is gettin' more an' more of their check, so each month they got less an' less to make the month on. 'Course, he'll gladly increase the loan, if you want 'time payments,' but by then people have paid in all their checks an' they got to put up their furniture, car, or maybe even their houses an' farms to get the money to live on."

"Farms?" Breedlove asked quietly. He had lost the logic of Joe Don's argument, but he knew that once the little man began planning a job and justifying his reasons, there was no stopping him. "I thought you said they were state workers?"

"It's like the goddamn company store!" Joe Don announced loudly, ignoring Breedlove as he sat up and opened a Samsonite briefcase where the plans and maps were.

"Look," Mike said as he recovered himself from laughing and plucked around in the cardboard bowl of French fries, "I don't care if we rob the son of a bitch blind. But let's skip the sermon, okay?"

Breedlove got the point. Mike wasn't in this business for the kicks or for some kind of perverse revenge against people who loaned money the way Joe Don seemed to be. Mike wanted the money. And Floyd seemed to be there for the profits, too. Neither one of them cared very much for Joe Don's sermons, as they called them. In fact, they didn't care much for the excitement or the danger—the things Joe Don seemed to love. Breedlove was convinced that their leader would go ahead with a job even if he knew there was no money in the place. He just wasn't interested in money. He seemed only to have taken a special dislike to loan companies and banks, but Breedlove didn't know why.

Another thing Breedlove didn't know was what *he* was doing there. He sure as hell didn't like the excitement or danger, had nothing in particular against loan companies, and he felt certain—and had said so more than once since their last job—that there was an easier way to make money. But he kept quiet and went along. He felt he couldn't get out now, at least not without getting hurt or maybe killed by one of these maniacs.

He almost laughed out loud when he thought about the money. He didn't have shit to show for the first job, since Joe Don had ploughed their "profits" into the second attempt without even asking them about it. They had gotten wildly drunk in Fort Worth the weekend after, and Breedlove lost count of the whores Mike and Joe Don brought back to their Hyatt Regency hotel room, but after the initial fling, they were back to spartan living and scrimping and saving like they'd had to do before their first robbery.

In the past seven months they had been in twelve or fourteen different motels and hotels, each cheaper than the last. They had planned to rent another house near Wichita Falls, but Mike checked and found that nobody had gone near the old one. Their tools and stuff were still in the garage, and the neighbors had even piled up the newspapers and junk mail on a table on the back porch. It was laughable. Joe Don moved back in and sent the landlord six months' rent in advance along with the back payments, explaining that he frequently had to go to Mexico on business and never knew how long he would be out of the country. It was goddamn stupid, Breedlove thought. Cops couldn't be that stupid, and if their luck didn't run out on the house, it would run out somewhere else.

But there they were on their second job, and all of Joe Don's assurances about their being "pros" had evaporated the second they had walked into the Holiday Finance Company office and Breedlove had felt the intense urge to piss. He fought it down, but he figured that they were all as nervous as he was, and at any minute the world was going to blow up. God, he thought, I want a drink.

Joe Don was pushing Alvin around, but he wasn't as hard on the manager here as he had been on Tom the time before. They couldn't count on using the *"plas-tique"* bluff again, but Joe Don knew of a back room with an outside lock, and they could shove Alvin and his employees and customers in there. Breedlove couldn't see the room from where he watched the hostages, but he hoped it was more than a closet, big enough for everyone. The coach was good-sized.

Mike, although not as cool as he had been the time before, kept glancing up and down the street and smiling at the hostages with an evil leer. He was showing his yellowed, snarled teeth and occasionally making kissing and sucking noises whenever one of the women looked over at him. An occasional car or pickup passed by, but mostly the downtown area of the small town was deserted in the afternoon norther's fury. Breedlove could see Floyd light up another cigarette in the rapidly fogging-up car, and he wished Joe Don would hurry. Then it all went sour, all at once.

Coach made a little movement, like he was scratching his back, and Breedlove watched him do it, then dropped his eyes down to the .45. It was a nifty pistol, he thought, and he was proud to have it. Joe Don had bought it especially for him, he said, because he raised so much hell about having to give up the .357 he took off the guard at Jolly. All of them had new guns—Joe Don's .38, Mike's .44 magnum—"Just like Dirty fuckin' Harry," he had said when Joe Don unwrapped it from the oilcloth—and even the two shotguns they kept in the car were brand-new. Joe Don had spent three weeks buying them, and he had driven all over Dallas and had even gone over to Louisiana for one of them to spread out the purchases. It had been a damned waste of time and money as far as Breedlove was concerned, but Joe Don had insisted on doing it in case one of them got caught or dropped one of the pistols in some kind of mix-up. Breedlove secretly suspected that Joe Don used the gun buying trips to try to score dope of some kind, but if he did, he never said anything about it, so Breedlove let Joe Don do as he wanted. He controlled the money anyway.

Breedlove was contemplating the pistol when he caught

sight of another handgun, this time emerging from under the coach's windbreaker. He thought very slowly: Okay, he's got a gun. So what? You got him beat all to hell. Just point the .45 at him and tell him to drop it. It seemed so simple, and Breedlove saw himself acting out the scene and receiving Joe Don's approving smile. "Nobody gets hurt," the short man always said, and that had always been fine with Breedlove.

Breedlove had long ago made the decision that if it really ever came down to shooting, he would just drop his gun and throw up his hands the way the bad guys always did in the movies. He wasn't a hero, he knew, and he wasn't about to get shot over a bunch of money he probably would never see anyhow. If bullets were flying, he had resolved, he'd just fall on the floor and scream that he gave up. The decision was firm in his mind, and he was certain he could do it, but he didn't count on something happening that would make his plan impossible.

Coach kept pulling the pistol out, almost as if he were moving in slow motion, watching Breedlove and flicking his eyes toward Joe Don behind the counter with Alvin. Suddenly the sickly old woman saw what he was up to, and before Breedlove could order him to drop the small pistol, she screamed, "Oh! No! Don't!!" and Joe Don whirled around. Breedlove's eyes left the coach for a fraction of a second to see what Joe Don was up to, and the next thing he knew an explosion deafened his left ear. He began to fall, feeling his knees buckling beneath him, then he caught himself. Suddenly everybody was shouting, and explosions continued to echo in the small office.

"Shoot the son of a bitch!" Joe Don was screaming as he held Alvin by his coat lapel and shook him back and forth. One of the secretaries was also screaming, and two of the others were bawling and crying. The male employee fell to his knees, crossed himself, and started praying. The last secretary was hanging onto Coach, trying to get into his arms, spoiling his aim as he blasted with the snub-nosed pistol in all directions.

Coach's gun wavered, and Breedlove saw a blast come

out of the tiny barrel, followed by what he swore was flame. He unconsciously followed the bullet's imagined trajectory and saw a black hole appear two inches over Mike's head. Mike held his head in his hands as he slid down the wall toward the floor. If he hadn't been sliding down like that, Breedlove dumbly commented to himself, he'd have taken the slug in the forehead. Breedlove felt detached from the chaos going on around him. Then he noted with horror that blood was spurting from between Mike's fingers. He'd been shot! The goddamn coach had shot him!

Breedlove's head snapped back toward the coach. He realized that the last bullet the struggling man had fired hadn't been meant for Mike at all, but for him. The silly woman had broken his aim and he'd missed, that's all. He'd missed Breedlove and hit Mike.

"Goddamn it to *hell*!" Joe Don screamed from behind the counter, "Shoot that son of a bitch before he kills somebody!" Alvin had begun to struggle with the shorter and lighter Joe Don, and Joe Don had all he could to do keep from getting slugged. His own pistol was gripped like a club, and he was trying to pound Alvin's head with it, but Alvin was too tall, and Joe Don kept struggling and weaving out of reach. Together, the two men looked as if they were performing some bizarre dance to the music of gunfire and terrorized screams, and Breedlove found it remarkably funny.

The humor of Joe Don's struggle with Alvin passed quickly, however, as Coach's pistol fired once more, this time into the office ceiling. Breedlove turned his attention to Coach. Breedlove didn't pause to think about what he was doing; he just pulled the trigger on the .45. The first sensation he noticed was that the gun started to rise of its own accord, and he realized that he was emptying the clip and eased pressure on the trigger before he riddled everyone in front of him. The recoil from the individual blasts was terrific, and he felt the gun pinch his hand as it barked. The sound of the shots reached his ears next. Whereas Coach's small pistol had exploded in spite of its size, the .45 blasted—there was no other word

for it—it sounded like a goddamn cannon. He saw
Coach's eyes enlarging as the flash from the .45 continued, and he noticed that the secretary's skirt that almost
touched the coach's leg began to ripple. Her mouth was
wide open, and she must be screaming bloody murder,
Breedlove thought, but the noise from the .45 covered it.
Then she pitched forward. Behind her three gaping, black
holes suddenly appeared in the paneling of the office wall.
But, amazingly, there was no blood. She had fainted in
time.

Coach stood stock-still for what seemed to Breedlove
like several minutes. He had an uncertain look on his
face, as if he expected to feel pain from his wounds at
any second, when nothing happened, he pulled his gun
hand up again in Breedlove's direction and prepared to
fire. Breedlove froze. This is it, he thought, but he
couldn't make himself move. All at once a ragged red
hole opened in one of Coach's blue eyes and his head
snapped back and struck the wall behind him. A stream
of blood shot out almost as far as where Breedlove stood.
The secretary on the floor was drenched with the gore,
and the praying man found himself splattered with bright
red drops. Another secretary and the sickly old woman
immediately drew themselves up tight, trying to avoid the
blood that now seemed to cover the entire area.

As Breedlove continued to watch, amazed, a second
circle of blood appeared on Coach's Ban-Lon shirt, and
he seemed to throw his whole body against the paneling,
then pitch forward, leaving blood and brains smeared on
the mahogany wall. He fell directly over the cringing
secretary, dropping his pistol. The back of his windbreaker was blown up, as if he had exploded from the
inside through his back, and something looking like his
stomach appeared in the hole. Breedlove felt his stomach
sink and his throat constrict. He had never seen anything
like this before, he thought. Hell, he'd never even imagined such a thing was possible.

The praying man moved slightly toward Coach's body
and, Breedlove noticed, toward the gun, which looked
like a very small-caliber automatic. "Don't," Breedlove

said in what he hoped was a firm voice, noting the silence that had descended on the small office, and the man moved back to his praying position and began to mutter.

Breedlove backed slowly up to the counter and looked over at Mike, who was now in a sitting position on the floor, holding his left hand over his cheek and eye and focusing down his right arm, which had the long barrel of the .44 at its end. The gun was still smoking. "Got the son of a bitch! Joe Don, I got him," Mike said, almost choking on the words. The .44! Breedlove realized, that's what had made that hole and blown the coach's guts clean out of his body. "Jesus Christ on a crutch," Breedlove whistled under his breath, "Deliver me."

Mike now had all the hostages covered. Those who were conscious were weeping softly, afraid to look up at the men who threatened them. Breedlove glanced over at Joe Don. He stood, also pointing his pistol at the fallen man, "Me too," he almost whispered. "I shot his fuckin' eye out." Breedlove noticed that Joe Don's scar, which was usually blood-red at moments of high excitement, was pale and almost blue. The rest of his face was drained of any color at all, and in his teeth the butt of a cigar he had been smoking when they entered the office remained bitten off. He seemed stiff armed, holding his pistol in his right hand and cradling both with his left in a three-point paramilitary style.

Alvin was slumped over a desk behind the counter. His face was bloody and pulpy with naked cartiladge sticking out his nose. Joe Don had pistol-whipped him into submission when the shooting had become too dangerous to fool around any longer. He was, Breedlove realized, unconscious or worse.

"Let's get outta here!" Breedlove heard himself say, surprised to find that he could speak in little more than a whisper. His throat was parched, and his tongue felt like leather. He noticed his hands were shaking. God, did he ever need a drink, he found himself thinking.

"Not without the money," Joe Don said, and suddenly as if a trance had held him and suddenly lifted, he broke his stance and began to gather up fallen bills and stuff them into a duffel bag.

"Fuck the money!" Mike cried out from his place on the floor. He still held his pistol on the hostages, who were now terrorized even beyond crying. They looked at the hacked-up corpse of the coach, which still lay atop the unconscious secretary, smothering her with entrails and blood.

Mike was hurt bad, Breedlove decided; blood still streamed from Mike's hand and covered his coat and shirt front. His voice was almost pleading. Breedlove reached into his coat pocket and pulled out a freshly loaded clip and exchanged it for the depleted one in his .45, glancing out to see if Floyd was still there. He was.

Joe Don had ignored Mike's plea and was sweeping up bills, knocking Alvin onto the floor to grab some more that were on the desk and under the chair where he had fallen. "Who knows how to open this safe?" he yelled at the group clustered around Coach's body. They had all turned to look at him with wide, expectant eyes. None of them moved or said anything. The praying man even shut up.

"Look, goddamn it," Joe Don shouted at them as he moved through the swinging door partition at the counter's end and pointed his pistol down at Coach's body, "We've got nothin' to lose now. John Wayne here seen to that! Now, 'less you want to join him in eternal fuckin' peace, you better goddamn open that fuckin' safe!" He was breathing hard, and his voice turned almost into a squeak as he finished his speech. His scar was flaming red again, and the cigar butt was still clenched in his teeth.

"You better do like he says," Breedlove found himself saying. The pistol was still hot in his hands. It burned his fingers, and his palm hurt where the mechanism had pinched him when he fired it. He didn't want to see any more blood. He didn't want to kill anybody. "Come on," he said, and silently added, Don't you see he's crazy? Open the goddamn safe!

After a long moment one of the secretaries stood up

and wiped blood from her hand on her pants' leg. "I can open it," she said, "but don't kill anybody else." It sounded more like a threat than an offer, but Joe Don stepped back and motioned for her to precede him through the swinging gate toward the steel box in the back of the office.

As she worked on the combination, finally getting the door open and standing aside while Joe Don shoved bills into the duffel, Breedlove noticed a foul odor in the office. He could smell the gunpowder, naturally, and that warm wet smell of blood and guts floating up from the coach's body too, but there was something else, something strong that added to the other smells. His ear was hurting from the first blast of the coach's pistol, and inside his head a ringing had started, but the smell was getting stronger. It smelled like shit.

He looked doubtfully at the coach's body. He'd always heard that dead men shit, when they lose control or something, but there was no stain on the dead man's pants, and the smell was getting stronger than ever. He shifted his weight a bit, wishing he could just lay the .45 down and walk away, out of the office into the cold wind outside. His jaw hurt, and he realized that he'd been clamping it shut ever since the whole thing started. He felt something wet trickle down his leg. I've pissed myself, he thought, looking down. No! he thought, suddenly filled with shame and terror, I've shit my pants. Like a goddamn baby! He felt awful. He wanted to vomit. Why not? he thought, fighting back the nausea, I've done everything else wrong today.

Joe Don came through the swinging doors behind him. He still had the cigar butt clamped in his teeth, and he shoved the duffel, which he had carried with both hands, into Breedlove's midsection. Breedlove grabbed it with his left hand and hefted it. It was heavy. There must be close to a hundred grand, he thought. "Come on," Joe Don said to him. "Help me with Mike."

They moved over to their wounded comrade, who had dropped his gun hand and was now semiconscious. They lifted him up between them, but they couldn't pry his

hand away from his face. He was still bleeding freely,
and both of them found his clothes sticky. Joe Don turned
to the hostages who had watched all their movements in
stark silence. The praying man was now squirming a bit,
his lips moving quietly. "Look," Joe Don said to them,
"we're gonna leave now. Don't nobody do nothin' stupid
till we've gone. Fifteen minutes. Please." This last he
added in a strange tone of voice that made Breedlove
think of a small boy asking for a special favor. But the
group didn't move.

Suddenly the praying man stood up and spoke in a firm
voice. "This man needs a doctor," he said, pointing
toward Coach.

Joe Don laughed his high, shrill, crazy laugh that
Breedlove had come to loathe. A hyena's laugh, Breed-
love often thought when he heard it, a jackal's laugh.
"Man," Joe Don said, "all he needs is an undertaker.
An' if I see anybody move outta here or try to use a
phone, you're gonna need one too!"

At that moment Breedlove realized that Joe Don was
supporting Mike with both hands. He recalled that Joe
Don had toted the duffel bag with both hands also. Where
was his gun? His eyes moved quickly to Joe Don's waist-
band to search for it, but it was gone. Where the hell
was it? Almost as if in answer to his question, the plate-
glass window in front of the office shattered into a hail-
storm of splinters, and noise and the bark of Joe Don's
.38 hit Breedlove's other ear.

"God fuckin' damn! She's got my gun!" Joe Don
yelled, dropping to the floor on top of Mike, who
screamed in pain.

Breedlove saw himself spin around and raise the .45
toward the figure of the secretary who had opened the
safe. She stood in a perfect three-point stance, cradling
the pistol in her left hand and squeezing off another shot
with her right. From the corner of his vision Breedlove
saw the shoulder of the praying man explode in a red
burst as the bullet clipped its top. Suddenly the .45
blasted in response. The explosions were deafening, and
Breedlove had to fight to keep the barrel down. Even so,

he watched as four black holes riddled a bulletin board
on the wall behind the safe. He was missing her. He was
frightened, and this time he felt his sphincter muscle relax and allow what was left in his bowels leak out. He
fought to aim at the girl, but his eyes clouded over and
he couldn't focus.

The girl had dropped to the floor as soon as he raised
his pistol toward her, and now she emerged from behind
the desk, dazed and startled, still holding the pistol in
her right hand, but not in a threatening way. Breedlove
almost laughed at the shocked expression on her face.
She looked for all the world like a lost child who suddenly finds herself in a strange place surrounded by mon-
sters. Her hair strung all about her face, and her cheeks
and mouth were streaked with the coach's blood, now
dry and dark like mud.

Breedlove held his fire. As soon as she rose high
enough to see over the counter, she spotted him standing
there with the smoking .45 in his hand, and she ducked
down again. He stepped over Alvin's still unconscious—
Jesus, I hope he's not dead, too, Breedlove thought—
body, and went over to the girl. She looked like a
cornered rabbit, but she handed him the pistol before he
got there really, butt first, as if it were red hot.

He took it and stuck it in his belt, grabbing her suddenly by the blouse to pull her up onto her feet. The
material gave way, and the buttons popped off, and he
caught a flash of white brassiere before she stuck a hand,
stained and streaked with blood, over her partly exposed
breasts, grasping at the remnants of the patterned shirt.
"You gonna rape me, too?" she asked him, fixing her
bright blue eyes on his in sudden defiance. But there was
no defiance in her voice, only resignation, as if she fully
expected him to rape her and then, he supposed, to kill
her. After all, she had tried to kill him—them—he suddenly thought.

"Just get over there with the others," he said, shoving
her gently by the arm, trying to make his voice soft,
understanding. She was pretty, he thought, in spite of the
hair, now sweaty and hanging in her face, the ripped

blouse, and the blood, which was everywhere on her. There was a big splotch of blood running down her neck, dried and almost amber in the office light.

She moved slowly toward the counter, tripping over Alvin a bit, and glancing back over her shoulder at Breedlove to see, he guessed, if he would shoot her in the back the way she had tried to shoot him. He wanted to tell her that this was all one big mistake. He was really not a bad guy. He wasn't a bank robber, a killer.

"Hey, shithead," Joe Don called. "What're you doin'? Shoppin' for a sex charge, too?" Joe Don was back on his feet and leaning on the counter; splinters of blood crossed his face where the glass from the breaking window had cut him. He held Mike up with one arm and trained the .44 on the huddled hostages, who were shivering now that the office's heat had disappeared into the arctic blasts that swept the street. "You know what I ought to do?" Joe Don sneered at the secretary, who swung the gate open defiantly and joined the huddle. "I ought to shoot every goddamn one of you."

Breedlove moved to the counter and swung over. He noticed the praying man leaning against the wall, still muttering. His shoulder was bleeding, but the cold was having its effect, and he didn't look that bad. "Let's get the fuck outta here," he said to Joe Don.

Joe Don looked at the people. He spat out the cigar butt all of a sudden, and then bent over and started heaving. At first Breedlove thought he had been shot, and, drawing the .38 out of his belt, he waved both it and the .45 toward the crowd, searching for the next hostage who had managed, somehow, to get a gun. The secretaries started screaming again, but Joe Don quickly recovered himself and straightened up. "You people make me puke," he said, and laughed his high, mad laugh once again. "C'mon." He gestured to Breedlove. "Let's go."

Breedlove picked up the duffel and followed Joe Don and the limping Mike out the door of the office. They could have as easily stepped over the window molding, as there was now a gaping hole in the office's front, but no one thought to go that way. As he left, Breedlove noticed the hostages were beginning to crawl behind the counter, dragging both the praying man and the unconscious secretary with them. "I'm sorry," he heard himself whisper, but before he could worry about whether or not they—or Joe Don—heard him, Joe Don broke in with a shout.

"God fuckin' damn!" he yelled over the gale that swept around them.

Breedlove spun around and raised his gun again, but his hand stopped halfway in its rise. He stared in disbelief at the empty parking space in front of the loan company. Floyd and the car were gone.

II. Lawman
August, The Present, One Day Before

Reloading the .44 Colt, Able Newsome finished his regular target practice in a pasture a few miles from Agatite and strolled back to his cruiser. It had been one hell of a week, he thought, shaking away droplets of sweat that ran into his eyes from his hat brim. First he found Eileen's body, then he had to deal with that jackass Jingles every day, sniffing around the office like a hungry dog, trying to get the jump on anything that turned up in the way of a clue. Then there had been the Castlereigh thing. God, he thought, leaning against the car as he lit a Hava-Tampa Jewel and drew the searing smoke deeply into his lungs. What the hell was happening to people? What a week!

He hadn't ever seen anything like the Castlereigh thing. He was almost certain there was more to it than anybody was telling. But they were keeping goddamn tight-lipped about it. Castlereigh's fingers had been broken, for one thing. Why? And that lifeguard, Vicki, had looked sicker than the corpse she had pulled out of the pool. Why was she fully dressed when Able got there if she was supposed to be on duty? he wondered. For that matter, where the hell was Castlereigh's suit? The whole thing didn't make sense, and they were playing him for a fool. Able didn't like that.

But none of them was about to talk, not even Jeff Randall, who should by-God talk, Able thought, since as soon as Doc Pritchard retired for good, Jeff was going to be county coroner, and Able needed to trust him. But none of them was saying shit, and Able was more concerned about the fact that they were all covering up something than what they might be hiding.

The Sandhill County sheriff had never liked or trusted Bill Castlereigh. He knew too much about what went on in the "consulting" sessions Castlereigh conducted in his office, since he had had more than one angry husband in the Sheriff's Office complaining about it. He also knew what Wilma did, too damned well, he thought with a rushing mixture of shame and embarrassment. She was the one black mark on his personal record, and she bothered him as a result. She was also the one thing that kept him from doing anything more about investigating Bill Castlereigh's death.

He had been getting calls about Bill and Wilma off and on ever since they moved into town. People had found out that their husbands, wives, sons, and daughters were being sexually involved with these two new people, and Able didn't know what to do about it. Without complaints by those who were actually having sex with either of them, or without witnesses to indecent behavior, there wasn't a thing he could do to them. And if he did make an arrest or follow up a complaint, what was he supposed to do with Bill or Wilma's partner, assuming the partner was of age and consenting? Mostly he just listened to outrage and indignation, but when Frances Brooks called him, he had to act.

Frances and he went back to high school. She had married Donald Brooks, an accountant, and they had one son, a boy, David, who was just now away at college. He had been barely out of high school, however, when he found his way to Wilma's back door with some regularity, according to Frances, and as soon as word got back to Donald, he exploded. Unable to keep her husband calm about it, Frances finally got him to agree to let Able handle it, but Frances warned the sheriff that if he didn't handle it, Donald was planning to take a shotgun and go over there and handle it for everyone in town. Able reluctantly agreed to talk to the Castlereighs.

He got to the Castlereigh home early one morning, hoping to catch both Bill and Wilma there—kill two birds with one stone, so to speak, tell them about all the complaints and let them know that he couldn't guarantee that somebody wasn't going to blow their brains out if they didn't cut out their sexual games. But Bill had already gone to an early golf date, and Able found himself sitting at their kitchen table while Wilma poured coffee.

He wasn't even sure how it happened, he thought, feeling a flush rise from his neck as he recalled the incident. She wasn't that attractive, particularly, not the sort of woman who would turn heads on the street or anything. Able had never even thought about what she might be like in bed. All he remembered about it was that it happened quickly. She was standing there pouring a cup of coffee for him, with her perfume wafting deliciously over him, then suddenly she was brazenly posed before him, her robe open, revealing a wonderfully inviting and sexy body, amazingly well preserved for a woman of almost fifty who had two nearly grown daughters. She held out her arms to him, wordlessly inviting him inside the robe, and he found himself on his feet, moving toward her and embracing her and hungrily finding her lips with his as his hands explored her body beneath the robe.

Within minutes they were on the daybed in her den, squirming and wrestling around, moaning and growling in their embraces, with her nails raking his naked back, although he didn't remember taking his clothes off. Finally he came as her moans became almost screams, and he found himself out of breath, his heart pounding. He gasped out a demand that she lay off the Brooks boy, and she agreed, teasingly twirling a lock of hair in her long nails as she reclined on the wrinkled daybed and smiled at him. Then he hurriedly dressed and left their house, ashamed of himself, and he never went back.

He dropped the cigar beside the cruiser and ground it out. She was a tiger, he thought, a by-God two-dollar pistol, that was for sure. And even though he had had other women besides Sue Ellen, even some of the whores in the Orient, none had given him the experience of raw, hungry sex that he had felt that morning in the Castlereigh home.

The other complaints had continued to come in, and he had been about to assume that Bill knew all about his and Wilma's one-time breakfast bang and to approach the man and tell him to curtail his affairs with young girls and married women when all of a sudden he was dead.

Able reached inside the cruiser, fetched a white rag, and bent down to wipe off his copper-colored boots. They were covered with red dust from the field, and he was reminded that he hadn't run for a week, not since he had found the girl's body hanging in Hoolian. A drop of sweat fell from his nose to the toe of his boot, and he shook his head as he wiped it off. This week had just gotten worse, day by day, and it promised not to get any better. On top of finding Eileen, on top of Bill's drowning, there had been that business of dealing with Eileen Kennedy's aunt.

She had been one of a kind, Able thought, straightening up and squinting up at the clean, clear white-hot morning sky. She showed up like she was going to church, and went into the icy morgue of the Sandhill County funeral home with Everett Hardin right behind her, then looked down at the horrible body of her niece through all that chiffon and lace, and didn't bat an eye. Finally she nodded quickly, produced a dainty lace handkerchief, which she held over her mouth, and strolled out just as if she had been judging pies at the county fair.

Able, who stood to her right, prepared to catch her if she fainted, couldn't even bring himself to look at the face, to reacquaint himself with the horror of what was there, and he found himself choking on the words when he asked her for the official identification required for the records. When they emerged into the warmer atmosphere of Everett's office, she turned to him and coolly appraised him, asking only one question, "Is that all?"

Able nodded briefly and gestured to a chair, which Everett was already offering her. The mortician then scurried about to make some tea while Miss Kennedy took out a small silver snuff box from her handbag and gently coated her gums with the brown powder. The task finished, she sat back and looked at Able again with her bright blue eyes and waited for the inevitable questions.

He learned little from her. Most of what she had to say she had already told the police when she reported her niece missing almost a month before, but she patiently and politely responded to Able's litany of official inquiries as if she were answering them for the first time. Finally he closed his notebook and looked at her as hard as he could.

"Miss Kennedy," he asked, "do you have absolutely no idea why this happened to your niece? Don't you have any clue as to who might have done it? I mean, people just don't do this sort of thing for no reason."

Her back stiffened perceptibly, and her lips made a thin line in front of the teacup she had daintily lifted toward them. She set the cup down, glanced over at Everett Hardin, who had remained silent through the interview and now sat obsequiously in a corner, watching and waiting. Then she glared at Able. "Sheriff," she said softly and as if she were having difficulty controlling her anger, "people do this sort of thing *all the time*! Don't you read the newspapers? I don't know who or what might have done this to my lovely niece, and it's not unlikely that she asked for it. She was a wild girl in some ways. But whatever sordid affair might have led to this was never a part of our conversation. I don't know anything I haven't told you."

Able fell silent, studying the brilliant blue of her eyes, which had not left him for an instant. He desperately wanted a clue from her, but she really knew nothing, he realized. She was the girl's maiden aunt, her only living relative, a person she felt obligated to visit from time to time, but she wasn't a confidante, just a fussy old pain-in-the-ass who occupied Sunday afternoons and sent Eileen crocheted Christmas presents she didn't want.

Aunt Vi waited a moment, then announced that she really needed to go. She was to catch the bus for Oklaunion to claim Eileen's personal possessions and begin disposing of them. Everett stepped up to the desk and began discussing the plans for the body. He did little to conceal his satisfaction in discovering that the funeral would be held in Agatite on Monday and that Eileen would be buried next to her parents in the family plot.

Then Aunt Vi was gone in a whirl of chiffon and lace and lavender perfume. And that had been Saturday.

Jingles was absolutely livid when he learned that Aunt Vi had come and gone and he hadn't had a chance to interview her. He had already been to Oklaunion to go through her "personal effects," as he called them, and he had sent one or both of his subordinates to Wichita Falls, where the D.P.S. had her burned-out car in a garage, to go over it with a "fine-toothed comb." But his investigation had yielded nothing more than a portrait of a fairly typical, attractive girl who somehow had fallen into a brutal and personal hell before she died.

Able pushed his body away from the cruiser and walked around to the driver's side. The ubiquitous and incessant insects droned and buzzed throughout the pasture where he came to shoot targets. Yes, he thought, Jingles, Aunt Vi, Bill Castlereigh, and, of curse, Eileen Kennedy had all made this one hell of a week. But nothing any of them contributed to the daytime aggravations could compete with the nightmares he had been having.

His dreams had been terrifying since Wednesday night, almost a week ago, the day they found her body. He kept waking up in the middle of the night, a scream in his throat, believing that he was choking on a wad of digested and packed paper, a wasp nest, jammed into his mouth so tightly that he couldn't close it. The dreams were inconsistent in most details, but most of them concerned the girl, sometimes seeing her hanging as he had found her, sometimes watching as she slowly rotted away before his eyes, turning from the pretty, smiling young

woman in her yearbook picture to the unbelievable terror
he had found strung from a rotting beam in an old outhouse.

About the only consistent element of the dreams was
the killer. He was faceless, nameless, but he was always
there, lurking in the background, sometimes illogically
bouncing the broken fingernails in the palm of his hand
and laughing. In his dreams Able had irrationally come
to the conclusion that she had been killed for the pieces
of fingernail, and they were all-important. When he tried
to ask the killer why, why he had killed her for such a
worthless prize, the man laughed louder, and Able started
yelling at him; then the choking would start and he would
awaken, the dream would vaporize, and he would find
himself covered with sweat, sitting upright in bed, holding his heart, terrorized.

Able got inside the cruiser and sat heavily behind the
wheel, cursing a bit because he had forgotten to roll down
the windows, and even now, an hour before noon, the
interior of the big car was unbearably hot. He flipped the
air conditioner up to high, idled the engine, and slowly
rolled down the windows to allow the superheated interior air to escape. From his shirt pocket he removed a
photograph of Eileen Ellen Kennedy. He had clipped it
from a high school yearbook from her senior year at Agatite High School. The photograph had become creased
and worn from being carried in Able's sweaty shirt pockets. It was a black-and-white photograph, of course, but
he remembered Vi Kennedy's blue, blue eyes, and he
filled in the colors the photograph omitted.

He stared at the picture as the engine idled, straining
now with the added burden of the air conditioner at such
low rpm's, and his eyes traced the familiar contours of
the girl's face, her soft hair, the clear skin, and white,
even teeth that smiled back at him from the crinkled photograph. He wanted more than anything else to find the
man who killed her and to punish him for hurting her,
for putting out the light in those eyes and turning her into
the macabre horror Able had found hanging in Hoolian.
God, he thought, he wanted that killer.

Jingles also wanted him. It shouldn't matter, Able told himself as he shifted the cruiser into drive and piloted it down the sandy road, who finds him, just so he's found. But he knew that to himself it did matter.

The thought of the pudgy chief of police caused the sheriff to grumble as he shifted his weight to accommodate the bumps in the rough field road. He was sick of Jingles snooping around the county, interrogating anyone who had ever known the girl, anyone who had ever gone into Mel's barbershop. The man was a fool and an egomaniac, and that made a dangerous combination.

As Able guided the cruiser onto the blacktop of the highway and pointed it toward Hoolian, he acknowledged that his corpulent nemesis was about half-right, even so. Jingles at least was *trying* to conduct an investigation, however stupidly he was going about it. Able hadn't done anything, really, except fail to cooperate every way he could with the Agatite Police Department.

The sheriff hadn't even gone to Eileen's funeral that Monday morning. It had been scheduled for nine-thirty. Miss Kennedy had sent for a Presbyterian minister from Memphis to conduct the service in Everett's chapel, although both Able and she agreed that few if any "friends" would show up. The Chamber of Commerce provided the pallbearers. Able figured at least some folks would come over from Oklaunion, but that was a long way, especially on a workday, and only a few people had shown up.

He eased the cruiser's speedometer up to seventy and grinned to think of Jingles worrying anybody who did show up with a lot of senseless questions. That man is an asshole, Able thought, shaking his head, a first-class asshole. It wasn't likely that he would turn up shit in spite of all the man-hours he'd already invested in the case.

As the cruiser ground to a halt in front of the Hoolian Barbershop, Able dryly noted that the chief of police had preceded him, his car pulled directly in front of the shop, blocking the ragged concrete walk that led to the porch. Mel sat on a wooden bench and raised his hand in a weak greeting as Able got out of the cruiser.

"Able," he said when the sheriff approached.

Able felt the sweat from under his shirt already driving away the cruiser's air conditioned cool, and he strolled up to the porch's shade, noticing a pint bottle in Mel's lap. He shook his head disapprovingly.

"Mel," the sheriff said as he raised himself up onto the porch, "you know that all of us know you drink out here, but goddamn it, you can't just keep it out in the open like this."

Mel grinned, but there was no humor in his face. "Shit," he said through a toothless set of gums, "what're you gonna do? Arrest me? Shit. After all this bullshit, an' cops crawlin' all over the place, an' that fat asshole of a police chief tryin' to arrest anybody who looks cross-eyed at him, ain't nobody goin' to come out here. Shit." He took a long pull from the bottle. "Ray don't even come 'round for checkers no more. I'm ruint, just fuckin' ruint." He clearly was beyond tipsy, Able noticed, and the whiskey, inadequately held in his mouth since he didn't have his dentures in, dripped down his chin onto his soiled barber's smock.

"You're old enough to retire," Able offered weakly. He realized when he said it that the old barber probably didn't have ten bucks in the bank, and he immediately regretted the suggestion.

"Shit," Mel said, shaking his head and looking down at his boots, "you know better than that. All I ever had was this place, an' now it ain't worth a pitcher of cold piss. People think it's haunted or somethin'." He was getting maudlin, Able thought, and he glanced around quickly. Even though Mel was an old bootlegger who insulted almost everybody he met, most people came to like the old country barber. It wasn't fair for something like this to ruin him. "Hell," Mel went on, wiping his nose with the back of his hand, "most of my business came from the greasers anyhow, an' with Jingles roustin' 'em ever' time they come 'round, there ain't nothin' I can do to get 'em to come by."

"People forget," Able said. "It's only been a week, less, for Crissake. They'll be back." Able listened to the insects buzzing and noticed a red ant bed afire with activity only a few feet from the porch. Mel fell into a musing silence. Suddenly Able noticed an Indian-red wasp droning around the porch's roof, and he found himself shuddering in spite of the heat. "Where is old Matt Dillon anyway?" he asked, trying to change his line of thought.

Mel waved his arm generally in the direction of the shop's corner, "He's 'round back, I suppose, prob'ly interrogatin' some rattlesnakes or somethin'."

Able shrugged and stepped around the side of the shop. Behind the building he spotted the chief of police ungracefully perched on an old Coke case, smoking a cigarette and apparently lost in thought.

Able studied the outhouse. Encircled by a white string with red strips of cloth attached, the old johnny kept its secrets in spite of the daily visits of the two lawmen. Not content to let it go without a thorough inspection, Murphy had ordered his men to scythe down all the weeds and brambles, sift through them, and carefully stack them alongside the perimeter, leaving the ground around the outhouse bare and sunbaked. All they found were a few snatches of cloth from the girl's dress that had caught on some cactus beside the trail leading up to the outhouse, confirming only that she had passed that way. Whether she had walked or been dragged, however, they couldn't say.

Suddenly Able noticed that a hole had been excavated next to the johnny's north wall, and he pointed with a fresh Hava-Tampa Jewel.

"What's that?" he asked.

"What?" Jingles looked up at him, reminding Able of how small and piglike his face was. "Oh. That. I had the idea of digging out the hole under the shithouse. Thought something important might've fallen down there."

For a moment Able waited for him to go on. They had never found the girl's missing shoe. It could be there. He wondered what they might learn from a crap-covered

shoe. Jingles said nothing, and finally Able was forced
to ask, "Well?"

"Well what?" Jingles shot back.

"Did you find anything?"

"Shit, no. Sons of bitches wouldn't dig it out. Quit on
me! Just like that!" He was clearly angry about it, and
Able realized that he had been brooding over the problem
when he came up. "Said there was a nest of snakes down
there an' they weren't goin' to stir 'em up. I told 'em I
didn't see any snakes, so they got all huffy an' told me I
could do the digging then." He shook his head. "Goddamn punks."

He was obviously referring to Hiker and Phillips who,
Able thought, had exhibited an uncommon amount of
horse sense in refusing to dig. "I doubt there's anything
there anyhow," he offered.

"Yeah," Jingles said, then as he stood up, " 'Course
you wouldn't know if there was. I mean, you really don't
know any more than anybody else about all this, do
you?"

Able felt the bile rising, but he swallowed hard and
said nothing. He was getting fed up with Jingles' insistence that he was hiding something from him. "Anybody
show up at the funeral?" Able asked, changing the subject.

"Oh, the old lady and the preacher from Memphis.
God-awful preacher, too. Everett was there, and there
was two women and a man from Oklaunion." Jingles
was trying to be casual about the whole thing.

"They know anything?"

"Hell, no. Told me they said all they had to say to the
deputy sheriff over in Oklaunion. I called him up, and
he said they was all clean. Shit, sheriffs are all alike."

Able again let the comment pass. "Your boys really
quit?" he asked.

"Nah." Jingles crushed out his cigarette. "They just
quit diggin'. I should've fired 'em both, but I didn't. I
got 'em out to Blind Man's Creek talkin' to some Mescans."

"Why?" Able asked, feeling the anger he had been suppressing beginning to boil.

"I figure Mescans is tied to this thing some way," Jingles said blithely, "I'm goin' out to some farmers' places later on an' talk to some more."

For a moment Able struggled with himself harder than he had for a long time. The outhouse shimmered in the heat, almost swimming in his eyes. The drone of the cicadas and other buzzing insects crescendoed.

"I mean—well, hell, Able, you haven't come up with shit," Jingles said, opening his hands in a gesture of innocence and nonchalance, "An' this country's full of Mescans. Wetbacks, most of 'em, an' I just figure one of them knows somethin' about this."

"Murphy," Able said, his voice dropping to low, angry tones, "you are about the dumbest son of a bitch I've ever known, and I've known some truly, righteously *dumb* sons of bitches!" Jingles stared at the sheriff, frozen in the shimmering heat, "And more than anybody I've *ever* known, *you piss me off!*" Able stood for a second or two, clenching his fists, then the fury finally broke. Looking into the chubby, stupid face of the chief of police, red as it was in the heat and lost as it was in complete, bigoted ignorance, the sheriff of Sandhill County lost control for the first time since he took office almost thirty years before.

"Goddamnit!" Able kicked the ground because he wanted to hit the fat cop so badly. "Goddamnit! I told you to lay off the Mexican people around here. God-*damn*it!"

Jingles opened his mouth as if to say something in protest, but Able cut him off. "These farmers need the Mexican workers, wetbacks or no, this time of year. They can't put up with you and your goddamn hoods running them off because you don't like them. Jesus fuckin' Christ, Murphy! Why don't you go off someplace and jerk off? It'd do about as much good as all this private-eye crap you've been carrying on around here. Jesus, you've run off all Mel's customers, and you've made a complete fool out of yourself. God in heaven, you're one dumb son of a bitch!''

Chief of Police Murphy was stunned into silence. He had never doubted that Able detested him, and he knew that the grudging admiration he felt for the sheriff was one-way only, but he'd never thought Able would lose control and come down on him like this. He was both afraid and embarrassed. He'd thought rousting some wet-backs would be a good idea—show that they were doing *something*—but deep inside himself he knew that it wouldn't have anything to do with the Kennedy murder. It was just something to do, something that would make him look good if, indeed, a vagrant Mexican had done it.

Able turned away from the chief of police and stormed around the side of the building. Mel, who had heard the whole thing, had produced another pint and was grinningly drinking it down, rocking back and forth in muffled laughter. Jingles slowly followed the sheriff around to the front of the shop and spotted Mel and his bottle. Able was leaning against one of the porch's roof supports.

"Goddamn it, Mel," Jingles said, "get rid of that bottle or I'll have to take you in."

"Fuck you, Murphy."

"Listen, Able," Jingles said, holding out his hand in a helpless gesture of friendship.

"Just shut up!" Able shouted at him, spinning around and slapping the hand aside. "Just shut the fuck up and leave me alone!"

Sheriff Able Newsome, gathering control back into his actions, took large steps over to his cruiser and opened the door. The bake-oven air came out at him in a rush, and he found his anger flaring as he flung away the Hava-Tampa Jewel and fired up the engine, threw the car in reverse, and wheeled out onto the ghost town's main street toward the highway.

Behind him in front of the barbershop with a fresh cigarette dangling from his pudgy lips, Chief Murphy lifted his hat and wiped his balding pate with a handkerchief. "That man's got a problem," he announced to the buzzing insects as he replaced his hat. He turned and looked into the shop, then brightened. "Hey, Mel," he yelled as he climbed the steps onto the porch, "gimme a drink, you son of a bitch."

III. Farmer
The Present, Afternoon

The ancient, rusty GMC pickup bounced over the culvert on the tractor cutoff between the all-weather road and the farm-to-market pavement, actually leaving the air and crashing down on the blacktop with a scream of protest from the balding tires and weary suspension. At the wheel, Claude Crane gunned the engine to its maximum power, bringing the truck out of its fishtail, and then he drew a mental bead on the horizon, beyond which lay Agatite and, he hoped, his wife and daughter.

Claude's hands were so tightly wound around the worn steering wheel that his fingernails were white in spite of the dirt beneath them, and the stream of air that swooshed past him from the open window did nothing to stem the flow of sweat from beneath his soil-encrusted gimme-hat. Behind his eyes, which flickered from the speedometer needle, which frustratingly refused to advance beyond the sixty-miles-per-hour mark, to the blacktop of the farm-to-market road, a headache pounded, and he could hear the throbbing of the pain in his ears as he calculated the time it would take him to reach town.

Gone, he thought, Cassie had gone. His rage was on the surface of his tormented mind, and both were augmented by the bad timing his wife had shown in leaving him on such a horrible day.

First the two Mexican boys had quit him cold. Right after dinner they had come over to him and asked him for their wages, saying they had to move on. They had been with him for more than two years, and even though he had cursed them almost every day for laziness and stupidity, they had gotten along all right. They had been good men, in fact, working from sunup to sundown on the farm, content to stay out in the bunkhouse, drink a few beers on weekends, and listen to their damned Mexican music on their tape machines. Claude knew they were probably illegal, wetbacks, but they worked hard. He paid them in cash, and it wasn't any of his business where they came from. This was the U.S.A., he often said, and he couldn't see any reason to ask them for proof of citizenship.

Then that asshole Chief of Police Jingles Murphy had come around asking questions, badgering every Mexican-American in the country about the girl they found in Hoolian. In the process of his investigation, Jingles had discovered a gold mine of illegal aliens, and he was running them in and calling buses from the Immigration Service faster than his two moronic deputies could process the paperwork. So Frank and Rudy had quit, nervous about being caught and shipped back to Mexico, and Claude was left with a mountain of ploughing to do, hay to get in, cows to tend, and nobody to do it, except for the two college boys he had put on for the summer, who weren't worth a horse fart if they were put together.

Then the tractor had broken down. The old International Harvester had simply sputtered and died, and he had had to walk almost two miles back to the house to go into town for parts to try to patch it up again—it would be the fourth time in as many weeks. Then he had found the note, taped to the icebox door:

Claude,
I've taken the baby and gone. Don't try to follow me and don't bother the folks. They don't know I'm going and they don't know where. I'm really sorry, Claude, I truly am, but I just can't stand it anymore. I don't love you anymore. I don't want to talk about it and I don't want to hear from you. There's cold chicken in the icebox. Potato salad too, and there's a pot of beans simmering on the stove. Good-bye, Claude. I'm sorry.
　　　　　　　　　　　　　　　　　　Cassie
P.S. The truck will be parked in front of the bank.

He had stood in the hot kitchen, sweat dripping off his face onto the pink notepaper, and read it over and over again. Unbelievable, he had thought. He tried to comprehend what she had written. Gone. How? Where? Why? The questions assaulted his mind, giving him the headache that had been sneaking around his brain's edge since the Mexican boys quit an hour before, since the tractor broke down ten minutes after he started the afternoon ploughing.

He had practically fallen into a kitchen chair, and he was still sitting there, dazed and in shock, when Mrs. Sitwell came in from his father's room for more ice cream. She had asked him what was wrong, and he showed her the note.

"Why, law?" she had exclaimed. "If that don't beat all. She didn't say nothin' to me about it. But she did ask me to stir them beans. I thought she was goin' out to the barn again on a lark, an' I told her that I wasn't hired to be no cook—"

Claude didn't hear her words. While she went on, he noticed on the large funeral home calendar over the telephone on the wall that Cassie had written "3:35" on today's date. A bus, he realized. She was taking a bus from Agatite to somewhere, and he had to find her, to stop her. He raced out the door without a word to Mrs. Sitwell, who was still going on about her duties and the low pay.

Cassie had taken the best pickup of the three he kept in the yard, and, unfortunately, the only one that was running today. The GMC needed a new starter and the battery was dead, and he began breaking down parts from the older Chevy half-ton that sat, covered with dust and surrounded by weeds, near the henhouse. Cursing and banging his knuckles, he managed to get the starter off the Chevy and installed on the GMC; then he dragged a battery cable out of the back and jumped it off a tractor battery he kept in the toolshed. The process had eaten up most of an hour, and it was after three o'clock by the time he had put the all-weather road to his farm behind him and was heading into Agatite on the farm-to-market road.

Claude's first reaction had been to blame other people. He was certain she was going to join her worthless sister out in California, even though Cassie hadn't even mentioned her sister in years. Claude had never actually met Cassie's sister, and he remembered her only as the older girl in the family who found herself pregnant and unmarried by the high school football star, disgraced and left literally at the altar, when the boy—what was his name? Claude tried to remember—chose running away to marriage. Since then Cassie's sister had simply been referred to, when she was mentioned at all around the house, as ''Cassie's sister,'' and except for a picture of her as a high school junior that sat atop a bookcase in their parents' den, Claude had trouble believing that Cassie's folks had ever had another daughter. In fact, she looked so much like Cassie that he often mistook the photograph for one of his wife, or at least one of her before they were married.

But the more he thought of it, the less likely it seemed that Cassie would run to her sister. She hardly knew her. More likely, she had gone south to that maverick aunt of hers in San Marcos, the one her father disliked so much. The aunt was some kind of artist, and she lived with men half her age and drank and probably used drugs, if what Cassie's father said was true. That was likely it, but he knew he had to get to her before she got away. Once she got into the clutches of that wild woman down there, he might never see her again.

There was another possibility that Claude didn't like to think of. The Moorely creep. He had been back in town, Claude had heard, and he wondered if his presence had been known to Cassie. She had made two trips into Agatite since Moorely returned to see to his mother's business after her death, and Cassie had always been taken with the freak, so maybe he was the one she was going to.

The very thought made Claude clench his teeth and tighten his large farmer's hands into fists around the smoothly worn steering wheel. Claude knew all about Moorely's telephone romance with his girlfriend back in high school, and he had done something about it. It had been after graduation. Moorely was pushing his fat body around a construction job and making everybody there mad with his holier-than-thou attitude. Claude had joined in with his buddies in giving Moorely a hard time every chance he got, but he really paid little attention to the fat, bespeckled, unpopular boy until one hot afternoon in July that same summer.

Claude had been on his way to see Cassie as usual, after he got done moving pipe or ploughing for his father, when he had run into her mother on their front porch. She had just checked the mail, and she handed the bundle to Claude to take in to Cassie, since she was going to stay outdoors and work in her garden. Going up the stairs, Claude had glanced at the magazines and stuff addressed to his girlfriend, and then he noticed the letter from Moorely. It even had his return address on it, and Claude instinctively pocketed it, saving it to read later.

It was a love letter. There was no other way to describe it. It not only had a full account of their telephone romance; it also contained a profession of passion that was almost embarrassing to Claude as he read it in his pickup parked in front of the Dairy Mart later that night. It also had an apology for all the nasty things he had said and, incredibly, an attack on Claude himself that sent him into an anger so deep that he had trouble reading the carefully penned letter under the neon lights of the drive-in restaurant. Moorely called him a "bumpkin," an "ignorant jock who will be lucky to find his way around a ploughed field," a "useless loser whose future is only slightly less bright than the village idiot's," and other similarly worded insults. He went on to offer Cassie a better future, with *him*, suggesting she leave home now, move to New Orleans with him, marry him as soon as she was of age, and live with him and share his life in the meantime.

Claude's rage was overwhelming. It was all he could do to keep from going over to the Moorely home and attacking the fat slob right then. But he got control of himself and bided his time. Then, with two friends, he managed to run Moorely down one early evening and talk him into "riding around" with them. They had then driven the flattered and confused Moorely out to the country and had beaten the living shit out of him.

Claude remembered the scene when they had gotten ready to leave the battered boy five miles from town with no ride home. His nose was a bloody pulp smeared across his face; his glasses, broken and missing, left him mostly blind in his blackened eyes. Claude believed that Moorely had lost several teeth as well. All three of them had hit him, but neither of the other two boys had struck him with such force, such anger, such mindless fury as had Claude.

Moorely had stayed close to home after that evening, going out only to go to work. And then, a month later, he left Agatite more or less forever, returning only to visit his mother for a while, spending most of his time elsewhere, and never again intruding into Claude's life.

Claude had thrown the letter into Moorely's bleeding and battered face that night, and the only thing he could remember the victimized boy saying was, "She's a bitch to show you that! I was right the first time." But Claude had kicked him again at that point, and that had been the end of it.

And now Moorely was back, a successful man. But then, maybe not. Gossip had come Claude's way that the checks he had generously spread around town to cover his mother's bills were bouncing all the way back from the California banks he had drawn them on. And while he seemed to be spreading around plenty of cash as well, Claude had also heard that he was anxious to sell his mother's house quickly, and for whatever he could get. And he wasn't a successful husband, either, Claude had heard, not if his track record of two wives already gone and another leaving him was any indication. He was just as big a fake now as he was then, Claude deduced, but he also figured that no matter how phoney Moorely was, Cassie would never believe it. There had been something between them all right; judging from the letter, it had

gone both ways. She had the wool pulled completely over
her eyes back then, and there was no reason to think that
she had changed her mind. Cassie never listened much
to gossip, especially the back-of-the-feed store variety.

Claude wrinkled his soiled brow. Cassie always believed what anybody told her. That was her greatest failing, and, he acknowledged, her greatest virtue. But if
she ever learned that anyone had lied to her, she never
forgave him. She hated dishonesty worse than anything,
and she could carry a grudge about it for years. He ran
a hand over his mouth and almost lost control of the
loose-steering pickup as it careened down the uneven
pavement. A jolt of fearful regret shot through him and
made his stomach weak. What if she had finally learned
about what her husband had done, had discovered his
interception of her mail and the beating he'd given her
telephone lover? She'd be mad about that, he knew, madder than she'd ever been about anything. But would she
be mad enough to run to him, away from her husband
and her home? His eyes blinked rapidly to flash away
drops of perspiration that flowed from under his cap.

Claude didn't think so. Her aunt seemed to be a far
more reasonable possibility; he really didn't think Cassie
remembered Moorely much at all. She never mentioned
him, and he couldn't have been that important in her life.
Claude thought he knew her better than that.

He thought he knew her better than to think she would
run away, too. But beneath the anger and pain, beneath
the shock of finding her gone, the anxiety of trying to
get to town before the bus—if it *was* a bus—left, he realized that he knew what had driven her away, and he
couldn't believe it.

Cassie had been his rock, his steady prop through all
the backbreaking work and worry of the farm. He knew
her life hadn't been easy, and he felt bad about having
had to deny her things that would make it easier. But he
thought she understood. He had to keep the farm the way
it was. His father would never have understood about the
whirring of blenders and dishwashers, about air conditioning or anything like the things Cassie always wanted.

His father had given him the farm, *given* it to him. *Him,* the youngest of the three brothers. And his father hadn't asked a thing for it. Of course, he'd planned to work it a few more years before he turned it over, but he couldn't, and so it fell on Claude's shoulders, he felt, to run it exactly as if the old man were still master and his mother were still alive. It was a poorly formed theory in his mind, and he didn't think about it much. It was just the thing to do, to keep the farm as much like it had been when he was just a boy as he could. For the old man, for his brothers to come visit. But what he did think about, what obsessed him, was an idea of how to escape the farm. It only depended on the old man's finally dying off.

Claude had not forgotten the dreams he and Cassie had shared when they were dating in high school. His father's stroke and the need for him to take over the farm had come as a surprise, and Claude hadn't considered it as more than a temporary situation from the start. He believed his father would die soon, and he had been believing it for years, but he knew that he couldn't do anything until the old man was gone. Even though his father was a drooling vegetable who sat in front of the TV the whole time he wasn't sleeping or the nurse wasn't spooning some awful gruel into his gaping mouth, Claude couldn't bear to have him think that his youngest son was ungrateful, unmindful of the honor the old man had bestowed on him by making him the owner of the best goddamn farm in the county.

But Claude didn't want to be the owner of the best goddamn farm in the county, because it wasn't his farm, by right or by ownership, not really. The old man had built the farm himself, set in motion a rotation of crops, a routine of work that Claude, and Cassie when his mother had died, inherited and were responsible for. It wasn't *his,* it wasn't theirs, and that bothered him. So he had decided to sell it to his brothers just as soon as the old man died. He had become worried about the deal for a while, since hail and rain had ruined both brothers' wheat for two years running, reducing their yields by more than half, and at the same time in the measureless caprices of climate, his crops had made bumper yields, increasing his wealth three-and four-fold.

Each year he banked his profits, not wanting to spend a dime on the old place, holding out for the time when he and Cassie could find their own piece of land, one they could work themselves without help, without hands. But one year led to another, and the old man kept on living his useless life, and his brothers kept complaining about their rotten luck and Claude's charmed life.

He had never told Cassie about his plans, but he was certain she knew. She must have known all along that she didn't want to spend his entire life working himself to death, too tired to sleep most nights or even to talk to her, worrying about the weather, the condition of his worn-out equipment, about the endless details involved in running a farm of this size. She must have known that he wouldn't forget all their dreams. Or did she?

He realized, as he shoved the old pickup as fast as its antique body and engine would stand, that she had been working awfully hard all these years, just as he had. He never really thought about how hard it must have been for her. She was a woman, after all, and cooking, cleaning, looking after Claudine—all that was her job, her responsibility. As for the milking, the livestock tending, the gardening, those things were also part of the housework of a farm wife. Surely she understood that.

He conjured up a picture of his wife in the dirty windshield of the pickup. But he didn't see the overweight, dowdy farm woman who was, at that moment, pulling into a parking space in front of the First Security Bank in Agatite. He saw the Agatite Eagle Mascot, a cute, eighteen-year-old girl, perky and bright, who worshipped him, and whose bright blue eyes made him melt inside. This was the Cassie he always saw when he looked at his wife, and while his love for her had been unsated and undemonstrated for a long time, it was still strong, and it tore at his heart in waves of panic and fear as he raced toward the small town.

Claude's blind vision of the reality that was his life was not restricted to Cassie. He hadn't seen himself in years either. When he shaved, the face that looked out of the mirror at him was that of a twenty-year-old youth, a man who had so much in front of him and no regrets behind him. He was tough, lean, handsome, and strong. He didn't see the older man, weathered in the face that was as cracked and lined with wrinkles, as baked by the sun, as the arroyos down by the river that bordered his farm. He didn't see the slight stoop in his shoulders, the hands cut from machinery and scarred by hard, hard work, above his undershirt the sunburned skin that was rough and cured like leather. He saw himself only as a youth. He didn't recognize the image of his father looking out through the troubled eyes of a workingman's face.

He had been proud of his daughter when she was born, and he wanted a son, but his fatigue and Cassie's indifference to him had prevented their having any kind of lovelife since Claudine's birth. He had tried to give Cassie outings in town, providing money for her to spend as she wanted, just so she didn't try to alter the house any, just so she didn't upset his father or his brothers with changes to a way of life that Claude didn't recognize as being their own. But he dimly realized that he had told her none of his feelings, that he had shared nothing of his emotions and troubles with her or offered to share hers, and the revelations of what he had done wrong were deeply buried behind the throbbing in his head and the anger at his departed wife for picking on him when so much else was going wrong.

The pickup hardly slowed for the stop sign where the farm-to-market road joined U.S. 287 just east of Agatite. Turning sharply onto the highway and narrowly missing a semi as it roared by, Claude cursed loudly at both the truck and his situation. He was mad enough, his father would have said, to chew nails, and from his red-rimmed eyes the hatred seemed to fuel the pickup's engine, forcing it faster and faster along the ten miles left before he would reach Agatite's city limits.

"Goddamnit, goddamnit!" he said harshly, blowing the words across gritted teeth. "Cassie, you picked one hell of a time for this nonsense. Goddamnit!" He reached

behind him and felt the .30-.30 in the gunrack mounted
in the cab's rear window, and he remembered with a grin
that a full box of shells was in the glove compartment.
He felt the urge to kill something, and inside him the
younger, more hopeful man was desperately afraid that
he would do just that.

IV. Breedlove
The Present, Eight Months Before

They stood in the whipping wind that had brought the
chill factor down to zero and assaulted the street with
dust and debris from the prairies north of the small town.
They felt naked and foolish and stared hard up and down
the main street for a glimpse of the Chrysler. They didn't
see it anywhere, and the few vehicles that still moved in
the icy northern blast paid no attention to the three desperate men standing in front of the blown-out glass of
the Holiday Finance Company, two of them brandishing
pistols like Mexican bandits, and the third seemingly doing his best to bleed to death as he leaned heavily on
their free arms. They had to shout at each other to be
heard over the whistling wind.

"That fuckin' nigger son of a bitch split on us!" Joe
Don yelled. There was nothing but despair in his voice.

Breedlove looked up and down the street one more
time, but no Chrysler appeared. An auto dealer's showroom was on the corner, and he began walking toward
it, toting the heavy duffel on his left arm and carrying
the nearly empty .45 at the end of his right. The feces in
his pants no longer bothered him. He moved unsteadily
against the wind, leaning at almost a thirty-degree angle
into it, concentrating on the big Ford sign in blue and
white that wobbled in the gale.

Both he and Mike had refused to put on silly clothing
for this job. Therefore, instead of the heavy, hot overcoats they had suffered with on the last robbery, they
were dressed in light jackets, lined, but no match for the
blue norther they now found themselves in. Breedlove

cursed both of them for resisting Joe Don's idea. A change of clothes in the car would be welcome. But it didn't really matter, he told himself. Floyd had split, and there was no car, let alone a change of clothes.

"Hey!" Joe Don yelled over the screaming wind from behind him. "Where the hell you goin'?"

Breedlove turned and yelled into the wind, "Ford dealer!" and Joe Don looked beyond him toward the corner, seeing the sign for the first time. He nodded.

"Right!" he yelled back, but no sound came to Breedlove's throbbing ear. Joe Don prodded Mike, who was still holding his palm over his face, and all three of them bent into the wind. Mike suddenly started waving his arm, which was draped around Joe Don's shoulder, and yelling into his ear.

"What's he say?" Breedlove screamed in their direction.

"No good!" Joe Don hollered back. "He says they don't keep gas in the goddamn cars. We'll have to find somebody who has keys to his own car."

"Damn!" Breedlove said, feeling weary of the whole business. Everything I touch, he thought, turns to shit sooner or later. He found himself wishing the goddamn sheriff would just come along and arrest them and get it over with. He was sick of the cold and the fear and the frustration. The thought of rushing onto the showroom floor and jumping into a new truck or sedan and driving right out the plate-glass window had appealed to him, had made him move against the damned wind. The idea of a confrontation with more of the crazy people in this crazy town didn't appeal at all. He hoped he'd never have to fire a goddamn gun again. He leaned heavily against a building and wished he could cry, but he couldn't.

Mike, leaning on Joe Don, wavered with his supporter in the middle of the sidewalk in front of Breedlove. They were standing directly before a White's Auto Store, shielded from view of those inside by a large cardboard cutout display of chain saws and a mannequin dressed like Paul Bunyan. Breedlove's weariness almost completely overcame him. His ear hurt, and his hand stung from the .45's continued pinch. A new, vague, raw pain was coming from his rectum. This was one big fuckup, he thought and almost yelled in his frustration into the raging storm, one hell of a fucked-up mess.

None of them knew what to do. Mike had been revived a bit by the cold and was searching the sidewalk and street with his uncovered eye, while Joe Don's eyes were glazed with confusion, Breedlove thought. Breedlove himself was breathing heavily, as if he had been running, and the trio all believed that at any moment a herd of police cars would come helling around the corner, guns blazing, and it would be all over.

Instead, a horn started honking, and then it blasted, and they all turned to see the Chrysler turn the corner, screeching its tires as it pulled up parallel to them. Floyd leaned over and flung open the door in front, and Breedlove lunged for the opening on the passenger side. Floyd had one of the shotguns across his lap, and he leaned way over to the back and opened the back door for Joe Don and Mike to pile in. Breedlove dragged the duffel in between his knees, and Floyd, with barely a glance at the two in back, gunned the engine, peeling out from the curb with a scream of rubber before they got the doors shut. In seconds they gained U.S. 287 and were headed east toward Iowa Park.

When they drove past the Holiday Finance Company office on their way out of the small town, Breedlove thought to look inside the office. The secretary who had fallen unconscious under the coach's body was on her feet and screaming hysterically, but the others were nowhere to be seen.

"Is this your idea of some kind of fuckin' joke, you crazy nigger?" Joe Don screamed from the back seat as he tried to ease Mike away from him, pushing him too roughly, Breedlove thought, to the other side of the car. Mike cried out in pain.

Floyd looked into the rearview mirror and smiled. "Why, shoah, boss," he said in a broad Negro dialect, thick with irony. "Ah jus' had ta go tak a pee, an Ah

seen y'all genmum wuz in a bit a trouble, sos Ah figgered Ah had some tahm.''

Breedlove looked quickly into the backseat for Joe
Don's reaction, half afraid he would see what indeed he
did. Joe Don's scar was blazing from the wind's chafe or
from embarrassment and anger, and he picked up the .44
from the floorboard where Mike had dropped it and
cocked the hammer back. Floyd anticipated the move,
however, and he suddenly wrenched the wheel to the right
and drove the car roughly onto the shoulder of the highway. The jolt threw Mike on top of Joe Don, who pulled
the trigger and fired a bullet through the floor of the car.
The explosion was deafening. Breedlove's ear came alive
with pain.

"Goddamnit!" he yelled, but Floyd paid him no mind.
He jammed on the brakes, grabbed the shotgun from his
lap, and laid it across the front seat, pointing it directly
at Joe Don's abdomen. Breedlove was dazed, but he
blinked as he noticed that Floyd had also produced the
other scattergun with his left hand. It replaced the twin
shotgun on his lap and was pointed directly at Breedlove.

"I saw you guys had blown it all to hell," Floyd said
in a calm, cool voice, "so I went around the corner and
put in a call to the sheriff. I told him there was one hell
of a car wreck out on 287 about five miles. People killed
all over the place. By the time he gets out there and back,
we'll be halfway to Lawton."

Joe Don relaxed and blew through his lips, smiling at
Floyd, who turned back around and began to pull the car
back onto the highway. Joe Don was feeling guilty about
blowing up, but Floyd's actions, helpful though they
were, had been stupid. They could have been killed on
the street. He had no idea how gun-happy these people
were, Breedlove thought. By-God football coach carrying a piece. Who'd have believed it? Besides, Breedlove
concluded, Floyd had scared them shitless. Why hadn't
he just come inside and made the phone call?

"Hey!" Floyd said after about ten minutes of silence.
"One of you guys stinks. Who dumped the load?"

Breedlove felt a flush of shame come over him. The

car's heater was going full blast, and he could smell the mess in his pants rising around him in waves. He was about to confess when Mike spoke up in the back seat.

"It's me, goddamn it." He squirmed up to a sitting position, still holding his hand over his face. "This hurts like hell, and I guess I must've passed out a little. That's when it happened."

Breedlove breathed out easily. That took him off the hook. The pain in his ear continued, and his hand was throbbing. He looked down and realized that he was still holding the .45 tightly in his right fist. He let it drop to the floorboard between the duffel and the seat, and tingles and prickles suddenly shot from his fingers up to his arm.

"We gotta freshen you up, sucker!" Floyd grinned. He lit a cigarette, passed it back to Mike, then lit another for Joe Don, who was sulking in the backseat's corner. "I mean, I ain't drivin' no shit wagon here."

Breedlove reached into his jacket pocket for a pack of smokes and lit up as well. He wished to hell they had a bottle in the car. His whole body ached for a drink.

"What the hell happened back there, anyhow?" Floyd crushed the empty pack from his pocket and accepted the cigarette Breedlove offered him.

"It was one big fuckup," Joe Don admitted. "Things were fine until this big jock went John Wayne on us and started blasting. Goddamn near blew Mike's head off, and he was drawin' a bead on Breed here when I plugged him."

"I got him first," Mike said. "Did you see the hole that .44 made in him? Just like Dirty fuckin' Harry, goddamn it!"

"I think Joe Don hit him first," Breedlove said, not arguing, but trying to keep the peace. "But Mike sure as hell messed him up."

"It don't matter," Joe Don said, and he began to relate the whole story to all of them, as if he had been the only one there. When he got to the part where Coach pulled out his gun, Breedlove braced himself for the criticism he knew was coming. "I don't know where or how he got that gun," Joe Don said, pausing for a moment to think, "but he sure as hell had it, boy, and before you could say 'fuck a duck' he was blazing away at ol' Mike." He passed over Breedlove's freezing up. "He missed ol' Breed here by a hair, ain't that right?" Breedlove nodded, reaching up to touch his ear. "And then me an' Mike shot the hell outta the son of a bitch."

Floyd's smile was bigger than ever. "Who blew the window?" he asked.

"Some bitch of a secretary got hold of *my* gun," Joe Don admitted. "She damned near got me too. Shit, I'll be picking glass outta my face for a week." His face was a road map of red streaks where the shards of glass had cut him. "But ol' Breed here almost emptied a clip at her, an' she gave it up. What I don't understand, Breed, is how you could miss people at that range."

Breedlove cleared his throat and noticed that it was sore and raw. "Well, shit, I never claimed to be no—"

"Fuckin' .45's!" Mike's voice interrupted suddenly from the back seat of the Chrysler. "Most goddamn inaccurate weapon ever made. Can't hit the goddamn ground with it. It makes one hell of a hole, but if you can't hit anything with it, what damn good is it?"

Breedlove felt relief and rage at the same time. "Then why'd you let me go in there with it? Jesus, I might as well have had a cap gun if I had a gun that was no damned good!" He seethed for a moment. "Did you know that, Joe Don? About the .45's?" he demanded, furious at him.

"Sure." Joe Don grinned at him, the scar on the side of his face now showing the bloody tributaries of the glass cuts, "But what the hell, Breed? It was a goddamn intimidatin' weapon. It should keep people in line just lookin' at it."

"Besides," Mike added, "you pissed and moaned so much about havin' to give up that .357, I figgered you'd really shit if we didn't give you somethin' really impressive. Shit, this thing hurts!" He tried to move his hand a bit, and Breedlove saw a bloody mass beneath it.

Breedlove sat in silence, turning to stare down the stretch of frozen highway in front of the big Chrysler.

"Look, Breed," Joe Don said in a conciliatory tone, "nobody was *supposed* to get hurt, right? How'd I know some sky pilot was gonna go bullshit on us?"

The memory of the fallen coach swept over Breedlove like a fever. He was dead; that much was sure. They'd lucked out on the first job. The old guard hadn't had a stroke, after all. They'd been wanted for armed robbery but nothing more. Now they were murderers, too. That was twenty to life, maybe the death penalty. How'd they do it nowadays? Thoughts of Jimmy Cagney saying "The Big Casino" crossed his mind. It's curtains, Breedlove thought wryly. They didn't use the hot seat anymore, and he knew they didn't hang in Texas. The words "lethal injection" came to him. Shoot you full of juice, he thought. You just go to sleep. At the moment he felt so tired, so dirty, so damned worn out that the idea of going to sleep appealed to him oddly, even if it was forever. But he didn't want somebody else telling him when.

They made the car switch smoothly just east of Iowa Park, but instead of going straight back through Okla-union to the van, which was at a roadside park east of Vernon, they swung by the house to clean up and change into some clean clothes. It wasn't on the game plan, but Mike had started to whine about his fouled pants, and Floyd insisted that they were ahead of their schedule be-cause of the unexpected ploy of sending the sheriff on a wild-goose chase after the phantom car accident. They fussed around and grabbed stuff they decided they might want.

Mike wasn't hurt as bad as they had thought he was. What had apparently happened was that when he noticed the coach's gun, he had turned his head slightly and his mouth must have opened. When Coach opened up, the bullet must have entered his open mouth and then gone out cleanly through his cheek, breaking the bone but not doing much other damage. Floyd cleaned the wound and Mike screamed bloody murder when the alcohol hit the ragged edges of the hole, but when it was over, he had just a tiny hole in his face and some bruises and swelling under his eye. Floyd bandaged it, and in an hour they had switched to the van and were on the road to Lawton.

Floyd had been monitoring the C.B. he had installed in the van since their last job. They had already passed one Highway Patrol roadblock stopping eastbound cars between Oklaunion and Iowa Park, and they figured that there would be another one before they got to Vernon, this time on their side of the divided highway. Breedlove felt panic rising in him. They had dumped their guns at the house, putting them in the bathtub and pouring acid on them from a can Joe Don produced. "It won't destroy them," he had explained as the acid began to smoke when it made contact with the plastic and metal on the weapons, "but it'll fuck up fingerprints and serial numbers for a while, anyhow." They kept the shotguns, and Joe Don had a .22 pistol in a shoulder holster he wore under his coat.

Sure enough, a trucker began chattering about a road-block five miles east of Vernon, stopping westbound traffic. They were onto them. The wind had slacked a bit, and a light sleet was falling, icing up on the windshield when they first made the switch to the van, and making the road slick. Floyd slowed down to forty-five, and the trio of passengers began to sulk in the back of the van.

"What'll we do now?" Breedlove asked generally. "They're looking for four men, one badly wounded. We can figure that out. Mike's bandage is sticking out like a searchlight, and then they'll look in the back and find the bag and the shotguns if they've got any sense at all."

"Be cool," Floyd said, and he reached down and flicked the C.B. to Channel 9, the emergency channel. "This is the Lone Ranger, KKV 0987. Break for Emergency Information," he said in a singsong voice that betrayed nothing of his race.

"10-4," a man's voice cracked over the speaker, "Go ahead. This is KKR 2246 monitoring."

"10-4," Floyd responded. "You guys looking for four dudes in a Chrysler?"

"10-4," the voice answered.

"Well, I don't know if it's important or not," Floyd said, "but I passed four guys trying to push a '77 Chrysler out of a ditch two miles north of Harrold on Farm Road 2-2-1-2. One of them had a big white rag tied around his head and face. Over."

"10-4. That's a roger, Lone Ranger!" The voice sounded excited. "Thanks for the info. What's your 20?"

"Oh, I'm about sixteen miles west of E-lectra moving south on 2-8-7," Floyd answered.

"That's a big 10-4, good buddy," the voice crackled. "This is KKR 2246 over and out."

"This is the Lone Ranger, signing off." Floyd laughed into the mike and placed it back on its hook. "Now we'll see if they take the bait."

They had driven on in silence for a few miles when suddenly the flashing red lights appeared on the horizon, moving toward them on the opposite side of the highway. In seconds five Highway Patrol cars and three local sheriffs and city police vehicles screamed past them. In ten minutes they could see the lights of Vernon, and soon they had turned north toward Lawton, Oklahoma.

Two hours later they were eating Kentucky Fried Chicken in the Trail's End Motor Lodge in Lawton. Their second job was over, and they'd gotten away again. Breedlove wondered how long their luck could hold out.

2

I. Breedlove
The Present, One Month Before

The stupid old fart of a farmer with the red nose and a jaw full of Skoal was supposed to let him out in Kirkland, Breedlove brooded as he stalked his way eastward on Highway 287. From there he had planned to hitch south to Abilene and then straight across to Fort Worth on the interstate to meet up with Joe Don and the others, as planned.

The heat from the blacktop had long since penetrated his boot soles, and his whole body ached for a cold drink of anything wet, anything other than his own sweat, which was even beginning to play out as the afternoon's sun beat down on him. Over his shoulder toward the northwest he could see a cloud coming up, dark and purple against the bright blue of the summer sky. Coming, he thought, but not here, not yet. The sun still baked him, and he wanted to lie down and rest in the shade, but there wasn't any shade, only Johnson grass and scraggly mesquite lining the fences along the highway.

He dimly realized how dumb it was to be walking toward Agatite, then Oklaunion and Jolly beyond, but somehow the thought of turning back to Kirkland and Childress behind him wasn't inviting, and he reasoned that he could, with any luck at all, snag a ride through the dangerous areas. It was still dumb, he knew, to come back this close to this part of the country, but the whole past month had been dumb, in fact the whole past year. He couldn't see much profit in trying to change his luck by simply doing the smart thing. It couldn't be that simple.

After Oklaunion he had had, for the first time in his

life, more money to spend than he knew what to do with. To a man who had eaten ketchup and hot-water soup and jam and cheese sandwiches for days at a time, who was accustomed to hitchhiking and sleeping wherever the opportunity of the moment provided, the idea of having more than ten thousand dollars all at once was overwhelming. He hadn't even spent any of it until three months after they had split up the take, and then he blew it all in a month and a half.

They had all been jumpy and paranoid after the Oklaunion blowup. But soon they realized stupidly and in a daze that in spite of all the shooting and fireworks the silly, frightened people in the small loan office couldn't give the cops a single accurate description of one of them. Breedlove wasn't satisfied, even so, and he immediately began growing a beard, which he continued to wear, hoping somehow that the facial hair would hide his face from anyone who might recognize him and suddenly start shouting ''Killer!'' or ''Murderer!''

Then it dawned on them that they had gotten away with it. They were home free with almost fifty thousand dollars in cash—old bills, too, spendable cash!

As he aimed his boot toes one after the other along the blacktop, Breedlove fell into a kind of trance a man walking long distances in the heat often experiences. His mind wandered back to the motel room in Lawton where Joe Don had finally found a television station that was covering the robbery in Oklaunion. The announcer noted it was an ''Old West shootout'' style holdup, and there were several people hurt, one dead, and then he switched to Alan Crum, who had an ''On-the-Scene'' report.

The pictures had shifted to a view of the front of the Holiday Finance Company, the broken window all but blocked from view by heavily coated, uniformed men, all lit eerily by the bright lights of the camera strobes. Ambulance attendants were bringing out stretchers on which lay bodies—the praying man and, Breedlove realized, the coach, who was shrouded by a red blanket.

Alan Crum's squeaky voice continued the narration: ''The holdup began about three-thirty this afternoon in this small-town loan office, the Holiday Finance Company. Present in the office at the time of the robbery were the regular employees, including the company manager, Alvin Atwood, who was severely beaten by one of the holdup men when he tried to stop the bloodshed—''

''Shit,'' Mike snorted through his bandage, ''the only thing he tried to stop was pissing all over himself.''

''Two customers were in the office at the time the robbers entered, one of whom was Oklaunion's sheriff, Virgil Barry. Sheriff Barry was not in uniform at the time, as he had just returned from a vacation in Florida and, according to his wife, had stopped by the office to take care of some personal financial business when the desperadoes entered the company and held him at gunpoint—''

''Hell's bells!'' Joe Don exclaimed, and then he whistled through his teeth. ''He wasn't no coach! He was the goddamn sheriff!''

''No shit,'' Floyd said without sarcasm. He couldn't believe his ears. None of them could.

''Apparently at one point Sheriff Barry pulled his gun and attempted to arrest the robbers when shooting erupted. In the hail of bullets that followed, Sheriff Barry fell, mortally wounded by at least two of the men.''

The camera panned away to show the secretaries climbing into the ambulances. They were wrapped in blankets and coats. Breedlove recognized the pretty one who had shot at them as she stepped up into the rear of the vehicle.

''I thought you said you *talked* to the sheriff about that accident thing,'' Mike said to Floyd.

''Hell, I don't know who I talked to. I called the sheriff's number and I talked to somebody.'' He lit a cigarette and flicked the match at the TV screen. ''I can't believe you guys wasted a sheriff.''

''Sh!'' Breedlove hissed, Crum was coming back on camera.

''Also wounded in the incident was Jim Bob Billings, a part-time employee of the small loan office. He was shot according to witnesses, when he attempted to force the thieves to call a doctor for Sheriff Barry. Weaver suf-

fered a gunshot wound to the shoulder, and he is being
taken to Wichita Falls General Hospital—''

"Makes it sound like *we* shot him!" Breedlove said
bitterly. "Hell, *she* shot the shit out of that asshole all
by herself, trying to kill Joe Don." And *me*, he finished
his thought silently.

The camera began giving sweeping views of the interior of the office, gathering statements of off-camera witnesses who occasionally were brightly illuminated by the
camera's lights. The victims were still smeared with
blood, and the statements jumped haphazardly through
the events of the robbery.

"Well, they came in here and demanded that Alvin,
uh, that's the manager, open the safe. . . ."

"One of them seemed to be the leader. He was shorter
than the rest. That was the one Eileen shot. . . ."

". . . and when that window broke, I thought the Texas
Rangers or somebody was gonna come right in here. . . ."

". . . then the short one—had an ugly scar right along
here—started beatin' the shi—uh, excuse me, stuffin' out
of Alvin, while one of the others, the tall one, kinda
skinny, was blazin' away like Charles Bronson or somebody with this shiny, army-type gun. . . ."

"I ain't never seen nothin' like it in my life, an' I was
in World War II. . . ."

And so it went. Finally the pretty secretary who had
tried to kill Breedlove, Eileen Kennedy, or so she had
been identified as, appeared in front of the blinding lights
and squinted through her stringy, blood-matted hair at
the camera. The camera barely focused on her for a moment before returning to the office's interior once more,
where officers were digging slugs out of the wall, taking
blood samples from the floor and paneling, and generally
trying to piece together evidence of what looked like a
terrorist attack. As the cameraman followed the action,
Eileen's voice narrated, "They were plenty scared. I
don't know when I've seen men more scared than that. I
thought they were going to rape me or something, but
they were just scared. I was plenty scared, too."

Switching back to the studio, Alan Crum summarized

the details once more. Then the announcer came on and
warned citizens against approaching three or four armed
men in a late-model Chrysler—"Shit, they ain't even
found the car yet," Floyd laughed—who were known to
be dangerous. There followed a brief and inaccurate description of each of the three inside men. About all that
was correct was Joe Don's size and his scar, and the fact
that Breedlove was tall and somewhat thin. Then the news
shifted to other matters, and the four men fell silent.

The next morning they drove to Oklahoma City, where
they split up the money in a Holiday Inn. Breedlove took
his sack of bills greedily, and then looked inside. Almost
ten thousand dollars! He had never even seen that much
money in his whole life. He'd certainly never imagined
actually owning that much.

"I'll be down in Fort Worth the middle of July," Joe
Don announced as he stuffed his own paper bag full of
bills. "But first I'm goin' out to California an' try to
score some pussy an' somethin' more potent than these
pea shooters we always seem to wind up with."

Breedlove couldn't conceive of why he would ever want
to see Joe Don again. He certainly couldn't see himself
going along with another robbery. He had what he
wanted, and for once he intended to keep it. He had
actually gotten away with something, and he wasn't about
to risk his good fortune by hanging around this crew any
longer than he had to.

But Joe Don had been a bit more perceptive about his
companions and their sudden wealth. "I figure you
boys'll be ready for somethin' a little bigger by then—
that is, if you can manage not to piss away a whole ten
grand each before I get back."

He laughed his mad, high laugh, and then he called a
taxi and disappeared into the night. Mike Dix elected to
stay in the room, immediately taking over the telephone
and trying to locate a girl he thought he remembered
from the city, and Floyd took the van, giving Breedlove
a ride downtown, where he sat in the bus station with a
grocery sack full of bills and nowhere in particular to go.

Breedlove wandered around northeastern Oklahoma for

a while, working on a couple of construction jobs in Tal-
equah and Bartlesville, avoiding the big city cops of
Tulsa, and staying out of trouble. He expected to be arrested at any moment and tried to will his beard to grow
faster. When a couple of months went by and he was still
free, he began to relax a bit. He took to drinking a good
deal during the waning winter months, and by the time
spring had come to stay in Oklahoma, he was used to his
routine of buying a bottle and a six-pack, going home to
his trailer he rented by the week, and putting away all of
it while he watched a miniature black-and-white TV well
into the night.

After more time had passed, he was able to put the
memory of the frigid afternoon behind him, shut it out.
Dreams about the coach—sheriff—drawing out his pistol
and aiming it at him came too often, and he would sometimes wake up, finish whatever booze was left in the
trailer, and finally pass out into a semiconscious sleep
that freed him of the horrible nightmares. Eventually he
found that he passed out earlier and earlier, and when he
woke up, he forgot where he was. Finally, he just tried
to forget the whole thing. It became like the memory of
a bad dream to him, something that never really happened.

By the first of June he took his share of the money
from a bus station locker, where it had been hidden all
the time he had been busting his ass on construction sites,
and headed west. He found himself in Colorado, a place
he remembered as somewhere he had been when he had
no money at all, and he began to blow the whole wad.
He ate in fancy restaurants, and no goddamn chicken-
fried steaks, either, he promised himself—KC sirloins,
rib eyes—and he checked into fancy motels with color
TVs and swimming pools and hot tubs. He bought a
wardrobe of expensive clothes, a pair of hundred-and-
fifty-dollar boots, forty-dollar jeans and a custom-tailored
western leisure suit that had set him back almost eight
hundred dollars by the time he added two handmade shirts
and a felt hat. And, of course, there had been women.

He avoided pickups in honky-tonks and bars, but he

sought fancy call girls who came when he slipped the
manager or bellhop or night clerk a twenty, girls who
charged a hundred just to take off their clothes while he
watched. Good-looking girls. He wined them and dined
them like they were ladies, and he eased back and let
them make him feel good, although he found that he
couldn't function like he wanted to all the time, not after
a night's hard drinking of expensive whiskey and wine,
imported beer and champagne, but they never complained. How could they? he asked himself. They better
not complain. They were well paid.

Then he bought a car.

It had been his downfall, he thought as he kicked a
small rock out of his way on the sunbaked highway, but
he had always wanted a car of his own, and this was his
chance. He didn't have enough money for a new one, of
course, but he put a big down payment on a good-looking
used Olds Cutlass, T-top with tape deck and white walls
and rally wheels. It was a great sex wagon, he told himself. But then he got the bright idea of driving it down
to Las Vegas and trying to turn the thousand or so dollars
he had left into some kind of big winnings and on the
way he got drunk and wrecked the car. At least he had
had the sense to walk off and leave it. It was wrapped
around a tree someplace south of Boulder, and he knew
he was lucky to be alive. All he had to show for everything he had gone to Colorado with were the clothes on
his back, the fancy western leisure suit, the expensive
boots, and fifty bucks.

The imported wristwatch he had bought was pawned
in Santa Fe for about a tenth of what it cost him. The
rest of his clothes, all of everything he had left, was back
in the hotel room in Boulder in fancy new leather suit-
cases he'd bought. He had just planned to run down to
Vegas for the night, pick up some blackjack winnings,
and maybe some showgirl snatch, and haul ass back to
Boulder. But he never made it that far.

Breedlove didn't remember having been that afraid or
that broke before. He knew he was lucky to be alive, but
he wasn't very smart. That much he was certain enough

of by this time. He just accepted it as a natural fact. "Everything I touch," he said aloud to the buzzing insects beside the road, "turns to shit."

This situation was testimony to his stupidity right here. He finally hitched a ride with a farmer who agreed to take him all the way from west of Amarillo and let him off at the bus station in Kirkland. Then he fell asleep, slept right through the town, and he was left standing on the superheated highway with his dick in his hand and twenty-seven cents in his pocket, watching the stupid old fart bump his rusty pickup down an all-weather road that came out of nowhere to meet the highway. Judging from the sun's position and the movement of the dark cloud on the horizon, that had been almost two hours ago, and nobody had given him a lift or even slowed down to take a closer look at his outstretched thumb.

He felt awful. He hadn't had a bath since he showered at a truck stop in Santa Fe two days ago, and his beard itched. He hated it. The expensive boots were killing his feet, pinching and binding when he walked, and threatening to turn under whenever he stepped on a stone or lump in the blacktop. He had blisters on his blisters; he imagined them bleeding, open and running inside the boots, and he felt a bit like crying. His tongue was a lump of hot stone between gritty teeth. He felt like a bum.

A big car swooshed past him, and for a moment the heat was augmented by the rush of bake-oven draft pulled in its wake. Hitchhiking had gotten a sight tougher than it used to be, he thought, shifting the western leisure suit's jacket from his left hand to his right now that there was no reason to stick out his thumb. Used to be, people picked up folks easy. Now they're too suspicious. They don't even look. They just pass you by. He had never had trouble before, he thought. He was a by-God expert hitcher. It was probably the beard.

After a bit of huffing and puffing broken only by the passing of an occasional car or semi, he topped a small rise and saw the town of Hoolian down on his left. Hoolian, he thought dimly. He used to have a great-aunt who lived there in a big, ramshackle white house. There were almost no houses left there now; most of them had been torn down or moved into Agatite, but he could still make out the old barbershop where he and his old man had spent hundreds, it seemed, of boring hours listening to old farts gossip and sneak drinks from pint bottles while his mother visited her aunt nearby.

He figured he had been walking for more than ten miles, alternately wishing the coming storm would go ahead and sweep over him, drench him in a cool, soaking rain, and dreading the prospect of a north central Texas storm hitting him out in the open. He wished he had had the guts to steal a car—he should have, he knew. Joe Don had shown him how, but, damn it, it just wasn't his style—if he had a style. He couldn't run a bluff, not like Joe Don could, and he'd probably wind up picking on some dude with a hog leg in his pocket who'd blow his brains out.

In the shimmering heat, accented as the storm cloud rose on the horizon, he could make out the ancient Hoolian Garage, and he could see men moving around it, tiny in the distance. He also noted the outdoor crapper where he had had to piss when he felt the need and his old man wouldn't take him back to Aunt Maudie's. He hated that place, he recalled, with its smelly, dark, wasp-infested interior and the red ant beds and weeds and snakes that surrounded it. He recalled once, when he was nine, he had to go out there at his old man's insistence since they had just arrived for what looked to be a several hours' visit, and he had been barefoot. Ants attacked his feet right away, and the stings had been horrible. He had pissed all over himself, running and screaming and streaming pee down his legs into the shop, where his old man had poured cheap whiskey all over the bites and laughed at him and cursed him for being too damned stupid to wear shoes when he came out to "the country."

God, he hated that place. He associated it with so many unpleasant memories, and he thought of it as a permanent nightmare that surely must come back from time to time, although he couldn't recall thinking of it consciously for years.

He briefly considered cutting across country to the diminishing hamlet to beg a cold drink or even a ride. It was a safe bet that no one much lived there anymore, and all those men must be going someplace. But directly between him and the small buildings was an open pasture where a tangle of tumbleweeds and mesquite, Johnson grass and prickly pear forbade his entrance. With a potential gully washer bearing down on him in an hour or so, he didn't dare risk leaving the highway, and he doubted his fancy boots would take too much punishment in open country. He doubled his stride and fixed his mind on the cutoff to Hoolian, which he calculated to be about two or three miles on down the road, down the other side of the rise and around a slight curve.

When he rounded the curve he almost fell over backward. Parked right on the shoulder was a bright yellow Vega with the hood up. Breedlove stopped dead, and his jaw hung slack in amazement. He hadn't even noticed the car from the rise of ground where he had seen the town, now invisible behind the mesquite-laden pasture. But there it was, not fifty yards in front of him. Damn, he thought, I almost walked right into it.

As he drew closer he saw a woman sitting behind the wheel, her head resting on one hand, her elbow propped on the windowsill. From about twenty-five yards out he called in a loud, friendly voice, "Hello!" He didn't want to surprise some gun-happy woman who had stopped for a nap and was just waiting for her chance to empty a .357 into some hitchhiking cowboy bent on rape and robbery.

She jumped quickly when he called, banging her head on the car's roof. "Shit!" she swore loudly, then turned her head and peered out the window, rubbing her scalp.

Her eyes were fearful when they turned toward him, for the last thing she expected to hear was a voice calling her from out of nowhere. "Hi," she said tentatively, and Breedlove noticed she was rolling up the window as he continued to ease forward.

"Trouble?" he asked, and felt stupid. She would hardly have stopped for pleasure in this heat out in the middle of mesquite and rattlesnake country. He stopped his movement to show he had no harmful intentions.

"Darn thing won't start," she said, showing what was obviously an hour or more's exasperation. "It just goes *clunk* and sits there." She had stopped rolling up the window, but she was making no move to get out. Breedlove noticed her bright blue eyes and admired her straight, even teeth that were showing in a friendly but cautious smile.

"Want me to take a look?" Breedlove asked, sticking his hands out in front of him and shaking out the Western leisure suit jacket to show he had no weapons.

"Sure, if you want," she said, hurriedly adding, "I don't have no money."

He got the meaning of her statement and sighed loudly. "Look, lady, I'm just a hitchhiker. You just stay there in the car. I'll have a look. Maybe I can get you going, and you can give me a lift. Maybe not. It don't matter."

"That's okay." She smiled suddenly and began rolling the window back down. "You probably could have snuck up on me if you'd wanted to. I think I fell asleep."

Breedlove moved up to the open hood and peered in. He didn't know much about cars at all, since, except for the Cutlass, which he hadn't had long enough to do more than put gas in twice, he'd never owned one. But he'd watched Floyd work on the getaway cars, and he felt he might spot something obvious. He felt stupid looking at the strange, dusty overhead cam engine. All the tiny little parts seemed to taunt him with their simple arrangement and elementary appearance.

"Giver her a try," he said in what he hoped sounded like a confident voice. She turned the key, and a clicking sound came from under the hood. "Could be the starter, or solenoid," he predicted, "but I don't know."

He poked and prodded around awhile longer, finding nothing as luckily simple as a loose wire, wondering where the hell the starter was on the car, when his eyes suddenly fell on the battery terminals. They were covered with white and yellow corrosion. Maybe that was it.

"You stop along here for any reason?" he asked, since he didn't think the battery terminals would make the car just quit going down the road.

"Uh-huh," she nodded, looking out the window. He noticed again how damned pretty she was. She looked fresh and bright in the yellow car, and he felt dirtier and sweatier than ever. Her bright blue eyes and brown hair complemented her bright face and wide, moist lips surrounding pretty, straight teeth. She's a lot prettier than the whores in Colorado, Breedlove thought, feeling a sudden hollowness inside him, a sense of inferiority he had come to know too well.

She smiled a bit and lowered her eyes, "I had to . . . uh . . . I had to pee."

He grinned at her and glanced down at the battery, feeling her embarrassment.

"You see," she went on, "I'd been visiting my aunt over in Memphis, and she fills me up with tea. Hot tea, iced tea, and more hot tea. I just couldn't make it another foot, so I pulled over for a sec." She reached into the seat behind her and held up a roll of pink toilet paper. "You see, I'm prepared!"

The image of her squatting in the bushes, exposed and vulnerable, swam over Breedlove, and he redoubled his efforts to free up the cables from the terminals. He felt himself growing erect and turned slightly away from her. That's the last thing I need, he thought, for her to see a bone in my pants and start going crazy.

"I flagged down a car about an hour ago, and the man said he'd go into Agatite for me and send somebody, but either he forgot or couldn't find nobody. I should have told him to go into Hoolian, but I forgot. I don't know whether anybody still lives there anymore anyhow." She pouted a bit, sticking her lower lip out prettily. "I guess I should have taken him up on his ride offer, but I think he had something else on his mind." She winked a bit at Breedlove, causing his erection to come up full. Where were you when I needed you, he thought disdainfully, in Colorado with those two-hundred-dollar-a-pop whores?

"Well, I don't think this is too serious," he said, trying to sound casual. "Ouch!" He banged his arm on the rear opening of the hood as he tried to pull one of the stubborn clamps off the terminal. "Do you have any tools? A wrench or pliers or something?" he asked, sucking his finger and tasting the corrosion on them.

"Oh, yeah! I forgot!" she said, her eyes brightening. "I got a whole mess of tools back there." She jumped out of the car and moved with the keys to the hatchback. He slowly followed her, noting for the first time that there was something he recognized about her. He wondered if she was someone he knew from Agatite, but he had been gone for years, and she was a lot younger than he was. Still, she looked familiar, like he had known her intimately someplace, sometime before.

She opened the hatchback, and he saw an enormous toolbox on the floor of the compartment. She opened it and began rummaging around, coming up with plastic envelopes of screwdrivers, wrenches, socket sets, and other miscellaneous tools and devices, all new, most with price tags still on them. "My aunt!" she exclaimed in mock disgust. "She worries about me driving this old clunker." She gestured at the yellow car. "I try to tell her that it's a good old car. It hardly ever gives me any trouble—at least not up till now. I've got over a hundred thousand miles on it, and it uses regular gas! Anyhow, she thinks a woman driving alone, even in a new car, should be able to fix it if it breaks down. So two Christmases ago she took this stupid toolbox down and made the Chevy House fill it with tools. It's *so* dumb. I don't know what half of them are for, and it takes up half my space back here. Poor Aunt Vi! I can't even change a flat. But I didn't have the heart to tell her. She's a dear old thing."

She piled the tools on the floor of the hatchback, sorting them absently. Breedlove noticed with pleasure the peach-colored suit and frilly blouse she wore. He could see her bra through the blouse, and he wondered about her breasts underneath. Her nails were brightly lacquered and reflected the sunlight that was suddenly brilliant in the storm-threatened sky. Insects buzzed fitfully in the pasture nearby.

"You wanted pliers, right?" She leaned over the hatchback, her skirt riding up, exposing the back of her leg. He caught a flash of white slip and lowered his eyes to where her foot raised partly out of the low-heeled shoe, revealing a perfect arch, and the erection that had retreated when he hurt his arm attacked again with a painful thrust.

"Yeah," he said dully, taking the tool and turning away. He walked quickly to the front of the Vega, casting his thoughts wildly about, trying to think of anything else but her graceful legs, her moist mouth, her slender ankles and feet.

"Look!" She giggled, running a bit toward him and catching him by surprise as he bent over the battery. Her right hand held an enormous open-end wrench, the sort used on semi-tractors and heavy machinery. It was two feet long and looked as if it weighed a ton as she held it up for him to see. It caught the final rays of the sun before it disappeared completely behind the now ominous cloud that covered three quarters of the northwestern sky. Breedlove started back, reeling, thinking insanely that she had seen his bone and was going to coldcock him.

"Hey!" he yelled, sticking a hand up in front of his face. But she began laughing and dropped the wrench to her side.

"Scared you? Shit! I'm the one who's helpless and broken down out here in an old car in the middle of nowhere!" She giggled and looked prettier than ever. He relaxed. "This guy I work for gave me this when he heard about my aunt's toolbox Christmas present. He thought it was funnier than hell. Damn thing weighs a ton!"

Setting the enormous wrench down on the fender of the Vega, she leaned over, watching him work the connections off the battery terminals. The scare she gave him had driven thoughts of sexual desire away temporarily, but now, with her so close again, he could smell her perfume, the freshness of her hair, and he could see the curve of her neck falling into the V of her blouse. Her cleavage was also visible. He wished she would go away, let him get on with his work, get the car started and drive him into Agatite, where he could hitch south to Abilene.

"You look awfully familiar," she said, and he realized she was looking at him intently. "You from around here?"

"Nope." He finally got one cable free and realized that it was so short he couldn't get to the other one without her holding this one out of the way. "Would you hold this?" he asked.

"Sure," she said, taking the cable in her long, beautiful fingers and ignoring the shake in his voice that revealed a fear that she might know him from Agatite or elsewhere. She wore a necklace watch that was dangling between her arms as she bent over, and it was banging against the walls of the engine compartment. "Here," she said, "just a sec." She handed the cable back to him and stood up straight, expertly flipping the watch around behind her neck, pulling up her hair with her other hand to expose a creamy neck that sent prickles up and down Breedlove's body. She dropped the pendent timepiece down her back, beneath her jacket. "Damned watch was also a present from Aunt Vi, and like almost everything else she does for me, it's a pain in the ass. You from Kirkland?"

"Nope." Breedlove handed the cable back to her and tried once again to concentrate on the battery. "I'm from San Antone. I been up in Colorado, tryin' to get work, but no luck."

"I thought there was a lot of work up there," she said, suggestively running one long, painted fingernail up and down the cable's line.

"I didn't find it if there was," he said, grimacing with the effort he was having working the clamp free from the terminal post. That was the way of things, he thought. One lie always leads to another. He had lied his way across the western United States, using names he couldn't remember, lying about who he was, where he had been, what he could do, where he was going. Some mornings he got up not even sure what the people he worked with thought was the truth, and he had the cold feeling of panic he always felt when people in a perfectly natural way asked him about a contradiction in history or facts about himself. He knew what was coming.

"What kind of work do you do?" She was looking intently at him again. His sexual hunger was becoming overwhelming.

"Oh, little of everything. Anything, really," he said, wondering why the hell he was doing this to himself. Then he added, "I rodeo a little." He then realized why he was doing it. He believed, as all itinerant cowboys believe, that country girls were suckers for rodeo riders. Shit, he'd only been to four rodeos in his whole life, and he'd never ridden anything in any of them.

"We got a rodeo comin' up over to Oklaunion," she said, suddenly trying to be helpful.

"That's nice," he replied. He was wondering how long this would go on, where it might lead, when suddenly the battery clamp came off the terminal easily, just as it should have. "There. That's part one," he said, digging into his Western leisure suit pocket for a knife, aware, as he fished around, of his erection's semidormant state.

She moved away a little at the sight of the knife, but she kept holding onto the cable, and she kept studying him. "You sure do look familiar. I'm from Agatite, originally. My friends call me Lee."

A giant semi screamed by, and they both bowed their heads in the afterblast, Breedlove reaching up to secure his hat in the terrible hot wind. He could smell in the rushing air the promise of rain and a lot of it soon to come.

The coolness hinted at in the approaching storm refreshed Breedlove, and the stirring at the back of his mind when he looked at the girl didn't fully register. That was the first vehicle to pass them the whole time he had been there, he thought absently, and he wondered at the vague discomfort in his mind. Something was stuck there. Something dangerous.

"So what's your name?" she asked, flicking out a lovely tongue to wet her lips.

He quickly searched his mind for a usable alias. He tried to remember the one he used in Colorado, but it wouldn't come. "Shit!" he cried suddenly as the knife slipped and cut a notch in his finger, drawing blood immediately.

"Oh!" she exclaimed. "I've got a first-aid kit in the car. Good ol' Aunt Vi to the rescue."

"No, that's okay," he said, sucking the finger. "Let's get these on and give her a try."

As he worked the clamps down, she commented, "That's a strange name, Shit." Then she giggled. Her voice was light, and her laugh like crystal.

"Well," he said, "it's better than my real one." His mind was racing through a tunnel of completely blank information. What *name*, goddamnit!

"What's that?" She looked carefully at him.

"You'll laugh," he said. "Everyone does." Okay, he thought, that did it. Now you don't just have to come up with a name, but a *funny* name. One lie always leads to another, he wryly reminded himself. For a moment he had a mad impulse to take her by her lovely shoulders and shake her. You silly bitch! he wanted to scream at her. You shouldn't be out here cock-teasing some hitchhiker you never met before. You don't know that I'm a by-God interstate felon, wanted in two states for robbery and conspiracy to commit murder—no, not conspiracy—for *accessory* to murder.

He thought for one horrible moment of the Oklaunion robbery on that freezing afternoon, of Coach with his guts hanging out, of his eye—no, not that, not now. He wiped the memory from his mind, something he hadn't had to do for months. Why now? What about this stupid, silly girl made that come up? Just because she was from there? Probably.

"Okay." He forced a grin. "You asked for it. Ronald . . . Ronald McDonald!"

"Oh, shit!" she squealed, and squatted beside the Vega's fender, laughing so hard she dropped the cable and held her head, "Oh, shit, shit, shit! It hurts. I gotta pee!"

A myriad of images hit Breedlove until he realized she wasn't going to the bushes again. He picked up the fallen cable and began working the clamp down on the terminal. "I told you you would laugh. Everybody does."

"I don't believe it!" She continued to laugh, and he found himself chuckling, glad to have lost the overwhelming sexual desire he had felt seconds before, glad that the vague discomfort he had felt because of her also seemed to have gone. This was better, he thought, and he was momentarily proud of himself for the quick lie. She stood straight up again, wiping tears from her pretty blue eyes, now transluscent with mirth. She chortled to herself again and shook her head, mimicking his deeper voice. "Ronald McDonald!"

"Why don't you give her a try now?" he asked, tightening the clamps down.

"Right," she said. She had recovered from the joke, and skipping to the driver's side to let herself in, she kicked her legs high—frisky, Breedlove thought idly—showing him a flash of thigh as she sat down. Through the windshield of the small car he could see right up her skirt, and she knew he could, but she made no move to put her legs together. The old longing feeling returned.

The car turned over right away, but it wouldn't start. It just cranked and cranked.

"Okay, okay!" he called out over the churning engine. "Save the battery." He could smell gasoline. "I think you flooded it. Wait a few minutes and try again." He glanced up at the sky and noticed that the purple cloud was now completely black and covered all but the easternmost horizon. In the distance he spotted lightning flashes. One hell of a storm was coming, he thought absently. "Say, you got a cigarette in there?"

"Sure!" she said, and she reached into the passenger seat and rummaged through her handbag. He moved back around to the passenger side of the car and fetched the pliers and overlarge wrench, setting them down on the other fender. She got out and handed him a smoke, holding another cigarette expertly on the tip of her lip, waiting for him to light it with a green Bic lighter she held out in her other hand. He reached over and, in spite of the fact that there was no wind at all in advance of the storm, cupped the flame in his hands. For a moment their eyes met, and as she drew in the smoke, two thoughts exploded in Breedlove's mind.

Both thoughts came, as it were, one on top of the other, tumbling immediately from the memory of a cold and stormy day months before, blown into the forefront of his consciousness with the same viciousness of a blue norther tearing down the street of a small Texas town. He never could have said which was first or which might have had more impact if he had been mentally ready and able to decide on his physical reaction. But there was no time for calculated movement. Less than a second passed.

The first thought, at least the one he always thereafter wanted to believe was first, was that he could take this girl right here, right on the highway, in the cramped backseat of the Vega or in the overgrown Johnson grass of the bar ditch nearby. This he was certain of, and he was equally certain that she wanted him to take her, to make violent love to her body, to make her cry out in ecstasy and make those beautifully long and polished fingernails scratch over his back.

The second thought canceled out the first, however. And it was this one that overcame his physical safeguards, his perpetual mask against reality, that forced his eyes to grow in terror and recognition and sudden understanding, and that triggered a similar and simultaneous reaction in the girl's mind. Oklaunion. Agatite. Lee— short for *Eileen*. The vision of the robbery returning now full and complete to torment him, the vague feeling of familiarity between them, all those things came together in one horrible vision of Eileen Kennedy with a pistol in her hands, blasting away from behind the manager's desk, her matted hair covered with Coach's blood, her blouse torn open by Breedlove's clumsy hand, her desire to kill him and the others overwhelming all other impressions

she might give. No wonder he hadn't recognized her! Her
hair was fresh now, longer, free from the sweat of fear
and the clots of gore. Her dress was intact, clean, no
bloody streaks running down her face and front. When
he'd last seen her, she had been a crazed woman with a
gun, not a flirtatious girl stuck on the highway. When
he'd last looked into her eyes, she was wishing him dead
with all her heart.

The horror of the afternoon swept over him in less than
a second, and his eyes widened in panic, in painful recognition of a ghost of his past he had thought, had hoped,
was finally buried. Racing around the bloody, battered
edges of his memory was a cold terror that she might
read his thoughts, his fantasies of her naked, of her wanting him, of her when he had lain with whores in Colorado, but it hadn't been this girl, this silly, giggly girl
with good legs and big tits who had taunted him on the
highway between Agatite and Kirkland. It had been the
girl in the office. It couldn't be the same girl. Life didn't
work like that. It wasn't the same girl! But he knew it
was.

Just as the two thoughts crossed Breedlove's mind like
twin beams of light, her mind in that curious way humans
have of intuiting thoughts registered the same scene. The
praying man's shoulder exploding from the bullet, the
shattering glass, the confusion, the pain, the screaming,
and as she remembered, she saw his eyes turn from the
soft, warm, lusty desire she had been cultivating all the
time since she first saw him that afternoon to cold, hard
terror with the same glassy, fixed stare he had shown her
months before in the office of the Holiday Finance Company, where she still worked. She recognized him as well.
She knew that the man she had thought of as a knight in
armor, showing up to rescue her and probably fuck her
senseless that same night, that same man standing terrorized before her with an unlit Winston in his mouth,
that man was the man she had tried so desperately to kill
only a few months before, the man she had said many
hundreds of times she would love to kill, to "blow his

balls off,'' she bragged to Alvin Atwood when he called her Annie Oakley and teased her about her rotten aim.

For another two or three seconds they stood silently, frozen, staring into each other's eyes, allowing the knowledge that they both suddenly found to admit itself to their respective realities, to creep over their bodies and force them into action.

II. Lawman
The Present, One Day Before

Doc Pritchard fussily lit his pipe and drew in deeply, blowing smoke out over the top of the bowl and extinguishing the match he had used. Across the desk from him, Sheriff Able Newsome frowned over the final autopsy report on Eileen Kennedy. His lips moved as he read the heavy Latinate words that filled the narrow typed lines of the report. Glossy black-and-white prints were attached to the papers, gruesome in their stark revelations of what Eileen had looked like before Everett Hardin restored her for burial.

''I can't make head or tail of this, Doc,'' Able finally said, running his hands through his hair.

''Well,'' Doc Pritchard said, a halo of smoke surrounding his bald head, ''read on through to the end, and maybe together we can decipher it. Those kids down in Austin don't know how to talk to real people.''

Able worried his hair some more and tried desperately to concentrate on the technical medical terms and descriptions. It had been a bad day so far, what with the scene with Jingles still bothering him, and he was having trouble focusing his attention on all the jargon and legal descriptions in front of him.

After he got back to the office from Hoolian, he had stewed and fumed, wrestling with his conscience because he had actually let the fat police chief bully him into losing his temper. He skipped lunch again and drove immediately back, pulling up again beside Jingles' cruiser, and got out, cursing the blast of heat that seemed to be increased by the argument going on between Jingles and Mel in front of the shop.

As he strolled up, he found out that Jingles had deduced that the electrical cord used to hang Eileen had come from Mel's back room, a conclusion the chief had come to after barging into the small rear of the shop in search of a drink Mel had denied he had for the policeman. After locating a half-full bottle, Jingles had blearily noticed the tangle of wires up over the box of liquor in the dusty, cobwebbed back room. After a few moments' cogitation, helped by the bourbon he drank while he thought, he began browbeating Mel until Mel, himself far from sober, finally admitted that the cord "could have come" from the tangle of old wires and junk, but he couldn't say for sure. He also admitted that the lock on the back window of the shop was broken and always had been as far as he knew, and that the day before they found the girl's body, the morning before they found it, he had "felt" like somebody had been inside the shop fooling around with stuff, but he didn't think much about it since nothing he knew of was missing.

The two men were standing clear of the porch in the bright heat of the midafternoon sun, toe to toe, screaming at each other. Jingles held a tangle of cords in his hand and kept whipping his leg with them, and Mel kept waving his arms, an empty pint bottle extended from his right hand. Both men were covered with sweat, with briny trails running from their foreheads into their eyes and mouths.

"Why in *hell* didn't you tell me about this before?" Jingles yelled.

" 'Cause I didn't think it made any nevermind!" Mel yelled back. "I told you that a hunnerd times all right, but you're just too pigheaded to hear me!"

"But if somebody *was* in the shop, he might have been the killer!"

"Well!" Mel screeched, his voice cracking from the effort. "If I'd aknown there was a body out in the shithouse, don't you think I'd a'taken a special interest in it?'' He was panting in the heat. "You think I'm as stupid as you are, you dumb son of a bitch?''

Clearly the argument had been going on for some time, and Able resolved not to lose his temper or become involved. He had come back to smooth things over between him and the chief of police, not necessarily to apologize, but this wasn't the time, he realized. He had long suspected that the cord came from around the barbershop somewhere, and he had long ago decided that it didn't make any difference.

"Maybe, just maybe," Jingles went on, ignoring the sheriff and concentrating on his old adversary, the barber, but lowering his voice and trying to appear as professional as possible under Able's watchful eye, "Maybe we might've found something last Wednesday that would point out who killed that girl, you dumb shit. Now, after a week, it's not even a good shot. And maybe"—the police chief's eyes went narrow with suspicion—"maybe *you* found something and are hidin' it. Maybe one of your buddies is involved in this.''

"For Christ's sake, Jingles—"

"What was that?" Police Chief Murphy's eyes widened in outrage and renewed anger. "What did you call me?''

"*Jingles*! Goddamnit, *Jingles*! Ever'body calls you that, you fat fuck! You're too dumb to hit the ground with a rock! You come out here an' run off all my business, all my friends. You're out here ever'day askin' all kinds of stupid questions, an' you're drivin' me crazy. I don't know nothin' 'bout that girl! Nothin'! Nobody out here, even that Mescan kid, knows nothin' either. What's the matter, God-awful-high-an'-mighty policeman? You worried 'bout your job or what? I checked with Harvey Connally, an' he told me you're not even in your rightful jury-iss-diction out here! You got no rights a-tall." Mel was warming to a climax, his face bright red under a steady flow of perspiration so profuse that Able worried that he might have a heart attack. "Well, I tell you somethin', Chief *Jingles* Murphy, I ain't answerin' no more questions for you or nobody else! I told you what all I

know a hunnerd times, an' if you wanna arrest me, you
go right ahead an' do it. But you better have some goddamn charges, 'cause I'm gonna put your ass in a sling
'less you do!''

The police chief of Agatite, Texas, stood stunned,
sweat running down his chin and dripping onto his soaked
uniform blouse. He shot a look at Able, who had stood
silently during the outburst, one hand on his gun butt,
the other holding a Hava-Tampa Jewel, his head bobbing
almost imperceptively as Mel's tirade hit a crescendo.
Insects buzzed crazily in the silence following the barber's speech, and Mel fished a handkerchief from his hip
pocket and mopped his head and face. He was spent,
done, too hot and tired to be angry. With a final look at
Able, Mel climbed the barbershop's porch steps and disappeared inside the building.

Jingles looked after him a moment, still keeping silent,
then he shifted his gaze to Able who had still said nothing and remained in the same position. "I got to call
in," said the policeman matter-of-factly, and he went to
his car, wiping his head and face with the sleeve of his
soaked blouse.

Able turned and strolled around back and sat down on
the upturned Coke case where Jingles had been that
morning. He figured any "clues" Murphy had ferreted
out of the situation didn't amount to a popcorn fart, and
as he gazed at the shimmering building and wondered
what secrets it held, he realized that they knew less now
than they did when they started.

He clung to the idea that the broken fingernails might
lead to something. He had remembered them too late to
ask the girl's aunt about them, but he'd called Eileen's
employer over in Oklaunion the night before and found
out that her nails were the girl's pride and joy. Another
call to Miss Kennedy confirmed the fact and added the
information that the nails had all been intact when Eileen
left Memphis. It wasn't likely she had cut them herself,
especially only a couple of them. Somehow, some way, Able
believed, those nails would lead him to the killer, but he
didn't have a notion of how that might happen.

They had fixed the date of death as Sunday, over three weeks before they found the body, based on when she was seen last in Memphis, but he didn't know for sure that she had been killed on that date, only that she had disappeared then. Her car's odometer showed no extraordinary mileage from its last oil change on the Sunday before she visited her aunt, the number duly recorded on the paper sticker in front of the door and still legible after the fire. But where had she been killed, and why? The questions just led to answers that led to more questions.

Suddenly Jingles came rushing around the corner, his utility belt and accessories confirming the accuracy of his nickname.

"Chrystal says your boys got a suspect in your office," he announced, breathing hard between words.

Able jumped up, almost too fast for the heat of the afternoon sun. His head swam and he felt his balance slipping. "Who?" He shifted his feet and squared himself.

"Didn't ask," Jingles said, turning to go. "Let's move!"

They got into their respective cars and raced into Agatite. Jingles ran his siren all the way and must have topped one hundred ten as he left Able behind. "Asshole," was Able's only comment as he fought the urge to speed to keep up.

Finally arriving at the courthouse office, Able walked into a scene of unbelievable tension. John David Hogan had placed himself between Jingles, who was still sweating profusely, his shirt soaked and globs of perspiration running down his face and fat cheeks in spite of the circulating fans' full-speed hum, and a small man dressed in a baggy suit and seated uncomfortably in a chair next to Able's desk.

"This is the sheriff," John David said, side-glancing at Jingles, who also received a quick shooting look from the little man who was clearly uncomfortable in the presence of the chief of police. Jingles, Able suddenly noticed, was holding a pair of handcuffs in his pudgy fists.

"Keep your seat," Able said, moving easily, now that

he was on his home turf, to his desk and sitting down. He opened his notebook and took a pencil from the tobacco can on his desk. "Has this man been given his rights?" he asked John David.

"Rights?" The deputy was perplexed.

"What I want to know," Jingles interjected, "is why the hell he's not in chains? Where do you train your men, Able, down to the Baptist Sunday School?"

"What rights?" the man asked generally of Able and John David, visibly shying away from chief of police.

"Excuse me, sir," Able said, still holding calm in the storm that was spewing from Jingles' mouth in the form of panting disbelief. "John David, my information was that you had a suspect in custody."

"Gosh, no, Able," the deputy said, his mouth hanging open, "This is Mr. Hollis Carlson, and he's come forward with some information about seeing the girl alive. That's all." He looked around to Jingles, who made a pained noise in his throat. "Who the heck said anything about a suspect?"

"Never mind," Able said. Jingles cursed under his breath but avoided Able's eyes. "I'm very sorry, Mr. Carlson. I'm afraid I was given the wrong information." He placed the notebook in front of him. "Now, what do you know about Eileen Kennedy?" Jingles immediately began fumbling with his blouse pocket, trying to pull his own sodden notebook out.

"Well," Hollis Carlson began, looking around the room and beginning to sweat a bit himself, "I'm a salesman—implement parts and accessories. I hit all the dealers in this part of the state and over to Oklahoma. I'm on the road a lot. I may not know nothin'. I mean, I seen a girl on the road, broke down. But it was nearly a month ago."

"Go on," Able said. "Tell us what you know."

Hollis licked his lips. "Could I get a cup of coffee or somethin'?"

Able nodded toward John David, who moved to the coffeepot and poured some of the thick liquid into a cup.

Hollis sipped it nervously, frowned, and set the cup on the desk.

"Our coffee's pretty bad." Able smiled at him. He could see the man was scared to death. Was he hiding something? Was Jingles right? Was this mousy little man the killer?

"Do I need a lawyer or somethin'?" Hollis asked, glancing again at the chief of police.

"Lawyer!" Jingles cut in. "Why do you think you need a lawyer? 'Less you're involved in some way."

"Shut up!" Able ordered suddenly. "Shut up, Murphy, and let the man talk. Go on, Mr. Carlson, tell us what you know. I don't think you need a lawyer. If you do, I'll be the first to tell you." He smiled a fatherly smile at the little man, who managed a weak grin before he continued.

"Well, I was goin' from Amarillo to Dallas. I was supposed to be home on Friday, but I had car trouble an' it took most of Saturday to fix it—carburetor, I think— so I didn't leave till Sunday. After the Cowboy exhibition game. I love the Cowboys. I'd stayed up real late the night before watchin' the cable in the motel—we ain't got cable at home—so it was late an' I was pretty near whacked by the time I got this far." He glanced around and took another sip of the thick bitter coffee. "I was just this side of Kirkland when I spotted this little yellow car off the side of the road. I wasn't goin' to stop, but then I seen it was a woman in it. Pretty girl, too." He blushed a bit.

"What kind of car was it?" Jingles asked, ignoring a scowl from Able.

"I don't know," Hollis replied, "One of them little cars, not new or nothin'. I don't know much 'bout cars."

"I thought you sold tractor parts," Jingles said suspiciously. "Doesn't that mean you know something about mechanical shit?"

"I sell *implement* parts, accessories an' parts. You know, tractor seats, umbrellas, junk like that. We even got a line of radios an' cassette recorders for tractors, an' we're goin' to have TV for the big ones. . . ."

"Let's get back to the girl," Able said, shooting a stern glance at Jingles.

"Well, like I say. I wouldn't normally have stopped, but she was standin' there with the hood up on this car, yellow car, an' she was dressed real sharp. Pretty gal, you know." Able nodded, noting that his comment was void of lust. It was objective description. "Well, like I say, I stopped an' tried to help her. The car jus' wouldn't start. When she tried it, it jus' went *clunk* like the batt'ry was dead or somethin'. Like I say, I don't know much 'bout cars, so I offered to give her a ride into town. But she said she'd rather wait an' have me send somebody out. So I went on into Agatite, here. But, like I say, it was Sunday, an' it was gettin' late, an' there wasn't nobody like a mechanic 'round. Just some kid, an' I went on to Vernon, thinkin' I'd get somebody there. But I couldn't find no place open with a service truck there either. So I went on, but nobody was open. I asked about a tow truck or somethin' ever'where I stopped, but nobody had one. By then it was gettin' dark, an' a storm was comin' up, an' nobody would even talk to me 'bout drivin' back that far west. I guess I figured somebody else had stopped for her by then."

Hollis sipped his awful cup of coffee again, clearly relieved to have moved himself away from the girl before she was killed. He glanced over the top of the cup at Able, trying to see if the sheriff believed him.

"Why didn't you go back and get her?" Able asked calmly, fighting down a sudden anger he felt toward this small, wormy salesman who had left Eileen Kennedy out on the highway to die.

"Maybe he did," Jingles said.

"Like I say," Hollis said quickly, "I was already two days behind schedule gettin' home, an' late in the day to boot." He leaned forward conspiratorially. "Listen, Sheriff, I got me one mean wife, an' her mother lives with us, too. I mean, I *had* to get home. If she knew I'd picked up some good-lookin' girl on the road, even to help her out, she'd give me nine kinds of hell. Shit, if she even knew I stopped for her for a minute or two . . ."

He leaned back, considering his woes. "As it was, I had to do some fancy talkin', late as I come in. She never did like my bein' on the road. Says motels are full of whores lookin' for guys like me."

Able knocked the ash of his cigar into a spitoon next to his desk and contemplated the cowardly little man beside him. "Was she stopped for any other reason than her car wouldn't run?" He knew there couldn't have been too much wrong with the car. Somebody had managed to drive it more than a hundred miles before dumping it and burning it.

Hollis reddened down to his dirty shirt collar under the cheap, baggy suit. "Said she had to pee," he said. "Jus' like that." Jingles snorted. "That's what she said!" Hollis insisted as he looked around the room at the lawmen's faces. "Listen," he said, lowering his voice, "I think she was comin' on to me a little." Then, sensing laughter about to burst out from his questioners, he added, "I'm not shittin' you! I know I ain't much to look at, but damn it, she got me horny as hell just talkin' to her. I s'pose . . . I s'pose she scared me a little. Like I say, I got this mean wife. . . ."

Able cut him off. "Did you see anybody else on the road?"

"No. Least not nearby."

Able tapped his pencil on the desk for a few seconds. Hollis suddenly brightened.

"Well, there was a hitchhiker!"

"Where?" Jingles said.

"Down the road, toward Kirkland. I seen him get out of a farmer's pickup at a crossroad. He tried to wave me down, but I didn't stop. You think *he* killed the girl?"

"What did he look like?" Able asked, ignoring the question.

"Well, let's see . . ." Hollis lost himself in recollection. "I don't remember much about him. He had a nice suit on, I remember. Green, I think. An' a hat, cowboy hat. Straw, I think." Jingles was writing furiously in the soggy notebook. "I remember he didn't have no suitcase or luggage or nothin'. I figured he was a local boy. He looked like a cowboy, you know? Had a beard.''

"What about the truck that let him out?" Able asked, noting that Jingles nodded as if in agreement with the question.

"It was jus' a truck, an old one, I guess. I remember worryin' 'bout him not havin' no turn signals an' tryin' to turn 'round right in front of me. That's why I slowed down, an' the hitchhiker thought I was stoppin' for him an' tried to wave me down, I reckon." Hollis looked around the room again and reached for the coffee cup once more. "I know it was a pickup, if that's any help. An' he did turn off the highway, jus' like I figured he would, but I was by him by then."

Able thought for a moment. "How come you're just coming forward with all this now?"

Hollis' eyes got large with innocence. "I just found out about it. I was over to the John Deere place this mornin', an' I heard 'em talkin' 'bout it, so I came right over soon as I got back from callin' on some farmers who was havin' trouble over to Franklin's Crossin'." John David nodded from his position behind Hollis to indicate to Able that those were the facts.

"Why'd you come here instead of the Police Department?" Jingles asked.

Hollis looked perplexed, but Able broke in before he could answer.

"Listen, Mr. Carlson," he said, "we really appreciate the information. If you remember anything else or if we have any more questions, we may want to talk to you again. Do you have his address?" The question went to John David, who nodded, resignedly passing a pad across to Jingles, who began writing down the information.

"Now," Able said to Hollis Carlson, "I want you to take a ride with my deputy out to where you think you spotted the car. Also, I want you to show him where the hitchhiker got out of the truck. Okay?"

Hollis nodded and stood up, sticking out his hand for Able to grasp. It was a limp handshake, Able noted with disgust, and his contempt for the small man who had abandoned Eileen Kennedy came back in a rush he had to fight down.

"Think I'll tag along," Jingles said to John David, who looked up at Able to catch his nod.

"Mr. Carlson," Able said, "did you happen to notice anything about Ei—about the girls' hands?"

"Her hands?" Hollis frowned.

"Yes, her hands. Anything unusual?"

"No," Hollis said, scratching his chin. "Nothin' I can remember. Nope, nothin' at all." He turned to go, " 'Cept her fingernails," he said as his head turned.

"What?" Able shot at him, causing him to turn back, his eyes wide.

"Well, like I say, she was done up real pretty, an' I noticed she had these really long fingernails. She said she was a secretary, an' I asked her how she could type with them long fingernails, an' that's what I meant"—he glanced around sheepishly—" 'bout her given' me the eye. Said she didn't have to type that much, if you know what I mean. I mean, it wasn't what she said so much as the way she said it. If you know what I mean."

"Were they all there?" Able asked, trying hard not to look into Jingles' face, which was a picture of incredulity.

"All what?"

"Her fingernails," Able said patiently. "Were all ten there. Were any broken off?"

"Hell, Sheriff, I didn't notice. I s'pose they all was there. I wasn't really lookin' at her fingernails, if you know what I mean."

"Thank you, Mr. Carlson." Able waved him off in a dismissing gesture. "Murphy." He called the chief of police back, watching in silence as Hollis disappeared down the hall of the courthouse. "Don't badger that man." He held up a palm to stop the protest he knew Jingles was formulating. "Don't browbeat him, Murphy. Just stick to his story. It sounds right to me, and he's trying to be helpful. So *leave him alone*!" Jingles turned angrily on his heel and left Able's office.

"I still can't make out much from this," Able con-

fessed to Doc Pritchard. It was now nearly dark outdoors. John David had returned Hollis to his car and then
gone back with Jingles to interview some of the farmers
around the crossroads. Hollis was unable to find the exact
spot where he had seen Eileen's car, but the crossroads
he had located with no difficulty at all. Able was not
hopeful, however. A loose count showed more than fifty
families living within easy reach of the crossroad before
it deadended into the Red River to the north and into a
mesa some five miles to the south. Besides, they had no
guarantee that the farmer actually lived in the area anyway. They could be weeks finding the particular truck
that had let a hitchhiker off at the crossroads a month
before, and even if they found him, the chances of finding the hitchhiker were remote at best.

"Well," Doc Pritchard said, relighting his pipe, "what
basically is there is a confirmation of the salesman's story.
She died sometime in the afternoon of that Sunday. But
we had the broken watch for the time." Able shook his
head. "Cause of death was multiple blows to the head,
probably by some part of the car, like he just kept slamming her into it someplace. Since it's burned, there's no
real way of knowing that. Not that it makes much difference. There was grease and some paint flakes in her scalp
and hair. We know where she'd been that day, what she
ate, what killed her. But we don't know much more than
that." He puffed the pipe contentedly.

"What's all this about?" Able jammed a finger at a
paragraph near the bottom of the second page.

"It's about the jaw," Doc said. "It was busted, and
her tongue was bitten in two, or damn near, and two teeth
were broken, but we knew that, too. The stains on her
clothes and skin were mud and some blood. Hers and
somebody else's, likely the killer's." Able's eyebrows shot
up. "But don't get excited. Hers is there and there's some
O-Positive—common as spit. Looks like she put up a
fight of some kind," Doc Pritchard went on as Able created a scenario of her struggling violently, with the faceless man of his dreams, "but there's no evidence of rape,

like I told you before, none. It was just a killing. That's it.''

Able sat up straight and wearily stretched his arms above his head, noticing with a scowl that he smelled frightfully from the day's perspiration. ''What about the fingernails?''

''Like I told you, there was no tissue or blood. . . .''

''I mean the missing ends. The three that were cut off.''

Pritchard reached forward and took the autopsy report from the desk, flicking through the pages with the stem of his pipe, ''It's hardly mentioned,'' he said. ''They were cut clean, not chewed or broken or ragged—I remember that. I took samples and photographs of them since you thought they might be important, but the Austin boys apparently were unimpressed. We don't have the body anymore, or I could do some more work on them. Do you think it's all that important?''

Able rested his head in his hands. ''I don't know,'' he said. ''It's just something to hold on to. It seems to be something, but damn me if I know what. It's just a feeling I've got. I . . . I just don't know.''

Doc Pritchard knocked his pipe out in the desk ashtray and stood up silently. He wanted to say something meaningful to his friend, but he didn't know what. ''Able,'' he finally offered, ''you've got to let go of this thing. It's eating you up.'' The sheriff remained silent, his head cradled in his palms. ''I can give you something to help you sleep.'' There was a barely perceptible shaking of his head. ''You need sleep.''

Quietly he put his pipe in his coat pocket and left the office. Able remained at his desk, his head in his hands, his mind wandering in weariness.

''I don't know,'' he repeated to the empty room. ''I just don't know.''

III. Downtown
The Present, Afternoon

Wayne Henderson ignored the rush of heat dominating
downtown Agatite, aimed his feet toward the First Baptist Church some ten blocks to the south, and walked
slowly. He would be early if he wasn't careful, he knew,
so he dawdled in front of the windows on Main Street,
pricing items he knew he would never buy. The usual
downtown business was going on at its usual payday pace,
but the heat kept shoppers scurrying from store to store,
seeking the air-conditioned cool as much as possible.

It's payday at the mill, he reminded himself, which
meant that toward closing time people would be coming
in to pay some on their bills and to pick up needed hardware items they had put off until they were paid. The
fifteenth of the month, he thought sourly, and a funeral
to take him away. He prayed to no God whatsoever that
the service would be short, but knowing Bill Castlereigh's popularity, he doubted it would be.

As he passed in front of the First Security Bank, the
doors swung open and a thin kid almost ran smack into
him. The boy, whose hair was a shade too long for
Wayne's taste, automatically mumbled an "Excuse me,"
then stormed into the slow downtown traffic to jaywalk
across the street.

Wayne was incensed, and he almost called out to the
retreating youth to make him come back and deliver a
proper apology, but suddenly the headache that had been
flitting around his brain all morning burst forth, and he
found himself acutely aware of the street's heat. He
moved on, still angry, and more quickly than he wanted
to, he reached Third Street, the edge of downtown
proper, and knew that he would be far too early at the
church if he continued even at a slow pace. The bank's
clock, behind him now, told him it was almost forty minutes before the funeral was to begin, so he ducked across
the street himself and walked to the middle of the block
and Central Drugs.

A cold blast of air hit him, and immediately he noticed a feeling of slight nausea. His ulcer, he thought sourly, walking to a booth near the fountain counter. He would do almost anything to avoid going to this funeral. It would probably be open casket, too. The goddamn Baptists love open caskets. It made him feel sicker than ever.

Wanda Watkins drew him a fountain Coke, something Wayne had always believed cured headaches and settled stomachs, and he sipped it slowly, watching the seconds tick by on the bank's clock across the street. The temperature was already over a hundred, and the sun seemed to force it even higher by the second. Old Samuel, the bank's custodian, came in and waved briefly. Wayne tabulated with a moderate degree of satisfaction that this was one colored man who didn't owe him money, and lifted his hand in a brief gesture of recognition. Elwood Long, the druggist, moved behind the counter and hummed tunelessly as he worked, speaking loudly to Old Samuel, who took a seat in one of the rear booths.

Wayne swiveled himself around in his booth a bit and began pricing some of the small appliances on Elwood's shelves. He was undercutting the druggist on almost every item, he noticed with some satisfaction. He felt hungry, and in spite of the fact that he had eaten a sandwich at the store before he left, he splurged and ordered a tuna fish on toast from Wanda, who grinned at him and began preparing the sandwich. He told himself it was a reward for the hell he was about to go through, and suddenly his stomach felt better.

For a moment, while Wanda made the sandwich, he allowed himself to drift off in reverie. He found himself thinking about Roosevelt Grady and his recurring nightmare of the coffin, up on one end, the corpse, eyes open, dripping wet, pointing at him and trying to say something. The image was very clear in his mind's eye, and he shuddered and shook his head. God, he thought, removing a handkerchief from his coat pocket and wiping his face, I better not start having this dream in broad daylight. They'll have to put me away.

As Wanda served his sandwich and got him another

Coke, he noticed the young man who had almost knocked him over come bursting into the drugstore.

"Any luck?" Wanda sang out, but the boy shrugged his shoulders and said nothing. He mounted one of the stools at the fountain counter. "What'd he say?" she asked quickly, placing a large sundae in front of him. She must have had it made, Wayne thought, stuck in the freezer. It was enormous and made him sick to think of the sticky, sweet syrup running down its creamy sides.

"He said college loans were bad for business," the boy growled. "He said I should work my way through Vernon." He didn't touch the sundae.

"Well, maybe that's for the best," she offered, pushing the sundae closer to him.

"He said the board of directors wouldn't approve of it." He was close to tears, Wayne noticed.

"Well, honey," Wanda said, again nudging the ice cream toward him, "sometimes things are just like that."

"No, Wanda, things really aren't like that," he said. "I can't afford this." He gestured to the sundae.

"Hey, that's okay, hon," she said. "It's on the house. I made it to, uh . . . well, you know . . . uh . . . in case . . . well, you know . . ." She trailed off, her celebration ruined by the bad news.

"Thanks, anyhow," the boy said, pushing his hair back and loosening his tie. "I'm just not hungry. Just give me a Coke to go. A big one."

As she made the drink, Wayne studied the boy. He looked like one of the O'Hara kids, but Wayne couldn't put a name to him. He felt sorry for the youth. He seemed honest, and his hands were large and calloused. He's not afraid of some work, Wayne thought. He's smart, too, you can tell, and goddamn polite on top of what was apparently crushingly bad news. Why couldn't that little shit Warren be like that? Wayne wondered. Maybe I ought to fire Warren and offer this boy a job. Give him something to get him off that dirt farm and teach him a trade. Why not? The boy can't help it if his father's poor and he's just one of a bunch of kids. He seems respectable.

Wayne was about to say something to the boy when Wanda made one more effort to comfort him.

"Maybe you can try again next year," she suggested.

"Wanda, that man's a *prick,*" the boy said in a withering tone, "He wouldn't know what quality was if it bit him right on the ass."

"Oh, honey," Wanda said, looking around embarrassedly toward Wayne and Old Samuel, "Don't talk like that."

"I'm not kiddin' you, Wanda," the boy went on, warming to his subject and taking the paper cup of Coke off the counter. "He's given money to every kid in school whose old man is somebody, kids who don't have half my grades or anything. Well, I tell you something. I'm going to make it on my own. Fuck him!" And he swiveled off the stool and was gone before she could reply.

Wayne sniffed and finished his sandwich. That was an O'Hara all right! They were *Catholic,* he recalled, and they had no morals at all. Lived all together in a dirty shack out in the middle of nowhere. Boys and girls all sharing the same room, same bed for all anyone knew. Wayne's mind raged, and he felt his heart pounding with anger. Language like that! In public! To a woman, even Wanda, who was about the least attractive woman in the world! Wayne finished his Coke with a gulp, surprised to find his hand shaking. White trash! he thought, never amounted to anything, never will. And I was about to give him a break. Take his trashy mouth into my own store! It just goes to show you!

He glanced through the window at the clock again and realized to his horror that more time had gone by than he'd thought. He quickly paid for his meal and scurried out of the drugstore. He noticed with distaste that the kid was loitering by a parking meter, leaning on it, staring across the street at the glare from the Flex-Glo windows of the bank. White trash, Wayne thought as he hurried past him.

He looked once more at the bank clock and hurried along across Third Street. Damn kid's going to make me late, he thought.

IV. Breedlove
The Present, One Month Before

Breedlove moved first. He didn't want to hurt her, only to escape. He turned awkwardly to his right, dropping the unlit cigarette from his lip and spinning about-face to run away, down the highway. He prayed that the car was still stalled and wouldn't start in time for her to run him down, run over him, laughing crazily all the time, her bright blue eyes flashing in insane vengeance. But his ill-fitting, expensive boots buckled under his sudden footwork. Worn down by all the walking, they crumpled and sprawled him onto the blacktop, twisting his ankle. He braced himself for the nauseating pain he knew would come as soon as his brain recorded the torn ligaments, but when it did come, he was surprised, for it registered on his right shoulder, and it exploded into his head as if he had been struck by one of the lightning bolts he had seen approaching with the storm.

Eileen had reacted the same moment Breedlove turned away. She spotted the oversized wrench and leaped over his falling body to grasp its weighty handle from the Vega's fender. Breedlove was collapsed, unbelievably collapsed, at her feet when she looked down, and without hesitation, she lifted the wrench like an ax, with both hands, and aimed for the crown of his head. He shifted position at the last second, and the wrench found home just behind his right shoulder. He groaned and leaned forward as much as he could with his leg twisted beneath him.

She lifted the heavy wrench again, swinging down into him, but he looked up and saw it coming, and he deflected it with his hand. It thudded harmlessly into the Vega's front tire, bouncing back and almost striking her in the face. It clattered out of her hands as she jumped back from the recoil. Suddenly a single thought flashed into her mind: *get into the car.* She knew she had just tried for the second time in her life to kill this man, this

murderer, and he was hurt, and badly. He wasn't likely
to let her get away.

Breedlove stumbled to his knees, barely noticing the
pain from his ankle, and grabbed at the fleeing girl. His
fingers caught her right leg, the leg he had admired so
much only minutes before, and came away with a tatter
of stocking, which he dropped quickly, thinking for one
horrible moment that part of her skin had come off. He
pulled himself up to the car's level, then onto his feet,
and saw that she was moving toward the door. He
grabbed the wrench from the ground with his right hand
and made a wild, stabbing swing at her arm that was
fumbling with the door handle.

Eileen shrieked and backed away, jamming her fingers
into her mouth. The wrench had come close enough to
break three nails from her fingers, clipping them off
cleanly and evenly. Slowly she backed away from the
man who advanced toward her, the oversized tool hanging loosely at the end of his right arm, the other hand
reaching across to support himself on the Vega's body.
She backed to the rear of the car and cast a quick glance
over her shoulder into the dark and threatening clouds
that seemed to be almost on top of them. Then she turned
the corner of the car and got it between them.

Breedlove's shoulder was on fire. The swing with the
wrench had torn completely apart something the woman
had loosened. He could barely hold onto the giant tool,
but he had no choice. He didn't think he had the strength
or could bear the pain to fling it far enough away into the
bushes and weeds in the bar ditch, and he didn't dare
leave it on the ground for her to use on him again. He
was confused and angry. He didn't want to hurt her. He
just wanted to get away from her. Couldn't she understand that?

As Breedlove arrived at the rear corner of the Vega,
Eileen, on the opposite side of the car, reached into the
open hatchback and took a package of screwdrivers from
the pile of tools. She ripped the plastic envelope open
and pulled out a Phillips head screwdriver and held it out
in front of her like a lance. She didn't think it was much

of a weapon, but it had a point on it, and she was prepared to use it.

The sight of the screwdriver was so odd, thrust out like a spear in front of the girl, whose eyes now looked like a frightened rabbit's, that Breedlove began to giggle. His laugh seemed ominous and hoarse, even to him, but he couldn't help it. To her he appeared raving mad, rabid, but the one thought that possessed him was to grab her, make her sit still, and then to get away. He didn't want to hurt her, he kept saying to himself between laughs; he just wanted to get away. For Chrissake, girl, he thought, let me go!

He followed her around the back and far side of the Vega. She kept backing up, faster now, around the front of the small car and down the highway side. He followed, never allowing much distance to grow between them, still laughing madly. She passed the back again, up the opposite side to the front. He reached the rear of the engine compartment by the passenger's door and held onto the opening edge to rest, watching her carefully, but seeing the screwdriver held out in her left hand, he began to guffaw even louder. Suddenly with her right hand she pulled the hood forward, releasing the automatic catch, and let it fall, crushing his left hand's fingers, which were steadying his shaking body.

When the hood fell on Breedlove's hand, Eileen jumped away, almost too far. She had fixed her mind on two missions: to try to keep a part of the car always between them, and to gain enough ground to get inside. Why had she locked the passenger side? she wondered. It was probably Aunt Vi's idea, just as that stupid toolbox had been. Oh, Aunt Vi, she moaned to herself, what have you done to me? The man had been giggling and talking to himself in a mutter since he had risen from the ground. She believed that he had gone mad with pain; in fact, she was amazed that he was still on his feet. She had hit him hard with the wrench. Why had she let him know she recognized him? Why had she let him know she knew? He had screamed, no, *roared* when the hood fell on him, and jerking away his ragged, bloody fingers, he lunged for her, splattering her suit and blouse with drops of blood.

She retreated faster, to the back of the car again, and he stumbled after her, leaving bloody streaks along the car's body in his wake. His foot must be hurt, too, she realized, as he was limping and not able to run after her. It was a good thing. If he could run, he'd have caught her by now.

Breedlove was indeed almost mad with pain. His mind was on the verge of snapping. The falling hood had had a double effect. It had crushed his fingers, and the surprise of it had caused him to bite down hard on the inside of his cheek, drawing blood, and now pain seemed to come from every part of his body. His left ankle was a searing, tormenting, terror of hurt, and his right shoulder ached with a dull throbbing that filled his ears and pounded on his brain. His fingers were lacerated and crushed and throbbed with screaming pain, and now the inside of his mouth was filled with briny blood and hurt worse than all the rest put together.

He stumbled faster and faster after the woman, losing his breath as they rounded the car yet again. He noticed that each time she passed the driver's door, she tried to open it, but it wouldn't yield quickly enough before he was on top of her and she moved away. She was also losing wind, and he suddenly noted the absurdity of the deadly chase. It was like one of those big executives chasing his pretty secretary around and around his desk, like in the cartoons, he thought. He wanted to laugh again, but when he did, a howling protest from his torn cheek forced the laugh back into his throat, where it emerged as an inhuman growl, and he stumbled on.

Eileen's mind was also approaching the loss of reason. Fear had almost paralyzed her twice. The atmosphere had grown heavy and silent as the storm prepared to break. Crazily she could hear insects buzzing in between her gasps for air. Her resolve was breaking down, and she began to wish the chase would end, however it would end, but then she would look again into the reddened, swollen eyes of her pursuer and take another deep breath

and continue to back away and keep the length of the
small car between them.

They had rounded the car almost a dozen times, and
finally both were leaning against it, breathing heavily in
the sudden humidity, staring at each other, holding their
similarly useless weapons, panting. The vision of a horny
boss chasing his secretary around a desk hadn't escaped
Eileen either, and far from finding it funny or absurd,
she drew an inspiration from it. She knew that she had
to get him closer to her to use the silly screwdriver on
him. She also knew that if he got close enough, he'd use
the wrench on her. The memory of how it felt to hit him
with it, the way it had sunk readily into his back, punch-
ing it in like a pillow with a sickening *thunk,* was fresh
to her. She thought of him ploughing it into her skull or
chest, and she wanted to faint, but she believed that if
she could distract him, take his mind off the wrench long
enough, move in close so she could stick the sharp point
of the screwdriver into his gut, press it up to his heart,
kill him, kill him dead, she would be all right. But how
to get him close without letting him hurt her?

He rumbled erect again to continue his chase. His
breath was coming in short gasps, but clearly he was
fresher than he had been before his rest, and she realized
that the time to act was now. He would simply outlast
her otherwise. Shifting the screwdriver to her left hand
and dropping it to her side, trying to hide it behind her
skirt, she reached up with her right hand, looped her
broken fingernails into her blouse, and ripped it open.

"C'mon, you son of a bitch," she gasped at him,
thrusting her chest out toward him and locking her eyes
on his. "It's what you wanted in the office that day. It's
what you've been wanting all afternoon. C'mon, cowboy.
If you're man enough."

Breedlove reeled backward a bit when she ripped open
her blouse. The slip and bra still covered her breasts, but
her cleavage, covered now with sweat, heaved up and
down, not tantalizingly, but repulsively, as if she were
suffering from a heart attack, he thought. He hadn't forgotten about the screwdriver, stupid weapon as it was,

hanging in her hand. She couldn't kill him with it, he knew, but she could sure as hell put out an eye. What she was trying to do was so damned obvious he wanted to laugh again, to explain to her that this wasn't going to work, that he just wanted to go away. But the pain he felt drove any laughter or words away. Between tortured breaths, all he could do was register pain.

As the man lurched forward toward her, it took all her force of will to stand her ground, not to continue to back away. He wasn't reaching for his fly, she noticed, not even reaching out to touch her exposed breasts, for in her confusion and terror, she had forgotten that all she had revealed was some rather expensive lingerie. In her mind's eye, her breasts were naked and she was inviting him to touch her, to hold her, to embrace her just before she would kill him. It would be bloody, she knew, but she could do it. She could! She would!

Breedlove kept his eyes flickering between her bright blue stare and her slack left arm. He moved within five feet of her, then three. The wrench felt like a rope at the end of his weary, painful right arm, and he didn't think he could carry it another step. He dropped it.

When the metallic ring of the wrench hitting the pavement reached Eileen's ears, she dropped her eyes from Breedlove's to the ground. It was unbelievable. He'd dropped the wrench just as she had planned he would. Now was the time to stab him, she thought, and she raised her head and opened her mouth to say, ''I think I'll screw you instead, you son of a bitch!'' just before she plunged the screwdriver into his heart—just below the rib cage, she reminded herself quickly; can't strike bone on this one; you won't have a second chance.

But her mouth was dry, her lips felt like sandpaper, and she paused a millisecond to run her tongue over them to moisten them. In that one pause, the thousandth of a second, she realized she shouldn't have waited.

Breedlove had worked hard almost all his life. Except for the past month of good living, he had spent most of his days since he left Agatite, where he had been in top condition as a football team captain and quarterback, working on farms, oil rigs, pipelines, and other labor sites. Lifting heavy loads with both arms was common to him, and although he remained lanky, the biceps on his arms, left and right, were the size of medium cantaloupes when he flexed them, as he often did for the high-priced whores in Colorado. When he saw Eileen's eyes drop and her head turn down, he knew he had his chance. But he wasn't sure what to do. Grab her? Hit her? Where? Then she looked up and stuck out her chin, and instinct sharpened by a hundred bar fights and oil field squabbles took over.

The raging pain in his body and brain faded away in the same millisecond that Eileen wet her lips, and Breedlove's left arm, accustomed to getting in the first punch and making it count, swung directly upward, catching her chin squarely with the knuckles of his left hand, formed into a half fist to protect the lacerated and crushed fingers. Pain sparked in the hand immediately, and he almost blacked out but fought hard for consciousness.

Eileen's jaw snapped shut with the blow's impact, which, if delivered by a healthy Breedlove with a whole hand, would certainly have crushed it if it hadn't killed her outright. Her teeth cut her tongue almost completely in half, and blood spurted out of her mouth through her clenched teeth all over Breedlove's custom-made Western shirt. Her eyes rolled back into her head, and she took a half turn and collapsed into the open hatchback, beginning immediately to slide down onto her knees.

The pain in Breedlove's hand joined a new chorus of aches from his other injuries, and he completely lost control. Seeing her down in the hatchback compartment, sliding as her body weight tried to pull her out onto the pavement, he reached up and grabbed the top of the hatch, slamming it down on the back of her head once, then again, and again. Her face, resting on the edge of the hatch's opening, flattened against it, and blood began pouring from her mouth and nose. Her nostrils flared on the metal latch of the rear door's lock, spreading grotesquely wider with each violent slam of the hatch on the back of her head. She died on the third crushing blow.

After he slammed the hatch door the sixth time and watched Eileen's body weight pull her down onto the blacktop into a bundle of bloody rags, Breedlove came to himself. He looked at her dumbly and expected her to sit up, bruised and angry. He was forming an apology, an explanation, preparing her to finally let him go. A minute or two went by, and he realized that she wasn't going to sit up and say anything at all. She was dead. He had killed her. The finality of it hit him harder than she had with the giant wrench.

His fingers and knuckles on his left hand screamed. His shoulder ached, and his cheek was stinging sharply. His ankle was swelling in protest to the lurching walk he had forced it through chasing Eileen around the car. His whole body was wracked with wholesale pain. But panic suddenly swelled over him like a fever. He staggered to his feet and grabbed Eileen's body, hauling it up and stuffing it into the hatchback compartment. He rounded the Vega, picking up the wrench, his hat, his western leisure suit coat, the fallen screwdriver, the pliers, even the half-smoked and unsmoked Winstons on the pavement. Eileen's shoes had come off when she fell, and he tossed these in along with the rest of the junk on top of her body and slammed the hatch down one more time. He secured the hood, and then he collapsed by the side of the car away from the road just as a couple of cars passed each other next to the parked Vega. They didn't even slow down.

As he sat on the ground, unable to fight off the pain with adrenaline any longer, he heard the sudden silence around him. The air was deadly still and seemed ghostly green and eerie. He could hear his own heart pounding, and his breathing filled his ears. He slid farther down onto the ground, resting his swollen cheek on the road surface that still held the awful heat of the afternoon. He couldn't see very far, he realized, not even to the pasture on the other side of the road. It was getting dark.

Now he was a murderer for real, he thought. The other killings had happened with his consent, maybe; after all, he was there, he had a gun, he had shot at people, people who had never hurt him. But he hadn't actually killed anybody, even wounded anybody. This—this was more horrible than pointing a gun at somebody and pulling the trigger and maybe hitting them and maybe killing them. This was worse, far worse, he knew. They killed people who killed people like this.

A sudden rumbling and flashing found its way into his consciousness, and he figured that he might be dying. He wanted to die, to just give up, here and now. I didn't want to kill her, but she made me, he thought. It was her or me, he thought, almost aloud, and then he started to giggle in spite of the pain in his mouth. He couldn't stop. A hundred-pound piece of ass and Big Bad Breed, and I beat her to death with a Chevy. God, what a man!

The rumbling became louder and he felt a gust of wind hit his face, carrying dust and trash under the car along with it. In the dimming light he noticed three strange shapes wedged underneath the front tire on the highway side of the small automobile. He studied them for a second or two, trying to figure out what the hell they were, and then, unable to contain his curiosity any longer, he pulled himself up and hobbled around the car. The ankle gave with any weight on it at all, and his shoulder throbbed angrily with the movement. She really fucked me over, he thought.

Coming around the front of the Vega to the driver's side, he tried to bend over, but the pain was too much for him and he allowed his body to slide down the car's fender to the pavement. He realized that he wanted a drink worse than anything else in the world. Forgetting and not much caring about whether a passing car saw him or not, he leaned over and lay prone next to the front tire and searched for the odd objects.

At first they seemed to be gone, as if he had imagined them, but then his eyes found them, and he grubbed them up into his palm. They were three pieces of fingernail, hers, broken off by the close passing of the wrench when she had tried to open the door. He stared at them and then closed his palm over them and started to cry. What, he wondered, am I going to do now?

3

I. Breedlove
The Present, One Month Before

Storms in north central Texas summers come on quickly and furiously. They generally arrive in one of two ways. They may pass rapidly, dumping enormous quantities of rain in their wake, bringing tornados and other dangers, then leave everything fresh and clean smelling. Otherwise, they come in waves, the first attack bringing the brief but often damaging high winds and sometimes hail amid driving rain and flashing lightning, followed by a brief respite, and then by a warmer, gentler shower that fills arroyos and creeks and eases the heat of summer for a couple of days. Both types of storms have in common a sudden drop in temperature, accompanied by a darkness to rival midnight, and an awesome power manifest in the wind and water. The breaking of such a torrential storm can intimidate even the strongest individual.

The storm that broke over Hoolian on that July evening was of the second variety. Breedlove had all he could do to get inside the Vega and slam the door against the driving rain and hail. Drenched, he found himself in the driver's seat at last, shivering and childishly fearful of the exploding thunder and lightning that complemented the deafening tattoo on the roof of the small car.

He located Aunt Vi's Christmas-present-first-aid kit in the glove box and began binding his wounds as best he could. An Ace bandage wrapped around his ankle helped some, but he had to use his knife to cut the top away from the offending boot in order to get it off, and that had hurt almost as much as the sprain. He doubted that he would ever be able to afford such a nice pair again. Aspirin, five of them taken at a gulp, eased the pain in his shoulder, and iodine and more bandages had wrapped his swollen and cut fingers tightly enough to convince him that he was properly doctored, or as properly as anyone could be in a Vega in the middle of nowhere.

Few cars and trucks splashed by in the downpour, but they apparently paid no attention to the darkened Vega parked alongside the road. Breedlove ducked down when they passed, causing loud complaint from his shoulder, but he tried to keep from crying anymore. He was damned lucky, he told himself, that no one had come by while he was chasing the girl or while he was stuffing her body in the back. Of course, he thought ironically, if someone had come by and stopped him from killing her, that might have been good luck. What was done, he thought, was done, and now he turned his attention to a thornier problem—how to get rid of Eileen.

He couldn't leave her here. The farmer who had let him out six or seven miles back would testify to his being in the area, could describe him, and there had been that truck that came by when they were together, laughing and talking. Also, he recalled, there was the man she said she flagged down earlier, who still might be coming back. Even if he didn't, he would remember her. Who wouldn't remember a pretty girl broken down next to Hoolian?

Hoolian posed a number of possibilities. The old township was filled with abandoned wells, storm cellars, and other places a body could be buried and hidden, but Breedlove also figured a dog or a coyote would dig her up sooner or later, if birds and other creatures didn't alert people to her before that. Anyway, he didn't feel that he was in any shape for digging, and the one thing Aunt Vi had neglected to provide for her niece was a shovel. He sat in the car biting his fingernails and smoking the last of Eileen's Winstons, trying to come up with an idea and desperately wanting a drink.

He began scouring the car in search of a bottle. Eileen was just the sort to keep a pint hidden away, he figured, but he had no luck. The thought of whiskey inspired him, however, and his mind fixed on it. The barbershop! There would be something to drink there. The old barber—what was his name?—no matter—if he was still alive the place would have a bottle or two stashed away. Breedlove realized he'd have to break in, but what the hell? Breaking and entering was nothing compared to what he'd done this afternoon.

He turned the key in the Vega's ignition, and the car started up and began running smoothly, just as it might have done an hour before and saved him a good deal of anguish, he thought with a grimace at the pain in his shoulder caused by moving the small steering wheel. He steered the car out onto the highway through the pouring rain toward the Hoolian cutoff.

As he reached the town, the rain began to slack off, and when he pulled up in front of the Hoolian Barbershop, it had almost stopped completely, even though a light show was still being offered in the heavens. He left the car running, noting that it was three-quarters full of gas, and shut off the lights. The front door of the shop was locked up tight, but he prowled around to the back, hobbling on one boot and barefoot at the end of a swollen, sore ankle. He discovered that the window to the rear of the place was unlocked. He pushed up the window and climbed through; noting that his shoulder had settled into a dull throb.

The back room of the old shop was covered with dust and cobwebs. Breedlove lit Eileen's Bic lighter and looked around for a likely stash of booze, and then he spotted it, obvious as hell, he thought. A Cutty Sark box, weathered and mildewed, sat in the corner under a pile of rags. He moved slowly over to it, opened the top, and found half a dozen pint bottles of various types of spirits. A half-pint of Ezra Brooks was stuck in one corner, and Breedlove lifted it from its pigeonhole, opened it, and drank deeply.

The whiskey on top of the aspirin soon had a soothing effect, and he began to cast his eyes around the darkened room, which had a commode and a sink awkwardly installed in the corner. Careful not to touch anything besides the bottle, he hobbled around a bit. The ankle was hurting less and less, and the shoulder was now numb. His cheek burned from the whiskey when he first started drinking, but now the lacerations inside his mouth ached only in a dull, throbbing way, and his fingers, swollen and sore as they were, flexed okay, indicating that none was broken.

He sat down on the windowsill and finished the bottle. Probably the barber, whatever his name was, wouldn't miss it anyway. Most of the other bottles were open, and it looked like an ongoing collection of odds and ends he just kept around for special customers like Breedlove's old man had been. An icebox hummed away in the main room of the shop, and Breedlove figured a cold beer might be in there, but for the moment, the whiskey satisfied him. He had finally stopped shivering.

The problem of what to do with Eileen still ate at him as he looked out into the rain-soaked field behind the shop. Lightning was still flashing everywhere, and the electrical storm illuminating the mesquite and tumbleweeds also revealed in eerie silver light the ancient outhouse with its tin roof shining as if a spotlight danced on it.

The outhouse! Of course! A plan suddenly formed in Breedlove's mind, dulled as it was by the combined effect of the bourbon and aspirin. Hiding the body wasn't enough. Somebody would find it soon enough no matter where he put it. So let them. Let them think it was supposed to be found. Not murder. Suicide! These county cops around here wouldn't even autopsy if it was left in the right way. He wished for a gun so he could make it look really good, but there might be other possibilities.

He lifted himself out of the window after replacing the whiskey bottle and taking a nearly full pint of Jim Beam in exchange. He hobbled around to the car, killed the engine, and painfully pulled on the bottom of the cut-off boot. Then he moved around, opened the hatch, hoisted Eileen's body over his good shoulder, and began a half-stumbling walk to the back of the shop. The rain began again in a slow drizzle, and he cursed every time he had to put weight on the damaged ankle.

His injured shoulder came alive, and he almost dropped the corpse before he got her to the path that led to the outhouse. Finally she did slip from his grasp, but her fall was cushioned by the mass of cactus and weeds alongside the path. He pulled the outhouse door open with difficulty, and half dragged, half carried her inside.

It was blacker than the belly of hell inside the ancient johnny, and the rain, light as it was, assaulted the tin roof with a horrid noise that terrified him. Breedlove waited for several minutes, holding her body up off the floor, and swallowing hard to fight back the gags he experienced when the smell of the shithole beneath him rose to his nostrils. He thought his eyes would adjust, but they never did. It was just too dark outside. He set her down on the johnny's seat and returned to the car to search for a flashlight he never found. Aunti Vi apparently didn't expect her niece to drive at night.

He didn't know what to do next. He thought of cutting her wrists with his pocket knife, but he knew he must have light to do it. In fact, without a flashlight, he couldn't do much more than simply leave her sitting there. Coming back around and standing in the rain on the gravelly ground behind the shop, he chewed his nails and gingerly explored his shoulder with his fingers.

He decided to go back into the shop, and he pushed the window open again and climbed in. It took him five minutes to locate the barber's old lantern under a cabinet in the main room of the building, and with it in hand, he prepared to go back out and finish his business. On the way, however, he stopped and removed another bottle from the barber's cache, and he noticed a tangle of old extension cords, electrical wires and other junk hanging down from a shelf over the whiskey box. Breedlove went over and untangled a five-foot length of cord that still had a socket on the end.

He scooted out the window, landed painfully on his sore ankle, and then limped to the outhouse. When he entered, the lantern's beam fell directly on Eileen's face, and he yelled, ''Oh, God! No!'' before he realized that she was still dead, not staring at him, but merely with her blue eyes open in the confused terror of death. Her mouth was open too, ready to scream with a half-severed tongue now swollen and black lolling out of her mouth.

He climbed up on the bench of the johnny's hole and flashed the light up to locate the crossbeam. He looped the cord over the beam and tied it off in a square knot. There wasn't enough cord to make a proper noose, he realized, and he doubted that he remembered how from playing cowboys and Indians when he was a kid. "If they catch me," he said to the lifeless Eileen, "I can watch them make mine."

Beginning to sweat even in the cooled atmosphere of the passing storm, he finally made a loop on the end of the cord, a slipknot. It didn't slide very well, but he figured it would do if he could make himself do it at all.

Breedlove leaned against the inside of the outhouse, careful to keep the light away from the dead girl's face, and paused to work up his courage and stamina. "You're a sick, sick man, Breedlove," he said aloud. At that moment the thunder rumbled again, and he heard the warning sounds of heavier rain falling on the roof. The storm was far from over, he knew, and he needed to work quickly.

He pulled Eileen up by her arms and stood her up on the bench seat of the johnny. Her height forbade him from looping her into the noose without lifting her up, and as he did, he dropped the lantern from under his arm and it went out. In the darkness, standing as much as he could on his good leg, he lifted her by embracing her limp waist, propping up her shoulder with his good arm, and reaching up beyond her for the cord's loop.

Finally, after three tries, he managed to push her head through the hole in the cord, and with a final effort, he ignored the scalding pain in his shoulder long enough to pull her hair through and release her body. It swung free on the electrical cord, bringing a groan of protest from the old, rotten crossbeam.

He climbed back down on the floor and picked up the lantern. Shaking it, he received a weak beam, and he surveyed his work. He briefly considered trying to rebutton her blouse, but his mangled fingers would never manage it, he knew. Then he spotted her feet. Her shoes, damn it, be berated himself. Hobbling through the renewed downpour, he moved back to the car. He retrieved the shoes, took them back to the outhouse, and tried to get them onto the corpse's feet. One went on correctly, even though it hung down oddly, and the other simply wouldn't fit. He tried to force it, but it slipped off and fell, before he could catch it, into the crapper's hole. "Goddamn it," he swore, shining the lantern into the interminable blackness of the shithole. There was nothing he could do about it. The toes of her unshod foot stuck out at a stiff, almost humorous angle, and he shook his head.

He returned the lantern to its place in the shop, took a towel from a large stack underneath the counter, wet it in the sink, and carefully and thoroughly mopped up his muddy footprints in the small building. Then he left by the front door, after making sure nothing but the towel and the whiskey were missing or disturbed.

He mapped out his next moves. There would be a car wash somewhere down the road. As soon as he drove out of the rain, as late as he could make it, he needed to stop and clean up the car. Get rid of all the blood. Then he could drive until he found a place to dump the car, and he needed to dump it before she turned up missing in Oklaunion. No, he suddenly thought, dumping it won't be enough. I need to burn it, get rid of any evidence that might tie me to this car or that girl. Get rid of it forever.

As he drove out onto the highway, he realized he should have left a suicide note or something, but he really didn't know if he could pull it off. He did know that he wouldn't have the courage to go back into that outhouse. They'd just have to try to figure out why she would kill herself that way, he decided. They wouldn't worry about it too much.

He finished the bottle as he cruised quickly through Agatite and stopped in Vernon to wash the car and buy some cigarettes. He found Eileen's purse in the backseat and fished around in it until he came up with some bills, almost fifty dollars. So she did have money, after all.

A few hours later he found himself hobbling in great pain up an all-weather road in Clay County, the sky behind him lit by the burning car. He had driven it into a creek bed and, using his shirt as a fuse, had set fire to it. He had eliminated all signs of violence and of his presence in the car, and he was reasonably certain that no evidence existed that he had killed a girl in Sandhill County hours before. It was almost two miles back to the main highway, and there he hoped to hitch a ride to Wichita Falls, then south to find Joe Don. He needed help, he needed money, he needed a drink. Whatever kind of hard time Joe Don would give him for showing up broke and hurt would be better than trying to get by on his own. Something in him didn't want to go back to Joe Don; he knew Joe Don had been responsible for all this in the first place. But he had nowhere else to turn. He hadn't really thought it out, but then again he hadn't thought out much of anything lately. He just reacted. Joe Don would have a bottle for him, and he might get him a doctor. For the moment at least, that was enough.

His shoulder was hurting him awfully, and the ankle turned with every step he took, but he felt as if he had managed to accomplish something. He was a little disturbed at how coolly he had handled it all, how easily he had gotten rid of a body and a car, how quickly his mind had leaped to details and fundamentals.

"I guess I'm really a professional bad ass now," he said to the empty road, "a regular John Dillinger." As he walked the thought of the old farmer came to him, and he swore.

II. Lawman
The Present, Morning

Able Newsome sat in the Town and Country Dinette and contemplated life from a sour point of view. He hadn't slept at all the night before, awakened every time he be-

gan to drift with the face of Hollis Carlson meekly trying
to explain how mean his wife was and how he didn't want
to leave that girl to die out there. He had killed her, Able
knew, not in a way that he could arrest the timid little
shit for, but he had killed her as sure as the man who
hanged her in the outhouse had killed her.

The coffee he sipped burned his lips and made his
stomach churn. He did not feel well at all. He hadn't run
or worked out since he found the body, and he was weary
of concentrating so hard on the murder.

This morning, however, his problems were compounded by other discomforting thoughts. For one thing,
it was already unbearably hot outdoors, and it wasn't
even noon yet. The radio had warned that today would
set a record for temperatures above 100 degrees, and Able
had little reason to doubt it, noting the sweating of the
tar on the blacktop streets as early as eight o'clock that
morning when he came to the office.

For another thing, he was going to have to work the
speed trap that afternoon, since Jingles and his deputies
would be tied up with Bill Castlereigh's funeral and the
anticipated extra-long procession to the cemetery. Able
didn't want the task, but it was easier to go ahead and do
it rather than to argue with Jingles and that fat-assed
brother-in-law of his. Mayor Longman would be at the
funeral himself and would doubtlessly side with the chief
of police against the sheriff.

Able knew he could assign the duty to John David or
to Vernon, but he didn't want to do that either. It was
dirty enough work without the heat, and sitting for two
to three hours in a car during a record-breaking heat wave
was something he felt he had no right to ask one of his
boys to do. He would do it himself, but the prospect of
it rose on the horizon of the day like a great, dark cloud,
probably the closest thing to a cloud he would see that
afternoon.

He was further upset by the haggling he had just finished with Morris Tucker over some new tires for the
cruiser. Morris wanted about three times the usual price
for the set, Able knew, just because the county would be

paying the freight. He had tried to talk sense to Morris, explain that if the Sheriff's Department paid such high prices for the tires they wouldn't get some other equipment they desperately needed. But Morris held firm, and Able was left stewing and sucking his burned lips.

So lost in thought was the sheriff of Sandhill County that he almost didn't pick up on what Dinah Mae Cross was saying from behind the counter of the dinette.

". . . and I swear I never seen nothin' like it," she droned on to a half-listening and bored Les Whitehead, who was taking his third coffee break from the county clerk's office that morning. "I mean, I used to go 'round with an ol' boy who carried snake rattles in his pocket— for luck—an' once there was this guy who carried his dead kid's tooth around, but I never seen nobody with *fingernails* in with all his change an' junk! I *mean*, it was spooky! You know?"

Able's mind snapped from its half-dreamy reverie, and he turned around in his chair and looked intently at Dinah as she repeated the story for some customers who had just seated themselves at the counter. "What I was sayin' to Les, here, was that these two guys came in for breakfast 'bout an hour an' a half ago, an' when they got up to pay out, one of them comes out of his pocket with a handful of change, an' right there in with the dimes an' pennies an' such was these three fingernails!"

"You don't say?" Irma McElroy said as she poured sugar into her coffee cup. "How'd you know they was fingernails?"

"Oh, they was fingernails, all right." Dinah nodded with an air of certainty and held up her own fingers, displaying red polished claws of which she had been long proud. "I recognized them. They wasn't the whole nail"—she suddenly screeched out a laugh at the potential misunderstanding—"just the ends, like they'd been broke off or somethin'. You know, like they'd been cut clean off."

Able leaned forward to ask a question, but Irma asked it for him. "Who was they? Strangers?"

"I thought I knew one of 'em," Dinah said, wrinkling

her brow, "but I couldn't say for sure. The other one was a hippie or somethin'. He had on a T-shirt, you know, one of them rock-'n'-roll band names on it, an' he had this long, greasy hair, and he looked ugly an' mean. Had a scar right here!" She poked her cheek with one red claw. "I *knew* the other one, I think. But I couldn't put a name to him."

Able stood up and moved over to the counter stool nearest Dinah. "Tell me about it again," he said. In all the information released about Eileen Kennedy's discovery and the search for her murderer, nothing had been said about broken fingernails on her hand. It was a long shot, he knew, but he didn't have another lead. He had been prepared to give it all up, try to forget it, not even join Jingles out at Hoolian again for their regular inspection of the site, but now this. Maybe it was nothing. Maybe. But maybe it was something. Could the murderer just stroll into the Town and Country and order breakfast and drop a major clue right into the lap of the town's biggest gossip?

Dinah wound up her version of the story once again, pleased to be receiving so much attention from Able, whom she had secretly admired for years. "What did they look like again?" Able asked, taking notes in his pocket notebook.

"Like I say, I think I knew him. Or he seemed familiar, but, damn it, Able, I don't know. He didn't look at all like he was healthy, kind of sickly and pale—you know, the way some fellers look when they've been on a bender, the mornin' after. An' he walked kinda funny."

"Funny how?"

"Oh, sort of stiff-bodied, like there was somethin' wrong with his side or somethin'. He was kinda tall an' skinny, but not as skinny as the other one."

"Tell me about the other one."

"Well, like I said, he had this long, greasy hair tied back in one of them pony tails, an' a white shirt, a T-shirt, with a sayin' on it, like some of the kids wear, you know. He had on jeans an' a jeans jacket."

"What was the other one wearing?" Able asked, writing quickly, "The one you thought you knew. The one with the . . ." He stumbled on the word. "The one with the fingernails?"

"Let's see . . . he had on a kinda suit, one of them cowboy suits, you know. It was kinda green, but faded a bit, an' a white shirt, an' the oddest thing. He had this cowboy suit on, like I say, but he was wearin' tennis shoes, you know, them fancy kind the kids wear. He wasn't wearin' no boots, an' you'd think a cowboy suit would call for boots. Then, again, he didn't have much money. Like I said, he paid in change. That's how come me got to see them fingernails." She looked around with the pride of a hen which has just laid the biggest egg in the farmyard.

Able was writing furiously. This was too far-fetched to be real, he kept telling himself. But Dinah was right. Fingernails in a man's pocket were unusual, and it bore checking out, even if it led nowhere. "You sure you can't remember him? I mean, if you knew him?"

Dinah leaned down on the counter and made a large show of covering her head with her hands, thinking hard. "Able," she said as if in pain, "I'm tryin', but there's so many guys come in here. He could've been a trucker or somethin' who comes by regular, for all I know." She looked up, curious for the first time, "Why you want to know about all this?"

Able flipped his notebook closed and buttoned it into his shirt pocket. "Could be something," he said, half to himself. "You see which way they went?"

"No," Dinah replied, put out that he didn't answer her question. "I was busy."

"I seen two guys out by the Conoco station on the highway this mornin'," Les offered, trying to be helpful. "What's this all about, Able?"

Able stood up and moved toward the door. "I don't know," he said, and moved out onto the sidewalk and into the mounting heat. He really didn't.

The odds against this amounting to anything more than a couple of drifters with some odd habits of collecting things were tremendous. Able knew that. He walked across to the cruiser. When he got there, he found one of the tires was flat. With a curse he kicked the useless tire and stalked off toward Morris Tucker's tire store.

III. Dilettante
The Present, Noon

Maggie Meacham sat on the side of her bed and held a washcloth wrapped around ice to the back of her head. She rolled her head around on her neck, testing to see if the pain from where her cranium had struck the edge of the shower stall had lessened any, decided it had not, and cursed under her breath. Her eyes were closed, and her hair, unintentionally wet from her fall, would have to be dried before she could get dressed. She was going to be late for Bill's funeral, and she was very angry.

She stood up, wincing from the pain in the lump that had formed under the makeshift ice pack. She walked over to the window and looked out from the upstairs of the house toward the all-weather road that led two miles up to U.S. 287 and then on into Agatite. Her white bathrobe fell open, loose around her nearly perfect body, allowing her beautiful breasts to hang freely and fully exposed. In the dressing table mirror she assessed herself and smiled in spite of the headache. She was a beautiful woman, still, she thought, and James Earl Meacham III could go to hell.

This latest prank—for that was what she thought of his nasty trick with the shotgun—had scared the be-Jesus out of her. He was crazy. She had really believed that he was going to kill her, not just for a split second, but the whole time he had stood there grinning at her, after she almost fainted and fell backward in the shower and knocked her head against the wall. She recalled with a shudder the fear she had known when she saw the hammers of the ancient shotgun falling, almost in slow motion, and the horror of trying to escape the blast she knew would follow but somehow didn't. Then him just grinning that crazy grin, staring at her and saying nothing. ''The son of a bitch!'' she said to herself. He wasn't going to get rid of her that easy.

The shotgun trick had been vicious, she thought as she lay the ice pack down and picked up her hair dryer and began blowing her long blond hair dry. Previously he had been less imaginative and less obvious. She had found a live rattlesnake in the dryer last week, jerking her hand back at the first telltale warning of the snake's presence, and not too soon by a damn sight, either, she reminded herself. The evil head had struck violently at the dryer's door, stunning the snake and allowing her time to collect herself and get one of the men from the horse barn to come in and kill it for her. ''Don't know how he got in there, ma'am?'' the bumpkin had asked her as he chopped the head off with a hoe he had brought for the purpose. ''But he's a big 'un, an' you're lucky not to've grabbed onto 'im.''

She knew how he got in there, though, even if she couldn't prove it. For there had been other things. Rat poison turned up next to the box of artificial sweetner she kept in the cupboard, and an open can of gasoline had been mysteriously left in her studio next to the ashtray where she placed burning cigarettes when she was painting. These things didn't just start happening by accident. She was convinced that James Earl wanted her dead, or at least he wanted her crazy so he could pack her off to some institution the way he had packed off his mother, put her in a funny farm and then forget all about her. No way, she thought, brushing out her now semidry hair and frowning at the wrinkle lines that were turning up with her eyes. You don't get rid of Maggie that easy.

She knew he had cause to hate her, and she felt sorry for him because she knew it. But she also knew she couldn't help it, and she believed it was as much his fault as hers anyway. Their idyllic romance had ended soon after they were married. The demands of the ranch had all but taken James Earl away from her, but she didn't really mind that. The ranch paid the bills, and she liked to run up some bills.

She had help around the house whenever she needed

it, and she was free to go into town or even on long
spending sprees in Dallas or Houston with her husband's
blessing. He had bought her sports cars, diamonds, and
furs, kept her the envy of most of the women in Agatite,
and he had built—or had *had* built, she corrected herself—a special room for her to use to paint in, her studio,
where she could retreat for long afternoons to create boring and trite canvases which people in town clamored
after to gain the favor of Sandhill County's most beautiful
artist and socialite.

But he could give and give, money or whatever it would
buy, and it was a poor substitute for her real problem.
She was bored out of her mind.

While James Earl majored in the business of ranching
at A&M, she had majored in art and music at Baylor.
She was a more than competent musician, and she entered her drawings in national competitions, winning blue
ribbons and a great deal of recognition. She could speak
three languages, detect a fine wine by taste, and knew
all there was to know about dressing well, speaking well,
and setting a gourmet table. In short, between sessions
of passionate loving with her intended Sandhill County
rancher-husband, she acquired all the necessities of a sophisticated woman of the world, and it had been her plan
for her and her husband, as soon as he fulfilled the silly
business of military service, to travel in Europe, maybe
even to live there.

But it hadn't worked out. Her scheme to woo him away
from the ranch in Sandhill County had gotten off to a
poor start when he insisted on honeymooning in Mexico
rather than Europe, and she should have realized that his
father's untimely death and his mother's insanity would
spell out James Earl's life for him as the heir of the
Meacham Spread and the responsibilities it entailed.

At first she hadn't given up entirely. She kept up her
music and her painting, talking him into the studio right
away. But as time passed, she lost interest in the violin
and piano. It was boring to play alone, and the bulk of
people she knew in Agatite had no more interest in joining her than they did in listening to her.

Her art work had also deteriorated. She still painted, but rather than concentrating on the abstract canvases she had gotten so much praise for before, she now found that local yokels wanted to see something they could recognize and understand—which, in Maggie's opinion, was precious little. So she did landscapes, imagined seascapes, and portraits of her friends and acquaintances, all for reduced fees. But eventually even these had become boring, and their quality was so dubious that few people wanted their pictures painted or their pastures immortalized in oil or watercolor, so she simply sketched whatever was outside her studio window—which, again, wasn't much.

She had flatly refused to do a portrait of James Earl and a self-likeness to join the collection of monstrosities that lined the front stairs. It was bad enough, she thought, that she had to endure looking at James Earl, but to add his permanent image to the passage of time represented by that stupid family tradition of having portraits made of the major Meachams would have been too much. They had had quite a fight about it, she recalled, but he hadn't mentioned it in years, and she hoped he had forgotten about it.

Basically she was suffering from tremendous disappointment in life. From her early teens she had dreamed of marrying the tall, handsome football star, James Earl, living on his daddy's money—and hers, too, if need be—and spending her winters skiing in the Alps and her summers sunning on the Rivera in a tiny bikini that would display her wonderful body to the leering and jealous eyes of Mediterranean men and women. Instead, she was the mistress of an ancient house on an artificial hill in Sandhill County. She got to go to Colorado skiing, and she lay around the country club pool in her skimpy bikini and was admired and leered at only by pimply-faced boys and fat old men. Somehow being the chairwoman of the Agatite Art League and a member of the Agatite Eagles Marching Band Boosters didn't compare to being a patron of the Louvre and a regular subscriber to the London

Symphony. So after a few years of boredom she began
to strike back.

Now she put down the dryer and brush, regretting that
she hadn't felt like washing her hair after the incident,
since it was already wet, and began applying makeup to
enhance her natural beauty and hide her advancing age.
She was still gorgeous, she knew, but there was no point
in advertising her mid-thirties' failings, even at a funeral.

Her first fling had been an accident. She had discovered, quite by chance, that Bill Castlereigh read French.
He had been translating a letter in the drugstore for Mrs.
Simon, whose son had married a French girl he met in
college. The new daughter-in-law didn't speak much English, or write it apparently, and she had written her
mother-in-law a note thanking her for a wedding gift.
Mrs. Simon had been in the drugstore in a panic to find
anyone who could translate it for her and let her know
what her new relative had to say. Bill had immediately
volunteered, and Maggie had been pleasantly amazed.
She approached him about doing his portrait, asking him
directly in French, and he responded affirmatively, in
kind.

Visions of his coming out to her studio and sitting for
the portrait while they chatted in French excited her, and
she looked forward eagerly to their first meeting. But he
hadn't wanted to come out to the ranch, and he insisted
she do at least the preliminary sketches in his office, so
they met there. And on the first meeting they found themselves scrambling around on the imitation leather sofa in
the slanted light from his drawn venetian blinds, making
violent love and saying things to each other in French
she had never dreamed possible.

As she prepared to leave him after the first time, standing and making sure her clothing was properly arranged,
she felt confused and strangely satisfied. Her lovemaking
with James Earl had always been tender, gentle, almost
intoxicating in its slow, methodical give and take. Bill's
approach had been virtually that of a rapist, taking her
without notice of her cries of protest or pleasure. Gripping his buttocks with her feet, she had felt him plunge

into her again and again, each time striving to get deeper and deeper into her, it seemed, trying, she believed, to hurt her with his organ as he threatened to hurt her with his teeth. Even though she thought she should have been revolted, repulsed, she knew she liked it, this violence in sex, and she also knew she wanted it again. But he thought differently.

Their next meeting, two days later, had been all business. He refused to speak French to her, or German, or Italian, which he also knew, and he spoke only when she asked him something, finally cutting the sitting short by telling her he had to make some calls. He never mentioned what had happened the first time, and she didn't either.

The portrait progressed slowly, finally almost stopping altogether. After six months, when it became important for her to have proper light, she insisted that he come out to her studio, and he did, twice. Both times she dressed in her sexiest outfits, bathed and perfumed her body to allure him, even offered him brandy to stimulate him—which he refused—but none of it worked. She painted and he sat passively, politely, and quietly, never making a less than gentlemanly gesture or suggestion, being the soul of friendliness, but not making any move toward her. It blinded her with frustration and anger.

She tried to forget all about him, about the afternoon's pleasure she had experienced in his office, but it wouldn't go away. She got to a point where James Earl's gentle sexual advances disgusted her, and the orgasm that had come so easily once, almost before he entered her sometimes, now was something she found herself faking more often than not, not that her husband, occupied as he was with cows and horses, family traditions and long, boring stories, seemed to notice.

Then one afternoon she had gone into town for her usual weekly buying spree. It was a sultry day in early summer, and she was in a particularly bad mood since James Earl had just refused to allow her to take flying lessons, one of the few things he had ever denied her, because he felt it was silly and dangerous. She found

herself passing the corner near Bill's office and watched
him let himself in the door. Going on to Central Drugs
and sipping a Coke did nothing to lessen her resolve. She
had left her packages in the booth, had marched directly
to his office door and banged on it when she found it
locked, the shades drawn.

He answered her knock quickly enough, and she strode
in past him. She plunked her handbag down on his desk
and turned to face him, her legs spread apart and her
hands on her hips. "Bastard!" she hissed at him. "I'm
the best you ever had." He said nothing. "What do I
have to do?"

He came to her still without saying anything, lifted her
in both arms which he wrapped around her hips, and
plopped her down on the imitation leather sofa. He ripped
her skirt up and pulled down her pantyhose and underwear in one motion. With his other hand he opened her
blouse, ripped her bra from her breasts, and then he took
her. She didn't even remember him taking down his trousers, but she did faintly recall that he didn't remove his
shoes or his shirt.

Like the time before, he was violent, brutal, but unlike
the previous time, there was no love talk, in French or
any other language. Her cries of climax did nothing to
stop the thrusting of his penis into her, and soon after
she climaxed for a second time, he withdrew from her,
still erect, and forced her forward on the sofa, pushing
his penis, shiny from her own juices, into her mouth.
She cooperated until, at last, he pushed her back, away,
and entered her again, bringing her again to orgasm and
finally coming along with her.

She lay there panting, pulling the strings of wet hair
from her mouth and eyes, and he stood and pulled his
trousers up and fastened his belt. "You got what you
wanted," he said quietly. "Now, don't come back until
I say so. Ever."

She found herself crying as she pulled her clothes back
on, stuffing the ruined bra into a pocket of her skirt and
straightening her hair. She didn't know what to say. Even
though she felt dimly satisfied with it all, a nagging sense

of wrong made her feel dirty and sad, ashamed and cheap. She reached for her handbag, then realized that the blue clutch she picked up wasn't hers. She put it down and grabbed her own purse, and then left, returning to Central Drugs around the corner for her packages and her unfinished Coke.

Sitting in the booth, feeling sore between her legs and on her body where his giant hands had bruised her, she tried to piece it all together, figure out what had happened and why. The first time had been beautiful, but this time he had been awful. What was different? Why had he been even more violent and uncaring than before?

Helen Monroe, wife of Quincy Monroe, the Agatite Chevrolet dealer, came into the drugstore and picked up something from the cosmetic counter. Maggie nodded to her as she passed, noting that there was something odd, something strange about the way the usually friendly Helen strode by without much more than a glance. Then it struck Maggie all at once. She turned in the booth for another look, and sure enough, tucked under Helen's arm was the blue clutch purse from Bill's desk. She must have been in the back room of the office the whole time. Maggie almost laughed out loud, and it was all she could do to keep from calling Helen over to share in the great joke.

But she didn't. Instead she confronted Bill two days later, after a discreet phone call to his office for an appointment, and talked things over. He told her he had no interest in ''an affair.'' He told her he wouldn't be ''available for sittings'' more than once or twice every few months. To get together more often, he explained, was to invite unnecessary gossip. If she didn't want to ''finish the portrait,'' he said, continuing the euphemism through his broad smile, he would understand. And then his phone rang, and she left him talking in low tones.

She had returned to his office from time to time, often monthly, but the strange hunger he had awakened in her for exciting sex wasn't satisfied, and she found herself wondering about other men in the town, seeking them out and openly flirting with them whenever she could, finally bedding with some once or twice, but finding few who could stimulate in her the violent passion Bill Castlereigh had discovered.

At first James Earl pretended not to notice. He teased her a bit about her increasingly frequent excuses not to sleep with him, and he bristled openly and loudly about her request to move to another bedroom where she could "avoid his snoring" and have more room for her constantly expanding wardrobe. He had finally agreed, however, and after a while he stopped coming into her room late at night, seeking love and sex from the woman he married, and he ceased dropping not-so-subtle hints about a family to carry on the Meacham traditions.

Eventually they began taking their meals apart, and for more than a year they had moved about the great house separately, often going for days without seeing each other except for a passing glance across the lawn or from a window.

She was certain he knew what she was doing, especially since a few of her friends had taken the trouble to warn her about her lack of discretion on several occasions, but she really didn't care. Also, the fact that most of those friends had been regular "consultants" at Bill's office made her want to laugh in their faces. Still, she didn't feel perverse. Except for her infrequent sessions with Bill, she stuck to one man at a time, even if the time turned out to be short.

She selected a blue summer dress that was inappropriate for a funeral, really, but would be cool in the terrible August heat. It promised to be a large funeral, and she wanted to look good. But it would take *hours* for everyone to line up at the cemetery, and she didn't want to wilt in some dark, heavier dress just because it was more fashionable. It rankled her to sacrifice fashion for comfort, but that was one more disadvantage of remaining in north central Texas instead of enjoying the more temperate climate of the Continent.

Her head still hurt, but the pain had become a dull throb instead of the searing hurt it had originally been. She reminded herself to take a Valium before leaving the house. This promised to be an emotional afternoon, and she didn't want to lose control. But then, she thought, I've never lost control.

The pranks had started recently, right after James Earl had asked her for a divorce. Under the Texas community property law, half the ranch and everything else belonged to her. He was timid about it at first, but she hadn't been. She told him she would have half the ranch, half his cash, and half the stocks and investments he had made. Then he had exploded, and for the first time since they met, he yelled at her. For a moment she thought he would give in, give her half and let her go, but he had no intention of that. He would rather kick her out and let her go, and she couldn't count on her daddy to save her this time. He liked James Earl a lot, and he would more than likely see to it that she didn't get a pot to pee in. It was just as likely that he knew of her colorful career, since two of the men she had slept with had been in front of his bench in divorce proceedings, and her name had come up incidentally at least once in each of those cases.

But James Earl hadn't mentioned divorce again, not since that fight. Instead he became a haunting figure about the house, sneaking up to her bed while she was sleeping, leaving things like the gasoline, the poison, the snake. She didn't know whether he wanted to kill her or just drive her crazy, but she supposed he wouldn't really pose a serious threat either way.

He probably didn't have the guts to kill her, she thought. When the old collie dog they had run over on the way out of the ranch's drive one morning had just crawled up there and moaned in pain, James Earl couldn't even shoot it himself, but had left the job to one of the hired men. Except for dove hunting, he didn't even like to go out and shoot animals of any sort, and he brought home so few birds each season that she suspected that he missed them on purpose. Murdering her would mean he would risk the ranch. No, he wouldn't kill her outright.

As for driving her crazy, he had a long way to go on that score. Maggie believed herself to be tougher than her husband by a long shot, and she wasn't about to let a snake or even an empty shotgun pointed at her make her nutty. She'd learn to be more careful, to lock her door when she bathed, to look before she sat down or smoked or ate anything in the house. She'd outlast him for sure, and she'd have her divorce on her own terms, uncontested and giving her enough cash to do Europe right and permanently.

Maggie Meacham finished dressing and went into the bathroom, where she took two pills and washed them down with water. She wanted a drink, too, but the clock by her bed told her that having to dry her hair had thrown her off schedule and she would barely have time to get into town before the funeral started. She hadn't eaten either, not since Jeff Randall had brought some hamburgers back to the Ramada Inn room in Kirkland the night before, and her stomach rumbled as she thought of the refrigerator full of meat and vegetables downstairs.

He probably sent Cook off today, she thought angrily, recalling that when she went down for the ice she hadn't seen the elderly black woman who cooked their meals every day except Sunday. Maggie figured she could hold out, though. She and Jeff were to meet in Kirkland again that evening, after the funeral, and she'd make him go out for steaks this time.

The young physician had been her latest conquest, and she smiled as she gathered her things together in a handbag that matched her blue dress. She had scheduled an appointment for an examination with him, shunning the all-business approach of Doc Pritchard, who had been her doctor since she had come from her mother's womb into his even-then-ancient hands. She managed to seduce Dr. Randall in his examining room, getting him to send the pimply nurse down the hall to check on another patient, and inviting him to take her right on the table. It hadn't been very good, the table was too small and the stirrups kept getting in his way, but they had soon renewed their intentions in the Ramada Inn in Kirkland, and he had proved to be most satisfactory in bed. He wasn't nearly as good as Bill, but then that didn't matter much anymore, did it? she asked herself.

Poor Bill, she thought, snapping the handbag shut,

damn it. She knew exactly how he died, what he had been doing when he died, chasing that young snatch across the pool. Jeff had told her, laughing grotesquely as he described their having to break Bill's fingers to release the girl's bikini bottom.

Maggie had smiled in spite of herself. Bill had been his own worst enemy. He'd never liked women, only sex, and probably, although he never told her this, the only woman he'd ever loved was poor Wilma.

Maggie liked sex too, she realized, but she really had never known love, and her appetite for the kind of love Bill offered was more for the violence and brutality than for the man she was with or the sex itself. She prided herself on the fact that she had never masturbated. No. She and Bill were cut from the same cloth in many ways, but she knew the difference between them. She knew what she wanted and would have been content to keep it if she found it. She had found it in Bill, but he wouldn't let her keep it. Damn him.

She let herself out the front door and walked carefully across the lawn to the blue Porsche parked in the four-car garage. She inspected her path carefully, watching for boobytraps possibly set for her by her husband.

Suddenly a thought occurred to her, and she smiled a beautiful if sinister smile. What if she could drive *him* nuts, just by continuing to sleep with other men? Wouldn't that be great? What with his mother babbling away down in Houston, no one would doubt that he had merely inherited his insanity naturally. It runs in the family, she thought as she turned sideways to edge between the side of the big Lincoln and the Porsche. I'll have to explore that possibility, she said to herself.

She peered through the glass of the sports car before opening the door, checking for snakes or other possible reminders of James Earl's madness, for so she had suddenly decided to think of his pranks. She reminded herself to start a diary, keeping a tally of what he was doing to her in case she could ever get it to court, even her daddy's court. He'd have to believe her then and declare ol' James Earl III mentally incapacitated. Then she'd have

it all. The thought made her breath rapid as she anticipated wealth, Europe, men of the Riviera.

Something caught her eye in the Lincoln, and she
moved over to the driver's side to take a look. She wrinkled her brow in curiosity and bent down to peer inside.
It appeared as though someone had taken a can of red
paint and dumped it out all over the back and bench of
the front seat. Even the steering wheel of the car was
covered with what appeared to be sticky crimson enamel.
Outraged by the vandalism, she automatically reached for
the door handle, and then she jerked her fingers away as
if it were white-hot.

Blood! she thought, horrified. It was blood. Her eyes
raced upward to the ceiling of the tin-roofed carport,
seeking someplace to focus on other than on what she
imagined might have been so viciously slaughtered in the
Lincoln's front seat that it covered the whole interior with
blood. She sought the courage to look inside the car again
and prayed that no person, no human being, had been
killed there.

"James Earl," she said aloud, and she almost laughed.
He had killed some animal and left it for her to find.
Maybe he had saved the blood from a beef he had had
butchered. Or was it an animal? Jeff Randall's face swam
before her eyes, and without a moment's hesitation and
in spite of the horror of the thought, she leaned down
and searched the car's bloody interior.

At first she saw nothing that would indicate the source
of the gore, but then she spotted a cat's head, dismem-
bered and wide-eyed, placed carefully on the dashboard,
just over the speedometer. The mouth was open, and the
raw, ragged tear of its neck sat atop streams of blood that
ran down over the instruments and onto the floorboard.
Cupping her hands to see better through the tinted glass,
she inspected the backseat and floor, and there she located other feline body parts strewn about haphazardly.

He killed a cat, killed it, cut it up, and smeared its
blood and guts all over the big Lincoln, figuring that she
would casually open the door, get in, and find herself
covered with the sticky gore and confronted by the death

stare of one of Cook's former pets. What made him think she would take the big car? The funeral? Probably. He knew she would be dressed up and would want to look important at the services. But she had decided to take the smaller car since she was planning to drive over to Kirkland later. His plan to send her hysterical and screaming back into the house, ripping bloody clothes from her body and attracting the attention of the men in the barn, had failed.

Slowly she turned away from the Lincoln and returned to the door of the Porsche. She rolled down the window and sat, carefully inspecting again for signs of tampering or traps. Firing up the small car, she backed out and drove directly over to the horse barn where men were at work. She pulled up and honked. Henry Gonzalez came out.

"Gonzalez," she said, touching up her lipstick in the rearview mirror, careful not to look at him at all, "someone's made an awful mess in the Lincoln. Would you go over and try to clean it up?"

She turned suddenly and flashed her prettiest smile. "It seems that someone put a dead cat in there. There's blood all over the place."

"Yes, ma'am." Gonzalez stood turning his hat in his hands. "Who'd do such a thing?"

"Why don't you ask Mr. Meacham?" she said, taking a hand-painted Italian scarf from her bag and tying it around her golden hair. "I'm sure I don't know anything about it." With that she backed the Porsche directly out of the horse barn drive, covering Gonzalez with a spray of hot dust and gravel, spun the wheel, and sped off down to the all-weather road and the highway that led to Agatite and Bill Castlereigh's funeral.

IV. Lawman
The Present, Noon

Morris Tucker took almost two hours to change all the tires and bubble-balance them on the cruiser. He wanted to do a high-speed balance on them as well, but Able Newsome had finally lost patience with the tobacco-chewing mechanic, and he drove out with Morris yelling about the crucial needs of law enforcement vehicles. He had practically danced around on one foot while Morris puttered around changing the four tires. It seemed to take forever to tow the cruiser into the garage, then Morris had stopped to gossip with every old fart who wandered in, answered every telephone call, and would have taken off for an early lunch if Able hadn't practically threatened him with arrest if he didn't finish the job.

Able lit a Hava-Tampa Jewel and drove out Main Street, scanning the sidewalk in front of the stores. Then he turned and made for Highway 287. He tried to tell if the new tires felt any different, but they didn't. As he passed the First Baptist Church, he noticed official cars were already arriving and lining up for the funeral, and Patrolman Phillips was arguing with Maggie Meacham, easily recognizable in her little sports car. It was going to be a goddamn circus, Able thought sourly as he slipped the cigar out of his mouth, wincing from the coffee burns on his lip.

Elton Cranston came wheezing out to the cruiser as it pulled into the Conoco station. Elton weighed close to three hundred pounds, wore a full but scraggly beard, and suffered from asthma, a combination of physical problems that made him an easy candidate for the most obnoxious human being ever to walk the earth. He wheezed with every breath, and his vast bulk made movement a trial for him.

"Mornin', Able," he gasped as he rested his hammy hands on the cruiser's door. "Or I s'pose it's nearer noon! What can I do for you?" Elton knew that Able never bought gas for the cruiser from the Conoco station since the Gulf dealer downtown had the county bid for service and fuel.

Able glanced into the round, piggy eyes and noted with disgust the crumbs of Elton's enormous lunch sticking in his beard, "Just wondered if you've seen any strangers hanging around here," he said.

"Strangers?" Elton stood up and glanced around as if he was trying to locate someone who might fit the description. "Uh, nope. Not me. Not lately." He pulled at the belt of his oversized trousers and hooked his greasy thumbs through the loops. "There was some hitchhikers 'round here this mornin', long 'bout eight or so, but I tol' 'em to move right along. I don't 'low no hitchhikers bummin' rides off customers."

"What did they look like?" Able asked.

"Hell, Able, I don't know. They was just hitchhikers. Worthless bums, likely. I tol' 'em to move on or I'd kick some ass, by God." He drifted on into a discourse on the worthlessness of hitchhikers in general, and Able realized that he was going to get less than nothing from Elton.

The sheriff sat in his cruiser, listening without hearing Elton hold forth in breathy gasps, and he glanced up and down the superheated highway. As soon as he politely could, he thanked Elton and pulled away, leaving the fat man in a cloud of greasy dust.

It had been a foolish idea, Able thought as he guided the cruiser out to the edge of town and swung wide to make a U-turn. He switched on the air conditioner and rolled up the windows, flicking the cigar stub out as he did so. Even if the guy with the fingernails had been involved in Eileen's death, the trail was too cold. Hell, they had been downtown two hours or more ago, and now they were probably in Oklahoma.

Mentally he tried to assess the descriptions Dinah had given him and imagined he could see the skinny man in the green suit reflected in the eyes in the photograph. Pretty weak, he mused, noting a tourist in a large Chrysler pulled over to the side of the road, steam rising from his engine. He almost pulled over to lend a hand, at least a ride back up to the Conoco station, when the radio crackled.

"Able?" Vernon's voice came over the static.

"Yeah?" the sheriff answered irritably. He hated the radio.

"Chrystal's been raisin' hell for you to get out and relieve Jingles on the speed trap," Vernon drawled into the mike.

Able had forgotten all about working the speed trap, and he cursed under his breath. "Right," he said, then keyed the mike again, "Listen, Vernon." He paused, hating to ask him to do this dirty job, but, damn it, he wanted to take another swing through town. Maybe, just maybe, he would get lucky and spot one of the men. "Would you go out and relieve Fatso?"

"Sure, Able." Able noticed hesitation in his deputy's voice, and he picked up on it.

"You had anything to eat yet?" he asked.

"No," Vernon admitted, "but if you'll give me ten minutes, I'll get a hamburger and meet you out there."

"Right," Able shot back. "Take a half hour and get in out of the heat. There's no hurry." He replaced the mike and swung the cruiser around toward the speed trap. No, he thought, there's no hurry at all.

4

I. Funeral
The Present, 2:30 P.M.

In complete defiance of his direct orders and instructions, Police Officer Clovis Hiker strolled into the Agatite Police Station, removed his utility belt and holster, and set them noisily on the chief's desk. He squinted through his bad eye toward the station office's clock and noted that it was only 2:30, and he figured he had a good hour before he would be expected to manage cross traffic in downtown Agatite as the funeral procession taking Bill Castlereigh's body from the First Baptist Church to the Sandhill Memorial Cemetery passed Second Street. Clovis stretched his short body up to his fullest height and tried unsuccessfully to tuck his rapidly expanding beer belly into his uniform pants, cocked his cowboy-style uniform hat back on thinning blond hair, and removed a small vial of aeresol breath freshener from his shirt pocket prepatory to spraying his mouth.

In an anteroom off the main office, Chrystal Murphy sat snapping chewing gum in rhythm to her snap of pages in a magazine. She had just ignored Able Newsome's attempt to radio the Police Department because the sheriff refused to follow correct procedure, and she adjusted the volume on her portable tape deck to drown out his demands that she answer him. Since Blair Phillips and Clovis Hiker would be joining her father-in-law in escorting the funeral procession, she looked forward to a dismally boring afternoon, and as her eyes glanced at the ads in the slick magazine, she vaguely contemplated painting her toenails or bleaching her hair again during the dull, hot afternoon hours.

Clovis quietly opened the door to the radio room and

stepped up behind her without making a sound. Slowly he ran his hand down to her neck and under her blouse, into her brassiere, tweaking her left nipple with his fingers as the other hand expertly worked loose the bra through the blouse from the back. She looked up, startled, then her eyes grew wide with surprise and she opened her mouth to receive his tongue in a hard, passionate kiss that eventually led to her losing her balance on the swivel chair and tumbling both of them onto the floor of the cramped quarters of the radio room of the Agatite Police Department.

Giggling and laughing, they got to their feet and play-wrestled through the station office, down the stairs to the holding cells, and into cell number one, where Clovis finally managed to remove her blouse and bra. She practically ripped his shirt open, running her hands down his hairless chest and fumbling with his belt buckle and trousers' fly, finally opening them and grabbing his erection, leading him by it to the cot in the cell and then falling down, never letting go.

While he carefully scrambled out of his boots and pants with one hand, Clovis pulled her slacks and panties down with the other, and finally he mounted her as she groaned in ecstasy. Their bodies glistened with sweat in spite of the well-air-conditioned station house. Their kisses became longer and deeper, their bodies moving in rhythm to the heavy country-and-western beat coming from Chrystal's tape deck upstairs, its music completely drowning out the static and plantive calls coming from Able Newsome or anyone else in need of police assistance.

As the First Security Bank of Sandhill County's outside clock and thermometer registered 2:58 and 110 degrees, Cassie Crane slid the old pickup into an angled space in front of the bank and got out. She had recognized Breedlove as he walked up and down the streets of his old hometown. He had changed, she thought as she passed him. He was walking with a sort of limp and was wearing a coat in this heat, but it was him. She wasn't likely to forget him, no matter how much he changed.

The long-haired guy with him also disturbed her. While Breedlove had paid her no mind at all, his companion glared at her when she slowly drove past searching for a parking space near the bank. The town was crowded, what with the payday for the mill bringing the normal middle-of-the-month shoppers in and adding to the crush of people who always seemed to come to town whenever there was a big funeral.

As Cassie hauled little Claudine out and balanced her on one hip, she forgot about Breedlove, who was, by now, all the way down toward the depot at the end of Main Street. She spotted on of the O'Hara boys and smiled at him. He didn't even raise a hand in greeting, which Cassie found odd, but she shrugged and went into the bank.

Cassie went to the far teller's window and spoke briefly with Maribeth Hogan, who took Cassie's check and counted out the cash she desired. Cassie was nervous, and, taking the cash, she glanced out the bank's Flex-Glo front window at the large black man who was parking a van next to her pickup. He showed no interest in the luggage she had left in the truck's bed, however, and he strolled across the street to Central Drugs. It was very cool in the bank, and Cassie could almost feel the oppressiveness of the heat outside as she stared out the window.

Then she noticed a small red sports car cruising down the street looking for a parking space. Adam Moorely! She felt herself flush with embarrassment and had to fight the urge to look around to see if anyone in the bank had noticed her spotting him.

"Have to pee," Claudine said, pointing to the women's room in the rear of the bank. Cassie sighed. She ought to go to the toilet, too. Maybe she should take the time to wash her face and fix her hair a bit. Waiting for that bus was going to be a hot business, and she didn't want to look too seedy when she got to San Marcos. She turned and hauled Claudine from one hip to another as she passed the teller's cages and went to the women's rest room. She wondered if the bus would have a toilet.

* * *

If William Castlereigh had been alive as his body lay in
front of the white pine pulpit of the Agatite First Baptist
Church, he would have raised himself up to a sitting position and smiled his famous boyish grin out into the
congregation of people who had come to mourn his passing. He would have had good cause to smile, too, for the
pews of the church, which was the largest in the small
town, were overflowing with people, mostly women, and
they were all appropriately attired in funeral dark colors.
Some were softly weeping.

Only the front pew was vacant, waiting for Wilma
Castlereigh and her two daughters to make their tearful
entrance, down the rows that were even crowded with
folding chairs, and take their places. In the choir loft a
trio of sisters waited to sing the first hymn of three that
Wilma had selected for the rite, and behind the hand-
carved cross on the door the Reverend Dr. Randolph P.
Streetman nervously checked his notes and bookmark in
his oversized Bible, sneaking a peek through the well-
hidden spy hole at the enormous crowd.

But Bill Castlereigh could not sit up from the satin-
and-velvet-lined mahogany casket, which had been the
most expensive Everett Hardin had in his funeral home's
warehouse, and he couldn't smile since his lips were sewn
shut and his jaws wired closed. And to tell the truth, it
didn't matter to him one bit that anyone at all was present
in the church, or even that some of them were weeping.

Had he been alive, however, he would not have la-
mented his own death much. He had lived a good deal,
and he had enjoyed tremendously the past several years
as a celebrated figure in Agatite. Probably, he had figured more than once, he had been with more women than
any man alive, and he knew that in no case had one of
them left his bed, couch, backseat, or other trysting place
less than satisfied with his performance.

From his spy hole, the Reverend Streetman looked again
at the crowd, and he wondered about Bill Castlereigh.
He wished he had been able to blow away some of the
smoke surrounding the man he was about to eulogize,

but he hadn't, and it was too late now. He desperately
wanted a cigarette. He bent his head to his notes again.

In almost the exact center of the congregation sat Maggie
Meacham. She adjusted her dress a bit and looked discreetly
around her. She was aware that women in the church were
almost all former or current lovers of the deceased.

Her thoughts ranged from the open casket in front of
Jeff Randall, who sat with the pallbearers down on her
right. His broad back and tanned neck met her eyes, and
she anticipated the evening when she would lovingly ca-
ress that neck and run her hands across that back in ecstasy. She was vastly pleased to have driven the sports
car, not only because of the bloody trap her husband had
left for her, but because she was able to squeeze it into
the parked line for the procession to the cemetery, right
up front, three cars back from the hearse. That was fine,
she thought with a smile, and appropriate.

There had been some nastiness with that awful policeman about her butting in front of the line that way, but
she had handled that. There was a distinct advantage to
being the wife of the richest rancher in the county, and
she had let that uppity young punk know by ignoring his
waving arms and pulling in right behind the family car.
Who better than I to be right behind Wilma? she asked
herself. Helen Monroe? She glanced at Helen, who sat
on the other side of the church beside her husband. If
she had caught her eye, she might have winked.

As Maria Trimble continued to drone the organ music,
Maggie contemplated just leaving James Earl. To hell
with his money. The blood in the car had shaken her
more than she realized at first. He just might work up the
nerve to kill her, after all, or at least to maim her seriously. He wasn't stupid, and he was well-liked in town.
It might be dangerous to stay out at the ranch, especially
since he had also come out in the open with the shotgun
prank. Perhaps she should talk to Jeff about it.

But then she thought, no, she didn't want to give Jeff
any inkling of what might be going on. He might get
ideas about her wanting something more permanent between them, and whatever her plans for the future, they

did not include some small-town doctor who would only wind up being a poor substitute for a small-town rancher. Either was boring, and she was bored enough now. She had had enough boredom for any three people. No. She would have to make decisions like this one on her own. But for the moment she would go with Jeff to Kirkland. Then she would decide what to do.

She folded her hands in front of her and stared at them. She should have worn a hat, she mused, one with a large veil.

Next to Jeff Randall on the pallbearer's pew sat Wayne Henderson, who was squirming in his seat. He was feeling particularly bad, since his stomach hurt terribly, and the walk down from the drugstore had been too hot to believe. He had not yet confronted the problem of how he was going to get to the cemetery, and he contemplated begging off and not going at all. He honestly did not feel well, he argued with himself, but he also argued that going back to the store would look bad if he complained that he was ill. Going home did not cross his mind as a possibility.

He had noticed the limousine parked next to the curb behind the family car, and he wondered if the pallbearers were supposed to ride in it. He had never been in such a car, but he figured it was about like any other. At least it would be air conditioned, he told himself, uncomfortably noting that body odor was rising from either him or Jeff Randall, who was sitting uncomfortably close.

Wayne's eyes flicked rapidly around, carefully skirting the open coffin. When Bill Castlereigh had first moved to Agatite, he had traded with Wayne quite a bit. But the really expensive items needed for setting up a new home the Castlereighs had gotten through the Sears catalogue or from one of the discount places over in Wichita Falls. Wayne wasn't a man to bear a grudge, not really. He just didn't like Bill Castlereigh, and he suspected that the dead man had been exactly what he was, a gladhander, a phony, a class-A son of a bitch. He didn't trust him, and he didn't like him. Wayne thought Wilma was probably okay, but he really didn't like her either, and he knew that the elder of the two girls was dating that little shit Warren, and he doubted that any good would come of it.

Wayne knew nothing of Bill's sexual adventures, since he avoided gossip and no one ever came by to share any with him, but he suspected that whatever Bill Castlereigh was up to in Agatite, it probably hadn't amounted to very much, and it was probably as shady as he felt the man had been.

Wayne's stomach churned and he felt the stares of the people behind him. Taking a hymnal from the rack in front of him, he began leafing through it, knowing that the ordeal of the afternoon was far from over. He raised his eyes to try to get his mind clear, and found that he was looking directly into the casket. Behind the choir loft was the drawn curtain of the baptistry, and the image of Roosevelt Grady swam before his eyes. He lifted his hand to his forehead and wiped away the last traces of perspiration. He believed he was more miserable than he had ever been before in his life. What else could happen to make matters worse?

The cross-laden door opened, and the Reverend Dr. Streetman passed through, carrying his notes and his Bible tightly in hand. He was more nervous than he had been when he preached his first sermon, and he clutched the papers and book firmly to keep them from shaking and betraying his lack of confidence.

He was already running ten minutes late, having delayed until the last of the mourners filed in, and he was now prepared to give the signal to Cecil Logan, the head deacon, to send in the family. The church was awesomely silent beneath the organ's continuing drone, the only noise coming from an occasional cougher and the distant labors of the overburdened air conditioning system, unused to such a gathering in August midday heat. He dreaded the graveside ceremony, trying to be heard in the shimmering sunshine by all these people.

Quietly trying to estimate the size of the crowd, he walked solemnly to the podium and opened his Bible and laid out his notes. His eulogy was to be brief, since he had little information to impart. He hoped to do something worthwhile here, make these people glad they came, inspire them with some insight, but he had none himself. Like many of them, he imagined, he only wanted to get this over with.

He nodded almost imperceptibly, and the family began its descent to the first pew, draped in black. Flowers covered the front of the sanctuary, their perfume mixing with the faint odors of perspiration and colognes worn by the mourners, giving a sick, sweet smell to the church. The Reverend Streetman's eyes fell to the open casket, beheld the handsome aspect of the deceased. Bill was deeply tanned, not at all paled by death. In fact, Dr. Streetman remarked to himself, he looked healthier than most of the people here. God, he wanted a cigarette! he thought, and he promised himself one as soon as he could sneak away.

Wilma and her daughters had come about halfway down the aisle. She was crying loudly, and her children were softly weeping into handkerchiefs behind her. Not a few of the mourners were classmates and friends of the girls, and their raised eyebrows of recognition brought similar eye signs from the girls. Was this all a show? Dr. Streetman wondered in amazement. Were they really as unmoved as they looked to be? He suddenly felt foolish, out of place, and an overwhelming temptation to turn this into an inquisition flooded him. He longed to ask Wilma what was the truth about her husband. Where had they come from? Why had they come? What had they done to deserve such a show of affection and respect from the town? With difficulty he controlled himself and consulted his Bible as they slowly moved down.

Bill Castlereigh's funeral was not particularly different from others in the town Dr. Streetman had seen. It was larger, perhaps, better attended than the average, but most people were there to be seen or to see, not to mourn. Of course, the preacher mused as he sightlessly studied the onionskin pages before him, some of these, these women, were doubtlessly here to mourn, for in his particular way Bill Castlereigh was a special kind of man to them, the source of heartbreak and temptation, no doubt, but special nevertheless.

As Wilma took her seat next to her daughters in the front pew, the weeping behind her began to crescendo, and it seemed to move forward toward the casket in a slow wave of sobbing. As the trio of sisters began their first hymn, they had to adjust their volume to be heard above the rising crying that began to fill the church.

The Reverend Dr. Streetman coughed as the women finished singing, and he smoothed out the pages of his Bible one more time. He tried not to focus on the faces of women who had come to him in the past few years, wringing handkerchiefs and weeping over Bill Castle-reigh in a very different way. He felt hypocritical, and he felt dirty. This was a tax on his faith he had not bargained for. "God help me," he whispered inaudibly to himself, hoping the Diety would hear and respond, and he opened his mouth and spoke.

"Friends," he said, shocked to hear his voice sounding so small in the crowded church, "we have come together to pay our final respects to a beloved brother in Christ. . . ."

Out on Highway 287 Sheriff Able Newsome sat and sweated in his cruiser. He didn't dare let the motor idle in this heat with the air conditioning on, and he had become hotter and hotter by the minute. Sweat literally poured off his forehead and dropped onto his shirt in globs of saline.

His mood wasn't helped any by the fact that Vernon hadn't shown up as soon as he'd thought he would, and Able's attempts to raise anybody at the police department had been met by stony silence from that idiot bitch, Chrystal, who was probably down in one of the holding cells fucking the brains out of somebody while official business went untended to upstairs. This was one miserable day, Able thought sourly.

He couldn't figure out how Phillips and Hiker could stand sitting out here day after day in this kind of heat. So far Able had watched about a hundred cars and trucks go by, leaving hot, red clay dust in their wakes, and a good half of them had been speeding. But Able didn't care. The prospect of chasing them down and then having to deal with them in this heat was too miserable to consider, so he just let them go. Besides, his mind was not on speed traps, it was still on Eileen Kennedy and the man with the fingernails, who was, Able had finally convinced himself, still in town.

He tried again to raise Vernon by radio but had no luck. "Oh, hell," he swore, lighting a Hava-Tampa Jewel and gingerly moving it around so it wouldn't offend his burned lip, "what difference does it make?"

But inside him the thought that one of the two strangers might be or know something about Eileen's killer gnawed at him. It was unlikely that he might be connected to a month-old killing, but then again. . . .

A big semi making over eighty swooshed past him, ignoring the speed zone like it wasn't there and spraying the cruiser with a hot blast of gravel and dust. Able frowned into his rearview mirror and said to his reflection, "This is totally fucked," and then he nodded, allowing his sweaty face to agree with his mirrored image. Without further hesitation he started the cruiser and spun his new tires in the gravel of the road's shoulder as he pointed the car toward town.

The Reverend Dr. Randolph P. Streetman finished his eulogy for Bill Castlereigh with an overlong prayer. He felt he had done the best he could under the circumstances, and he breathed a final sigh of relief when the congregation mumbled a benedictory "Amen" at the prayer's conclusion.

The pallbearers helped Everett Hardin set the casket up for final viewing, and the family formed a reception line as the full congregation filed past, weeping and looking much sadder, Dr. Streetman thought, than the family they attempted to console.

As the final mourner went out to the bake-oven hot cars parked in a long parade around the back of the church and stretching for a dozen blocks down toward the highway, Everett closed and sealed the casket, and with the pallbearers behind him, he wheeled it out to the hearse. Attendants piled the flowers into the trunks of the family car and pallbearers' limousine.

The Reverend Dr. Streetman quietly went into his study and sneaked a cigarette from an almost empty pack, lit it, sucked the smoke in deeply, and wiped imaginary sweat from his forehead. The ordeal was almost over, he told himself, again sucking on the smoke harder than was necessary. He still had the graveside service to attend to, but that was virtually a formula. It was hotter than he ever remembered it outside. He took another puff from the delicious smoke, crushed the cigarette out, then picked up his Bible and went out to get into the hearse for the drive to the cemetery.

Wayne Henderson had made it through the funeral with less discomfort than he had expected. He went out into the blistering heat with the other pallbearers and lined up to aid Everett in setting the coffin into the hearse. It was heavy, and the men were sweating profusely through their heavy, dark suits. Once the hearse was closed, all hopes of escaping the graveside service were dispelled when Everett directed the six men to the third car in the procession, the limousine, which, blessedly, was already started and had the air conditioner running. Wayne got in the front seat next to Newell Longman, who would drive, and slammed the door. He really wanted to get out of the car, he realized, worse than almost anything else. As he contemplated how to ask Newell as politely as he could to let him off in front of his store on the way, the procession pulled out behind Jingles Murphy's cruiser, which was flashing its lights and goosing its siren at every intersection.

Downtown, ahead of the procession, traffic was grinding to a halt. A few perceptive motorists, spying the flashing lights of the funeral procession just as it pulled away from the church, moved quickly out of their parking spaces and turned the corner, but others who had been circling the downtown area looking for a close-in spot, jumped into the open spaces as soon as they were vacant.

* * *

Young Daniel O'Hara leaned on a parking meter in front of Central Drugs and sipped his fourth Coke in a row. His mood had not improved in the past two hours, and he was pondering how to go home and break the news to his family that he would not be going to school this September.

Directly opposite the drugstore in front of the bank, he noticed four men, three white and one black, meet. Two of them had come from a van that had been parked for a few minutes directly in front of the bank's front door. Glare from the bank's Flex-Glo windows hit Danny squarely in the face, and he couldn't see clearly what the men were doing. But suddenly the three white men entered the bank and had some trouble moving large duffle bags inside. The black man turned away from the bank's door and crossed the street to where Danny stood.

"They got a phone in there?" the giant black man asked the dark-haired boy.

"Sure!" Danny answered, sounding more cheery then he felt.

Floyd pushed past him and entered the drugstore. Danny munched ice and wondered what was going on. Probably some big-shit business deal, he thought to himself as he chewed the straw in the Coke cup. Anybody can get help in a bank but me, even cowboys and worthless niggers. He was bitter and disappointed about the afternoon's events, but he also felt ashamed of what he was thinking about the men in the bank and their friend in the drugstore. "What the hell?" he asked himself aloud. The heat of the afternoon did nothing to diminish his sense of dread for all the hard work he knew lay ahead in the coming months on his old man's farm.

Inside the drugstore in an antique wooden phone booth, Floyd Tatum scratched his chin and thought deeply. Something was wrong, but he wasn't sure what. He looked out toward the simmering street. All appeared to be normal. People moved up and down sparsely and slowly, but there were women and children everywhere, and there was no obvious cause for alarm. But something wasn't right.

No one answered at either the sheriff's office or the police station, and, damn it, that wasn't right either, not even in a little jerkwater town like this. He plunked a coin into the phone again and dialed the sheriff's department number that was printed in large red letters over the phone. No answer after five rings. He depressed the hook and collected the coin, inserted it again, and dialed the police department. No answer there either. He swore silently.

He left the booth and walked to the door and peered out into the street. The bank's windows threw hard sunlight into his eyes, but nothing, nothing appeared unusual in any way. He turned and aimed for the phone booth again when he spotted an old black man sitting alone in a booth way in the rear of the drugstore.

"Hey, Bro!" Floyd flashed a toothy grin and sauntered up to the wizened old man. "Wha's happenin'?"

Samuel Adams Christopher, the custodian of the First Security Bank, looked up from his coffee and studied the enormous black man who stood grinning over him. Old Samuel, as he was known all over the country, could recognize a fraud a mile away, and he'd spotted Floyd for trouble when he first noticed him coming into the drugstore. "Whacha want?" he growled at him.

"I jus' wanna know wh's goin' on 'roun' heah," Floyd drawled, sensing the man's hostility. "I mean, Bro, I never seen such a dead town. Any action 'roun' heah?"

"We gotta sheriff'll bust your black ass if you cause trouble," Samuel snapped. "We got good folks 'roun' here, an' we don' wan' no trouble."

"Right!" Floyd said, still pasting his grin on his face and hating himself for doing it. "Me neither. I jus' wanna know where to fin' that sheriff. I might have business with him." He studied Samuel's face for an opening.

Old Samuel didn't flinch a bit under Floyd's gaze. He didn't trust this man for shit, he told himself, and sending him to the sheriff might just be the right thing to do. "Well," he said slowly, pulling an abused pipe from his shirt pocket and sucking a match flame through the bowl, "there's a funeral over to the Firs' Baptist Church, an' I spek he's over there now. Mos' everybody else in town is.''

"Thanks, Bro," Floyd grinned, "What say you let me buy your coffee?" He pulled a roll of bills from his pocket and began to peel off a five spot.

"No thanks," Old Samuel said balking at the display of bills, "I gotta job. I go to work real soon." With that he took a slow sip of his coffee, and Floyd realized he had been dismissed.

Floyd turned away and felt confused. This was either very good or very bad. He didn't know. It sure as hell wasn't in the game plan, but neither was the street full of cars he saw outside. He should have asked the old Tom where the church was, but it didn't really matter. Hell, he thought as he moved out onto the sidewalk, a funeral could be as good as a car wreck if all the cops are tied up.

He paused briefly on the sidewalk and pretended to stretch and checked the pistol concealed in the small of his back under his jacket. God, he thought, it was hot. The bank's thermometer inched up another notch to 111 degrees, and Floyd felt the oppressiveness of the light-weight jacket he wore. He set his jaw and strolled across the street. Let the chips fall where they may, he thought as he reached the van and got inside. He tried to peer through the bank's windows, but the glare from the sun concealed anything from the outside. He adjusted the shotgun across his lap and waited.

Back on the sidewalk in front of the drugstore, Danny O'Hara had noticed Floyd's gun when the black man stretched. He wrinkled his brow and wondered again what was going on. As he observed Floyd going across the street and entering the van, he briefly thought of going inside and calling the police or Able Newsome—that, he decided was a better idea.

Just as he was about to move away from the parking meter, however, he spied Janey Pruitt driving by in her daddy's new pickup. She waved briefly toward him, but it was an automatic gesture she used for anyone in Aga-tite she recognized as being near her age and a potential vote for something she was running for. She wouldn't have been friendly to Danny on purpose, he knew.

"Bitch," he said softly. "You'll be screwing college boys by September, but you're too good for me," he finished in a barely audible mutter.

He leaned again on the meter, waiting for her to make her U-turn by the depot and return so he could get a closer look at her soft beauty. The bank clock registered 3:05, and he noticed that the temperature was really shooting up. It was one hot afternoon.

Chrystal's second orgasm was completely ruined by the telephone's ringing. She was just about to come under the sweating and grunting Clovis on the cot in cell number one when the telephone upstairs started jangling.

Panic-stricken, she pushed the confused policeman off her and gathered up her clothes, dressing as best she could as she stumbled up the stairs, leaving a cursing and spewing Clovis behind her. She reached the telephone on the fifth ring and jerked the receiver up only to hear the dial tone.

Cursing herself now, she half walked and half hopped back down the stairs and then burst into a shriek of laughter when she spied Clovis trying desperately to thrust a leg into the twisted pants of his uniform. Hearing her, he turned seriously angry, and fixed his clouded eye toward her. She feigned terrible fright, then dropped the blouse she had held up to her naked breasts and strutted provocatively toward him, noting with pleasure that he scrambled out of the trousers and rose to greet her.

In minutes they were back on the cot, groaning and perspiring at their work, and the phone started ringing again. Clovis only grunted, "Fuck it," when she started to climb out from under him. "Just fuck it."

"That's what you're doin', sugar," Chrystal cooed into his ear, squirming under him again, but this time they didn't even count the rings.

As the phone rang in the office, Sheriff Able Newsome was standing perplexed in front of the Town and Country

Dinette. He had quizzed Dinah one more time, trying to
force her to remember anything else she could about the
two strangers who had been in that morning. Since leaving the speed trap he had developed an absolute certainty
that he was going to miss something. He felt instinctively
that his one chance of solving Eileen Kennedy's murder
lay in finding that man with the fingernails in his pocket.
A panicky feeling that he was doing nothing while the
man wandered around Agatite, veritably flaunting his
crime in Able's face, ate at the sheriff and pushed him
onward.

Behind him in the small cafe, Dinah stared hard at
him, more than a little put out that he wouldn't let her in
on what was going on. She had told him nothing new in
the latest interview, and he had left her in mid-sentence
and now stood on the steaming sidewalk, his hat pushed
back on his head, his hands on his hips, looking up and
down the street as if he were seeing it for the first time.
"That ain't like Able," she said to the empty dinette,
"He's just not himself today."

Able fixed his eyes on the pedestrian traffic as people
moved up and down the sidewalks and disappeared
around the corner into the downtown district. Across the
street the court house shimmered in the afternoon sun,
and to his right a woman dragged her young son into the
clinic of the Sandhill County Memorial Hospital. The
boy was resisting every step of the way, and the mother's
cajoling was rapidly giving way to exasperated anger in
the heat.

Able squinted to his left and through the glare he spotted Clovis Hiker's cruiser parked in front of the police
station and grunted. Well, that was why Chrystal wasn't
answering the radio calls. He wished he knew where Vernon was, but above all, he wished he knew where the
man with the fingernails was. The anxiety that had been
growing inside him now began to solidify in the center
of his stomach. It rested there like a giant rock and
seemed to weigh him down to the sizzling griddle the
sidewalk under his feet had become. There was nothing
here but raw speculation, he told himself, nothing at all.

But mere logic wouldn't move the feeling of dread that held him down. Something was going on. He could feel it. Something bad was going on, and he felt powerless to stop it or even to find out what it might be. God, he thought as he pulled out a handkerchief and wiped his brow under his lifted hat, it was hotter than the paving stones of hell!

He replaced the hat and took a long stride toward the corner of Third Street and Main.

II. Breedlove
The Present, 3:10 P.M.

Breedlove's mouth tasted like chalk, and his head pounded. He barely noticed the people who lay prone on the floor of the First Security Bank of Agatite, Texas, who he was supposed to be guarding with the .12 gauge pump-action shotgun he cradled across his arm. His shoulder, torn by the giant wrench Eileen Kennedy had used on him more than a month ago, also throbbed with pain that had become so much a part of every waking moment that he had trouble remembering when it wasn't there.

What he was most aware of was how badly he wanted a drink.

He shifted his weight from one foot to the other and winced as the old tenderness from his ankle shot up his leg. Cursing the weight of the shoulder harness where the .357 magnum rested against his strong side, he shot his eyes for the hundredth time in five minutes up to the broad-faced clock over the tellers' cages. 3:10. They'd been inside for only ten minutes, but it seemed like an eternity. He saw Joe Don moving methodically from cage to cage, loading cash into the plastic tote bags they'd wrapped their shotguns in when they entered the bank. Joe Don was working his way toward the vault where, according to Joe Don anyway, there was more than a quarter of a million dollars in cash awaiting their eager hands.

In spite of the large number of people on the floor of the bank, four tellers, two load officers, half a dozen customers and a couple of secretaries, no one moved or said a word. Even Joe Don, unlike in the former holdups, worked methodically and quietly.

Breedlove was nervous. He had felt stares of potential recognition directed toward him from every corner of the small town, and just before they had met Joe Don and Floyd on Main Street in front of the bank, he had almost run right into a couple of people he knew he recognized. But he didn't know for sure whether they knew him or not. Still, the fear of being singled out nagged at him and intensified his need of a drink.

He glanced down at his charges on the floor. There wasn't going to be any screwup this time, he assured himself, not this time. He had come too close to getting killed in Oklaunion and again on the highway not to be careful about these people. One move and he would blow them all away. He wasn't ruthless, only hopeless. He had already killed, and there wasn't anything they could do to him more than they would do anyhow if they caught him alive.

This plan was much like the others, except instead of being some jackleg loan office, this was a bank. It was the biggest bank in the region, too, according to Joe Don, and it was supposed to be loaded with cash to payroll the gyp mill checks and cover withdrawals for midmonth expenses.

How Joe Don had learned all this Breedlove wasn't sure, but Joe Don seemed certain, and Breedlove was desperate enough for money to get far, far away from Texas to believe anything.

That morning Floyd had left him and Mike Dix out on the highway by a Conoco station and they had made their way downtown on foot. The idea was that they would scout around and see if anyone suspected a robbery was about to take place. Why anyone should suspect anything was a mystery to Breedlove, but that was the plan. And one thing he had learned about Joe Don was that he followed his plans to the letter even when they didn't make sense.

Of course, that didn't apply to Mike Dix, who had stopped following instructions as soon as they were in sight of a cafe and insisted that they eat breakfast. Then they had walked around the town and talked to some girls in cars who drove past and who Mile flagged down. High school girls, Breedlove sniffed, jailbait. Christ, he thought, Dix is a sick, sick man.

Finally they made their way into the bank for a few minutes to check for anything out of the ordinary. While Mike cashed a bill at one of the cages, Breedlove doodled on a pad and eavesdropped on a brief shouting match in one of the offices which was a prelude to an angry, marching exit by a young man who almost knocked Mike down when he passed. Breedlove had buried his face against the wall and tried to look as inconspicuous as possible as the youth stormed out of the bank's front doors. Mike had yelled at him as soon as they were back on the street.

"Man," he sneered, "you're some kind of paranoid!"

"I grew up here!" Breedlove shot back at him in a loud whisper as they hurried down the street, sweating freely in the rising heat. "People *know* me here!"

"Shit," Mike replied as he lit a cigarette, "that was *years* ago, man, centuries ago!" He flicked his ashes onto Breedlove's green suit coat. "What if they do recognize you? What the fuck are you, some kind of celebrity? What you think's gonna happen? They gonna want your autograph?"

Breedlove said nothing, but he kept his eyes open. He had felt panic twice already that morning. Once in the dinette when the waitress had recognized him he had almost cut and run. She had stared at the fingernails he pulled out of his pocket along with the change he used to pay for his coffee. He had no idea why he still had them, but something forbade throwing them away. So he carried them with him, like good-luck charms or reminders of something he didn't dare let himself forget, even for a moment. He wondered if the waitress had really noticed them or recognized them for what they were.

Breedlove was certain that the whole town knew by

now that he had killed that girl out on the highway. He had seen the newspaper story about them finding her body, finding out who she was. From that story, and the two they had run since, he knew they hadn't connected her murder with the robbery in Oklaunion, not directly. At least they hadn't told anybody about the connection if they had figured it out. Instead they claimed to be looking for some kind of psychopath, some sick individual who beat her to death and hung her out there as some kind of horrible joke. Such stories made him squirm. As usual, he thought, he had fucked up. He couldn't even kill anybody right.

The second time he panicked was when he saw her father coming out of the hardware store. He was dressed to kill, Breedlove noted, like it was Sunday or something, and he had a boutonniere stick in his lapel. He was too far away to have recognized the man who ruined his daughter, but Breedlove knew that if he did, he would probably try to start something. He wasn't the sort of man who forgot things people did to him—or to his daughter—and what Breedlove had done wasn't the sort of thing a man could forget anyway.

Mike Dix sat quietly on a chair by the bank's front door. His shotgun was pointed upward toward the ornate woodwork on the ceiling of the old bank building. He was watching the street and not commenting on anything except to say that Floyd was back in the van. All of them seemed more calm this time, Breedlove noted, even though he knew that hitting this bank was insane. But he went along easily enough, and he blamed his participation on the pain that wracked his whole body.

The chalky taste in his mouth persisted. It was the result of the twenty or thirty aspirin he had chewed since arriving in Agatite that morning. Aspirin and whiskey, he thought wryly. That had been Floyd's remedy for all his injuries. Aspirin and whiskey and Ace bandages. Breedlove doubted that any of it was doing him much good, but he also knew he was in no position to complain at all. At least he was alive and out of jail, and for a murderer—a psychopath, he reminded himself—that was staying ahead of the game.

He had stumbled into the motel room where the gang was holed up, waiting, he supposed, for his arrival. They'd almost given up on him, and when he practically fell into the room and passed out, Mike let him know that he was damned lucky they just didn't dump him in a ditch somewhere and call the police. Mike generally regarded the whole incident with the girl on the highway to be asshole stupid and dangerous for all of them to be involved in at all, and he was more than a little put out that Breedlove would visit it on them at the outset of a big job. At least that was what he kept telling Breedlove whenever he was conscious during the next ten days or so.

But Joe Don had stuck by him, more or less. He bought him a pair of cheap running shoes—he refused to waste money on boots, saying, "Maybe this'll give you an idea the next time some little pussy goes at you with a wrench!"—and a new shirt. He kept Mike off his back by insisting that it was too damned late to bring in a new man, and this was a four-man operation at the least. He had charged Floyd with fixing up Breedlove's wounds, and Floyd had ignored Breedlove's cries of agony as he bandaged his shoulder.

The aspirin and whiskey had kept the pain away, at least until yesterday when Joe Don forbade any of them, especially Breedlove who had passed the previous month in a constant state of semi-intoxication, to drink anything until the job was over. So today he had a motherfucker of a hangover, or so he had told Joe Don that morning, a three-week drunk hangover that threatened to take his head off completely if he didn't get something alcoholic into his system soon. But nothing had swayed Joe Don from his orders of sobriety, and Breedlove had been forced to content himself with extra aspirin instead.

He was fairly sure the Ace bandages were doing more harm than good. While they made it possible for him to move more or less normally, he still had a good deal of pain in his shoulder—"Something's broken in there," he kept saying to anyone who would listen to him—and his ankle was weak, although it only hurt when he put weight on it a certain way. He almost didn't get his shoe on that morning without a snort of whiskey to help, but somehow he managed. Yet the pain in his shoulder and ankle was nothing compared to the pain inside his skull. He felt like hammered dog shit, he kept saying to Mike and Joe Don or just to himself. It was a description his old man had used a thousand times, and Breedlove had never felt he completely understood it until now.

Aside from the lousy way he felt and the quiet that surrounded the whole operation, this job was different from the start. In the first place, they were driving new or relatively new vehicles. The triple switch was still set up, but they had not operated out of a house this time. Instead, they had taken a motel room over in Kirkland.

There were differences in their armament this time as well. Instead of mix-matched catch-as-catch-can arms, they carried identical weapons, except for Joe Don. All four of them had .357 magnum pistols, brand-new, and each carried over fifty rounds in their pockets and in the plastic tote bags. Additionally, they had .12-gauge pump-action shotguns, with the plugs removed so they could hold extra shells, and boxes of ammunition were in the tote bags.

Joe Don, however, had to be different, as usual. Dropping all his talk about nobody getting hurt, he was carrying a short-barreled machine gun that he claimed fired more than a thousand rounds a second, although Breedlove imagined that he was exaggerating. Joe Don had extra clips for the weapon stored in his jacket and taped to his body under his shirt. He also had the pistol, of course, and he announced that this time they were to take no chances with a trigger-happy lawman.

They had decided that Floyd's quick thinking in Oklaunion had paid off, so he went across the street to make a phone call to the local sheriff and police to report a bad accident on the highway west of town just as he had done before. Since they would be escaping north into Oklahoma and eventually Canada, they hoped this would work just as well as anything else. But there were switch vehicles parked along the highway to Oklahoma City just in case something went wrong. Joe Don had planned everything with care.

Breedlove's recollections of their long planning sessions was hazy. For those he stayed awake for, he found himself too drunk to do much more than nod. He knew Mike Dix wanted to dump him and wasn't about to put up with any argument from the "weak link," as he referred to Breedlove, for very long. Also, Breedlove was embarrassed because he had no money to pool with the gang's to buy the cars, the weapons, or even to pay for the motel room or the whiskey and aspirin Floyd kept insisting he take.

He still wore the same leisure suit he had arrived in, although it painfully reminded him of the encounter with Eileen Kennedy on the road. But it was all he had, and he was too aware of his personal debt to Joe Don to ask him to buy him clothes on top of everything else.

As he stood in the bank, he was amazed that this time he felt no real fear. Maybe it was the throbbing pain in his head, or maybe it was because of the aspirin he had been chewing. He didn't know. He only felt a detached dullness, a desire for this intermediate step in his life to be over so he could put it behind him along with the other steps he had taken, steps that never seemed to lead anywhere.

I wonder how this will fuck up? he asked himself as he contemplated the water fountain and wondered if he dared risk a drink while he was guarding the people on the floor. But deep inside himself he had been arguing that maybe because the odds were so much against him this time things would go well. It was reverse bad luck, he told himself; with so many chances to fuck up, maybe things would go right for a change. But he really wasn't convinced.

"Something will go wrong," he whispered to himself. "Something always does." He only hoped that when it did, he could handle it.

Mike got up from his chair and paced the front of the bank's lobby, secure in his concealment from the outside by the bank's Flex-Glo windows. "All's cool," he called to Joe Don, who looked up only momentarily and

grinned, allowing his scar to flash quickly, and then continued his work. By now every cop in the county would
be helling west for twenty miles, looking for the six-car
pile-up Floyd had reported, Breedlove thought, as he
watched Joe Don move from the second to the third teller's cage, methodically separating small bills from large
ones and stuffing them into the plastic totes.

After each cage he would vault over the half-partition
between them and check the hostages on the floor. There
was no enthusiastic shouting or orders like before, only
a quiet efficiency that marked their hard-earned professionalism, and Breedlove thought wryly of how things
had changed since their first experience.

On the floor the hostages lay face-down. They weren't
crying or whimpering as the women had done before.
The men were also very quiet. There was no guard. In
fact, the bank seemed abnormally empty, considering it
was a big payday. But Breedlove reasoned that it was a
hot day, and he figured that people had banked early to
avoid the heat of the afternoon.

There seemed to be something they should have done,
something they'd forgotten to do, but it didn't seem to
matter. It's just a question of time before it will all be
over, one way or another, he thought, and if we've already screwed up, then that's just the way it goes.

Joe Don finished working in the third cage and vaulted
into the fourth. He made short work of the cash drawer
and shifted the machine gun to his other hand, inspecting
the counter for hidden compartments he claimed all banks
had. "Almost done," he said in a calm voice to Breedlove and Mike, who had resumed his position in the chair.
Breedlove looked at the clock. 3:15.

III. Procession
The Present, 3:17 P.M.

Vernon Ferguson, Deputy Sheriff of Sandhill County, was
thoroughly embarrassed. As was his custom from time
to time, he stopped by the Dairy Mart and picked up a

hamburger and then drove out to check his trot lines on
Blind Man's Creek. He figured it wouldn't take more than
twenty minutes to make the round trip, and if he ate the
burger in the car, he could easily make it back to relieve
Able on the speed trap.

He had gotten out to the lines with no trouble, but as
he checked the last hook and began lowering the line
back into the water, he lost his footing and slipped into
the shallow creek. He was wet up to his waist, and his
gun and utility belt were soaked too. He was pissed off
about the whole thing. He didn't like letting Able down,
even in a small way, especially for something like this,
something so damned *niggerly*, running a catfish line in
a goddamn creek. But there was nothing to be done about
it now but to hurry. He wondered if Able had gotten tired
of waiting and called John David to come in early, but
he doubted it. John David wouldn't be able to get a baby-
sitter at such short notice.

Vernon had spent the better part of an hour trying to
clean the mud and muck off his pants and boots, but
finally he gave up and drove toward Agatite. At 3:17,
according to his wristwatch's digital readout, he entered
the city limits, swinging his cruiser to the right on First
Street to avoid the funeral he could see coming in his
direction. From the corner of his eye he could see James
Earl Meacham III emerging from the hardware store with
a rifle in his hand. That was funny, the deputy thought,
since Able had remarked a dozen times how odd it was
that a man with all that land hated hunting as much as
James Earl did, but Vernon dismissed the thought and
spun around side streets, trying to work his way as
quickly as he could out to the highway speed trap and
Able's relief.

James Earl Meacham III was coming out of the hardware store with a new Browning 30.06 lever-action rifle,
complete with scope and strap, cradled in his hands. He
had wanted a fancy leather case for the rifle, but Wayne
didn't stock them, and he'd had to have that damned kid
order one for him. He'd taken a long time picking out the
gun, handling and aiming and fooling around with every

rifle the store stocked, and now as he ran his hands up and down the cold blue barrel of his purchase, enjoying the fresh, factory-made feel of the stock and hardware of the piece, he could feel the tremendous sense of power it gave him.

The shotgun trick had been a good one, he thought, a by-God scary stunt that had frightened Maggie but good. He hadn't dreamed it would work half as well as it had. She had actually fainted, and for a moment he'd thought she'd cracked her skull when she fell. But she hadn't, he remembered with slight disappointment. She just got up and sort of looked around before she got really pissed off.

He had only a small hope for the bloody car trick. For one thing, she'd probably spot it before she got into the car. Maybe. But maybe not.

It was all kid stuff, and he knew it wasn't going to work. None of it. It was stupid. She'd never just leave him or even just go nuts. So he decided to buy the rifle.

All the whiskey he had consumed that morning had left him with a raging headache, and he decided to stop by Central Drugs to drink a cup of coffee. The heat in the street was unbelievable, and he wondered if it was too hot for coffee. The bank's clock registered 3:17 and 111 degrees, and the temperature half of the digital sign was flickering as it always did when it was about to change. "Going up," he said to himself.

A paper sack full of cartridges for the rifle swung from his left arm, and with a sudden recollection he stopped and gazed up and down the street. He remembered that he had seen someone earlier, before he went in to buy the rifle, who had reminded him of an old friend, an old high school classmate, an old teammate, but he wasn't sure. Maybe it was the whiskey buzz that had caused him to see something that wasn't there, but he stared at the people lining up on the street to pay respects to the funeral procession, and he tried to find the green western leisure suit he had seen earlier. As he looked up and down, he spotted Maggie's sports car in the funeral line, three back from the hearse, and thoughts of finding the familiar face fled from him.

"Damn!" he swore, then caught himself. She hadn't taken the big car, after all. He had ruined the Lincoln's interior for nothing. Oh, well, everything couldn't work out. This plan, this new plan with the rifle, was more surefire.

It was Maggie's custom, he knew, to spend all day Saturday painting in her studio. The studio was mostly made of glass to let in the light necessary for her work, and he knew she liked to sit with her back to the window while she splashed paint onto the canvas.

By pure coincidence he had discovered a small prairie dog village at the base of the artificial hill on which the Meacham house sat. Prairie dogs had become almost extinct in Sandhill County years ago, but for some reason, probably because of the hunting out of all the predators that once preyed on them, they had made a comeback. They posed a hazard to horses and cattle with their ubiquitous holes, and they played hell with Cook's garden. Eradication was almost impossible. Poison endangered the dogs and cats around the ranch, and the prairie dogs were almost impossible to trap in sufficient numbers to make any difference.

So James Earl had decided to shoot them. At least that was the story he prepared for Abel Newsome if he asked about it. Of course, he reasoned, most people would know that a 30.06 was too much rifle by a bunch for such a small rodent, but James Earl wasn't most people. It was widely known that he disliked hunting, and except for the old shotgun and some other rusty relics in the closets of the Meacham household, he didn't own any other gun. It was typical of a rich man such as he was to go out and buy the most expensive gun in Henderson's store, even it was the wrong kind for what he wanted. And James Earl counted on its looking typical.

It was also typical, James Earl reasoned, for an inexperienced hunter to miss, to overshoot his mark, to aim directly at a prairie dog in his scope and put a bullet through his wife's head while she sat two hundred yards beyond in a house painting a picture. He would be real sorry it happened. Real sorry.

He watched in amusement as Jingles Murphy waved

his arms and argued with a semitrailer tractor driver under the flashing light at Third and Main. The truck had
turned into the intersection oblivious to the oncoming
funeral, and Jingles had apparently stopped him and
forced him to get out. Behind the half-turned truck, James
Earl could see the funeral procession idly waiting in the
heat. What a fucked-up mess, he thought, and continued
to walk toward the drugstore.

He stopped again to admire some jeweled watches in
the window of Peterson's Jewelry. Maybe he should go
inside and buy Maggie a watch. She already had about a
dozen, but if he bought her one, and if Peterson *knew* he
bought her one, just because he loved her, not for a special occasion, it would all look even better, even more
typical. The watches all had different times on them, and
James Earl pulled out the solid-gold pocket watch that
had been handed down to him by James Earl Meacham I
and snapped open its handmade case. It said 3:18.

On the extreme eastern end of the town's city limits, the
3:32 freight highballing from Fort Worth on its way to
Denver, carrying one hundred empty coal cars and a caboose, blew its first warning whistle. It was more than
ten minutes early that hot afternoon, and the engineer
and conductor were pleased to be able to reduce their
speed as they were bound by law to do when passing
through small towns. The intersection where the tracks
crossed Main Street in Agatite had always bothered the
engineer anyway, since people anxious to be somewhere
always tried to get across ahead of the engine in spite of
the flashing red lights and warning whistles from the
train. This was a long train, he knew, and it was hot, so
that meant a long wait today, especially since the train
would be moving more slowly than usual. But regulations were regulations, he told himself, and he blew a
warning whistle for another crossing coming up.

At the opposite end of Main Street from where the train
would cross, Claude Crane's GMC pickup's tires squealed as
he rounded the corner off Highway 287 and Main. They
squealed again as he hit the brakes with both feet.

"Shit fire!" he yelled through clenched teeth. Ahead of him was the funeral procession, and he had almost run right into it.

The ancient pickup shuddered to a stop along the curb as Claude fumed in the cab. The heat of the afternoon, partly dispelled by the wind tears from the window as he had driven into town, settled on him like a blanket, and sweat ran down into his eyes.

"I can't wait for this, goddamn it," he yelled through the cracked windshield. He rammed the pickup into reverse and backed up to the corner, wheeled around, and raced back down two blocks to find a side street that would take him downtown as quickly as possible.

All the side streets had stop signs on every corner, and Claude was forced to slow down for each one. He scanned each street for a sign of one of Jingle's boys ready to hand out a ticket to him, and he cursed every time he downshifted the old truck before speeding toward the next intersection.

The bank, he thought—she would have to go to the bank first. That's where I'll catch her. He gunned the tortured engine of the GMC as he passed another intersection, checking to see how far along the funeral procession was. He prayed he could make the corner of the bank ahead of the hearse.

Vernon had spotted Claude's two-wheeled turn onto Main Street, but he didn't slow down. He was late enough already and didn't wish to worry about what that crazy farmer was doing. He figured he was in for a good ass-chewing himself as soon as he got to the speed trap spot, and he hoped, for once, that Able would really give it to him. He was angry, hot, embarrassed, and uncomfortable in his wet clothes.

As he reached the famous spot Jingles had picked out long ago as the prime location for catching unwary motorists, he noted with dismay that the sheriff wasn't there. Swinging the cruiser around in a wide U-turn to pull into the vacant space, he was narrowly missed by a Corvette with out-of-state plates zooming out of town. "You son of a bitch!" Vernon yelled, downshifting the automatic transmission of the cruiser for

maximum pickup and spinning gravel from the shoulder out
behind him as he gave chase to the speedster. His wristwatch
told him that it was 3:22.

IV. Breedlove
The Present, 3:30 P.M.

The First Security Bank of Agatite, Texas, was what in
the parlance of professional bank robbers would be called
"a crackerbox." There was no alarm system, no closed-
circuit video camera, no guards. With one or two aborted
attempts, the most recent occurring more than forty years
before, as exceptions, no one had ever tried to rob it, and
there wasn't much good reason to do so. In spite of Joe
Don's assurance of hundreds of thousands in cash, the
bank rarely had enough money to cover more than a hundred thousand dollars in withdrawals, and if such an unlikely eventuality occurred, it would have to send to
Wichita Falls for more money.

Constructed just after the turn of the century, the interior had been remodeled a half-dozen times. The newest improvement had been refrigerated air conditioning
that had also called for the installation of Flex-Glo windows on the street front plate-glass window. The window
faced the west and now reflected the hot exterior light of
summer like a mirror and made view from the outside in
impossible during daylight hours.

Twelve-foot ceilings, dark wood paneling, and indirect
lighting added to the dim antique atmosphere of the lobby
that was in no way diminished by the frosted glass doors to
the bank's offices and rest rooms lining the rear wall. Originally there had been a side door leading out to Second Street
a few feet from where it intersected with Main; however, this
had been permanently locked years ago, and now, except for
a delivery entrance and firedoor that fed into the alley behind
the building, the only working door was the double glass
Flex-Glo panels that opened onto Main.

Breedlove was uncomfortable because of the windows.
People lazily passed by the bank's front, looking directly

inside, and Joe Don's assurance that "they couldn't see shit" through those windows did not diminish Breedlove's constant feeling of being watched. He wished Joe Don would hurry. He wished they were already across the state line into Oklahoma and on their way to Canada. Things were just too quiet. Things were going too well.

Joe Don vaulted out of the last cage and into the lobby, where Breedlove painfully stood shifting the long-barreled shotgun from one arm to the other. Joe Don looked at Breedlove and smiled boldly. He had changed quite a bit since Oklaunion. Spending time in California, where he had located the machine gun, he had also acquired a deep tan and bleached his hair blond. He had lived well, Breedlove noted, and he was amazed that the ugly scar had somehow toned down a bit in the time since they had parted a few months before. It still glowed when Joe Don was excited, but without the wrinkles and worry lines surrounding it, it didn't seem to be as threatening or angry as it had been.

"Which one of you citizens had the keys to the boxes?" Joe Don asked of the helpless figures on the floor. No one responded. "Listen," he said, his voice hardly rising above a whisper in the mausoleum atmosphere of the bank's lobby, "we got no time for you to play hero. We're desperate men. We'll kill you soon as piss on you, so you best answer up."

"Leona, uh . . . she keeps the keys . . . uh, she's off today. She's gone to—" One of the tellers was speaking, rising just a bit off the carpet.

"I don't give a shit where she is," Joe Don snapped at her, "an' don't look up, sweet pants, if you want to see anything else again!" The teller buried her face in the carpet. "Who's in charge here?"

"I know where they are," said one of the loan officers.

"Get up," Joe Don ordered him. "But don't look at me or him or nobody!"

The man struggled to his feet, his eyes fixed on the lobby floor and then lifting as he turned to the back of the bank to stare at the office doors. With Joe Don gently prodding him with the muzzle of the machine gun, the man moved to a desk near the vault and opened a drawer. After fishing around for a few seconds, he came up with a jangling ring of keys.

"Now, look," Joe Don said, putting his hand on the man's shoulder and pushing him more gently than not toward the vault's door, "we ain't got all day. I ain't got time to go on no huntin' expedition. You know who's likely to have good shit in his box an' who ain't. So let's cut the crap, get the book out, an' go for the gold!"

"Sir," the man said, and Breedlove suddenly thought he seemed familiar, an old face from the past that he knew he should recognize but couldn't. Was he some friend's father? Would the man recognize him? Panic crept up his spine and he pulled more aspirin from his shirt pocket and chewed them. "I can assure you I have no idea—"

"Look, shit for brains!" Joe Don tapped the man's skull with the machine gun's barrel as he injected his voice with the old viciousness Breedlove recognized from the previous holdups. "I told you, I ain't got time for all this fuckin' around. Now you know who's likely to have somethin' we might want, so let's get it!"

The man carefully opened the book on the desk and began thumbing down the list of box holders for likely stashes of wealth.

Joe Don signaled Mike to come join him, and he nodded at Breedlove to watch the street as well as the hostages, and then he followed the man with the book into the vault. "Check for the cash," he ordered Mike over his shoulder, ignoring the glance from the man, whose eyes widened in a questioning look toward one of the women on the floor.

Breedlove allowed his eyes to fall into a pattern of movement. Down to the hostages, up to the clock, over to the door, and out the windows onto the street. He noticed the van, motor running, parked at an angle in front of the bank, next to a battered pickup, and through the glare he could barely make out Floyd's dark form at the wheel. Now and then a whoop would come from the vault when Mike came across someone's supposedly buried treasure, but the pattern would be broken, banging in Breedlove's ears and the throbbing in his head. Still, he couldn't get over the feeling that they were being watched, that disaster was about to fall on them as if from the ornate ceiling overhead.

Indeed they were being watched. From his office, the crouched Alexander Bateman, President and Chairman of the bank's board, peered through the keyhole of his door and literally writhed in agony. What he was witnessing through the tiny opening was creating all sorts of problems for his already overworked heart and anxiety-ridden stomach. The doors to the offices had all been checked, of course, but his had been locked, and the bandits—or so he had come to think of them—had merely rattled the knob.

His door, like the others, was older than he was, and each had an antique handle and lock that functioned with a long, old-fashioned key. The keys to the others had long ago been lost or carried off and forgotten. But Alexander had found a locksmith with an overdue note who had cheerfully duplicated one for his own door, and he kept it with his spare cigar cutter in his desk.

When the bandits had come into the bank and announced their intentions, they had put an end to all work immediately. The cessation of his secretary's typewriter, the end of the noise made by one of the calculators in the teller's window nearest his office, and the sudden quiet after the almost constant chatter of his lobby workers had alerted him immediately that something was wrong. He was almost to his office door, ready to spring on them and alert them to the fact that even though he had given more than half the employees the afternoon off for that damned funeral, he expected a full day's work from everyone else, when voices penetrated the frosted glass in his door, and he stopped.

Joe Don yelled, "Nobody move!" and Alexander Bateman froze in his tracks, his pudgy hands on the door-knob. When another voice, Mike Dix's yelled for all the employees to come and lie down on the floor, Alexander almost turned the door handle and walked out, thinking that in some bizarre way the bandits could see him. It took almost all his will power to reach into the pocket of his three-piece suit, secure the key, and quietly lock the door before the men in the lobby came back to check the office doors along the rear wall. He then went to his desk and picked up his telephone, but in seconds—even one second, he proudly thought—he returned the receiver to its cradle, pleased with his quickness of mind.

He had suddenly realized that on each desk in the lobby, immediately surrounding the three men he could see through his keyhole, were other telephones. On the bottom of each instrument's face panel was the normal row of buttons, buttons that lit up whenever someone was on a line anywhere in the bank. If he called Able or even that useless jackass, Jingles Murphy, he reasoned, the bandits would see the light and know that there was someone behind the locked door of his office. That would be close to suicide.

Alexander Bateman was never meant to be a hero. But he knew that his workers knew he was there. He doubted they would ever forgive him for doing nothing to save the situation. He looked forlornly at the Flex-Glo glass of his office windows, sealed shut after the refrigerated air conditioning system was installed. No one could see him even if he waved and signaled, even if anyone ever walked down Second Street anymore, even if he put a sign in the window. The privacy he had reveled in since the windows were installed now seemed imprisoning, and he felt panic swelling in him like the gas from his lunch that now sat sourly on his stomach. He didn't know what the hell to do, and he felt like crying.

Mike continued rifling the deposit boxes as the man, who, Breedlove discovered by looking at the name plate on the office door, was Jim Sheppard, father of Billy and Leslie Sheppard, former schoolmates of the man who now held a shotgun on their father's co-workers, called out numbers. Still the hostages remained quiet. Things were going very well. There was no sign of panic, no sign that there was anything to worry about, and this disturbed Breedlove even more.

He considered briefly the few employees in the bank. This

was obviously a skeleton crew, and while it seemed odd that such a small group of workers would be present for such a big business day, there could be some sickness going around today. Something big might be going on elsewhere. Or, he thought darkly, it could be a trap. But there ws no sign of a trap. Nothing, in fact, to suggest that this was anything but a normal Wednesday in August.

From inside the vault an argument erupted.

"Man, there's no cash in here." Mike's voice came out.

"Don't give me that shit." Joe Don's answer came quickly. "I know there's big bucks stashed in here someplace. Where is it, citizen?"

Jim Sheppard said something Breedlove couldn't hear, but he did hear the sickening crunch of metal meeting skin and bone as Joe Don obviously lost patience with the bank officer.

"Please, mister." One of the tellers spoke, addressing Breedlove. "We'd give you all the money there was, but there isn't anything like a bunch of cash back in that vault! I'm begging you, mister. You got to believe me!"

Breedlove instinctively knew she was telling the truth. "Hey!" he called, and Joe Don stuck his head out. "I don't think there's anything back there."

For a moment Joe Don's face twisted into an ugly mask of hatred. "What do you know? Cripple!" he said, but then he looked again into Breedlove's eyes. "Are you shittin' me, man?"

"I think you got it wrong," Breedlove responded, gesturing toward the hostages. "These people don't want to die for money that ain't even theirs."

Joe Don hesitated, then nodded. "Okay, man, but you better be right." He reentered the vault. "On your feet, citizen, we're going to check some more boxes."

Alexander Bateman breathed a sigh of relief at the bandits' decision not to kill anyone for money that wasn't there. But he was not the only one who was listening to the drama unfolding in the bank's lobby. Inside the women's restroom, Cassie Crane tightly held on to her daughter and waited and listened. Her hand was clasped over Claudine's mouth, and the youngster wriggled and writhed to free herself from her mother's fierce hold. But Cassie held on.

She had been adjusting her clothing and checking her hair for a final time when she heard Joe Don's command. Like the bank president, she also froze, but when she was certain that a robbery was indeed going on, when she heard the order to lie down, all she could think of was the news stories from Oklaunion months before, and of the crazy man who had killed the girl out on the highway. She felt her nerves were about to snap, but she bit her lip, grabbed Claudine up and enclosed herself and her daughter in one of the stalls. Standing in an uneven balance on the toilet's rim, she had breathlessly waited until she heard the door open and the scuff of shoes outside the stall. It had been a careless check, she had thanked the Lord, and the robber was quickly gone.

After a bit she sat down, and although her watch told her that more then twenty minutes had gone by, she still held Claudine's mouth closed, mindless of the discomfort the girl was suffering.

Cassie strained her ears to catch any signal that the danger was over and they could leave. She realized that she had missed her bus, but that was not her chief concern at the moment. At the moment her prayer, her heart-felt yearning for her big, strong husband to burst into the bank and save her was overwhelming. "Claude," she whispered soundlessly. "Where the hell *are* you? Why don't you come?"

She forgot the fact that he wouldn't return to the house until nearly dark, and instead she concentrated on remembering the note she had left. What could she have said that might make him abandon hope right away? What might prevent him from chasing after her and trying to stop her before she got away? She couldn't think of a thing. But time passed and he wasn't there yet. She knew that he knew she would have to go to the bank. The goddamn truck was right outside! A blindman couldn't miss it! Sweat ran down into her eyes in spite of the refrigerated air of the bank. "It's all right, honey," she whispered to Claudine, who continued to struggle. "Daddy'll be here in a minute." She prayed even harder.

"That's enough," Joe Don announced, pushing Jim Sheppard over to the others and guiding him down onto the floor next to the tellers. A stream of bright red blood ran from under Sheppard's gray hair and onto his gray suit coat, but he didn't appear to be hurt badly.

Mike came out of the vault, zipping up the tote bag and tossing it next to the three other, all bulging with money, valuables, and ammunition, on the bank's countertop.

"Folks," Joe Don said, "this has been a real quiet little operation, an' to show our appreciation, we're not goin' to hurt nobody. If y'all 'll just mosey on into the vault, we're gonna see to it that we're not followed for a spell, an' then we're goin to get the hell outta here." His tone was dripping with folksy familiarity.

Without another word, the hostages began to get up and move toward the vault. Finally Jim Sheppard spoke up. "You can't lock it," he said.

"The hell I can't!" Joe Don shouted at him, suddenly losing the genial tone he had been using.

"No," Sheppard continued, and Breedlove was suddenly filled with admiration for this incredibly brave man. "What I mean is, it won't lock. It hasn't locked in years. We never close it. Not really."

"The hell you say," Mike said, going over to the vault door and trying to move it. He motioned for Breedlove to help, and Breedlove moved over and put his strong side against the heavy door. It wouldn't budge, but the pain in Breedlove's body roared in protest. "Hell, Joe Don, it won't even close," he said.

"Well, I'll be fucked," Joe Don said, and Breedlove smiled. Maybe this was it, he thought, maybe this was what would go wrong. If this was all it was, maybe he still had a chance. For a moment they all stood absurdly in front of the vault, waiting for someone to say something.

"Shit," Joe Don finally said. "Get in there anyway." He waved the machine gun, and Mike and Breedlove helped herd the hostages inside. "Now listen," Joe Don continued as they slowly filed in, "if any of you stick your heads out, you're going to lose them. Got it?"

"There are no heroes here," Jim Sheppard announced loudly.

Turning and winking at Mike and Breedlove, Joe Don smiled broadly. "Let's go!" he said. Without a word they picked up the totes and started out the front door of the bank, watching over their shoulders to see if anyone emerged from the vault.

Breedlove glanced up at the clock. 3:30. The whole robbery had taken just a half hour. He was pleased. Floyd and the van waited only fifteen feet from the bank's front door. This was a cakewalk, just as Joe Don had said it would be. In spite of all their guns and fears, nobody but Jim Sheppard had even been roughed up, and his injury was apparently slight. Maybe they were getting good at this, Breedlove thought. But it didn't matter, not to him. This was his last job. This time he would use his money wisely, he would get himself fixed up right by a real doctor and try to live like a real person should, not like a bum. He felt the cringing need for a celebratory drink, and he fervently hoped Floyd had a bottle in the van.

After a final look at the vault, the trio stepped through the bank's front doors abreast onto the searing sidewalk in front of the building. For a few seconds the bright sunlight, made more intense by the 112-degree heat and by its reflection from the cars in the street, blinded them. They shielded their eyes as best they could, waving their shotguns and crossing their arms over their faces.

Suddenly Mike screamed, "it's a setup! It's a goddamn setup!"

That was the last thing Breedlove heard Mike Dix say, for everything else was lost in the thunderous noise of gunfire.

5

I. Cops and Robbers

When the bank's clock registered 3:21, Sandhill County Sheriff Able Newsome shifted a Hava-Tampa Jewel from one side of his mouth to the other and rounded the corner of Third and Main Streets, heading north into the heart of the business district of Agatite, Texas. His shirt was soaked with sweat, although he had walked less than two blocks from the Town and Country Dinette. But the dreadful weight in the sheriff's stomach, the feeling that something awfully wrong was happening or about to happen, had not diminished in his walk across the oppressive heat of the court house square toward the downtown district.

At the same time another feeling, a guilty one, crept around his mind. He shouldn't have left the speed trap untended. There would probably be hell to pay for that, especially if he came up empty, as he fully expected he would, in his search for the two strangers. He also was not a little concerned that Vernon had let him down so badly. It was unusual for his main deputy to fail to show up on time. When he turned his face northward, he could feel the incredible heat of downtown, and he cursed. He figured that even the cellophane wrappers of his remaining cigars wouldn't keep them from soaking in his pocket.

Able felt more than a little foolish. The whole idea of putting so much effort into finding some nut who might have had fingernails in his pocket, and then into making a connection between the nut and the mad killer of Eileen Kennedy, was absurd. What was worse, he knew, was to imagine that the killer, if indeed it was he, was just hanging around town waiting for Able to find him.

On the corner, next to the Auto Parts of Agatite store, began the series of small offices and shops that housed lawyers and bankers, accountants, a barber, and a couple of more businesses that had carved up an old furniture store and remodeled it to look too modern for the century-old storefronts that marked the rest of downtown. Oh, well, Able thought, glancing across the street. The bank's new windows gave it some odd sort of ultra-modern look, too. He passed the shops and stopped in front of the Ben Franklin store and looked long and hard up and down the street. Able checked the bank's clock against his own wristwatch and shook his head. The weather was something to discuss, all right.

Able rubbed his chin and felt sweat streaming from under his hat, down his forehead, and onto his cheeks. Even on the shady side of the street he could feel the intensity of the afternoon August sun. Downtown was full of people in spite of the afternoon's discomforting temperature. Albe recalled it was payday at the mill, but he noted that most parking spaces were filling up rapidly. People were anxious, it seemed, to be off the street.

Turning his attention southward toward the opposite end of Main Street, he saw why. The flashing lights of Jingles' cruiser were going as the official car parked awkwardly in the intersection where a semitrailer had begun a turn, oblivious to the funeral procession that was now backed up for a mile or more down Main. Jingles was screeching at the truck driver and waving his arms. Finally the driver climbed back into his cab and drove the rig on down Main, and Jingles began waving the hearse in behind it.

Able walked deliberately but slowly down the street as the rig moved, staring again into the Ben Franklin store, and finally coming to the door of Central Drugs. In a back booth he could see Old Samuel sipping a cup of coffee. Sam raised a bony hand in greeting. Wanda Watkins also waved, but no one else was in the store except the druggist, Elwood Long, who was behind his counter.

Poor Elwood, Able thought, shaking his head and turning around. Since the Gibson's store had opened over in Kirkland, Elwood hadn't been able to sell shit except pills. His store was full of small appliances and beauty aids and other junk that was dusty from lack of customer inspection.

As he walked out to the edge of the sidewalk next to the noses of parked cars and trucks, Able spotted Adam Moorely sorting papers in his sports car down in front of the lawyer's office, and in the other direction he spotted James Earl Meacham standing in front of Peterson's Jewelry, looking in the window. James Earl was holding a rifle, Able noted, wondering what he would do with it. It must be a present for someone, the sheriff thought. He knew James Earl hated to hunt.

The hearse was now between the bank and the drugstore, and Able removed his hat and stood silently as the dead man passed by. The family car followed, then the pallbearers in the limousine. In the distance Able heard the familiar sound of the 3:32's whistle as it approached the crossing down the street, and Able had trouble suppressing an ironic smile as he realized what was about to happen. In a few seconds the semi would be at the tracks, and seeing the flashing lights, the truck driver naturally would stop. That would mean that the whole funeral procession was going to be stopped for God knows how long while the train slowly cleared the tracks.

"This is going to be one hell of a mess," he said aloud, replacing his hat after wiping out the sweat band with a soaked handkerchief.

He had made the comment idly, not addressing anyone in particular, but Danny O'Hara, who had been idly sipping the remains of a Coke while he leaned on a parking meter, spoke up. "Yeah, I'd say the odds against gettin' the hearse across are three to one."

Able grinned at the boy, whom he had always liked. "You'd think ol' Everett would learn or at least start bettin' on the come," he said. Danny smiled and nodded, and Able suddenly thought of something. "Say, you been standing here long?" he asked.

"Pretty long," the boy said, suspicious of the question.

Able notice Jingles coming up the wrong side of the street, his lights flashing and his mouth working in serious protest to the train's crossing the funeral's path.

"You see a couple of strangers around here?" Able asked Danny. "Fellow in a green suit and a side-kick in a jeans jacket?"

"Uh, I don't know." Danny said, taken aback by the question. He rubbed his hair and tried to think. Then he remembered, of course—in the bank. He opened his mouth, but before he could answer, events began to take place that left that logical progression far behind.

A siren suddenly swooped from Jingles' cruiser, as the chief of police grew impatient with the train's slow progress and wanted to signal the engineer to hurry it up, in spite of the fact that the engine was now a quarter mile beyond the intersection.

Able was about to yell at the imbecilic officer when he spied some men emerging from the bank who were yelling and waving. Before he could focus on them, however, on the corner of Second and Main, next to the bank, an old, battered GMC pickup came helling up out of nowhere and crashed directly into the funeral's family car, knocking the doors open on the side away from the impact and spilling Wilma Castlereigh and one of her daughters out onto the sunbaked pavement. Able recognized the driver, Claude Crane, standing full up on the useless brake pedal, his elbows locked on the steering wheel, and his mouth wide open in a scream that was swallowed in the earsplitting sounds of crashing metal and breaking glass.

Before he could react, however, the yelling across the street in front of the bank became more intense and was joined by another sound that was distantly familiar to Able. He swiveled his head again to the trio of men coming from the bank, and he remembered that he had noticed something odd about them before when first he first spied them.

They had guns! He screamed to himself, "Jesus! They're robbing the bank!"

It was so unbelievable, so improbable to be happening

along with everything else that had occurred in the past few seconds, that Able tipped back the brim of his hat and lay his hand on the butt of his holstered .44. He couldn't accept what his eyes and ears told him were three frantic men looking left and right up and down the line of cars, seeing the flashing lights of Jingles' cruiser, and the approaching lights of Phillips' patrol car as he raced up to find out what was going on. The whole street was now blocked off, and Able recognized what the men thought they saw. They believed this was a trap of some sort, Able knew, and he almost yelled at them that this was merely a screwup, only a funeral, when he realized that the distantly familiar sound he heard was that of a machine gun, an automatic weapon, and it was firing a tattoo up and down the street.

Less than five seconds had passed since Claude's accident, and Able hadn't moved a muscle. He watched, fascinated, as one of the men, the one with a long pony tail, dropped his tote bag and pointed a shotgun directly across the street. A billow of white smoke came from the barrel. Able felt he should do something—duck, move, anything—but he was rooted to the spot.

In what seemed like slow motion he felt himself being lifted and flung backwards through the display window of Central Drugs. "Oh, shit!" he yelled as his body rose, and then he heard the crash of glass as he fell through the front window of the store.

As soon as Mike Dix yelled, he started shooting. So did Joe Don. Breedlove's eyes had not yet adjusted to the brilliant sunlight that flooded Main Street, but as soon as they did, he was shocked at what he saw.

The street was full of cars, all neatly lined up, it seemed, to prevent the van from backing out, and two police cars, their lights flashing brightly, were parked on the opposite side, obviously lining up for a classic road-block. Clearly, the whole town was laying for them, and he dropped the tote bag he was carrying and switched the shotgun off safety.

To his right a pickup slammed into one of the cars in

the intersection, a useless move, from Breedlove's point
of view, since the street was blocked with a freight train
and a large semitrailer tractor at the other end, and nobody was going anywhere. People were screaming and
shouting, and not a few were running up and down the
sidewalks, their hands over their heads as bullets and flying glass showered them. The noise was deafening, and
the headache he had had all morning and afternoon
reached new heights of pain as the battle in the small
town's main street raged.

The man in the pickup was trying to climb out the
cab's window, holding his arm in an awkward, twisted
position, as if it were broken, and Breedlove watched
him fall down onto the pavement. Another figure, a cop,
a sheriff of some kind, was standing directly across the
street from the bank. He looked as if he were directing
operations. Breedlove glanced at Joe Don for instructions
to fire his gun, but Joe Don was already firing, and Mike
suddenly aimed his shotgun at the officer and pulled off
a shot. When he looked again, Breedlove noticed the
officer was not in sight.

Mike and Joe Don now began firing rapidly, filling the
confusion of the street with as much lead as their weapons could deliver. Mike was blasting cars, systematically
working his way from left to right, pausing only to flip
the shotgun over and reload, while Joe Don, with a look
of panic and crazy glee on his face, laughing his high,
insane laugh, his scar flaming with rage and excitement,
was sweeping the machine gun's barrel in great arcs up
and down the storefronts across the street. Plate glass
shattered in the wake of the tattoo of the automatic
weapon, and the staccato blast of Mike's shotgun punctuated the chorus of screaming, shouting people with
regularity.

Breedlove imitated Mike by dropping to one knee and
raising his .12-gauge pump and firing. His injured shoulder screamed with pain at the recoil, but he saw a car
window explode from his blast. He fired again, but this
time he braced the gun against his torn shoulder improp-
erly, and the shot went wild. Ejecting the empty, he fired

a third time, and suddenly he found himself pumping and firing in a syncopated rhythm with Mike. Then he realized he was dry firing, and he flipped the gun over the reload.

As he fed shells from his pocket into the gun's breech, he shouted as loudly as he could to Joe Don, ''We gotta get to the van!'' But Joe Don didn't hear him over the machine gun's rhythmic fire. Breedlove looked desperately for help from Floyd, but Floyd had flung open the rear doors of the van and was himself blasting away at cars and potential police positions as he scrambled through the narrow space alongside of the van and onto the sidewalk. He had realized what would happen when the funeral procession came up the street too late for him to do anything about it, and cursing himself for not figuring out what it would look like to his accomplices inside the bank, he had sat in the van and stewed while the whole operation blew up in his face. He figured their only hope was to shoot their way onto a side street, steal a car, and get the hell out of town.

Suddenly one of Joe Don's bursts found a car's gas tank, and a superheated shell ignited the fuel, exploding the whole car in the middle of the street toward the Third and Main intersection. The entire street was now effectively blocked at both ends. Bright yellow flame shot up higher than the building fronts on either side of the street, and black smoke climbed from the downtown district. Other drivers, panicking with the noise and continued firing, began trying to maneuver out of the center of town. The entire thoroughfare was now jammed, and those cars not yet moving were trapped in a jumble of steel, smoke, and fire that had become an unimaginable storm.

People scrambled from their vehicles or lay prone on the floorboards and prayed that their own cars wouldn't blow up as well. The din was deafening, and instructions shouted by Patrolman Blair Phillips or by his chief, Jingles Murphy, evaporated like steam from their mouths.

Breedlove emptied his shotgun again and flipped it over to reload. He didn't think he had hit anyone yet, and he was fairly pleased with the fact. A small flame had erupted from the car that had been hit by the pickup, and he noticed some men crawling to it to drag the people still inside to safety. Neither Joe Don nor Mike seemed to notice them, and Breedlove decided to let them alone, feeling that they weren't trying to do him any harm, and that the car was about to go up anyway. He felt terrible pain from every part of his body, and he desperately wished everyone would just calm down and let them go.

Floyd ran along the sidewalk, dragging a tote full of more ammunition behind him, and began yelling at the trio, who were now firing in all direction. Breedlove strained to hear what Floyd was yelling at them, but the noise of the blasting guns and the burning car was too great. He could only try to read the man's lips, and finally he understood.

"Nobody's shooting back at us, you assholes!" Floyd yelled.

Breedlove nodded and turned to touch Mike's shoulder and get his attention. If no one was shooting at them, he reasoned, they still might be able to get out of this thing alive.

He grabbed Mike's shirt just as Mike emptied his shotgun again. He turned to face Breedlove, his snaggly teeth showing in a grin, and the hole in his cheek dragging his mouth and eyes down in a bizarre expression of sad mirth. Before Breedlove could say anything, however, Mike's face contorted strangely, causing Breedlove to drop his hand away. Winking oddly, Mike dropped his shotgun to the sidewalk and brought his hand up to the throat of his "Gotta Have Rhythm" T-shirt, where immediately, between his fingers, a spout of blood formed.

Breedlove stepped back in horror as the blood splashed out, then Mike did an almost obscene bump and grind as red holes seemed to sprout from his T-shirt and he collapsed at Breedlove's feet. An odd pause in the noise occurred at the moment Mike's shaggy head struck the sidewalk with a crack, and from behind him Breedlove heard Floyd's low whistle.

"Man!" he said. "They're shootin' back now!"

Seeking cover as best he could behind parked cars in

front of the bank, Breedlove spotted a cop standing behind one of the police cruisers, with his pistol cracking off shots in their direction. Breedlove didn't even think. Raising the shotgun and ejecting the empty at the same time, he fired twice toward the cruiser. The pain from his shoulder was blinding, but when his vision cleared, he noticed the cop was gone and so was the flashing light bubble from the top of the car. He made no connection between his action and the death of another human being. All he knew was that, for the moment at least, a source of danger had been removed.

Bullets were now whining everywhere around the three men left alive on the sidewalk. Joe Don, noticing Mike lying on the sidewalk in a growing pool of blood, was firing short, controlled bursts from the machine gun, pausing only to replace the magazine clip with a fresh one when he emptied the awesome weapon. Suddenly the Flex-Glo window behind them exploded in a shattering crash, showering the robbers with glass and a cold blast of air as the air-conditioned atmosphere inside the bank escaped. They crouched as the window disintegrated, and then they resumed firing.

Breedlove now fired in any direction he could find a target. He glanced at the wrecked car to see if there was anyone there. An instant later it also exploded, sending flame and smoke all over the streets of Agatite.

As he reloaded again, now reaching into Floyd's tote for more shells, he noticed that his two companions were similarly firing with regularity at anyone who moved or fired back. Main Street had become a vicious no-man's land of flying lead and smoke, where no one dared to move except to tighten up under a car and hope a ricochet didn't find him.

From inside the display window of Central Drugs, Able Newsome had a unique viewpoint. He was high enough, propped up as he was by bottles of perfume and boxes of tissue, to see what was going on in the street, but his body lay beneath the level of the tops of parked cars and he was out of the direct line of fire. He had blacked out and now was slowly coming back to consciousness, and he found movement difficult if not impossible, but mostly undesirable. His body was numb, and his head seemed to spin as if he had been whirling around.

He could see people scrambling for cover. The crying and screaming didn't penetrate the ringing in the ears, and when the car exploded, he was more taken with the brilliant colors and flush of heat than with the horror of the concussion or the screams of those around the inferno.

In the distance he was sure he could hear gunfire from a variety of weapons, but the only person he could see with a weapon was Chief Jingles Murphy, who was shouting at patrolman Blair Phillips from the relative safety of the pavement on the near side of his cruiser. Jingles had his pistol out and was waving it around, but he wasn't shooting at anyone. Instead he was screaming into his radio mike in between his shouted orders to Phillips.

Phillips finally drew his own weapon out and leaned over the top of the cruiser, professionally snapping shots with his Police Special .38 in the vague direction of the opposite side of the street. Able's attention was distracted by the several ugly black bullet holes in the car's white hood. He wondered who was shooting at the officer, and he shook his head, trying to get a clear picture of what was going on.

Lifting himself up a bit, Able noticed Wilma Castlereigh, bloody and bent over, trying to drag her daughter's limp body from the burning car. Fire seemed to be all around her, and he remembered Claude Crane slamming into the large sedan just before things got fuzzy in his mind. He sought out Claude's truck and found it in time to see Claude trying to pull his rifle from the rack in the cab of his wrecked pickup, which had bounced away from the family car after ramming into it. One of Claude's arms was stiffly jammed close to his body, and Able immediately deduced that he had injured himself in the crash.

He returned his attention to Phillips, who was now

freely blazing away with his pistol, firing four or five times
and then dropping down behind his car to reload. Suddenly recalling that in the past week his opinion of the
former street thug had elevated, Able began to admire the
cool professionalism of Phillip's firing procedure. Just then
Phillips reeled backwards and fell between parked cars.
Immediately he scrambled to his feet, crouched down, and
crawled to the side of his cruiser, his hands clasped over
his face, which was spouting blood. Able frowned. What
the hell was going on?

All at once a pair of hands seized the sheriff and jerked
him backwards over the wooden back of the display window and into the drugstore. Another pair of hands broke
an ammonia capsule under his nose, and pain and a
complete picture of the past few minutes' events came
flooding into his head.

"Sheriff! You gotta do somethin'!" It was Old Samuel, and Able struggled to a sitting position, painfully
recoiling from the wound in his left side. He seemed to
be bleeding all over.

"What the hell's goin' on?" he yelled, noting the prone
body of Wanda Watkins sprawled on the slat boards behind the fountain. She was dead, he saw, killed by a burst
of automatic weapon fire that had followed his body
through the drugstore's front window. Able saw that her
head was half gone, and he gagged.

Just then another car went up in a tower of flame and
smoke, and the blast's concussion shattered the mirror
behind the soda fountain. Able thought he saw a body
flying through the air, and now he could clearly hear the
screams and gunfire from the street. People are dying in
my town! Somebody's robbing the bank, and people are
dying!

Elwood appeared with bandages and antiseptic, and he
and Old Samuel began working on him. Able pulled out
the pistol and checked the load on the .44. It was turning
out to be the worst day of his life, he thought, shaking
his head sadly. The absolute worst day of his life.

"Go call Chrystal and tell her to get us some help!"
Able ordered Old Samuel. Samuel turned his head du-

biously toward the drugstore phone booth and shook his head. The booth was riddled with gunshots, and the phone inside dangled from its cord.

"I already done that," Elwood said, feverishly working to wind a bandage around Able's waist. "Ain't nobody there." He began tying off the bandage. "Listen, Able, you ain't hurt too bad. They took a chunk outta you, but I think you'll live till Doc Pritchard gets a look at it."

Able shook his head. What to do? The machine gunner made another vicious pass through the store, and glass and wood splintered and showered the three men. "This is one hell of a mess," Able said.

When the noise started downtown, Officer Clovis Hiker was going for a record. With Chrystal mounted on top of his sweating, lunging body in cell number one of the police station's basement, the two lovers were trying for four simultaneous orgasms in a row. Chrystal had read in a magazine that if the man was *really* a man, a *virile* man, he could give his partner such a gift. She had challenged Clovis with the article, and he had happily agreed to prove he was as virile as the next guy.

"Wonder what that is?" Chrystal asked between gasps, as the muffled sound of the first car's explosion reached them.

"Beats the shit outta me," Clovis answered, grunting between clenched teeth and muttered curses at himself.

The second car's explosion caused him to move. Coming suddenly, he rose and shoved Chrystal rudely off him onto the concrete floor of the cell. He ignored her cursing and accusations as he hopped on one leg, trying to get his pants on and climb the stairs at the same time. That had been one *big* explosion. Something was very wrong. The goddamn phone upstairs hadn't stopped ringing all afternoon, and he knew Jingles well enough to know that he'd better get himself out and do some looking around.

He buckled his pants and was buttoning up his shirt as he hit the door of the police station. When he looked up Third Street toward downtown, his mouth fell open and his fingers grappled unfeelingly with the zipper in his uniform pants. Columns of black smoke climbed into the bright blue sky. Cars turned every which way, and people were running around crazily. Clovis could see that some of them were carrying guns, and others—his hands went automatically to his eyes to clear his vision—others were *bleeding*!

He looked across the street toward the volunteer fire department, but the trucks were still parked behind their garage doors. Half the firemen were in the funeral party. Hell, the chief was a pallbearer, and probably nobody was even at the station. Clovis stumbled down the steps and started to get into his cruiser, then he hesitated. He ought to put in a call to somebody. He started back inside, but then he picked up a sound he hadn't heard before—the cracking and popping of gunfire. My God, he thought, what the *hell* is going on?

Perspiration dripped down his face and into his eyes. Gunfire! Fire! Car wrecks! "What in the name of sweet bleeding Jesus is goin' on?" he demanded of the shimmering air. He stepped haltingly toward the cruiser's door again, but thought better of trying to drive into that mess and took off at a half-jog toward downtown.

II. Breedlove

In front of the bank Joe Don had ripped off his coat and opened his shirt and was peeling extra clips from his body and shoving them into the machine gun. It might not fire a thousand rounds a second, Breedlove admitted to himself, but it was goddamn efficient weapon. Every time Joe Don made a sweep across the storefronts opposite the bank, a magical trail of black holes appeared in the wood and brickwork, and windows disappeared as if they had been sucked up by a vacuum.

Breedlove himself was now kneeling so low behind the parked cars in front of him that he was almost lying down, carelessly blasting away with his shotgun, pausing only to reload. Instead of aiming at anyone in particular, he contented himself with busting out store windows or windshields on the jammed cars in the street, and with making as much noise as possible to keep these hick-town morons from shooting back with any regularity. He wanted to throw down his weapon and run away, but there was really nowhere to run. Guns sprouted from behind every conceivable barricade, and he figured that to stand up was to die, as Mike Dix had died, terribly and painfully.

As he reloaded, fishing shells out of the ammo tote and noting that soon they would have to root around in the money bags for the remainder of their shells, he noticed Mike's body, grotesquely sprawled against the low brick wall in front of the bank. Mike's eyes were open and his mouth was wide in a snaggle-toothed grin that reminded Breedlove of his former comrade's cruel nature. Motivated by Mike's dead stare, he stood and emptied his shotgun quickly, pumping and firing at nothing in particular, but taking a perverse, almost humorous pleasure in the cessation of return fire in the face of such bravado.

As he shoved more shells into the shotgun's breech, he looked down at his feet and noticed the blades of yellow, dead grass that poked their way up through the cracks in the sidewalk, and he began to count the number of sweat droplets that fell from his face each time he flipped the weapon over to reload. God, it was hot, and he was going to say so, but his mouth was stone dry and tasted bitter from the smoke and brimstone that permeated the atmosphere.

He thought he wouldn't be able to stand another minute of this; then some asshole would start firing from yet another storefront or from behind another car, and he would frantically lay down as much buckshot as he could in that direction to keep the defender of the bank and town under cover.

From time to time he would glance over at Floyd who, surrounded with empty shell casings, was firing his shotgun less frequently and less carelessly than Breedlove, and more effectively. Floyd's teeth were bare and white against his face, and he, like Joe Don, had settled into his work with a single-mindedness that seemed familiar to them. No one was saying anything.

The shot that had burst the window of the First Security Bank had been fired from in front of Peterson's Jewelry by James Earl Meacham III. He was kneeling by the simulated rock front of the store, resting the new rifle in its sling as he had been taught in basic training so many years ago, and he was trying his best to hit something he was aiming at. Thus far he had managed to miss with every shot, and he was swearing loudly as he ejected cartridge casing after cartridge casing onto the hot sidewalk.

The scope on the new rifle had been factory adjusted, and he was no marksman in the first place. He kept trying to sight in on one of the robbers' heads, but as soon as he would squeeze the trigger, the man would move and the shot would go wild. His aim was further confounded by smoke from the burning family car in the funeral procession that still fumed in the intersection between him and the bank building on the kitty-corner. Once he had actually hit a woman in the West Texas Utility Office next door to the bank, but he had seen her get up and stumble out of sight, so he knew he hadn't killed her at least.

It seemed that people were shooting from everywhere, and no one knew what was really going on. People were leaning over cars and trucks, irregularly peppering the front of the bank building, but no one was taking the time to aim. They just emptied their weapons and then crouched down and reloaded. Some were grim-faced, but others were smiling and shouting encouragement as they went about the business of defending their town.

"Sons of bitches are goin' to be hitting each other!" James Earl said as he jammed more cartridges into his weapon's breech, trying not to remember the woman in the office he had hit earlier. One thing was certain, he said to himself, the men in front of the bank weren't in any greater danger than the townspeople, especially those crouched down behind their cars or still in their vehicles, jammed as they were in the middle of the street.

As James Earl sighted in on the green leisure suit, he thought for the second time that day that he recognized the man who wore it. Pausing for a half second to make sure, he blinked sweat from his eyes. When he focused again, though, the man ducked down with a bright burst of red appearing on his forehead, and James Earl lost sight of him in the scope.

Cursing, he lowered the rifle and squinted through a billow of black smoke coming from another car that had exploded down the street. It was then that he spotted Maggie's Porsche, smashed and jammed in between the car behind her and a Chrysler New Yorker that had tried to back out and had instead run into the hood of her car. The windshield was splattered with something black, probably oil from one of the explosions, and he couldn't see if she was still inside.

All at once James Earl pumped four shots into her windshield, as low as he could, levering out the empty casings onto the sidewalk beside him. He was satisfied to see how well the scope was working now, and in spite of the sweat on his face that kept clouding it, he felt he could now count on its accuracy.

As he reloaded the rifle, he noticed that the Chrysler's gasoline tank was directly over Maggie's car. Levering a round into the chamber, he sighted low on the car and fired. Nothing happened, but through the scope he could see a small hole in the Chrysler's lower rear fender.

"This is too good to be true!" he said half-aloud, checking to make sure that his fellow citizens were filling the air with shot and lead, and he aimed and fired again. There was no explosion this time, either, although his bullet had gone a bit lower. He relaxed, pulled a handkerchief from his hip pocket and wiped his eyes and the scope's glass as he waited for another black cloud of smoke to clear. He had plenty of time, he thought; no need to hurry and blow the chance of a lifetime.

* * *

Inside the pallbearer's car, which was immediately behind the blocked-in hearse, a slow panic was building.
The back window had been shot out, and Jeff Randall
was hunched forward with blood flowing freely from his
unconscious head. The other six men, including the
portly Mayor Newell Longman, who was driving, had
scrambled onto the floorboards of the limousine when the
blast had hit them. Even with the motor still running and
the air conditioner going full-blast, the heat inside the
car was overwhelming.

Cowering on the floor of the front seat, Wayne Henderson felt his stomach tearing apart. His natural fear and
anxiety were compounded by claustrophobia and by the
horrible knowledge that his own storefront was only fifty
yards away. As pain took over his entire mind, reason
fled, and he had convinced himself that whatever was
going on out front was the result of his letting that idiot
kid Warren handle the firearms in the store. But the time
or two he had dared to peep out the window of the limousine, he had seen the folly of trying to leave the car
and check on things in his place of business.

He finally spied Warren standing openly in the store's
doorway, a rifle in his hand, looking as best he could up
the sidewalk to where all the shooting was coming from.
Wayne crouched back down and groaned aloud. He wondered how much of this he would be liable for, and the
thought made his stomach churn even more.

Checking once again, he spotted the caboose of the freight
that had blocked traffic passing by the giant truck in front of
the hearse, and he shouted to Newell Longman.

"The train's moving past! Let's get the hell outta
here!" But the Agatite mayor didn't move, and Wayne
had to grab him by his suit coat and practically wrestle
him in place behind the wheel.

Newell's eyes were practically frozen shut. He was
scared worse than he had ever been, and without glancing
ahead of him at all, he rammed the gearshift into drive
and floorboarded the large car smashing it into the rear
of the hearse, which was still waiting for the eighteen-
wheeler to start moving.

For a moment or two Newell sat motionless, and the other passengers in the limousine were too stunned to say anything. Glancing over the dashboard, Wayne saw that the eighteen-wheeler was finally getting under way and that Everett Hardin was having trouble restarting the hearse, which had died when Newell had rear-ended it.

As the semitrailer crossed the tracks behind the caboose, Everett finally got the hearse started, but its bumper was locked with the limousine's, and neither car was about to move forward. Everyone started yelling at once, and Newell, trying to follow what seemed to be the wisest choice among the advising voices, pulled the gearshift into reverse and backed up just as quickly as he'd gone forward, smashing the wrecked and burning family car behind them, and jerking the rear door as well as the bumper off the hearse.

Wayne's eyes widened with horror as he saw Everett Hardin, free from the anchor of the limousine, finally get the hearse under way, and peel out into the open space behind the semitrailer. So rapidly did he take off that the coffin containing the body of Bill Castlereigh slid down the rollers of the hearse's bed and crashed on its end in the street, standing straight up in front of the limousine, weaving and tottering as if it were trying to decide which way to fall.

Newell was totally, incoherently panicked. Jerking the car into drive and twisting the wheel sharply to the left, he rammed the nose of the limousine into the slant-parked cars, neatly clipping Bill Castlereigh's coffin and knocking it across the street, where it broke open and spilled the corpse out onto the pavement.

The movement of the automobiles had drawn the machine gunner's attention, though, and a quick series of shells struck the long car, blowing out the back window and leaving Jeff Randall and the other pall bearers covered with glass and exploding metal.

Wayne had had enough. Newell Longman was struggling unsuccessfully with a jammed door on the driver's side, and Wayne doubled up his fists and pounded on Newell's broad shoulders and head in an attempt to urge

him to get the door open so they could get out. But the
door wouldn't budge. As the mayor continued to jerk
fruitlessly at his door handle, Wayne felt his throat constrict with a claustrophobic sense of being trapped. He
pulled up hard on his own door handle and spilled out
onto the sizzling blacktop, planning to crawl, if he had
to, to get away from the noise, blood, and death all
around him.

He scrambled up to all fours and looked around,
searching for the best escape, when his eyes fell on Bill
Castlereigh's broken coffin and the body of the deceased
sprawled between Wayne and the safety of the cars in
front of the hardware store. For a moment Wayne hesitated, swallowing hard to stop a moan from climbing up
inside him and bursting into a scream. His mouth was
dry, his stomach was on fire, and his vision blurred as
he beheld his old nightmare coming to life before him.

He couldn't face it. And he mustered all the will he
could, thinking to retreat to the limousine that still contained the struggling figure of Newell Longman and the
bloody backseat occupants who had not found their way
out of the blasted car. Before Wayne could move, however, a neat tattoo of holes raced up the pavement in his
direction and he jerked to his feet just before the line of
small bursts crossed the spot where he had been lying.

He backed away quickly from the symmetrical black
holes now forming a barrier between him and the limousine, and as he moved, Newell turned and gestured for
him to leap back inside the car and out of the line of fire.
But Wayne's mind was spinning. He thrust out his hands
toward Newell's waving figure, trying to ward off any
attempt by the mayor to come and get him. Then he
turned and ran, strength welling up in him from a source
he didn't know; he had to make his legs pump harder and
harder with each fleeing step. His heart thudded under
his coat and his breath rasped with every intake, but he
finally made it to the end of the block down by the depot,
where he stopped and fought for air.

The gunfire had turned in another direction, and slowly
Wayne made his way back up the safe side of the street,

out of sight of gunmen down the block and back to his storefront, where he discovered Warren crouching in the doorway with a shotgun in his hand and a frightened look on his face.

"Get the hell back inside and put that up!" Wayne gasped at him, feeling pain from deep inside him throbbing. He suddenly ripped off his suit coat, unable to bear the heat of the afternoon any longer. His head was splitting, his stomach burning, but he forced himself to duck down and creep between the parked cars until he was directly in front of the broken coffin and the dead body, which was grotesquely arranged on the pavement. For a moment he stared at it and stepped a bit closer. Then, suddenly unmindful of the loss of cover and safety afforded him by the cars, he stood straight up and moved over to it. He was waiting for the body to rise and speak to him as it always did in the dream.

Then something in his stomach seemed to burst, and pain enveloped his body, bringing him to his knees. It took every muscle he could command to keep from turning and running away. Darkness seemed to cloud his eyes, tunneling his vision and focusing his attention entirely on the corpse's face. He was oblivious to the deadly chaos around him, and slowly his legs automatically bent, lowering his buttocks to the pavement between the cars where he finally sat down, hugging his knees to his chest and staring mindlessly into the broken coffin until he blacked out completely.

III. Lawman

In the doorway of Central Drugs, Sheriff Able Newsome crouched down and smoked a cigar. His mind was now clear, his memory of the afternoon's incredible events whole, and he was trying to decide what to do. Even though he estimated there were only three or even as few as two men returning fire now, their fire *power* was deadly. The shotguns were intimidating as hell, though they were considerably less threatening than the machine gun.

Smoke and steam cascaded over Main Street in great sweeps, blocking vision and fields of fire for thirty seconds at a time, but, of course, that didn't stop every damned fool with a firearm from pumping lead into the clouds. There was a kind of mania about it all, and the temptation to draw out his weapon and join his fellow townsmen in indiscriminately firing toward the bank was strong. Able's hand actually fell to the butt of his pistol before common sense took over and he shifted his fingers forward to his knee, where they drummed nervously as he tried to think this out. God only knew how many people had been hit out there, and probably most of them had been hit by their own friends and neighbors. The one thing Able was sure of was that something had to be done to stop the firing and quickly. People were dying all around him.

"Samuel!" he yelled, and the old man scrambled on his knees up beside Able. "Get over to the police station and tell Chrystal to get off of whoever she's fuckin' and call the highway patrol or somebody. Try to raise my deputies, too. Goddamn it, get the fuckin' National Guard!" Able glanced to his left as a new spate of firing commenced. "We got some kind of situation here!"

"I'll do it, Sheriff!" Samuel announced, nodding, and he was almost on his feet and headed down the sidewalk before Able could catch him by the shirt and pull him down.

"Go out the back way! You dumb son of a bitch!" Able screamed at him over the noise of breaking glass and shrieks of terror from next door.

"Damn!" Samuel swore, grinning through yellow teeth at the sheriff, and he started duckwalking to the rear door.

Able turned back to the street. Cupping his hands over his mouth, wincing from the pain in his side, he yelled, "Murphy!" The chief of police was still crouched down beside his cruiser, yelling into the radio mike. "Goddamn it, Murphy!" Able screamed, noting at once the uselessness of trying to make himself heard over the din and realizing the strain it put on his voice.

Frustrated, he raised his .44 and aimed as best he could from his kneeling position. Certain, he fired, and the window of the police cruiser just above Jingles' head shattered, causing the officer to sprawl onto the pavement and fumble with his own revolver to meet what he was sure was a flank attack. As soon as the chief caught sight of Able still pointing the .44 at him, he began moving his mouth in absurd motions, which doubtlessly were sending all sorts of curses that were lost in the noise.

"Bullhorn!" Able yelled. "Bullhorn! Goddamnit!" But Jingles shook his head. He couldn't hear. He kept gesturing toward the radio mike, but Able suddenly noticed that in his excitement Jingles had pulled it loose from the transmitter and its cord dangled uselessly.

"Bullhorn!" Able repeated, then took a deep breath and shouted with such intensity that he felt himself hurting in his wound, "Bullhorn!" But Jingles couldn't hear him, or wouldn't, Able thought.

"I'll get it, Sheriff." Able looked around, mystified at the voice that seemed to come from under the parked car immediately in front of the drugstore. "Where is it?" It was Danny O'Hara, the kid Able had spoken to just before the world exploded. He apparently had taken refuge beneath the car, and now he poked his head up to curb level and spoke again. "Is it in the car?"

"Yeah," Able yelled back at the kid, who was now climbing onto the sidewalk, careful to keep himself down, out of sight of the shooters in front of the bank. "It's in the trunk. You'll have to get the key from the chief."

He watched as the kid belly-crawled over to Jingles' car and began arguing with the chief of police. Able could see that Jingles wasn't going to hand over the keys of the police car to the kid, and he wasn't about to expose himself to get the bullhorn either. They were both screaming at each other, although no sound penetrated the noise of gunfire and the crackling, burning automobiles on the street.

Able was distracted from the argument in the street

when he saw the men in front of the bank scrambling over the low wall that had been the building's windowsill, retreating into the bank's interior. He saw the black go first, then the other two standing up, blasting away with their weapons, forcing their opponents to stay low and let them get inside.

Able stood up. He had the perfect opportunity. Since no return fire had come from the drugstore, they weren't paying any attention to him. He pulled his .44 up and painfully took a three-point stance, cocking the weapon and choosing the taller man as his target. He was about to squeeze off the shot, mindful only of the fact that this was his first experience at firing a gun in anger since he had become a lawman, when he hesitated. The man he had in his pistol's sight was the man he had been looking for! He was wearing a green leisure suit. To pull the trigger was to eliminate him forever, but it was also to seal the mystery of why he had killed Eileen Kennedy.

Able Newsome debated. He had a perfect reason to kill this man, to avenge the girl's death, to expunge his dreams. But he also was not completely sure that this man was the killer, not sure enough, and he had to be sure. He had to take this man alive! It was the only way. He had to question him, to see if the objects in his pocket were fingernails, Eileen's fingernails. He had to know.

As he waited, the men continued to empty their weapons, stepping backwards as they fired, and Able shifted his gun to the right, trying to find a lethal target on the shorter man, the one with the machine gun. Then he noticed that the man was stitching a pattern of deadly fire directly toward him, and instead of firing his .44, Able ducked. If he had fired, if he had waited another second, the machine gun would have cut him in half, and he counted himself lucky to have such good reflexes, wounded as he was.

As the shorter man continued his sweep of Main Street, Able stood up, noting that the green-suited man had now dropped down behind the low wall. Able fired, and he felt a well of satisfaction as he watched the short man jerk backwards and fall inside the bank.

Able's tongue involuntarily ran out and licked his lips, and he was amazed at how dry they were. His whole mouth felt parched, and as he commanded his arms and shoulders to relax from the tension that had braced his shot, he felt himself shudder. War hero or no war hero, he thought, you never get used to shooting a man.

"Here, Sheriff." Danny's voice came from below him, and Able dropped down on one knee and accepted the dusty bullhorn from the boy. The kid had a nasty red mark on his cheek, and he didn't look happy at all. Able started to say something, but he interrupted. "Had to knock him out. Coldcocked him with this." Danny held up Jingles' service revolver. "He hit me first, an' I think he was going to kill me," Danny concluded, holding out the gun for Able to take.

Able saw Jingles lying peacefully prone in the street next to the cruiser, holding the useless mike in his hand.

"Keep it," he said as the boy again thrust the revolver out toward him. "But I hope to Christ you don't need it."

As the words left the sheriff's mouth, pistol fire came in heavy doses from across the street. One shotgun soon joined the firepower from the bank's blown-out window, and return fire from Agatite's citizens intensified the noise in the street one more time.

IV. Breedlove

Breedlove had been enjoying the relative safety of the space between two parked cars when he had been hit. The bullet had burned more than it had done anything else when it creased his skull, but the wound took away the headache that had plagued him all day. He still wanted a drink, though, worse than anything short of getting out of the mess he found himself in.

Floyd had pulled him into the space, and then he and Joe Don had taken turns covering the street from their respective sides. They were running low on shotgun shells and machine gun magazines, and their frantic dig-

ging in the money bags for their extra shells had scattered
bills up and down the sidewalk on that side of the street,
some of them fluttering down and landing in the pool of
blood that had formed under Mike Dix's body.

Breedlove wanted to give up. He tried twice to get
their attention and tell Floyd and Joe Don that he had
just had it, but Joe Don signaled for him to get up and
help him lay down covering fire for a move back inside.
Glancing at the busted window of the bank and seeing
Joe Don jam his last clip into his machine gun, Breedlove
struggled to his feet, fighting the lightheadedness that hit
him. Joe Don laid down a murderous pattern from left to
right across the street, and Breedlove found himself firing rapidly to the right of the bank, forcing the town's
defenders to duck down low and stay that way for a while,
anyway. Floyd struggled over the low brick wall, pulling
the last ammunition bag in with him, and then Breedlove
began to move back with Joe Don, firing as they went.

As Breedlove dropped over the wall, he looked up to
see Joe Don emptying the final clip, a murderous grin on
his face. Suddenly Joe Don jerked backwards as if a string
had been attached to his shoulder and pulled him off balance. He dropped the machine gun and came crashing
into the bank.

"God fuckin' *damn!*" he yelled when he landed, and
Breedlove saw blood come surging from beneath Joe
Don's torn shirt. Breedlove removed his pistol from his
shoulder holster and cocked it. Floyd hurriedly fashioned
a tourniquet from Joe Don's shirt and began wrapping
the wounded shoulder. Breedlove tried to catch his
breath. Firing had stopped for a moment, and again he
was about to give it all up. Just stand and put your hands
up, he tried to order himself, but before he could act,
Joe Don shoved Floyd back, jerked his own .357 from
his holster, and began firing. Floyd grabbed his shotgun
from the shattered glass that seemed to be all over the
floor where they lay and also took up a steady fire, resting the barrel of the gun over the low wall.

Breedlove raised his own .357 and cocked it. Well, he

thought grimly, at least there were plenty of pistol ammo left. Might as well use it. He fired blindly into the street.

Maggie Meacham was well aware that someone was trying to kill her, and she wasn't just thinking of the men in front of the bank. She had spotted them just before the firing broke out and, thinking quickly, realizing that she was hemmed in between two cars, she grabbed the lever on the bottom of her driver's seat and quickly reclined it all the way. She was then comfortably out of the line of fire that ripped through the windshield of her sporty import just over her prone body.

When someone had jumped into the large Chrysler that was parked next to her and tried to back out, ramming her first, then ultimately running up over her hood before stopping. She had almost panicked, and she did pee all over herself when she heard the two cars explode near her. One of them—she wasn't sure which—sprayed black oil over her small car, but she grimly hung on, satisfied that if she couldn't see out, the gunmen couldn't see in.

She had rolled up the windows as best she could from her position right away, then she started playing a deadly game with the bullets that occasionally flew through her vehicle. She tried to judge when she was being fired upon by the sounds of the blasts to her right. She reasoned that no shots at all were penetrating the car from her left, but her door was tightly jammed and wouldn't open, at least not from the leverage she could exert from her reclining position.

So from time to time she would rise and glance quickly into the street to her right and left to check the progress of the forces of law and order in saving her from this mess. Whenever she scanned the street through the few clear places in her windshield and door windows, she would try to pull the handle and open the door, but it wouldn't work, and she would lie back down quickly.

After one attempt, she lay back down just as four shots in rapid order splattered into her windshield. A new fear seized her for a moment, and she found herself disoriented and confused. Those shots had not come from the bank.

"Who the hell is that?" she wondered aloud.

After a moment when the shots didn't repeat themselves and the blasts from the bank drifted away from her, she raised herself and looked out to her left.

"James Earl!" she yelled as she spotted her husband reloading his rifle. "You son of a bitch!"

Anger filled her, and, without thinking, she jerked the door handle violently. It finally gave, tumbling her out onto the street. He still hadn't looked up from his business of unloading, and smoke quickly settled between them. She kicked the door behind her and crawled across the pavement to the gap between two parked cars. From there she watched with horror as he methodically placed shell after shell into the big Chrysler that sat atop her car. The sudden deafening explosion of the pallbearers' car down the street clued her as to what he was trying to do, and she brought her hand to her mouth.

"Well, I'll be damned," she said aloud, and she continued to watch her husband trying to kill her right in front of a whole town full of people. "He's finally lost his mind."

In that instant the Chrysler's gas tank exploded in a cloud of yellow flame, pushing her backward onto the pavement and taking her breath away.

Just as Maggie's car went up, Vernon Ferguson and John David Hogan screamed into downtown Agatite. The black deputy had been in the process of writing his third ticket of the afternoon out on the highway when he heard the first automobile exploding, and he had driven quickly to John David's house, collected the younger deputy and his child, whom they had had to drop off at John David's mother-in-law's house, and hauled for downtown.

They could see the towers of black smoke climbing skyward from the town's business district, and they could distinctly hear the gunfire. Vernon guided the cruiser around the back of the courthouse and up onto the lawn. He was cursing because he hadn't been able to raise

Chrystal or anyone in authority anywhere in the whole town. As soon as the car stopped, they leaped out, bringing riot guns from the front seat with them, and they crouched down behind their cruiser and tried to assess what was going on.

"Goddamn civilians are shooting the shit out of somebody!" Vernon announced, noting that John David had gone pale with terror. He's scared to death, Vernon realized. He's just a kid. He hasn't been in a firefight before, nothing more serious than a dove hunt. Shit! Vernon spat in disgust.

About that time, John David pointed toward the alley behind the business district where Old Samuel was making his arthritically painful way toward them, waving and shouting unintelligibly. Vernon jogged over to him, talked briefly, then returned.

"It's a goddamn bank robbery," he said when he got back to position, and he noticed that sweat was pouring off John David. He knew it was hot out here, especially with the inferno of downtown only a block or so away, but that kid was making his own heat, Vernon thought.

"Bank!" the young deputy said. "Goddamn! My wife's in the bank!" He jumped up and started to bolt toward the fire zone that downtown had become, and Vernon barely managed to get a good hold on his uniform shirt and bring him back behind the car.

"Listen," Vernon said, forcing John David's face directly into his own and trying to make him pay attention. "Here's what we're going to do."

Vernon saw a wildness in his young partner's eyes, and he feared that he would simply go to pieces any second now. "I don't know about you, Vernon," John David screamed, "but I'm gonna get my wife!"

Vernon's heart went out to this man, but in spite of the rush of admiration he felt as he watched him shift from terror to courage, he knew that blind action wouldn't do much more than get both of them killed. "Look, man." He increased the pressure of his grip on John David's shirt. "*I'm* the senior officer here, and you *will* do what I tell you." He waited to see if his command was registering, then he continued. "There's a good chance I can work my way around Mill Street and come up Second or First. Samuel said they were in front of the bank, and if I can get to that old side door on Second, I can outflank the shit out of them."

After a second, John David nodded and wiped the blanket of sweat from his forehead. "What'll I do?" He desperately wanted to do something, Vernon knew, even die if he had to.

"You cover this end of town. I figure if they make a break for it, they'll come this way. Samuel's gone over to get Chrystal on the radio, and you might monitor to make sure she gets through. If she doesn't, then go over and get on the horn yourself and try to raise somebody. We're going to need fire trucks and ambulances. Lots of ambulances. You might try to get hold of that bastard Harvey Connally. Tell him to get his ass over here on the double and bring some firepower. Samuel said they got a machine gun."

"That's it?" John David asked, and Vernon noticed a brief flash of relief in his eyes.

"That's it," Vernon continued in a firm voice, and suddenly he turned and jogged down Third Street. He reached the intersection of Main and Third, quickly cut between the jammed cars, and ran across. Bullets whistled overhead as he made the safety of the Goodyear Tire Store, and he stopped to catch his breath and count his blessings.

"Damn!" he swore as he tried to survey the situation from his poor vantage point. He had forgotten to bring the riot gun, and he wasn't about to go back and get it. He waved broadly to his partner, who stood slightly hunched behind the cruiser. Then Vernon turned and ran to the corner of Mill and Third.

In the police station Old Samuel came out of the private rest room of the chief of police, chuckling and buckling his aged, striped pants. He hadn't been able to find Chrystal when he arrived in the office, but without too much trouble he had figured out how to use the dispatch board and had made calls to the Highway Patrol and to the emergency frequency to fetch ambulances and fire trucks to Agatite.

Then nature had called Old Samuel. He cursed his bowels at first, but then the great joke of taking a shit right in Chief Murphy's private crapper seized his sense of humor, and be happily relieved himself right there, chuckling as he looked through the array of sex magazines Jingles kept on a rack by the commode.

He'd almost managed to get his arthritic hands to master the belt buckle when he noticed that a white man was standing in the office doorway. He was holding a gun, and Old Samuel froze, his belt buckle still undone, his chuckle still echoing in his ears.

The glare of sunlight made the man a mere shadow in the eyes of the old black man, but it was clear that he was watching him closely and had observed him coming out of the corridor where the private rest room was located. Boy, you've had it now, Old Samuel thought to himself.

"I said, where's my wife?" the man said, and Old Samuel realized that he must have been talking to him all along. "Where's Chrystal?" the man repeated.

Samuel suddenly recognized the shadow. It was Morris, the chief's son.

"I don't know," Samuel said, allowing his hands to fall open, palms up, and his trousers fell down a bit.

"The *hell* you say!" Morris Murphy yelled, pushing Samuel roughly aside and scouring the office with his eyes. "What the *hell*'s been goin' on here?"

Downstairs, still lying naked in cell number one, Chrystal Murphy was concentrating hard on finishing what she and Clovis had started earlier. Her mind was deeply committed to her actions, and her hips moved rhythmically as her one free hand caressed her breasts and stomach.

Then her thoughts were interrupted by the clamoring of feet on the stairs. She raised her head and spotted her husband, pistol in hand, face blackened by soot and streaked with blood, standing before her. He looked wild and crazy, and she was immediately terrified.

''Morris! What's wrong?'' she yelled at him. ''What happened at the funeral? Jesus, Morris . . .'' Her hands covered her naked body, but her eyes were riveted on his wild appearance.

Morris stared at her, his mouth open and the pistol hanging loosely from one hand. He was having trouble focusing his eyes, which were rapidly filling with tears of frustration. ''Oh, my God,'' he said, his voice choking with rage and sorrow. ''Oh, my God in heaven. I always knew you were no damn good, but oh, my God, Chrystal, a nigger? An' that old, old nigger? Oh, Chrystal!'' As he spoke the gun came up and Morris directed it at his wife, who was frantically crawling to one end of the cot, trying to make herself as small as she could.

He aimed the gun with a wavering hand, but blinded as he was by the tears in his eyes, he paused to pull a filthy sleeve across his eyes. Chrystal took advantage of the momentary distraction and jumped up and pushed past him, knocking him backward and off his feet. The pistol discharged, sending a thundering echo up and down the cellblock, and Chrystal scrambled up the stairs as he swore at her and tried to grab her legs when she raced past.

Reaching the hallway that led into the office, she practically leaped to the outside door. She had it halfway open when she remembered that she had no clothes on, and she hesitated. Behind her, Morris' footfalls on the steps told her she had no time for contemplation, so with a quick, deep breath, she swung the door open wide and bounded down the steps of City Hall and toward Clovis' patrol car. She wrenched open the door when she arrived and flung herself into the front seat. She lay down as low as she could and prayed.

Morris made the outside steps just as she ducked out of sight. Then he turned his eyes toward the black section of town, in which direction Old Samuel's distant form could be seen moving as quickly away from City Hall as his painful, arthritic legs would allow him.

''You nigger son of a bitch!'' Morris screamed, and he took off after him, waving his pistol and shouting.

V. Breedlove

Inside the bank, Breedlove rolled over onto his back and reloaded his pistol. He couldn't hit anything with it, he knew, and he was glumly content simply to empty it over the low wall and then reload.

From where he lay he could see the clock over the teller's cages. Although the paneling and woodwork around the time machine was splintered and pockmarked from spent cartridges, the clock kept right on going. It was only 3:47. They hadn't been in this mess more than a few minutes, but it seemed like hours.

Joe Don, smaller than either Floyd or Breedlove, was able to squat behind the low brick wall and snap two and three shots off into the street, but Breedlove doubted that any of them were hitting anything important.

Floyd rolled over next to Breedlove to reload, and for a moment their eyes met.

"Man, this is fucked," Floyd said as he shoved cartridges into his pistol. The shotgun still lay by his side.

"Yeah," Breedlove said, "I guess we ain't got a prayer." Then he realized for the first time that afternoon that he was going to die. In only a few minutes, perhaps seconds, he would be dead. The thought chilled him, and he shivered.

"Shit, man," Floyd said, "we ain't got a fart's chance in a hurricane. I mean, them folks is out for blood." Almost in response to his comment, a rapid spate of gunfire erupted from the opposite side of the street, and they all ducked low as more wood splintered and glass shattered in the bank's interior.

"You know, Breed," Joe Don said loudly, and Breedlove lifted his hands from his face to look into the wild, scarred face of his leader, his comrade, his friend, "I can't help but think that this is all your fault!" Joe Don suddenly reared up and fired three quick shots, then dropped down and paid no more attention to his two companions.

Luck can't last forever, Breedlove told himself, even

bad luck, and he acknowledged that Joe Don was right. This was his fault, all of it, and this time there was nowhere to run.

By the time Claude Crane managed to wrestle his battered body from his battered GMC pickup and wrench the .30.30 from the gun rack, he was in terrible pain. From inside the long sleeve of his khaki shirt he could feel that his right arm was broken, and pain shot from his knees and ankles up both legs.

Ignoring the pain and gritting his teeth, he managed to work his way to the other side of the pickup, but the effort forced him to lie prone on the sticky, steaming pavement and rest for a while.

He wanted to pass out, just drift off into a haze of pain and confusion, but he had spotted Cassie's truck parked in front of the bank, directly before the three men who had been blazing away at all the cars and people they could see. The knowledge that Cassie was in the bank someplace kept him conscious and determined.

After a while he dragged himself and his rifle up onto the front fender of the pickup, wiped a mixture of sweat and blood from his eyes, and surveyed the situation. He had a fantastic line of fire. Nothing lay between his rifle barrel and the three men but open pavement and sidewalk, and he could completely cover them, take them one at a time. If he was lucky, he thought, they would never see where the shots were coming from.

He reached into open the glove box, pulling out a dusty box of cartridges, and proceeded to load his bolt-action .30.30. He managed to lock a cartridge into the breech and then limped painfully back to the pickup's hood.

Laying the rifle across the smashed hood of the truck, he sighted on the tall black man nearest him and prepared to pull the trigger. Just at that moment a car exploded and he was knocked back to the pavement, shocked and confused.

By the time he managed to resume his position, sighting again by resting the rifle on the hood, he discovered that the men had retreated inside the bank. He saw that one of them lay dead on the sidewalk in a pool of blood. Claude cursed as he spotted a random assortment of bills floating around in the smoky atmosphere of the street.

Claude was dizzy with pain, and the frustration of not being able to spot a target for his big rifle caused him to grind his teeth and to make a low, growling noise. Through the smoke that clouded over the center of Main Street, he spotted Adam Moorely darting from one parked car to another. Whenever the firing lulled to any degree, Moorely would jump from car to car, briefly exposing himself through the black smoke in his attempt to make the corner of Third and Main and relative safety.

Claude shifted the barrel of his rifle and fired blindly through the newest billow of smoke toward the point where he had last seen his old rival crouching. When a clear space appeared between the clouds, Moorely was gone, and for a moment Claude was sure he had gotten lucky and hit him. This is all that fat little prick's fault, Claude said to himself as he ejected the shell and loaded in the next cartridge. He checked the empty sidewalk in front of the bank once more, and then looked again toward Moorely's last position. As the smoke wafted past, he spotted him rounding the corner, gripping one arm with the other, his sport jacket splotched with blood.

There was no time for another shot, but it didn't matter to Claude. Moorely was out of the picture. Now he had to go get Cassie. Aside from a now maniacal obsession about saving Cassie from the men in front of the bank, he could only concentrate on killing somebody who was causing so much noise and chaos.

James Earl Meacham III had all but given up trying to blow up the car atop Maggie's sports car when one of his shots was followed by an explosion that engulfed both automobiles in flames and shattered any as yet unbroken windows up and down Main Street. He grimaced as someone jumped from the Chrysler and ran into the shattered window of the West Texas Utilities office, but he figured that someone there would help whoever had been foolish enough to remain in a wrecked car in the line of fire. He hadn't meant to hurt anyone except Maggie, and when her car exploded from the flames, he jumped up.

"Good-bye Maggie!" he yelled at the top of his lungs. "You whoring bitch!"

He saw across the street, coming up Second along the side of the drugstore building, Police Officer Clovis Hiker gaping openmouthed at him. Clovis had seen the whole thing, and owing to a lapse in the firing at that moment, he had heard what James Earl said. Clovis wasn't yet sure what was going on downtown, but he had worked his way to the Main Street area and now was shocked to see one of the most prominent citizens in town deliberately blow up his wife's car and scream obscenities at her.

Without wasting any time, James Earl Meacham III dropped to one knee and fired four quick shots in Clovis's direction. The officer backed up against the wall, wincing as he felt one of the slugs hit him in the side and knowing that each thought he had might be his last. But none of the other three shots hit him, and he suddenly discovered his legs and took flight down Second Street, limping and bleeding as he went, but not taking time to look back over his shoulder and give the rancher a second chance at him.

James Earl swore loudly and reloaded his rifle. He hoped that at least one of his shots had taken effect. Wiping sweat from his eyes, he knelt again and began pouring fire into the bank with a random carelessness that indicated his newfound boredom with the whole affair in downtown Agatite.

VI. Lawman

Able Newsome had finally located the proper batteries from Elwood Long's stock, and he had the bullhorn working. In the street people had gone mad. In less than half an hour they had managed to arm themselves to the teeth, and they were pouring fire into the bank at a murderous rate. The bullets they were flinging in there were as likely to hit any bank employee left alive inside as one of the men.

The return fire from inside the bank, however, was considerably reduced, since none of the men could risk exposing himself long enough to aim, and they were merely throwing occasional shots over the low wall that shielded them, each one bringing a torrent of answering gunshots from everywhere in the battle-torn street.

Through diminishing black smoke from the burning cars that now merely sat and flamed up and down Main Street, Able tried to see if there were any bodies inside the bank. But the gaping black hole that had been the building's front window told him nothing, and unless the sun got low enough to light the whole interior of the lobby, he wouldn't be able to see much beyond the first fifteen feet.

"Hold your fire!" Able shouted through the bullhorn's mouthpiece, wincing as the squeal of feedback deafened him. He lowered his voice and turned the instrument up and down the street. "Hold your fire! Hold it, dammit!"

Slowly, with a final pop or two, firing ceased, and except for the moans of the wounded, the crackling of flames from the burning cars, and somewhere, off in the distance, a baby crying, complete silence descended on downtown Agatite, Texas.

That's more like it, Able thought, as he depressed the horn's trigger and spoke. "You in the bank!" he said. "This is Sheriff Able Newsome. Please hold your fire so we can get some of these people off the street!"

Then he simply waited. Straining his ears and his hopes for the sounds of sirens and help on the way, he shook his head. "What now?" he asked of no one in particular, but before he could answer, the cease-fire was broken again, this time from inside the bank, and the deafening sound of gunshots resumed generally up and down the street.

Able dropped his Hava-Tampa Jewel to the sidewalk in front of Central Drugs and ground it out. He rubbed his chin. His side hurt like hell, and the heat from the blast furnace on the pavement before him made his stomach ache. He wanted to vomit, but he fought the feeling. He was helpless.

The Reverend Dr. Randolph P. Streetman was not feeling well either. After Everett Hardin brought the hearse to a crashing halt in collision with a parked wheat truck around the corner of First and Main, they had spilled out of the black car. The Reverend Streetman had been dumbfounded by it all, and he turned to see Everett with both fists jammed into his open mouth, his eyes wide, crying loudly as he saw the bloody and flaming remains of the finest funeral he had ever staged laid out behind him.

Streetman knew he could be of little help in the battle in the street, and Everett, for all his suffering, was not hurt at all. Still, the pastor reasoned, people were dying out in the street, and they needed comfort, maybe medical aid of some kind. Surely he could do something. He knew Doc Pritchard was fishing, as it was Wednesday, and Jeff Randall was in the blasted limousine. He could even be dead.

Turning away from the sobbing Everett, the Reverend Streetman moved up the alley between Main and Howard Streets and started toward Central Drugs, where he could find medical equipment and bandages. His breath, he noticed, was shorter than it should have been.

When he reached the alley opening at Second Street, he stopped and glanced up and down the street. Still unsure what was causing all the shooting, he wanted to be certain not to walk into anyone's line of fire. He spotted officer Clovis Hiker sneaking up the side of the drugstore building, and he almost stepped out to rush and join him, when suddenly he realized the policeman was being fired upon and was, in fact, bleeding.

As Clovis ran past him on the opposite side of the street, the Reverend Streetman waited in horror. Things must be much worse than he'd realized at the outset, and he breathed a small prayer before starting across.

He reached the alley and began to congratulate himself on his safe passage when the brickwork on the building burst and exploded just over his head. He spun around

and twisted his ankle, neatly sitting down and facing
James Earl Meacham III, half a block away, who was
potting at *him*.

The minister raised his hand to warn off the rancher,
but he suddenly realized that this was the same man who
had shot at Clovis Hiker. The Reverend Streetman half
crawled and half scrambled to the safety of the alley.
Finally he got to his feet and painfully limped to the back
door of the drugstore. Friends were shooting at friends.
He was terrified, and he threw one frightened look over
his shoulder as he entered the drugstore's back door and
made his way to the counters.

Inside, he spotted Elwood and Able kneeling down in
the doorway in front of the store. The whole place was
shot up, with broken glass and splintered wood and plastic everywhere. He crawled, wincing in pain, to the aisle
behind the drug counter and spotted Wanda Watkin's
body a few feet from him. He gagged at the sight of her
exploded head, and he brought both hands up to cover
his face.

After a bit he heard Able yelling through some sort of
loudspeaker, and he found the courage to look around a
bit. He examined the rest of the store and understood
that whatever was going on was worse, far worse, than
anything he could ever have imagined in his descriptions
of the final wrath of God. He tried to pray but he couldn't.
The thoughts just wouldn't come. He tried to make himself crawl out to Able and Elwood to see what he could
do to help, but he couldn't. His legs just wouldn't obey
his brain's command. Instead he sat helplessly behind the
counter and waited.

Over his head, he discovered, was the store's cigarette
display. Quickly rising, he selected a pack of Pall Malls
and a book of matches from the tray next to the cash
register. He lit up and thoroughly enjoyed smoking one
after another in a continuous, mindless chain.

Inside the bank's office, Alexander Bateman was in agony. Sitting in the uncomfortable chair, he realized that
he had done nothing but hide, but from the chance

glances he made through his keyhole, he could tell that the battle in the street had come inside the bank. The shattered glass of his office door no longer offered him protection, and for a while he had crouched down behind his desk and tried to squeeze his bulk into as small a package as he could.

His stomach hurt, his heart was pounding so loudly that he could barely hear anything, and he needed to go to the bathroom. The pain in his kidneys and bladder had slowly increased until it was all he could think of, so he moved to the chair and tried to decide what he should do. He considered going where he was, in his pants, or on the floor, but something in his nature forbade that. So he just sat there, comfortably out of the way of the shattered door, and sweated and suffered.

Able's voice coming from across the street demanding a cease-fire, and the brief pause in the shooting that followed, inspired him, and he jumped up. Unreasonably, he assumed it was all over, and aside from relieving himself, he wanted to be highly visible at the episode's conclusion. He stepped carefully and quickly, crunching glass underfoot as he opened the broken door of his office and emerged into the outer office area in the rear of the lobby. He somehow thought that Able Newsome would be standing in the ruined lobby of the bank, and he intended to begin by giving the sheriff a piece of his mind for ever allowing such a horror to happen in the town's only bank. His mouth was actually open to begin his lecture when he sighted the three prone figures reloading and moving about beneath the low wall in front of the lobby.

Glancing quickly into the vault, he saw only the terrified and bloody faces of his employees as they had literally climbed over each other to avoid ricochets. He flapped his jaw noiselessly, and then he threw up his hands the way he'd seen it done in countless movies and announced, "I give up!"

Floyd, who had taken the opportunity of Able's call for cease-fire to shove the last shells he had into his shotgun, heard Alexander Bateman's announcement, and adroitly rolled over and fired in the direction of the sound. From his prone position, he couldn't manage a decent shot and the load went high, cutting the banker's hands almost completely off and sending him flying backwards into the doorway of his office.

Jumping quickly to finish the job, Floyd pumped out the shell and started toward the rear of the lobby. Joe Don, who had turned at the sound of the blast, rolled back and quickly fired over the wall to give him cover, but it didn't work.

Bullets shattered Floyd's body with a terrible ripping force, and Breedlove, who had turned his head around to see what Floyd was after, watched with horror as Floyd's skin literally fell apart under the terrible fire. Blood and organs collapsed through Floyd's torn clothes and littered the lobby carpet around him. As the huge man fell onto the mess on the floor where the hostages had been only a while before, Breedlove started to rise to go to him, but Joe Don stopped him.

"Look out, Breed! Goddamn it!" he screamed. "Stay down!"

Breedlove rolled his head over and put his hands over it. I'm going to die, he thought, feeling bile rise in his burning throat. I'm going to die any minute now, and I can't do anything about it. God, I want a drink. If I'm going to die, at least let me have a drink first.

Vernon Ferguson had move up the street toward Main, had reached the alleyway behind the bank and discovered that the service door was securely locked. Cursing, he emerged onto Second Street again and moved up the side of the bank building slowly from behind.

He watched with horror as James Earl Meacham III shot at the fleeing Baptist preacher, and he saw Claude Crane struggling again to get to firing position behind his battered truck.

"The whole fuckin' town's gone crazy!" Vernon said aloud, and he continued to creep slowly up beside the wall of the building, hoping to get Able's attention and find out what, exactly, the situation was.

Looking around the corner of the bank turned out to be a very bad idea, for no sooner than his head appeared around the building's side than the brick wall began to crumble as rifle and pistol fire from across the street ate away at it. One or two shots, he was certain, had come from *behind* him, where the gun-toting citizens could clearly see he was a lawman. He jerked back and retreated.

Pressing his face against the Flex-Glo window of Alexander Bateman's office, he tried to get the banker's attention, but he couldn't knock loud enough to be heard. He was about to use his gun butt to smash it out when he heard Able calling for a cease-fire.

He hesitated, then he saw, incredibly, the banker rising and moving out into the lobby. He knocked on the window, but the fat man was moving toward the doorway. Vernon tentatively moved a few steps toward Main Street to see if the men had decided to leave the bank and make a break for it. Satisfied that they were still inside, he reached the window again and peered through his cupped hands into the office's interior. He saw that the banker, incredibly, was gone. Vernon hesitated for a moment, then, thinking quickly and not wanting to make any noise, moved to the side door of the bank, a portal that hadn't been opened in years. The glass in the door had been artificially frosted over, and he couldn't see inside, but he worked the knob furtively, hoping to force it open just by strength of will. It remained locked. When he heard the shotgun blast from inside the bank and the quick resumption of gunfire from the street, he smashed the window of the door with his pistol and grappled with the lock on the inside.

He found the horrible scene of Floyd's body disintegrating only a few feet from him, and then he saw the other two men aiming their guns at him. He had them! he realized, but with the bullhorn blasting out in the street and continued fire coming into the bank, he was disoriented. From the corner of his eyes he could see the frightened hostages peering out from the vault, and he raised his pistol toward one of the robbers who was

bleeding from a shoulder wound and was about to fire at
him. He pulled the trigger and nothing happened. The
gun misfired.

"You *dumb* nigger!" Vernon shouted at himself as he
continued to jerk the pistol's trigger. The dunking the
gun had taken in the creek earlier that day had ruined his
ammunition. But he knew it was too late. He saw the
muzzle blast from the .357 magnum just as he realized
he had fired his sixth dead cartridge, and he felt himself
being thrown back onto the sidewalk next to the bank's
outer door.

VII. Breedlove

Breedlove watched dispassionately as Joe Don gunned
down the black cop. He kept thinking maybe, maybe with
some luck they could still get away. Yelling at Joe Don,
he checked the load in his pistol and realized that he had
no more shells. The fire coming into the bank was now
steady and flew over their heads, like a deadly sheet of
lead only inches from where they lay. Out in the street
that sheriff with his bullhorn was again trying to get people to stop shooting, and his words evaporated into the
noise. Finally Breedlove reached out and grabbed Joe
Don by his good shoulder and rolled him over, forcing
him to listen by hollering right into his scarred face and
pointing toward the open door.

"It's a buttfuck, man!" Joe Don yelled back at him.
"You go out there, and you kiss your ass good-bye!"
Breedlove realized that Joe Don had lost his mind, that
he was reconciled to dying right there, in the bank with
a pistol in his hand. That's fine for him, Breedlove
thought; all his wild fancies are now coming true. But
what about me?

Gradually the gunshots from outside slowed down and
Joe Don got a wild look in his eye. Checking his pistol
quickly, he jumped to his feet. Breedlove looked up from
the floor and almost cried out, but he realized that nothing he could say would stop what was going to happen.

Wild-eyed and crazy, Joe Don smoothed back his hair and grinned down at his companion.

"You know, Breed," he said calmly, "I never wanted to hurt nobody!" He looked out into the street. "But *them*. They been wantin' to hurt me ever since I was born. The sons of bitches got everything! They just got everything!" He cocked his pistol. "Well, they ain't got me," he said, "an' I intended to take a few of them along with me." Then without another word he stepped over the low wall and out onto the sidewalk.

Breedlove lowered his head.

VIII. Lawman

It had taken almost five minutes to effect the second cease-fire, and Able Newsome's voice was hoarse from yelling into the bullhorn.

He had watched helplessly as people had fired on each other, not just toward the bank, as cars and human beings blew up in the street right in front of him, as other people bled to death or burned up right on the main street of his own town.

It was all his fault, he thought, and he couldn't really blame Jingles, who now sat cross-legged in the street where the O'Hara boy had dropped him, rubbing his head.

Able had seen Vernon poking his head around the corner of the bank, and he figured him for dead, in view of the volume of fire that had greeted his black face. Able was almost sure one of the men in the bank fell, too, but why he had stood up that way was beyond Able.

But, then, nothing this afternoon had really been understandable. A routine funeral procession, even a routine bank robbery, if such things could be said to be routine, and a routine investigation of a somewhat unroutine murder had all become an unbearable tragedy that this town was going to be a long time getting over. Maybe it never would, he surmised. He sure as hell wouldn't.

The drugstore's clock had been shattered, and Able's

own wristwatch had stopped at 3:32, but the bank's clock, incredibly, was still functioning. He had been on Main Street for almost an hour. He had sent Old Samuel for help almost thirty minutes ago, and still there was no sound of sirens coming in to assist them.

He desperately wanted to talk to the men inside the bank, especially to the green leisure suit, if he was still alive, since Able just knew that this was the man who held the answers to Eileen Kennedy's death. He wanted to end it, but how? They had already made it clear that they did not intend to be taken alive.

Besides, he thought as he painfully shifted his weight to relieve the pressure on his side, which raged from the squatting position he had maintained, how could he measure all the carnage he saw in the street in front of him against the death of one girl, however horrible it was? No, he thought, setting his teeth, there isn't a way in the world I can expect to talk to those boys, not now, not ever. What I've got to do is find a way to kill them, the way Sheriff Ezra Stone Holmes shot his bank robber right here in this very drugstore years and years ago.

Suddenly he saw a short man rise from his hiding place on the inside of the bank's wall. Maybe they were giving up, Able thought excitedly; maybe it was to be after all! He saw the man speaking to someone down on the floor and then step over the barrier.

"Hold your fire!" Able screamed through the bullhorn. "Everyone hold your fire! I'll shoot anybody who fires a shot!"

Spotting the O'Hara boy crouched down by a car, Able tossed the bullhorn over to him. "Keep yelling that," he ordered, and he stood up.

Incredibly the short man came right out to the middle of the street, then he started shooting in spite of the bullhorn's continued warning. He didn't have a target, and he was weaving around, apparently weak from blood loss caused by the wound in his shoulder. Even though the shots were wild, Able instinctively dropped down and raised his .44, taking careful aim on the man's midsection.

Joe Don kept shooting and waving, shouting unintelligible curses as he swung the pistol to and fro, and then finally running out of ammunition and clicking the revolver uselessly in the air. Able lowered the .44 a bit, checking to see if there was any way of taking him alive. Joe Don began fumbling in his pockets for more bullets. "Breed! Breed!" he screamed. "Bring me some more shells!" His words were slurred, and he suddenly brightened as he came up with one live shell. He broke open the .357 and emptied the casings out onto the pavement, then he tried to feed the single slug into a chamber. As he was working with the gun, trying to close it, Able raised his .44, sighted directly between the young man's eyes, and pulled the trigger.

He blinked with the blast from the big pistol. He never saw Joe Don fall. One second he was there, weaving around and searching for the stability to aim his own gun, and then he was gone. It was like magic, but the jolt from Able's pistol when it discharged told him that there was nothing mysterious about it.

The sheriff stood completely still, his pistol held in position, thrust out in front of him like a lance. His eyes fell to the sprawled figure of his target, slumped down between two parked cars where the impact of the bullet had flung him. His head, or what was left of it, was hidden from view, and Able decided that he was just as glad. There's no satisfaction in this, he thought, no goddamn satisfaction at all. Cautiously, he relaxed and dropped the gun to his side. Behind him Danny O'Hara was still crying out through the bullhorn the warning not to shoot, and Able noticed that the boy was holding Jingles' pistol at the ready, covering the sheriff in case something went wrong. Able felt a deep gratitude and admiration for the scruffy kid who was proving his worth and keeping his cool all at the same time.

6

I. Breedlove
The Present, 4:25 P.M.

Inside the bank, Breedlove had seen Joe Don fall when the sheriff's bullet struck him. Peeking over the top of the low wall, he winced as Joe Don's head snapped sharply and the back of his skull popped open as if the pressure of brains and blood had become too much. Breedlove tried to find something to admire in Joe Don's bravado, his ability to stand up and face the town, defiant and undefeated even in the face of death. But he couldn't. It was all just too sad, too crazy and too sad.

He watched as the bank employees from inside the vault clambered over each other for the door on the opposite side of the lobby. Some, including James Sheppard, had been hit by misspent bullets, but as Breedlove counted them, he knew that they were all still alive. They peered at him anxiously as they filed out, afraid he thought, that he would suddenly decide to do them in out of a perverse sense of vengeance. But he didn't feel vengeful. He just felt numb, miserable and numb. He lay on the floor, taking cover, although no more fire was coming into the bank, still gripping the pistol in his hand, although he had no more bullets to fire, still sure he was about to die.

He knew that as soon as he saw someone in authority, someone who wouldn't kill him on sight, he would just give himself up. But he had no illusions about how much the town wanted to kill him. He was already a bank robber and a murderer, and on this very day he figured he had probably killed some more. He felt certain he had killed that cop, and he had seen enough TV shows to know what other cops did to people who killed cops.

He hadn't meant any of this to happen. It was all some

kind of crazy accident. He wasn't a killer, not really. He didn't have the courage to be a killer. Hell, he thought, as the last hostage made the doorway and escaped, he didn't even have the courage to face up to a pregnant girlfriend. He had just run away. And that's what he would like to do right now. But there was no place to run, and he knew it.

He was parched, and squeals of pain from wounds both old and new came from every part of his body. His head throbbed, and the searing gash across his forehead had reopened, streaming blood into his eyes. His shoulder was a continuing agony, and his ankle was swollen and sore. In addition to the fuzzy, dry tongue that lolled in his mouth, he felt the internal thirst for a drink of something strong, alcoholic, and hot.

He was dirty, grimy, and, closing his eyes, he just wanted to sleep, to shut out the horror around him and drift off into a peaceful sleep. Out on the street only the sounds of the burning automobiles came wafting in, and he breathed deeply, drying his tears and trying to decide what to do next.

His ears were still ringing from all the gunfire that had exploded around them in the past hour, but in the distance he could hear the sounds of sirens—lots of sirens—moving closer, and peeking over the top of the low wall, he could see uniforms moving through the shattered window of the drugstore directly across the street.

He rolled over and began painfully searching the pockets of his suit for unused cartridges, but all he came up with were some coins and the girl's fingernails, parings he had kept since that horrible night that now seemed so long ago. Something about them was valuable to him, and something about the memory of his mania and his pain made them almost sacred.

He stared at them in the sweaty, blood-streaked palm of his hand. Reason told him that there was no connection between his killing that girl and the trap the town had laid for them outside the bank, but in the back of his mind he continued to connect the two events. Agatite, he thought, Agatite. Hoolian wasn't Agatite, but it was close enough. And now he was about to die in Agatite.

He looked up at the clock and noted that it was nearly 4:30, that in spite of the splintered wood and shattered glass surrounding it, the second hand was still sweeping along, checking the time, making sure that not a second of his agony was lost. He watched the small red hand make another revolution and then another. Time meant nothing, he decided, nothing at all. He was the same loser he had been in this town twenty years ago.

Around him shotguns, spent cartridges, pistols, broken glass covered the carpet of the bank's lobby. The ruined body of his friend, Floyd, lay where it had fallen. Not a pane of glass, not a piece of wood was without its bullet hole or ruination. It was as if a great wind had swept through the bank, bringing with it sharp objects that shredded the entire building and destroyed everything in sight. Everything but him.

He pulled himself to his feet, almost crying out in pain, and stumbled over to the water fountain. He pulled a handkerchief from his hip pocket and wet it. He could hardly believe the machine was still working since it had several bullet holes in it, but it was, and he bent down and swallowed an enormous mouthful of water, wishing it were whiskey. Than he wiped his face and mopped the sweat and blood from his forehead and neck.

He was aware that he was completely exposed to fire from the street, but it didn't seem to matter anymore. The game was over. As usual, he had lost. The only question this time was what had he lost? His life? It wasn't worth much, he said to himself. He wished, almost, that another torrent of bullets would come through the window and cut him down, end his pain, and the weariness that seemed to envelope his entire body, would be over.

He filled his mouth with water one more time, rinsed and spat onto the ruined carpet of the lobby. In his right hand the empty .357 dangled uselessly at the end of his arm, and he turned and looked around the room where only an hour before he had satisfied himself that everything that could go wrong had already happened. He felt terrible, lost, ashamed. He could feel the fingernail parings pressing into his palm against the gun butt, and he found that he enjoyed the additional discomfort in the chorus of complaints coming from every other part of his body.

"Here I am!" he tried to yell, but his voice was little more than a croaking whisper. "Come get me! Big Bad Breed! Son of a gun! Son of a bitch!" He wanted to cry, "Son of the town drunk, son of—"

And then the tears came. They ran down his cheeks and salted the inside of his mouth, which hung open in huge, gaping sobs. Nothing ever worked out for him, he cried silently to himself, swallowing the sobs and trying to stop. Everything fucked up every time. Other people got away with murder. He couldn't get away with shit.

All at once the vision of a young boy, himself, standing in front of a double-glass pane in a house of mirrors in an amusement park not far from where he now stood in the lobby of the First Security Bank of Agatite, Texas, came before his eyes. The boy was frantically trying to scrape the taped twenty-dollar bill from the window, but he couldn't do it. The frustrated boy tried harder and harder, running his hands around the edges of the glass, but he would never get the twenty.

He saw himself somewhat older, being beaten senseless by some big cowboy in some nameless bar in some anonymous town, then being cheated by some whore, then being almost run down by a big semi on some stretch of hot, sunbaked highway, then . . . then . . . then . . . He saw all his life in one quick rerun, like an old movie that had no ending but was cracked and jerky with age, just one absurd, tragic scene after another, spilling out of the past, documenting the endless stupidity of his personal history.

"It's okay, Roy."

At first he thought the voice was part of the dream vision he was having, but he suddenly located it in the room, and instinctively he spun around and raised the .357 at the woman and child who stood in the bank's lobby near the outer office area. He almost pulled the trigger on the empty gun before his eyes focused, and he began to shudder and pushed his hands out in front of him in a defensive posture.

"You!" he exclaimed, and then he shook his head to see if what he saw was real or imaginary.

When Cassie heard the shooting stop, she decided the time had come to leave. It didn't matter that the danger could still be in the lobby, and it didn't matter that the ricocheting bullets had penetrated the entire bank, including the women's rest room where she had cowered in her stall and prayed unceasingly and unreasonably for Claude to come to rescue her and Claudine. What mattered was getting the hell out of there.

"If they're the sort of men who will shoot a woman with a baby in her arms," she said to Claudine, "then we probably don't have much of a chance anyhow." And with that, she had gathered herself and her baby up and walked into the lobby of the bank. She arrived just in time to see Breedlove standing helplessly in the middle of the ruined lobby. She could hear some boy's voice on the bullhorn in the street insisting that people not shoot, and she suddenly gathered an understanding of what was going on. She also recognized the bloody man in the dirty green suit who stood broken in the center of the lobby, next to the grotesquely sprawled figure of a black man who still clutched a shotgun in his lifeless fingers.

That was when she spoke.

II. Lawman

Across the street from the bank, Sheriff Able Newsome was in hot debate with Police Chief Jingles Murphy and Harvey Connally of the Texas Highway Patrol, who had finally arrived, alone, and had come into the drugstore's back door just as Joe Don fell dead in Main Street. Harvey was trying to explain that he hadn't taken Old Samuel's call seriously at first, and that by the time John David Hogan had gotten him on the radio, he was nearly in Kirkland and had to turn around.

Jingles and Able, however, weren't much listening to the Highway Patrolman, as they were growing angrier and angrier.

"I say just give me my gun an' I'll shoot the shit outta him, Able!" Jingles yelled. "After all, you got the one in the street, an' I got jurisdiction!"

"Fuck you, an' fuck your jurisdiction!" Able screamed at him, completely losing control. He pushed Jingles roughly out of the way and into a display shelf with a crash. Jingles hadn't found the courage to crawl into the drugstore until he had seen Able shoot Joe Don, and even then he had crouched down, looking up only to see if he could still spy the figure in the green leisure suit standing in the lobby. "I'm running this show, and you can damn well like it or not," Able went on as Jingles pulled himself to his feet.

"Well, goddamn," Jingles looked around through his piggy eyes, one of which was swollen shut by the blow Danny O'Hara had delivered with the very pistol he now wanted.

"Where the hell's my gun anyhow?"

"I gave it to somebody who'd use it," Able snapped, and he turned away. Now that the shooting seemed to be over, he had made up his mind to try to take the green-suited figure alive. He had to know, he told himself; he had to be certain if there was a connection between Eileen Kennedy and this hellish day. He was determined to capture the man in the bank and get the truth out of him, even if he had to beat him to death to do it.

With his wound throbbing, Able limped between the parked cars, but when he finally saw inside the bank, he tried his best to run forward.

III. Breedlove
Omega

Cassie moved toward Breedlove slowly. She reasoned that she could get past him easily enough if she moved quickly and at the right time. She remembered Roy Breedlove well, and as she listened to him crying, sobbing to no one in sight, she also felt a kind of understanding for him. She pitied him, and, in a way, she loved him. She was amazed that somehow she didn't find it in her to be afraid of him. Maybe, she thought, I'm just too tired.

Breedlove did not see Cassie Crane standing before him, inching her way toward his protesting hands, one of which still held the pistol pointed slightly in her direction. He saw *her*. The ultimate torture of his life was standing there, holding the child that had become the symbol of his guilt. He had never known if it was a boy or a girl, and now seeing that it was a girl—a woman child—ate deeply into his heart.

It didn't matter to him that the child he had fathered and the woman he had abandoned pregnant at the altar years before would be much older than this sweaty, frazzled farm girl and year-and-a-half-old standing before him, for all the horrors of his life again began their parade before his mind's eye, burdening his soul with the bitterness and struggles of a lost man who could never go home again.

He also remembered the face of Eileen Kennedy, standing as she did with her chin up, flirting with him, daring him to come closer and to touch her, then as he last saw it, staring blankly at the outhouse's interior, her mouth open in a silent scream.

The memories flooded his consciousness, and the irony of his life's end became clear. All he wanted was a drink, just like his old man would have wanted. He was just a drunk, just like her father feared he would be. He'd been wrong from the start.

He wiped his eyes with his free hand, and stepping toward Cassie a half pace, he choked out, "Oh, I'm so goddamn sorry."

Cassie also stepped in his direction, planning to push past him in a second, but suddenly she recoiled in horror as a great red hole appeared in his upper chest and red blood shot out all over her and Claudine.

Screaming, she fell backward as he lunged forward, toward her, his eyes bulging out as his body flew in an absurd dive that left his head resting on the toes of her shoes.

She kicked her legs hard, backing up onto a desk behind her, holding Claudine as high as she could, and scrambling away from the fallen boy who had just moved her with his pained look. Then she saw her husband's grimy face. He stood in the shattered front door of the bank, holding his rifle down toward the lobby floor. Claude Crane had come at last.

IV. Able
The Present, Midnight

The clock in front of the First Security Bank of Agatite read three minutes after midnight, 89 degrees, when Able Newsome climbed painfully and wearily up to the courthouse steps' top level and sat down. From that vantage point he could survey the wreckage of the downtown area in the dim glow of what streetlights were still working. He breathed deeply.

From the pocket of his sweat- and blood-stained butternut uniform blouse, he drew a pack of Camels and lit a cigarette with a match, flicking the small flame into the bushes at the base of the steps, drawing in the smoke and enjoying the pain of it all.

His copper-colored boots were ruined, he thought, staring briefly down at them. They were so stained with blood, soot, and other indefinable junk that he might just as well throw them away. His trousers were also soiled beyond recognition with the foulness of the afternoon's carnage and the evening's cleanup.

The amazing thing, he thought for the thousandth time in a few hours, was that more people hadn't been killed. Twenty-two corpses, including Mrs. Thomas, who had a heart attack just before the shooting began, lay at Everett Hardin's funeral home awaiting attention from the still shocked mortician. Of course, more than a hundred people were in the hospital, and a good third of them were critical. Many had burns and injuries other than gunshot wounds, but some were just plain blown up, and not all by the thieves from the bank.

He had spoken with Alexander Bateman as he was being loaded into an ambulance for transfer to Wichita Falls where his hands would both be amputated, Able had learned. The fat banker was raving on about how it was all the fault of that "damned O'Hara kid," who, for some reason, he believed was behind the robbery. Well, Able thought, I'll have to set him straight on that.

The sheriff had also helped load Wayne Henderson onto a stretcher for removal to another hospital, Wichita Falls or elsewhere, Able couldn't remember. Wayne was unconscious, but Able didn't know what was wrong with him. He hadn't been shot, and he was alive. That was all they could tell.

Wilma Castlereigh came to Able's mind, and he wondered how she was doing. Although not seriously hurt at all, she was hysterical, and both girls had been injured by the collision with Claude Crane's pickup. It's been a hard week for her, he thought. But, it's been a hard week for all of us.

After Claude Crane had gunned down the Breedlove boy, Able had hurried past Joe Don and Mike Dix's corpses to the bank. Stepping over the low wall beneath the blown-out window, he was shocked to see inside. The bank's interior looked as if a tornado had come through it, carrying broken kegs of nails. It was amazing that anyone could live through the fire storm that had swept through the small bank. He found Breedlove's eyes glazed. He was bleeding to death, a gaping hole in his chest bubbling with frothy gore. Incredibly, Cassie Crane was kneeling down beside him, mopping his forehead with a dirty Kleenex, and Claude was covering the whole thing with his rifle.

Able was so overcome with anger than he knocked the severely hurt Claude down and would have kicked him to death, probably, if his own wound, reopened with the effort of striking Jingles minutes before, hadn't hurt him so badly.

He left the semiconscious Claude on the bank's floor, and moved over to the fallen thief who remained alive in his stained and bloody green leisure suit. As the young man came around a bit under Cassie's ministrations, Able ges-

tured that she should move away. She did so, still clutching
her daughter to her tightly, Claudine now wide-eyed and silent in fear and horror of what she saw around her.

"You know him?" Able asked as he studied the face
of the fallen man.

"Yeah," Cassie muttered. "Sort of. He's Roy Breedlove." Able wrinkled his brow and set his hat back on
his head. "You remember, the son of the old drunk."

"I'll be damned," Able said.

"Only he was better than that," Cassie said, surprising Able with the staunchness of her defense of this
bloody killer who lay at the sheriff's feet. "He was always all right."

Breedlove groaned and moved his hand and Able
started back, realizing that the criminal still held a pistol,
although he doubted that there was any strength left in
the body. The gun fell free, and Able knelt even lower,
coming face to face with the young man, and then he
reached into his pocket and pulled out the sweat- and
blood-soaked picture of Eileen Kennedy and held it up
in front of the dying man's face. For a moment the sheriff
feared that he was too far gone, but at last Breedlove's
eyes registered on the limp, creased photograph, and a
brief smile of recognition crossed his lips.

With great effort Breedlove lifted his hand, opening
his palm, and revealed to the sheriff three fingernail
pieces embedded in his flesh, in his hand, like museum
exhibits set for viewing.

"Why?" Able asked, trying to put as much meaning
into the single-word question as he could.

Breedlove opened his lips, and blood froth came out.
"I don't know. I really don't," he said. Then he was dead.

Able closed Breedlove's eyes. He probably just tried
to come on to her, he thought, and she wouldn't go
along—or, he contemplated with discomfort, the opposite took place—but it didn't matter anymore. This was
the killer, and the hows and whys died with him. It wasn't
like the sheriff had imagined it would be. There was no personal confrontation, no laughing maniac with a taunting,
mad attitude. There was just a poor, confused, second-rate

holdup man with a bullet in his back and a history that was probably sadder than anything Able could ever imagine. The sheriff stood up. The nightmare was over.

Able crushed out the Camel he'd been smoking. At least, he hoped, the case of Eileen Kennedy was closed. He wondered if the afternoon's events would spawn new nightmares, but then he shook his head. This had been too much like a war, and he had never dreamed about his war experiences, since, he reasoned, that was part of his job. Sheriffing was part of his job, too. But being a sheriff did not mean one had to find bodies hanging in outhouses.

Even so, he decided as he lit another Camel and puffed deeply on it, there was something too horrible about it all. It just wouldn't end, it seemed.

Jingles had gone completely off his rocker when Morris was brought back to City Hall with a first-class concussion from a baseball bat Old Samuel had turned on him when the irate white man had spent all his bullets and tried to attack the old custodian physically. The chief of police had thrown Old Samuel in jail and directed Morris to the overcrowded hospital, but then, according to John David at least, Chrystal had appeared, buck naked, and cleared Old Samuel and demanded protection from Morris, who, she asserted, had tried to kill her. "The whole damn town's gone crazy," Able said aloud through a cloud of tobacco smoke.

The chief of police was now at home, heavily sedated. One of his subordinates was hanging onto life by his fingernails with half his face shot away, and the other had apparently disappeared. No one had seen Clovis Hiker since this afternoon.

And so, Able thought, with Vernon laid up for a long time, it seems, I guess me and John David's the law in Agatite *and* Sandhill County. I wonder if I've got *official jurisdiction* now, he sadly asked himself. He thought of calling Newell Longman and asking him, but then decided that it would be too cruel a prank even to play on Newell, who was still suffering from shock.

He shook his head and flicked the Camel out onto the lawn. From behind him the courthouse door opened and John David, as if summoned by the sheriff's thoughts, emerged into the night air.

"Able?" he said. "Shouldn't you be in the hospital?"

"No room," the sheriff said, coughing from the cigarette. "They gave me a shot for pain and told me to go home and rest. I'm not hurt that bad. Doc Pritchard took a handful of shot out of my side, but nothing serious is hurt."

John David stood waiting.

"Uh," he said, "How's Jeff Randall? He able to help any?"

"No," Able replied. "Doc Pritchard said he'd live, but he's cut up pretty bad, and it'll be a while." John David shifted his weight from one foot to the other and continued to wait. "What's up?" Able finally asked.

"Well, uh . . . ." The young deputy hesitated, then took a deep breath. "Maggie Meacham just called. She found James Earl out in the barn. He shot himself." He looked relieved to have gotten it all out at once.

"Good Christ!" Able exploded, feeling a sharp pain in his side. "Why?"

"She says she's got a good idea," John David replied, "but she wouldn't tell me. Wants to talk to you."

Able tried to rise, then sat back down heavily. "Well, she can't," he said with finality. "Call Harvey Connally and get him or one of his people out there. I've seen enough blood for one day." He recalled that Vernon had tried to tell him something about James Earl when they were loading him into the ambulance, but the black deputy hadn't been able to speak with all the dope they had shot into him to keep him quiet. Able also remembered that Maggie's car had been one of the ones that had blown up.

"Yessir," John David said, and started back inside.

"Say," Able said, stopping the young deputy, "how's your wife?"

"She's over to her mama's," John David said, "Doc gave her a shot, and he said she'll be all right after a bit." He paused. "Baby's okay, too," he added.

"Well, you make that call and get on over there to her.
She needs you worse than any of the yahoos around here
do. I'm going home myself in a few minutes. I figure we
got a long day's paperwork ahead of us tomorrow." He
thought guiltily about Sue Ellen. She had been at the
hospital, and he had raged and stormed at her to go on
home and leave him alone. She was a better woman than
he deserved, he knew.

John David disappeared inside the courthouse, and
Able stood up and began making his way down the steps.
He mentally catalogued the dead, and he wondered how
many fell to bullets fired by their friends—or old ene-
mies—rather than the four desperate men in front of the
bank. He knew damned well some of them had been
killed by "friendly fire," as the phrase went. Adam
Moorely, Able mused, had been the only one to say anything about it, though. His shoulder was damn near gone,
and from the garbled account the man had given the sheriff as he was being loaded into an ambulance, there was
little doubt that he was shot by "some farmer with a
rifle," as he put it. Able didn't wonder much about who
it might have been. He shook his head. It didn't really
matter, not now. "It was mass insanity," he said, remembering a phrase one of the television newsmen had
used in front of the hospital where the wounded and dead
were being unloaded from ambulances and pickups. Mass
insanity.

He lit another Camel and sat down on the lowest step.
How could this happen in his town? he wondered. He
thought briefly about resigning, about just handing in his
badge to Newell Longman and heading north after the
ghost of Ezra Stone Holmes, maybe relaxing and waiting
to die. After all, he argued with himself, this had to be
his fault. Old Sheriff Holmes would have said so. He took
care of his town.

But he knew he wouldn't leave. This was his job. His life.

"Able?" A man's voice came from the shadows.

"Yeah?" Able responded, recognizing Mel as he
emerged from the dark.

"Is it all over?" The old barber moved closer to the sheriff and gazed into the downtown area.

"God, I hope so," Able said.

"Hear it was pretty bad," Mel said, shaking his head.

"Pretty bad," Able agreed.

For a moment neither of them said anything. They shared the silence of understanding that comes from living in a small town all their lives and knowing the truth of things without having to talk about them.

"Hear Jingles made an ass of himself," Mel said timidly.

"You might say that," Able said in a flat tone.

Again they fell silent. "You know, Able," Mel said at last, "I think I knowed this was gonna happen." Able said nothing but noted the strong smell of whiskey on the old barber's breath, "Soon's you found that gal hangin' in my crapper, I knowed somethin' bad was gonna happen." Able still said nothing. "You reckon all this had to do with that? Findin' that gal, I mean?"

Able was stunned. Weary and hurting as he was, he couldn't help feeling a shiver of excitement at the old man's suggestion. He rubbed his hands across his face as if he were washing it.

"You might say so," he said. "You really might, but I don't know . . ."

"Well"—Mel reached into the pocket of his overalls and produced a pint bottle, which he thrust out toward Able, who accepted it without comment—"I'll be goddamned."

"We probably will be," Able said, pulling deeply on the pint bottle. Then he handed it back to the barber, who wiped the top of his sleeve and finished it off. "You know, Mel," Able said in almost a whisper, "We probably will be."

Epilogue: The Cemetery

It was a week before the body of Roy Lynn Breedlove, age thirty-eight, was buried in Pauper's Corner of the Sandhill County Memorial Cemetery. He rested between the unmarked graves of his father, who lay next to his wife's also unadorned mound, and an itinerant drifter, Roosevelt Grady.

The cemetery was alive with fresh-cut flowers that week, marking the graves of the newly dead, but Breedlove's grave had only one bouquet of yellow daisies on it, placed there sometime after dark by a pudgy girl driving a heavily loaded and battered, rusty pickup. She waited silently over Breedlove's final resting place for a few minutes, then got into her pickup, quieted her squalling baby, and headed south. She was never seen again in Agatite.

Not far from Breedlove's grave lay the Kennedy family plot, wherein Eileen Kennedy's abused corpse also rested. There were almost twenty-five new graves in all in the cemetery, and had someone passed by daily for a week or so, he would have figured an epidemic had taken place in the small town. What he would not have seen, however, was the Reverend Dr. Randolph P. Streetman praying over any of the graves, even those belonging to longtime members of the First Baptist Church. The Reverend Streetman would never preach another funeral for as long as he lived.

Breedlove's accomplices, Mike Dix and Floyd Tatum, were each buried elsewhere, as obscure and forgotten next of kin claimed the bullet-torn bodies and interred them separately. The fourth member of the gang, Joe Don McBride-Franklin-St. John was buried in Kirkland in the St. John family plot.

Eventually most of who the four men were would be forgotten. Time would take their memories even from the old men who sat and whittled and fouled the sidewalk in front of City Hall in Agatite. Even the merchants who would remove the boards that covered their broken windows would forget most of their names in time. And life would go on. Eventually, one would have to search in the tumbleweeds and red clay dust over the mount of Roy Lynn Breedlove for the cheap, tin nameplate that Everett Hardin used to mark his grave.

Although he had made no real mark on the world, done no real good with his life, and enjoyed not even a few moments of real happiness, Roy Breedlove had, in his living, given something to the town's people that would keep them from forgetting him even if they couldn't exactly recall his name in years to come. In the Town and Country Dinette, Central Drugs, and the Goodyear Tire Store, in the domino parlors, around the filling stations, feedlots, and everywhere people gathered to gossip and remember old times, they would recollect the day he came home to Agatite.

He would never be publicly linked to the horrible discovery that was made in an outhouse behind a barbershop in Hoolian, but he would be remembered as the son of a town drunk who led a gang of thugs home to rob the bank and died trying. His accomplishments on the high school team would also pass from memory along with his name, but the day his gang shot up the whole town would always be recalled as the day time stood still in Agatite.

Agatite would continue to die its slow death, and the fear that gripped the citizens for so long would return to envelope the streets once more in a nameless belief that the end of something was always near. Young people would still leave, and tourists would still hurry past, cursing the heat, the cold, the incessant wind, but Agatite would always feel a perverse kind of gratitude for what Roy Breedlove did, for the one brief moment of unique violence that gave the town something as hard and lasting as the stone for which it was named.

"He was a bad 'un," the old men would say, "one mean son of a bitch!" But while they would never understand the uselessness of his life, they would always try to imagine something of the wildness of his spirit. And that his how they would remember him.